Jules Van Mil is passionate about living a creative life. Her career spans education, fashion design, styling and writing. When she isn't writing, Jules loves to escape to the country. She lives in Sydney with her husband.

You can find Jules at www.julesvanmil.com
or on Instagram @jules_vanmil

A
REMARKABLE
WOMAN

JULES VAN MIL

MACMILLAN
Pan Macmillan Australia

Pan Macmillan acknowledges the Traditional Custodians of country throughout Australia and their connections to lands, waters and communities. We pay our respect to Elders past and present and extend that respect to all Aboriginal and Torres Strait Islander peoples today. We honour more than sixty thousand years of storytelling, art and culture.

This is a work of fiction. Characters, institutions and organisations mentioned in this novel are either the product of the author's imagination or, if real, used fictitiously without any intent to describe actual conduct.

First published 2022 in Macmillan by Pan Macmillan Australia Pty Ltd
1 Market Street, Sydney, New South Wales, Australia, 2000

A catalogue record for this book is available from the National Library of Australia

Typeset in 12.5/16 pt Sabon by Post Pre-press Group

Printed by IVE

The author and the publisher have made every effort to contact copyright holders for material used in this book. Any person or organisation that may have been overlooked should contact the publisher.

For GB – And all our days at WH

PROLOGUE

Tours, Loire Valley, France 1945

The boy stared ahead and gently worked the reins between his fingers, encouraging the mare forward over the uneven cobbled road. The late afternoon sun lit the crumbling sandstone walls of the abbey as the horse cautiously picked her way towards the front gate. A sudden gust of warm wind swept across the field of cowslips and wood violets and tumbled over the buggy and its passengers, causing the horse to shy. The woman cried out in pain as the left wheel slid into a deep crack between the stones. Her slender fingers clutched the driver's arm. With eyes closed, her head rocked sideways, coming to rest on his shoulder.

The buggy creaked to a stop in front of the steps. The boy secured his reins then gently manoeuvred the young woman upright, so her back rested against the seat.

'We are here, Madame,' he said. 'I'll help you down.'

He jumped to the ground and ran around to the other side. The woman's arms were lost amongst the folds of cotton dress fabric, as she cradled her bulging belly.

1

'Please, give me your hands. You have to get down, Madame.'

For a moment she rocked forward, then her body slid sideways across the back of the seat, her head landing where the driver had been sitting.

'Help me,' she groaned, 'please help me.'

The boy charged up the weather-beaten stone steps and pounded on the wooden doors. He stared back at his passenger and banged on the door again. Harder, longer and louder than before.

'Hello,' he shouted. 'Hello! Is anyone there? Can anyone hear me?'

If Sister Marguerite had been in the vegetable garden, then perhaps she wouldn't have heard the call for help so quickly. But she'd been sitting at the open window in an upstairs room, writing, and had seen the horse and buggy approaching.

The heavy door swung open and together they hurried to the buggy. The lad scooped up the passenger's basket from behind the seat and slung the straps over his shoulder. Sister Marguerite and the boy guided the mother-to-be down from the bench seat, onto the footstep and to the ground. With their arms around her torso, they walked her carefully up the steps and into the security of the abbey.

Sister Marguerite steered the distressed woman down a long corridor and into a large, sparse room. The spring sunlight flickered through the tall leadlight windows, throwing shadowy leafy shapes across the floorboards and several narrow beds, up and over a jug and wash basin that was sitting on a long table. The room was surprisingly cool.

Sister Marguerite sat the woman on a bed and removed her well-worn shoes, then slowly swung her legs up and onto the blanket. She positioned the pillow under her neck and shoulders, then brushed a mass of tangled brunette curls off her face, lifted her tiny wrist and took her pulse. She was younger than Sister Marguerite had first thought, nineteen, twenty at the most. Her belly, disproportionately large compared to her thin body.

Sister Marguerite motioned for the boy to come closer. He took the wicker basket from his shoulder, set it down lightly and removed his cap.

'What has happened?' Sister Marguerite asked.

'I don't know, Sister. I snuck into Chateau de Vinieres to pick fruit. I didn't think I would see anyone. The lady – she was wandering in the garden. She told me to bring her here.'

'Chateau de Vinieres?' Sister Marguerite repeated.

'Yes,' the boy said, nodding.

'You've done the right thing. What is your name?'

'Louis Moulin.' He waved his cap as if to indicate some form of direction. 'I live on the other side of the village with my grandmother.'

'Louis, I need your help.'

Sister Marguerite sent Louis to the kitchen and told him to start a fire in the stove and to boil two large pots of water. She unlocked the doors to the armoire behind her and collected towels and sheets, thread-bare yet clean. From another shelf she took bandages, a medical kit and scissors, and efficiently laid the equipment along the table. Then she removed her cardigan and rolled up her shirt sleeves. When Louis returned, she sent him to fetch the lamps from the rooms next door and candles and matches hidden behind the bookcase. She asked him to retrieve her journal and pencil from the desk upstairs, which he did without hesitation.

'In the room next to the kitchen you'll find a baby's bassinet. Please, fetch it for me.'

He did as he was asked, then Sister Marguerite and Louis pushed two beds together. He helped her turn the mattresses and surprised her by tucking in the newly laid sheets with efficiency and precision.

The light had almost disappeared when the wind strengthened and began to whistle through the gaps in the window frames. Louis stood beside the basket, shifting from one foot to the other. He stared towards the darkening evening sky, twisting his cap nervously in his hands.

'I have to get the mare back,' he said, glancing at the floor. 'Or I'll be in trouble.'

The sister sensed that the horse may have been taken without permission and she did not want to see the lad punished.

'On your way home, go back to the chateau and tell someone that the woman who is having the baby is here with me. If no one is there, find some paper and leave a note on the kitchen table. God bless you.'

At the door Louis stopped and looked back at the figure stretched out on the bed. His big dark eyes drifted upwards to meet those of Sister Marguerite.

'She'll be all right, won't she?' he said with a nod towards the bed. 'The lady and her baby.'

'I'll take good care of them both.'

Sister Marguerite dipped a cloth into a basin of tepid water. She prayed for the young woman and her unborn child as she dabbed her brow. She looked carefully at the refined features of the face before her. There was something familiar in the shape of her nose and her dark green eyes. She took the woman's clammy hand in her own and stroked her fingers, feeling the hardened callouses on her palm. Her only piece of jewellery, a delicate gold watch. She half opened her eyes as Sister Marguerite gently wiped the beads of sweat from her chest.

'I'm Sister Marguerite,' she said, her voice calm and full of kindness. 'I'm a nurse and I'm going to help you deliver your baby.'

'Where am I?' the woman said, almost too soft to hear. 'Are there soldiers nearby?'

'You're at the abbey in the town of Tours. There are no soldiers here.'

Suddenly the woman's eyes flew open, fully lucid. She grabbed Sister Marguerite's arm and tried to pull herself up on her elbows.

'Please, don't leave me. Don't let them take me,' she pleaded.

'No one will take you. I'll not leave your side. I've delivered many babies in my seventy-two years. What is your name, dear?'

The woman's lips quivered, and she closed her eyes as her head sank back onto the pillow. A large single tear pooled in the corner of her left eye, rolled down her cheek and slid onto the pillowcase. 'Sister Marguerite, it's me. Avril. Avril Montdidier,' she whispered.

'Lord be praised,' said Sister Marguerite. 'Yvette's girl.'

*

By the time Avril's contractions were five minutes apart and building in intensity, she'd been in labour for more than twelve hours. The baby was in a breech position but Sister Marguerite knew the birth was imminent. When she saw the baby's tiny feet, she guided Avril through the last moments of her delivery.

Avril's baby finally entered the world with Sister

Marguerite's assistance, his first cries echoing off the walls. Sister Marguerite clamped and cut the cord and placed the baby on Avril's chest. Somehow, Avril found the strength to bring her arms around her son. Tears spilled from her eyes as she gazed at his face and tufts of dark hair. 'My beautiful baby,' was all she could manage to say.

While Avril held her son, Sister Marguerite skilfully carried out the post-birth tasks.

'I need to bathe your baby,' Sister Marguerite finally said. 'What will you call him?'

'Philippe Montdidier.' And for the first time, Avril kissed her baby's forehead.

Sister Marguerite bathed the little boy in the porcelain basin, fashioned a nappy from a hand towel, dressed him in the only baby garment she had, then wrapped him in a crocheted knee rug. She placed the baby in the bassinet then turned her attention to Avril. She washed her body, rolled away the bloodied bed linen and helped her into a clean nightdress.

'I'm going to move you onto this bed here,' she said, pointing at the beds pushed together. Once on the bed, Avril fell asleep almost immediately, her chest gently rising and falling with each deep breath.

Sister Marguerite cleared the room of all instruments and carried them to the kitchen. She restoked the stove and put water on to boil. She sat down at the kitchen table and then, for the first time in more than twenty-four hours, she briefly closed her eyes.

'Chateau de Vinieres,' she said to the empty room. 'Of course.'

*

Several times that morning Sister Marguerite checked on mother and baby, satisfied that both were sleeping peacefully. When she heard Avril wake around midday, Sister Marguerite hurried to the kitchen and returned carrying a lunch tray. She placed the cheese sandwiches and slices of peach on the chair beside Avril and turned to pour two cups of tea. 'You need to eat and drink, dear,' she said. 'Even if it's only a couple of bites.'

Avril lifted her head and peered into the bassinet bedside her bed. She reached down and stroked her son's cheek and flinched.

'His face is blue,' she cried. 'Why is he blue?'

Avril flung the bedcovers away and tried to stand. A sharp pain ripped through her abdomen, and she fell back on her elbows. Sister Marguerite scooped up the baby and placed him on the bed. With two fingers on his chest, she began pushing in pulses and gently blowing against his mouth.

'What's wrong? What's wrong?' Avril screamed.

Sister Marguerite turned the baby on his side and moved her hand in a circular motion over his spine. Once more, she laid him on his back and blew gently against his lips. She repeated the process over and over, but Sister Marguerite knew the newborn was no longer of this world. He was gone, of that she was certain. There was nothing she could do for him.

Finally, Sister Marguerite stopped. She stroked the baby's head and wrapped the rug back around his tiny body.

'No!' Avril sobbed. 'No!' She reached up, took her son from Sister Marguerite, cradled him to her breasts and howled.

*

Throughout the afternoon, Avril's cries rose and fell. She spoke to her baby in hushed sing-song tones and traced the outline of his eyes, nose and lips with the tips of her fingers. At nightfall, Sister Marguerite lit a fire in the hearth at the end of the room, the air quickly filling with the scent of pine cones and oakwood. Avril would not release her baby and Sister Marguerite didn't request it. Avril held her son all through the night.

In the morning, Sister Marguerite chose her words carefully and explained to Avril that her baby would need a resting place.

'You will need to let him go, my dear. When you are ready, we'll go together, into the garden, and find a place for him.'

Avril stared at her baby. She said nothing and Sister Marguerite allowed the silence to hang between them. There would be time for Avril to tell her story. Avril eventually looked up, her face pale, her eyes raw and swollen.

'Do you still have fruit trees?' she asked.

'Yes, quite a few,' said Sister Marguerite.

Avril stroked her baby's head, staring at her son's beautiful face.

'Below the branches and leaves and blossoms,' she said. 'That's where I'll place him.'

Later that day, Sister Marguerite wrapped a shawl around Avril and her baby and together they walked through the abbey and out into the garden. The earth was damp and the orchard was littered with ripened fruit, torn from the branches by the previous night's storm.

At the beginning of the second row stood a huge peach tree.

'Here.' Avril nodded. 'I'd like this to be his place.'

While Sister Marguerite dug the grave, Avril wandered

down between the trees, her arms rocking her baby slowly. The hem of her nightgown dragged behind her, changing the colour of the wet grass from pale mint to vivid green.

When it was time, Avril kissed her baby and placed him in the wooden fruit box lined with linen that Sister Marguerite had prepared. Sister Marguerite said a prayer and then, side by side, they prayed together in silence. When Sister Marguerite lowered the small box into the rust-coloured earth, Avril collapsed to her knees. The mud stained their hands and oozed through their fingers as Avril and Sister Marguerite pushed the soil into the grave. When the burial was completed, Sister Marguerite forced a small white wooden cross into the earth. Leaves rustled overhead and the smell of the turned soil folded around them.

The bells from the church in the village below began to ring out, the rhythmic toll rolling over the roof of the abbey. Avril and Sister Marguerite turned in the direction of the village. The peal grew louder and down the valley they heard joyous shouting.

Up through the row of trees, someone ran, coat flapping widely, arms waving above their head. As the figure drew closer, Sister Marguerite saw it was Louis Moulin.

He cupped his hands around his mouth and cried out. At first, his voice was inaudible, but his words soon became clearer.

'*L'Allemagne s'est rendue. C'est terminée. La guerre en Europe est enfin terminée.*' 'Germany has surrendered. It's over. The war in Europe is finally over.'

Sister Marguerite helped Avril to her feet and cradled her in her arms. Louis stopped a short distance from the grave, a look of shock on his face, and pulled his cap from his head. Avril and Sister Marguerite turned and headed back towards the abbey as Louis stared at the newly turned soil. Then he watched as a blue wren swooped and landed on top of the cross. The tiny bird hopped sideways, fluttering its wings, swivelling its body left and right, then as if lured by the call of the bells, darted away.

PART 1

Love all, trust a few, do wrong to none.

William Shakespeare

PART 1

CHAPTER 1

Melbourne, Australia, Summer 1950

A vril Montdidier stood on the deck of the *Harmony Prince* and leant against the railing. A golden halo crowned the pinkish glow that had begun to break over the horizon. The wind whisked her hair from her face, and she closed her eyes. She drew the salty air into her lungs and listened to the hum of the engines and the rhythmic surge of the waves against the bow of the ship. At least for a short while, this tiny piece of paradise high up on the aft deck would be hers. This had been her little haven, the place she'd come to almost every morning for the past four weeks, to look out across the ocean, to be alone with her thoughts, her dreams. Ten thousand miles of Avril's memories lay scattered over the Atlantic and Indian oceans. Soon, the rest of the passengers would wake and clamber for the best vantage point as they steamed towards Port Phillip Bay, their new lives and the city of Melbourne.

The small bench against the wall was protected from the wind. After breakfast Avril would settle into her spot, with her thermos of coffee and her sketchbook, and draw the fashions of Paris or work on her own designs. Her mind turned to the countless hours of cutting and sewing she'd carried out over the past three and a half years, as her hand moved fluidly over the paper. She was determined to start her own fashion business and the sooner the better. She'd worked too hard to let anything hold her back and, in a new country, a new city, she was free to chart her own course.

There were times on the voyage when an unexpected feeling of exhaustion would overtake Avril. She'd close her sketchbook and eyes, turn her face towards the sun and allow her thoughts to drift away with the swirls of the wind and the sound of the ocean. And that was exactly what she was doing the day she met Louise and Gabriel.

A woman in tight black pants and a black and white polka dot shirt raced up the stairs, ran to the corner of the railing and threw her hands up in the air, laughing.

'Hurry up!' she called as the wind tossed her light brown curls. 'Take the picture.'

The handsome young man with fair hair clicked and wound his camera several times in the direction of his model. Then he paused, turned the lens towards Avril and took a photograph. He dropped his camera to his chest, smiled and shrugged his shoulders. 'I couldn't resist,' he said, winding the film spool. 'A record of a moment in time,' and he moved towards Avril, his right hand extended, and introduced himself as Gabriel Dupont.

On that first day, the three travellers had talked for hours, trading stories and discovering Avril had lived only a short distance from Louise and Gabriel in Paris.

'I certainly would have taken your photograph if I'd seen you in the Marais,' Gabriel had said. 'Your face. So easy to capture in any light.' He crossed his legs and lit a cigarette.

'What if I didn't want to have my photograph taken?' Avril had laughed. 'What then?'

Gabriel blew the smoke skyward.

'That would not surprise me. True beauty doesn't need to seek attention.'

There was an awkward silence for a moment, until Louise snatched up the packet of cigarettes and lit one for herself. She circled her hand in the air.

'That's the trouble with my brother,' she'd said, 'he's a casual romantic but he's very serious when it comes to his photography.'

Avril, Louise and Gabriel were not, however, a private group of three for very long. This secluded space soon became known as 'Deck Paradiso'. Anyone who happened upon Avril, sitting on the bench, her hair tied back with a paisley scarf, was instantly drawn to her radiant smile. When a young woman stood on her own against the railing, Avril waved and called, 'Please, come join us.' She knew too well the pain of being alone. Or the morning when two small children broke free of their father and rushed over to see what was in Avril's lap, she simply hoisted the girls up beside her and passed them her sketchbook and pencils.

One evening, as the *Harmony Prince* surged across the Indian Ocean, three Belgian men arrived with their violins, and the space was soon filled with music and clapping. A couple of Greek boys insisted on dancing with Avril and Louise. The brothers from Crete twirled and spun their partners while Gabriel captured the dancing and the different faces in the crowd.

'You are going to have this all your life,' Louise had said to Avril, once the gathering had cleared and it was only the two of them, lying on the wooden deck, staring up at the night sky.

'What do you mean?' Avril pushed herself onto her elbows and looked at Louise.

'You have a gift. You draw people together. You make them feel safe.'

'No!' Avril said, embarrassed. 'It's just the music and the laughter that makes everyone feel good.'

Changing the subject, Avril pointed to the sky and said, 'Right there, Louise, look. That bright one. That's Venus.'

For a long time, they lay still, searching for patterns in the stars. Then Louise drew her knees up, lit a cigarette and quietly said, 'We were always hungry, Mama, Gabriel and I. So often, all we had for dinner was a cigarette.'

Avril closed her eyes and listened to the surge of the ocean. They'd not spoken much about the war, about the pain and the darkness inside them all. Their conversations had focused on the future, their dreams and what they hoped their new lives would be like.

'And now look at me.' Louise laughed. 'I'm as fat as a pig and still smoking. There's no justice in this world.'

Avril did not need to look at Louise to know that underneath her laughter, her eyes were full of tears. She knew that Louise and Gabriel's father had been killed not long after the invasion of France, and they'd lost their mother shortly before the war had ended. She reached out and held Louise's hand. And in that moment under the night sky, Avril's heart broke open and her own past washed over her and she returned to another time and place. She could see her mother's face, as clearly as if she was in front of her, as if they were back in her mother's workroom, rolls of fine fabrics lying on the cutting table.

*

Yvette Montdidier leant over the shoulder of her fifteen-year-old daughter and looked closely at the newly stitched hem of the dress.

'Beautiful work, Avril,' said Yvette. 'A light press, then you can take it up to Madame Leon. I told her it would be delivered this afternoon. And don't take the shortcut through the vineyard. Go up the main driveway. I don't want you turning up at the chateau in dirty shoes.'

Avril hummed a tune as she carried the pale pink and white striped box through the ornate iron gates, past the sign that read *Chateau de Vinieres*. As with all her garment deliveries, Avril wore an outfit her mother had made, a flattering yet simple boat-neck dress in lemon cotton voile, belted at the waist and finishing at her calves. As she walked, her long loose ponytail swished across the row of covered buttons.

Her eyes searched the branches of the plane trees for Guy. She knew he would be hiding somewhere, waiting to spring out and surprise her. She did not have to wait long. A short way up the drive, he dropped from a nearby tree, landing with a thud on the gravel.

Guy rushed over to Avril and kissed her on the lips. Although he was three years older than her, he was only slightly taller. With his broad shoulders and strong physique, he was often mistaken for a man in his mid-twenties. His dark eyes lit up as he smiled. 'I'll meet you behind the stables,' he said, blowing Avril a kiss as he dashed off through the shrubs.

Brigette, the housekeeper, opened the front door and showed Avril through to the main salon, where Madame Leon was rearranging some flowers.

'Good afternoon, Madame Leon,' Avril said, placing the dress box on the settee.

'Oh Avril. How lovely to see you,' she said and kissed her on both cheeks.

Madame Leon opened the box, removed the tissue paper and held the garment up to admire the lovely fall of the fabric. For cocktail dresses, evening gowns and shoes, madame went to a couturier in Paris. But for luncheon and afternoon tea dresses and most of her hats, she preferred to use the services of Yvette. Madame Leon knew Yvette was a widow with a young daughter, and she tried to give her as much work as possible.

She was also acutely aware of the attraction between Guy, her only child, and Avril. It was not hard to understand. Avril Montdidier was growing into a beautiful young woman, and it wasn't just her grace that Madame Leon noticed. Avril was a girl without malice. She was polite to all the house staff, genuinely so, and Madame Leon looked upon Avril with great affection. From an upstairs window, she would often see Guy and Avril ride out together, racing their horses through the vineyard to the hills beyond, and was delighted with their association.

'Brigette, could you please take this to my room?' said Madame Leon, placing the lid back on the box. 'And you'll have to excuse me, Avril. I have quite a bit to do before our guests arrive this evening.'

*

At the back of the stables, Avril found Guy and they sprinted, hand in hand, down the row of poplar trees. They climbed a wooden fence next to a field of sunflowers and made their way to the grassy bank of the river. As they sat and watched the ducks swim by, they talked about the coming summer. When Guy had first told Avril that he wanted her to come to Paris with him and his parents for two weeks, Avril had been excited.

'I love it whenever Mama and I go to Paris,' she'd said. 'But it's only for a couple of days each time we visit.'

Guy described the shops, art galleries and cafés he wanted to take her to. 'I'll love showing you around the city,' he'd told her. But that was six months ago and now everything was changing so quickly.

'Papa's gone to Belgium on business,' Guy said as he twisted a long strand of grass between his fingers. 'He's also trying to convince his sister to come back to Tours. He says she'll be safer in France.'

But it wasn't going to be safer. The nightmare was only just beginning, and as Avril and Guy kissed and lay in each other's arms that spring afternoon in 1939, they had no way of foreseeing the horrors ahead.

By the following year, Yvette and Avril stood shivering, huddled together in the snow, and waited for Avril to receive her identity card, a document all French citizens over the age of sixteen were required to carry. When the enemy first arrived, Yvette was instructed to repair the damaged uniforms brought to her by the German soldiers. Then she was told to make dresses, sometimes suits, for the officers' girlfriends. Avril had numerous hiding places she quickly went to whenever the soldiers arrived. She would never forget the terror she felt, cowering behind the bolts of fabric as steel-capped boots paced decisively up and down the rows of merchandise. By 1942, what little fabric remained was confiscated, leaving only some buttons, a few reels of thread and one box of sewing needles. The Haberdashery Montdidier, once brimming with wool, crepe, satins, the finest cotton and lace, was empty.

At the beginning of the war Yvette had packed away

all of Avril's brightly coloured dresses and she made Avril trousers and dresses out of navy gabardine.

'Wear nothing bright,' her mother had told her. 'Nothing that will draw attention to yourself.'

Avril could still feel the clip, clip, clip of her mother's shears against the back of her neck as her long wavy hair fell to the floor.

'It's only hair, Mama,' Avril had said when her mother had cried. 'It will grow back. Perhaps I will start a new fashion.'

When they had no stock to sell and no fuel to heat their home above the store, Madame Leon insisted Avril and Yvette move into the chateau. As the months become years, the Chateau de Vinieres saw many women and children in need of food and shelter come and go. No one was turned away. Those who stayed longer than a few days were set to work, doing the farm chores the men used to do, tending to the vegetable garden and vineyard. Sometimes, one of the handful of nuns still living at the abbey would cycle down from the convent and deliver a basket of freshly picked fruit or vegetables. And once or twice a nun called Sister Marguerite had called to attend to someone who was unwell.

Guy and Monsieur Leon joined the Resistance shortly after the war had started. Father and son came and went, often staying away for weeks or months at a time, only to reappear in the dead of night, exhausted and hungry. Under the cover of darkness, parcels of food, matches and warm clothing were hidden at pick-up points in the vineyard for the Resistance fighters. By first light the parcels had always been taken.

Another Christmas and new year came and went, and by January 1944, Yvette Montdidier lay desperately ill in one of the upstairs bedrooms of the chateau. The snow was five feet deep at the windows when Avril took an axe to what was left of the fence surrounding the dressage arena. She loaded the pieces into her arms and carried the wood up to her mother's room to keep a small yet constant fire burning. Yvette had stopped eating, her breathing slow and shallow. Avril hardly left her mother's side except to fetch wood or to make soup.

On one of her searches, Avril found an unfinished piece of embroidery in a small bag of threads and needles in a trunk in their room.

'Look, Mama,' she said, holding up a doily. 'They're daisies. Your favourite. I'll finish this for you.'

Avril sat on the bed and took her mother's limp hand in hers.

'Daisies,' Yvette Montdidier whispered through her thin grey lips. 'Such pretty little things.'

And then, her mother's eyelids closed, and Yvette didn't speak or breathe again.

*

Avril was hanging out laundry when something appeared across the field. She shielded her eyes from the morning sun and squinted. At first, it looked like a low-flying bird. Whatever it was, it was gathering speed as it travelled. Then she saw.

'Guy,' she tried to call, but her voice seized.

They raced towards each other, his arms stretched wide. He flung his rucksack skywards as he swung Avril off her feet, around and around she flew. He kissed her, holding her face in his hands.

'Have you heard?' he said. 'Do you know?'

She clung to him. 'What has happened, Guy?'

21

'Paris has been liberated,' he shouted. 'The Resistance and our Allies marched down the Champs-Elysees yesterday. Our country is back in the hands of the French. You should have seen it. Avril. People came out from everywhere. They were singing and dancing in the streets.'

'Is the war over?' she cried. 'Is it really over?'

'Yes. It's over for France. Let's pray it will soon be over for the rest of Europe as well.'

*

Word soon spread that there was to be a celebration at the chateau. By lunchtime the courtyard was full of people from the village and surrounding farms, with a spread of bread, cheese and wine on the trestle tables. At sundown, Guy lit a small fire pit, drawing the singing revellers around the glowing embers. Guy had not seen his papa since they'd parted company in Limoges three weeks earlier, but he reassured his mother that his father would soon be with them. Throughout the festivities, Madame Leon kept glancing in the direction of the driveway, hoping.

A rendition of 'La Marseillaise' struck up as Guy took Avril's hand and they slipped quietly away from the fire and into the darkness. They raced around to the other side of the chateau, through the kitchen and up the servants' stairs that led to the first-floor gallery, along the long corridor and into Guy's bedroom. He locked the door and pulled Avril into his arms.

'I love you, Avril. I always have.'

'And I love you, Guy.'

His lips found the nape of her neck as she unbuttoned his shirt and ran her hands down his back. They tumbled onto the four-poster bed, his hands freeing her of her dress and caressing her breasts. And for the first time, Avril and

Guy gave themselves totally to the desire and love they felt for each other.

Avril awoke to the sound of the larks singing in the nearby trees and Guy gently stroking her hair. He stared into her eyes, locked his fingers with hers and kissed the back of her hand.

'I have no intention of moving, so you won't mind if I don't go down on one knee?'

She smiled at Guy.

'Will you marry me, Avril Montdidier?' he asked.

Avril's heart felt like it was lifting to the sky.

'Yes, yes! A hundred, thousand times, yes.'

She reached out and pulled him closer, pressing her lips to his.

'You have no idea how long I have wanted to ask you,' he said.

'How long?' she whispered.

'Forever. It's always been you. It will always be you.'

*

Avril would later remember the months that followed Guy's proposal as if every scene, every face she recalled, moved in slow motion, fragmented. Images of the chateau and the people who came and went were never quite in focus.

Madame Leon was delighted when Guy told her he'd proposed to Avril.

'We don't want to wait,' he'd insisted. 'We want to marry straight away, in September.'

If the war had shown Madame Leon anything, it was that happiness must be seized with both hands. That life was unpredictable. The date was set for Saturday twenty-third of September at Saint Michael's church in Tours, followed by a wedding breakfast at the chateau.

It was Guy who answered the telephone and spoke to his father's lawyer a week before the wedding. Monsieur Fortin sounded agitated and said he needed to see Madame Leon and Guy in Paris immediately. Guy had repaired the engine of his Deux Chevaux and he'd even taught Avril how to drive. As he placed the luggage on the back seat of the car, he commented on how fortunate they were to have a vehicle.

'We'll be gone four days at the most. Home by Wednesday,' Madame Leon reassured Avril as she kissed her goodbye.

Avril and Guy wrapped their arms around each other.

'I wish we did not have to go, right now,' said Guy, 'but we'll be back in no time and besides, you'll be busy putting the finishing touches to your wedding dress, I'm sure.'

'I love you, Guy,' said Avril.

'And I love you. I'll be back before you know it. I promise.'

'Hurry home,' she called as Guy closed the driver's side door. She watched the small grey motorcar as it went down the driveway and Guy's arm appeared out the window. Avril waved back, and kept waving, long after they'd turned the corner and disappeared.

The following evening when the telephone rang, Avril dropped the piece of lace she was stitching and sprinted across the room. Monsieur Fortin explained that Madame Leon and Guy had not kept their appointment that morning and he wondered if they had been delayed. He said he'd telephoned the Leons' house in Paris, but the phone had rung out several times.

There was still no sign of either of them by Wednesday and on the Friday morning, the day before the wedding was to take place, Monsieur Fortin arrived unexpectedly at the chateau. He explained to Avril and Brigette that he'd gone to the home of Madame and Monsieur Leon in Paris and found Guy's car parked in front of the house. The luggage was still on the back seat, but so too was Madame Leon's handbag and gloves, and this disturbed him greatly. Avril excused herself as she ran to the kitchen and was sick.

'Paris may have been liberated,' Monsieur Fortin said when Avril returned, 'but the city is far from safe. Food and electricity are still rationed and much of the city is in ruins.'

'What do you think has happened?' Avril asked.

'To be honest, I really don't know. But it cannot be good,' he said.

'Guy and his father were with the Resistance,' said Avril. 'Could that have something to do with it?'

Monsieur Fortin's gaze dropped to the floor.

'I have something to tell you, Avril, and it is not easy to say. Monsieur Leon was killed, some time ago it seems. Shortly after Guy left Limoges, apparently. I wanted to give the news to Guy and his mother personally. This is why I needed them to meet with me. There are legal matters that need to be settled, now that Guy will inherit his father's estate.'

Avril comforted Brigette as their tears flowed, both acutely aware that there would be no wedding.

'What happens now?' Avril finally asked.

'We wait. I'll return to Paris straight away and see what else I can find out,' he said.

Avril sank onto the settee and tried to process everything they'd heard. *Please bring them home. Please bring them home,* was all she could think.

*

Throughout the autumn months, as Avril's belly grew, she kept herself busy tending the vegetable garden, caring for their small brood of chickens, and helping Brigette with household chores. In the most unexpected yet natural way, Avril assumed the position held by Madame Leon. One by one, men drifted back to the Loire Valley and Avril allocated work to the fieldhands in return for food and lodgings. The poplar and plane trees transformed into a blaze of crimson and orange, and the winter which followed was a cold and lonely one. By the time the first flush of spring buds appeared in March, Avril was no closer to knowing where Guy and his mother were or what had happened to them.

Brigette had gone to town for the afternoon and the fieldhands were working a long way from the chateau when Avril doubled over in pain and grabbed hold of the kitchen table. She was sure the discomfort would pass as the baby was not due for a fortnight. If need be, she'd go to the neighbour's farm. There would be someone there to help her. Avril gathered some personal belongings and placed them in a basket, in case she needed to leave. Walking helped to ease the discomfort and so she wandered into the orchard, oblivious of how her life was about to change, again, forever.

CHAPTER 2

On a blue-sky February morning, two days after Avril's twenty-sixth birthday, the *Harmony Prince* docked at Station Pier in Melbourne. The passengers were dressed in their best clothes, saved especially for this auspicious moment. Men in their dark suits and white shirts. Some wore ties, others open-neck shirts. Women in jackets over straight skirts or fitted dresses. Children in polished black shoes.

Avril had pulled her dark wavy hair into a loose bun at the back of her neck. Her face had the glow of sea and sunshine and she'd applied a red lipstick which intensified her deep green eyes. Before leaving France, she'd changed the colour of her court shoes from beige to navy, to match her crepe dress. Her silk stockings, a farewell gift from Remi, a friend she had worked with in Paris, she'd kept for this very moment. The long panel lines of her dress flattered her slim figure as the hem swayed freely above her ankles. Her only jewellery was her gold watch and a pair of pearl earrings. The tan leather bag slung across her body held her passport, immigration papers and a collection of photos, while everything else she owned was in the suitcases beside her.

At the top of the gangway the purser held the waiting passengers at bay while the last-minute docking formalities were carried out. Avril laughed when she saw Louise and Gabriel at the front of the line. They turned and waved as they led the procession off the ship. Avril had already made plans to meet with them at the end of their first week. She took her newfound friendship with Louise and Gabriel to be a good sign. Friendships had been formed amongst the passengers on the voyage, strong friendships that would last a lifetime. Avril's thoughts turned to the people she'd met on board who were arriving without a friend or family member to greet them. She felt blessed.

Avril felt her heartbeat quicken. The last time she'd seen her aunt and uncle, she was a child. Josephine and Albert Dubray had emigrated from France in 1935, *'to escape'*, Avril's mother would always say whenever she talked about her younger sister and brother-in-law. Albert had followed the social and political changes that were occurring in Europe since the early 1930s and with each passing year, he warned his friends and family that they should leave France for America or Australia.

Avril was nine years old the night she crept out of bed and sat on the top step of the narrow staircase that led to her bedroom above her mother's shop. She'd tucked her knees up under her chin and listened, peeking through the railing, watching the pale yellow candle flickering on the kitchen table. She saw her aunt reach across and take her mother's hand.

'Come with us, Yvette,' Josephine had pleaded. 'Claude has been gone six years now. What is here for you? And we have money.'

Avril thought of the photographs beside her mother's bed of the father she did not remember.

'You mean Albert has money,' she heard her mother say. 'Besides, Tours is our home. And I have my business to run. What would I do in Australia?'

'What you do here. Yvette, you could have your own atelier in Melbourne. We could help set you up. What do you say?'

Avril watched as her mother sipped her coffee.

'You and Albert will do well, wherever you are, and I don't wish to be answerable to him!'

So Josephine and Albert sold their bakeries, packed up their home and left to make a new life, *'as far away from Europe as possible,'* Albert had said, the last time they'd come to dinner.

*

Avril peered over the sea of hats and heads in front of her as she made her way down the gangplank. Many of the passengers broke into their native language, their excited chatter drifting throughout the inspection area. Family groups and individuals fanned out and joined one of the many queues in front of the immigration desks. Avril sensed the nervous excitement around her as she slowly worked her way to the front of the line. The young man behind the desk looked up and returned Avril's smile as she said good morning and handed him her documents. He checked her passport and immigration papers.

'And you're staying with relatives, is that correct?' he asked.

'Yes, my aunt and uncle. Collins Street in the city.'

The clerk signed and stamped the documents and slid them across the desk.

'Welcome to Melbourne,' he said, 'and good luck, Miss.'

'Thank you,' Avril replied. She hesitated for a moment, intrigued by the sound of his accent, then turned and jostled her way through the doors to the arrivals area.

She recognised Josephine and Albert almost immediately from the photo they'd sent her before she left Paris. They were standing beside a grey pillar, their chins lifted, their eyes fixed in her direction. For a moment Avril froze. Josephine looked so much like her mother. It was the colour of her hair and the way she'd placed her small pillbox hat to the back of her head. Then they both saw Avril and waved. Her aunt called Avril's name and brought her hands up to her face.

Avril dropped her bags to the floor and hugged Josephine, stood back, then hugged her again.

'You're here, at last, you are here,' Josephine cried.

Josephine reached out and stroked Avril's face and kissed her hand. The photograph did not do her aunt justice. Josephine's light brown hair was coiffured into a sophisticated French roll that finished at the base of her neck. Her face was expertly made up with a touch of blush, her eyelashes heavy with mascara and her lips a peachy nude. Although Josephine had recently turned fifty, with her flawless skin and high cheekbones, she could easily pass for a woman ten years younger. It was obvious to Avril that her aunt's navy and white polka dot silk voile dress was not off the rack, and she recognised Josephine's lightweight navy swing coat as a Dior original.

Albert embraced Avril warmly, kissing her on both cheeks. She hadn't seen him since she was a girl, and even then, only on a few occasions. He wasn't a good-looking man – his nose dominated his face and his eyes were closely set – though he was stylishly dressed in an open-neck shirt and tailored linen jacket. He stood with an air of confidence, his broad shoulders compensating for his lack of height. As a couple, Josephine and Albert Dubray looked like the essence of French chic.

'Come,' said Albert, taking charge. 'Let's get out of here.'

He picked up Avril's suitcases and cut a path through the crowd. Avril and Josephine linked arms and followed, talking all the while.

'Oh, it's so good to finally have you here.' Josephine could not stop looking at Avril or squeezing her arm.

Years later, whenever Avril was asked what she'd noticed when she first started living in Melbourne, she'd always say, 'Everything! I couldn't stop looking at the sky, the trees, the people and what everyone was wearing, the buildings and the cars and trams. And the light. I'd never known the sun could shine so brightly.' She'd talk about the scent from the frangipanis and the roses in Fitzroy Gardens. The taste of the ocean spray on a windy day as she walked along the water's edge at St Kilda Beach. 'I felt like I'd been set free,' she would say. 'I felt like a big adventure was waiting for me.'

And so it was.

Avril drank in every detail of the buildings and signage as Albert drove down City Road. Josephine pointed out the Melbourne Cricket Ground, the Treasury Gardens, and the Yarra River in the distance. Avril was surprised to see that Melbourne, like Paris, had very few tall buildings, but unlike Paris, the streets were devoid of people.

'Where is everyone?' said Avril as she wound down the window.

'Ha!' laughed Albert. 'You're not in the Montmartre now. Hardly anything is open on a Sunday. Some cafés, a couple of cinemas. After lunchtime on Saturday, the city is almost deserted all weekend.'

Josephine swivelled around and placed her forearm along the back of the seat. 'I still can't believe you are finally here. I'm pinching myself,' she said.

The car rolled to a stop in a tree-lined street in front of an elegant sandstone building.

'Here we are,' said Josephine. 'Our city abode. Work and home.'

Avril stared up at the grand building and counted five levels from the ground floor to the top. *Bistro Dubray* was in white cursive writing across the black canvas awning that framed the restaurant windows. Her mother's words to Josephine rang in her ears, '*You and Albert will do well, wherever you are.*'

Josephine unlocked a door to the right of the bistro.

'Welcome to Collins Street,' she smiled. 'The Paris End of Collins Street, they call it.'

A narrow hallway led to a long flight of stairs and on to a large open landing. At the other end of the landing the staircase continued upwards. 'We live on this floor and the one above,' Josephine said. 'The top two floors, we let.'

Avril felt as though she'd walked into an apartment in Saint Germain. The entrance floor was covered in black and white tiles. A huge gold gilt mirror hung on one wall and a large vase of white hydrangeas took pride of place in the centre of a side table that ran along the wall opposite. The lounge room was enormous, with pale blue drapes framing the front windows that overlooked the street. A long rectangular coffee table sat between a pair of taupe velvet sofas. The room was tastefully appointed with paintings, cushions, matching rugs and occasional chairs. A floor-to-ceiling bookcase covered part of one wall, with the bottom shelves housing a substantial record collection. A half-wall partitioned off the dining area, where a long pine dining table stood with seating for twelve.

Josephine opened a small gold case, took out a cigarette and lit it. She snapped the lighter closed and leant against the wide doorframe that led to the kitchen.

'Josephine, your home is exquisite,' said Avril as she moved about, running her hands over the texture of the cushions.

'I should have been a decorator,' said Josephine. 'Come. See your room.'

Avril followed her aunt up the sweeping staircase, guided by the glossy banister as they climbed to the floor above.

'I hope you like it,' Josephine said as she opened the door.

Avril was speechless and tears filled her eyes. Her room was more like a small apartment than a bedroom. It was luxurious and the opposite of the damp grey quarters she had shared with Simone, another seamstress, in Paris. Their studio was so small they couldn't walk three paces without running into each other, though it hardly mattered when all they did was work and sleep. 'It's . . . it's wonderful,' she finally managed to say.

Josephine opened one of the street-facing windows and a fresh breeze drifted in. A long single drop of voile curtain billowed lazily.

'Why don't you unpack and freshen up? Come down when you're ready. There's no rush. Albert's making us something to eat.' Josephine turned to leave but stopped to embrace Avril again. 'I'm so glad you're finally here.'

Avril removed her shoes and jacket and looked around her rooms, barely able to believe that this would be her new home. There was a small kitchen area where she could make herself coffee and a light meal and behind that was a modern bathroom. Plush white towels hung from the rail and a small vase of lavender had been placed on the vanity. In the main room was a small sofa, two matching armchairs, and a well-used trunk served as a coffee table. Albert had already placed Avril's suitcases next to a desk. Behind three delicately painted oriental screens in the far-right corner of the room was a double bed, dressed with a blue and white damask bedspread and flanked by a pair of small tables with matching lamps, the colour of cornflowers.

Josephine had thoughtfully placed some novels and fashion magazines on the coffee table. An illustration of a young woman wearing a straw hat and holding daisies in her gloved hands graced the cover of *The Australian Woman* magazine. The daisies immediately reminded Avril of her mother, and she was overcome by sadness. She recalled how she had searched for firewood and blankets during Yvette's illness and wondered if her mother would still be alive had she left France with Josephine and Albert.

At the window, Avril pushed the curtains to the side. She rested her elbows on the windowsill and looked out onto the street. Trees filtered her view but she could see a park or large garden not too far away. It was a glorious summer's day and she reminded herself that she'd vowed to leave her past in France. *How lucky I am to be here*, she thought. *This is where I'll make my fortune.*

*

Josephine was a natural conversationalist so it was easy for Avril to listen intently as they shared the meal which Albert had prepared. Quiche, roasted tomatoes, aubergine

34

and the finest cheese and wine Melbourne had to offer, it was a far cry from the fare aboard the *Harmony Prince*.

'For eight years we ran those bakeries, seven days a week,' Josephine said. 'Two on St Kilda Road and another one on Lygon Street, not too far from here.'

'We could barely keep up,' said Albert proudly. 'Customers waiting outside every morning.'

'It was almost impossible to locate decent coffee and olive oil,' Josephine went on, sipping her wine. 'And do you think we could find a carpenter who could build shop cabinets the way we wanted them?'

Albert smiled at Avril as he topped up their wine glasses.

'I always had my eye on this building.' His eyes swept around the room. 'I knew one day it would be mine. *C'est la vie.*'

He told Avril how he had purchased the Collins Street building six years earlier when the owner had hit financial difficulties.

'War can be good for some, not so good for others,' Albert shrugged.

'I don't think war is good for anyone,' said Avril.

Albert's eyes narrowed on her uncomfortably.

'Oh, no. Of course not,' Josephine agreed quickly. 'Albert's talking about business opportunities.'

There was something about Albert's manner that made Avril feel uneasy. She wasn't sure what it was but it was there, hovering below the surface of his smile. Was it a sense of entitlement? Or his self-confident tone, or the intensity of his stare? She remembered her mother's words: *I don't wish to be answerable to him!*

Josephine tapped her cigarette in the ashtray, blew a smoke ring and continued as if the awkward exchange had never occurred. She explained that the ground floor of the building had been converted into the restaurant, and once she'd decorated the upper-level apartments, lifting the rooms out of their drab, pre-war heritage, they had leased quickly. The fourth floor to a barrister, and the top floor to a man in banking. 'We hardly ever see them. Only when they come into the restaurant for dinner.'

Albert expressed his annoyance about the antiquated laws regarding the serving of alcohol in restaurants and the restrictions around opening hours. But he relaxed when he spoke about the success of the bistro and in particular, Duncan Campbell, their head waiter, who had worked with them since they'd first opened. Albert described him as a boy from 'nowhere', who didn't know a soufflé from a flambé when they first met.

'So, what do you think you'd like to do for work?' Albert asked, as he poured their coffee. Without waiting for Avril's reply, he continued, 'Something in fashion, I imagine. Perhaps a position at Georges department store or as a seamstress in Flinders Lane.'

Avril suspected that Albert was more of a talker than a listener, and as Josephine went to speak, he cut her off.

'You could try your hand at modelling,' he said. 'It's become a booming business now that the war's over.'

Avril took a moment to think before she spoke. 'I'm not sure exactly what I want to do. I've worked for three and a half years, six days a week, often seven. I know the hours you need to work in the fashion industry. But yes, I see myself doing something creative.'

Albert leant forward and pointed his finger at Avril. 'With references from Dior you could get a job with any of the top couturiers here in Melbourne,' he said. 'I wouldn't waste any time if I were you.'

But you're not me, Avril heard her inner voice say. Then, *Be wary.*

'For heaven's sake, Albert,' Josephine said. 'She's only just arrived. Give her time to get to know the city.' She turned to Avril. 'And you need to have some fun, make friends, go dancing.'

Josephine knew that while she and Albert had been sheltered from the horrors of war, Avril had not. Over the years, Avril and her aunt had corresponded regularly and there'd been times when Josephine had wept as she read the letters. In almost all her correspondence Josephine had tried to persuade Avril to leave Paris and come to Australia.

'Would you like to work a few nights a week in the restaurant, as a hostess?' Josephine suggested. 'Take coats, seat guests. Earn some money while you're settling in.'

'What an excellent idea,' said Albert. 'Now, why didn't I think of that.'

Avril was quick to assess the offer. She'd have a small income which would add to her savings and still be able to explore Melbourne during the day. Above all, she'd feel less indebted to Josephine and Albert for allowing her to stay rent free with them.

'I'd like that very much,' she said.

'See,' said Albert, 'you're not here five minutes and you're already employed.'

Eager to take the focus off herself, Avril said, 'Oh, I have something for you. Excuse me for a minute.' She left the table and went upstairs to her rooms, took a few long steadying breaths, and returned with gifts for her aunt and uncle. Cigars for Albert, perfume and a silk scarf for Josephine. She'd also bought some ground coffee in the marketplace when the ship had docked in Lisbon. 'And I thought you might like to see some newspapers from home,' she said, handing Albert copies of the *France-Soir* and *Le Parisien*.

'Oh, *merci*! What a treat.' He seemed genuinely pleased.

Josephine stood. 'Let's go for a walk and stretch our legs,' she said. 'You must be dying to have a look around?' Avril did not need any convincing.

'Albert, will you join us?' Josephine asked.

'With these to read?' Albert scoffed, holding the newspapers aloft. 'Enjoy yourselves.'

CHAPTER 3

That afternoon, Avril and Josephine walked through Fitzroy Gardens. They'd changed into slim pants and flat pumps and strolled past the picnickers who had taken up position in front of the bandstand, where a string quartet was playing a piece by Schubert.

While Josephine fetched ice-creams for them from a nearby vendor, Avril took a seat on a bench and smiled as she watched three young children play tag beside the fountain, where a statue of a woman and two dogs stood. There is nothing like the sound of laughing children and for a moment her thoughts turned to what might have been with her own child. She would not feel sad today, she told herself, and as quickly as the door to her memories had opened, she closed it. It was something she'd learnt to do over the last six years that had helped her to look forward, to believe that life would get better.

Josephine returned with two ice-creams accompanied by a tall young man with fashionably cut red hair. 'Look who I've just run in to,' said Josephine. 'Duncan, may I present my niece, Avril Montdidier.'

'*Bonjour!*' Duncan said with a big smile in a grating French accent, planting quick kisses on Avril's cheeks. 'Head waiter at Bistro Dubray and Josephine's right-hand man,' he said, pointing to himself. 'It's lovely to finally meet you.'

Avril was immediately taken by Duncan's open, friendly nature.

'Lovely to meet you, Duncan, head waiter and right-hand man,' said Avril with a smile.

Duncan waved towards the bandstand. 'There's a group of us sitting just over there,' he said. 'Why don't you join us? We have plenty to eat and drink.'

'We'd love to,' said Josephine. She wrapped her arm around Avril's waist. 'You see. I have you making friends already.'

*

It was late afternoon when they returned to Collins Street. Josephine flicked on the light and they continued chatting as they climbed the stairs. Josephine called out for Albert, but there was no reply. They kicked off their shoes and sank onto the sofas.

'He probably took the papers over to Maxim's – one of his card-playing friends. He'll be back when he's finished drinking Max's best wine.'

Avril stretched out and gazed up at the detailed pattern in the plasterwork on the ceiling. She pulled the tie from her hair and let it fall over the back of the sofa cushion. 'I can't remember the last time I laughed so much,' she said. 'Duncan and his friends are such happy people.'

'Wherever there is light, there is also shade,' said Josephine, spontaneously, then hesitated. 'So, you already have a date planned for tomorrow? Duncan will make an excellent tour guide.'

'He will. I'd like to see the department stores first of all. And I hear Melbourne has many arcades and laneways to explore.'

'So, tell me. What do you really want to do?' Josephine asked, her eyes steady on Avril but with a kindness that reminded Avril of her mother. 'Albert was quite persistent at lunch about his ideas for you. I know he can be a bit overbearing at times. Just ignore him when he does that. I know I do.'

Avril felt that she could confide in Josephine. Plus she wanted to hear what her aunt thought of her ideas.

'I want to go into business for myself.'

'Perhaps a couture salon of your own?' Josephine suggested.

'Possibly,' said Avril. 'Or maybe there's more opportunity in ready-to-wear garments. I'm not sure.'

'But fashion. Yes?'

'Definitely something in fashion.'

'Fabulous,' Josephine said enthusiastically. 'That's what I was hoping you'd decide to do. You have a talent, like your mother.'

Avril blushed from the compliment and the warm memories of her mother's workroom, but she knew the hard work which lay ahead. 'First, I need to explore the retail and wholesale side of fashion here in Melbourne,' she said. 'Who sells the best fabrics and trims. Where the cutting and making is done. That sort of thing.'

'I'll help you with the connections I've made and financially any way I can,' said Josephine. 'Although I'll have to run the money side of things by Albert first. He manages the books. He has investments in all sorts of businesses, you know.'

'That's kind of you to offer to help finance me,' said

Avril, 'but I will have to think about that. I've been used to doing everything for myself for so long.'

Perhaps it was the memory of her mother's words, spoken that night in the candlelit kitchen, that made Avril innately cautious about Albert. Or that Albert, like most married men, made the financial decisions for themselves and their wives. But in that moment, on her first day in Melbourne, Avril instinctively knew she would never let Albert be involved in her business, monetarily or otherwise. She did not want to be beholden to anyone. She had her savings from her time at Dior. She had excellent pattern-making, cutting and sewing skills and was confident about running her own establishment.

Josephine went to the bookcase and found the catalogue from the 1948 Dior parade held at David Jones. They pored over the designs, and Avril described the process involved in making the garments, two of which she'd hemmed. Josephine knew from Avril's letters that her niece had been fortunate to gain a position at Dior, which was emerging as the leading couturier after the war. And she knew of the arduous hours and dedication that Avril had put into learning her craft. But she inwardly worried that starting a business would not be as easy as Avril hoped, no matter how talented and determined her niece was. Melbourne was still a man's world, and Josephine knew that all too well.

That night, Avril dreamt she was sitting at her table in the atelier at 30 Avenue Montaigne, Paris, sewing tiny stitches through the red silk lining of a black silk faille jacket. A light dusting of snow drifted past the window, and she looked up to see Guy's face reflected in the glass. *He's come back! He's here!* Then she woke with a fright, disoriented by her new surroundings, and checked the clock; it was two in the morning. She thought she could hear raised voices but didn't know where they were coming from. She lay there listening but when she heard nothing more, she turned on her side and eventually went back to sleep.

*

The following morning, Avril and Duncan were among the first through the doors at the Foy & Gibson department store. Women, in their floral dresses with matching shoes and handbags, streamed past the glass counters, fanning out in every direction. Avril's eyes swept over the beautifully displayed merchandise on the ground floor. Well-groomed sales assistants busied themselves behind the cosmetic and perfume counters, making final adjustments to the products on display, eager to assist the early shoppers. Avril had little opportunity to browse the department stores when she lived in Paris. She worked long hours and always accepted any overtime that was offered. Even if she'd wanted to shop, there was very little available, and what was for sale was quickly procured by the wealthy.

The simplicity of Avril's aqua linen dress, with its collarless neckline and capped sleeves, set her apart from the sea of boldly printed frocks. Never one to wear large hats, she had placed a small white crescent-shaped band above the chignon at the back of her neck. She'd removed her wrist-length gloves as she'd entered the store, unclipped the bamboo-handled bag Madame Leon had given her, and tucked them safely inside. Her unique ensemble drew the attention of the young saleswomen, who gave her compliments as she passed by and in doing so made it easy for Avril to strike up a conversation with them and, more importantly, ask questions.

Avril could tell that Duncan was enjoying looking at the merchandise as much as she was. She was fascinated by the way he casually browsed and chatted to the staff with camaraderie, often eliciting a burst of laughter, while displaying an amazing eye for detail – and quality. He stopped to feel the texture of a towel, all part of a beach theme displaying hats and sunglasses.

'Some shells and sand on the tabletop would have made all the difference, don't you think?' he said. Avril whole-heartedly agreed.

'And perhaps some large beach umbrellas hanging over-head,' Avril added.

Duncan grinned. 'I agree.' Then he sighed somewhat wistfully. 'I could transform this whole first floor given half a chance.'

Avril sensed some hidden ambitions in the head waiter of Bistro Dubray. 'What would you do to that counter over there to showcase the perfumes?'

Duncan's face lit up as he described the props he'd use to bring the perfume counter to life. A Moroccan theme, he envisioned, with spices and tapestries and moody lamp lighting.

'You remind me of my dear friend, Remi, who I worked with in Paris,' said Avril as they made their way towards the elevators. 'He was so creative, so original. Always coming up with innovative ways to display Monsieur Dior's accessories.'

'You worked for Dior?'

'For more than three years. And it was wonderful. Hard work, but I learnt so much in my time there. Not just about fashion, but people too. And myself, I suppose.'

'Now, that's a story I'll need to hear over lunch! My mother was a beautiful sewer,' said Duncan with unrestrained pride. 'She would have given anything to have worked in a proper fashion house. I can still see her sitting at her machine at night. The clickety-clickety sound of her machine willing me to sleep like a metronome.'

Duncan stopped and turned to Avril. 'She's gone now, but oh, how she would have loved to have known you.'

'I can tell her creative spirit lives on in you,' said Avril, and she reached over and squeezed Duncan's hand.

In the elevator, Duncan suggested they meet in an hour as he wanted to go up to the third floor to look at the menswear.

Avril agreed and when the elevator stopped, the doors rattled open and the conductor announced, 'Second floor, Ladies' Fashion, day dresses, skirts, blouses and suits,' she stepped out.

Avril wandered around the ladies' department, studying the vast range of garments available and noticing which designs were being taken to the change rooms and, more importantly, being purchased. To Avril's surprise the shoe department carried a wide assortment of styles, colours and heel sizes. The hat selection was equally impressive.

The hour flew past and she met Duncan outside the store as planned.

'Where to take you next?' he said, looking at the streets around them before smiling broadly. 'I know!'

He took Avril's hand and they dashed across busy Bourke Street before the next tram approached. The moment they turned the corner, Avril felt a sudden surge of excitement. This was Flinders Lane, and she would soon discover that it was the heart of Melbourne's fashion district. A treasure trove of wholesale haberdashery, fabric merchants and millinery suppliers lined both sides of the lane. There were pattern makers, fabric cutters and garment makers, all housed in an area between the city centre and dock-lands on the Yarra River. Avril grabbed Duncan's arm and beamed up at him – she was in her version of paradise.

Cars and delivery vans haphazardly lined the narrow one-way street. Avril read every overhanging sign as they weaved their way down the bustling footpath. Bloomfield's Buttons, Gordon & Frank Fabrics, Brayer Millinery Wholesalers, Parker's Tailoring. The variety of services and fashion suppliers seemed endless and every conceivable item needed for garment making could be found on the lane. The clang and the clatter of the garment makers rang out from behind half-opened doors, and the air carried the heavy scent of sewing machine oil. Avril felt like she could have been in one of the many laneways that made up the fashion district of Paris.

As she peered curiously around the doorway of garment makers Almen & Sons, she saw a woman at a cutting table, running a piece of chalk around the edge of a cardboard pattern. The woman glanced up at Avril, and over the hum of the machines shouted, 'No vacancies, love. Try Hoffman's, this side, further down. They're hiring.'

Avril hadn't asked the woman about work but replied, 'Thank you,' acknowledging the suggestion with a friendly wave.

By mid-afternoon, Avril and Duncan had walked all over the city, down every laneway and arcade, ending up at Pellegrini's for a late lunch. Avril spoke to the waiter in Italian, who was delighted to suggest a dish for them that was not on the menu, then she chatted excitedly with Duncan about everything she'd seen.

'Your accent is adorable! I could listen to you talk all day,' Duncan said. 'What other languages do you speak, other than French and Italian?'

'A little bit of Spanish,' she said, holding up her thumb and forefinger, 'but only a little. And my mother taught me English, which we often spoke at home. She used to say, *If you have another language you have another culture.*'

'Well, what do you think of Melbourne so far?' Duncan asked as they waited for their meals.

'This city is really wonderful. And I must admit, I'm surprised at the range of fashion merchandise. And everyone looks so, so healthy.' She laughed. 'You know, Duncan, there is so much life here, so many possibilities.'

'From Dior to Flinders Lane,' Duncan said with a smile.

'And tell me about you, Duncan. Where did you grow up? Do you have family in Melbourne?'

Duncan said that he was born and raised in a country town called Bendigo. 'Let's just say I couldn't wait to get away.' He had one sister, Elizabeth, who was a nurse and lived in Sydney. He seemed reluctant to say more than that, so Avril didn't press him and he quickly changed the subject, asking about her work in the Paris fashion house.

Avril enthusiastically explained the running of the atelier and the work carried out by the seamstresses, then she started giving him a detailed account of what was involved in organising a seasonal collection. She stopped suddenly and looked down at the starched tablecloth. 'Oh, there I go, rambling on,' she said, embarrassed.

But Duncan just laughed. 'I'm happy to hear your rambling,' he said. 'I want to hear more. Tell me about your plans to start your own business.'

Avril smiled, feeling fortunate to have already made a friend in Duncan. They had similar interests and instinctively she felt like he was someone she could trust. 'I want to get it right,' she said. 'The world is changing, Duncan.

Fashion is changing. I can feel it. I discovered that when I worked at Dior.'

'Well, here's what I think,' he said. 'One day, people are going to point and say, *That's her. That's Avril Montdidier.* I think you're going to be a big hit in this town.'

'And I think we're going to be great friends, Duncan Campbell, head waiter, right-hand man,' Avril said, laughing, though she genuinely believed they would.

'I think so too,' Duncan replied.

'Now, tell me all about these horse races I've heard they have here in Melbourne,' she said. 'Apparently, the fashions are spectacular.'

*

As arranged, Louise and Gabriel were waiting for Avril the following Saturday morning outside Gibby's Café. Once seated, they wasted no time exchanging stories. Louise and Gabriel were living in a garden apartment at St Kilda Beach which was a popular location for European immigrants and the Duponts were already fully embracing its rather bohemian lifestyle. They had both found jobs at the *Melbourne Times*, Gabriel as an assistant to one of the senior photographers while Louise, for the time being, would be stuck in the typing pool.

'I told the simpleton at the interview that producing invoices was a waste of my journalistic talents and I should be writing features. He laughed and said, "I don't care how good ya English is, luv, take it or leave it,"' said Louise, mimicking the interviewer. 'I tell you, what would he know?'

Gabriel and Avril laughed. 'You see, Avril. My sister is impossible,' Gabriel teased, but he was no more content with his lot. 'I don't want to be photographing politicians and government officials for long. How terribly boring.' He made a disgruntled face. 'Fashion, advertising, that's where my passion lies. I already have my eye out for a studio.'

It had been less than a week but Avril had missed the banter they shared on the ship, as well as their more serious discussions about the careers they hoped to have. They had seen how war had destroyed opportunities for young people in their homeland, and had vowed to make the most of their new lives.

Avril told them about her new friend Duncan and her job at the bistro, describing the patrons that included prominent businesspeople, women of the social set, members of the European community and the artistic elite. Avril had already worked two evening shifts, which, to her surprise, she had rather enjoyed. She'd learnt that many of their clientele were regulars and since it had opened, Bistro Dubray had become renowned for its *boeuf bourguignon, filet mignon* and *canard à l'orange.*

The city bustled around them while they laughed and ate their breakfast. The footpath was busy, mainly with female shoppers, many of them free of the responsibility of household chores and children for a few precious hours. The department stores and speciality shops were doing a crashing trade as customers hurried to make their purchases before closing time at midday.

Louise pushed her breakfast plate away. 'You should be producing your own designs, Avril, not showing people to tables,' she said. 'There's so much happening in fashion right now. I had no idea there were so many stylish women in Melbourne. Have you seen the couture they have here? *Magnifique!*'

'Louise is right, Avril,' said Gabriel. 'You need to start looking for some premises.'

'We've only been here a week!' Avril countered with a smile. 'I want to get to know the city first.' But she was impressed by how quickly the Duponts were chasing their dreams and it spurred her on towards her own.

*

Over the following weeks, Avril came to know every garment retailer and wholesale business in the city, especially the couture businesses that specialised in upmarket day and evening wear. In a small black notebook, she recorded all their names and addresses, their trading hours, what they sold and the people she spoke to. *Miss Rodwell, Foys, Ladies shoes, assistant manager, very helpful. Brayer Millinery Wholesalers, Mr Brayer, quality buckram, straw and felt, COD.* All the while, she kept her eye on potential shops that might be suitable for her own business.

She returned time and time again to the millinery and fashion shops she'd discovered down the numerous arcades and laneways. She browsed the Block Arcade, with its beautiful glass ceiling, taking note of the selection of imported and locally made accessories. She visited every department store at least half a dozen times, including Ball & Welsh, Buckley & Nunn, Georges, which were three of her favourites, making a mental inventory of the women's fashions, shoes, handbags, hats and accessories.

Employing her good manners and French charm wherever she went, Avril easily engaged the sales staff in conversation, always taking note of their name tags and addressing them personally. Sometimes a shop assistant would get up the courage and ask Avril about her appearance. 'Where did you get your dress?' they would say quietly. 'How do you get your hair to stay like that?'

Avril would happily reply that her dress was one of her own designs and explain how she applied a touch of hairspray underneath her hair, not on top, to keep the style in place. She was always keen to find out what the sales assistants would buy, given the chance. For as much as she loved couture, producing made-to-measure clothing was costly and labour intensive. Avril was now sure that the future lay in innovative ready-to-wear clothing, wonderful designs that most women could afford.

One morning, while in the Myer department store, Avril was chatting to the sales assistant with whom she'd established a rapport. 'Miss Thompson, what would you buy if you had, say, twenty pounds to spend on some dresses?'

She knew that this was more than a month's wages and something all the shop assistants dreamt of being able to do. The young woman wasted no time in selecting several dresses from the rack, explaining what she liked most about the style, colour and fabric. Avril then casually enquired about which labels were selling well and which ones weren't. For it was the salesgirls, on their feet, day in and day out in the department stores, who truly knew what the customers favoured.

As often as possible, Avril also tried on the garments – dresses, skirts and suits – to gauge the fit of the label. Once inside the change room, she turned the clothes inside out to see how well they were made. She looked at the quality of the stitching, the finish of a hem, whether a dress was fully lined and how generous the seam allowances were.

It didn't take Avril long to work out which labels were the best sellers. Time and time again, two names kept coming up as the preferred choices of both wishful sales assistants and their customers – it seemed nearly everyone wanted to buy a Miss Collins or a Barbra Vance dress.

Each department store had an entire floor specifically for haberdashery supplies and dress fabrics. At Foy & Gibson, Avril examined the silk, lace and cotton fabrics, most of which had been imported from Switzerland and France, and spoke to the sales assistants, often in French or Italian.

One lunchtime, Avril struck up a conversation with a lady in the cafeteria in Manton's department store. Mrs Rossi, who was the head of Women's Alterations on the fifth floor, was only too happy to talk about the type of work they did, once Avril had explained she'd only recently arrived from Paris and was a seamstress herself. Avril knew that anyone who worked in alterations would have a wealth of information about the local fashion manufacturers – who was the best and who should be avoided.

'As soon as a customer says the zipper has broken, I know which label it will be straight away,' Mrs Rossi said, flattered to be consulted.

'The Miss Collins and Barbra Vance labels have some lovely designs,' Avril prompted.

'Now, there's quality,' Mrs Rossi eagerly replied. 'We might have to take up a hem if the frock is too long, but I've never had to replace a button, zipper or seen a faulty seam in any of those garments. And I've been here for twelve years.'

'Are they made in Sydney?' Avril asked.

'Oh no,' scoffed Mrs Rossi. 'Those labels are made right here in Melbourne by Lewin & Son. They have quite a few of their own labels in the stores, and they manufacture for other fashion labels as well. They have a very good name in the trade. Treat their staff well. If you're looking for work, that's the place to go.'

Avril didn't want to work for Lewin & Son. She wanted them to work for her, and at nine-thirty the following morning Avril was in Flinders Lane, knocking on their door.

*

Mr Lewin appeared in the doorway of the small reception area, dressed in a dark tailored suit, and warmly shook Avril's hand. At five foot seven, Bert Lewin was a little shorter than Avril, in his late sixties, clean shaven and immaculately groomed. Over the top of his wire-framed glasses, his eyes sparkled as he scrutinised the cut and cloth of her elegant navy coat dress, trying to identify which label she was wearing, though of course it was one of her designs.

After their introductions and small talk, he asked, 'How can I be of service, Miss Montdidier?'

'I was hoping you might be able to make up some samples for me.' Avril did not hesitate to make her plans known. This was not the time for subtle research or questioning.

Mr Lewin motioned towards a door. 'Please. Come through to our showroom.'

Avril placed her drawings and fabric samples on the table for Mr Lewin to see.

'I know my order is small, but I'm hoping to find a manufacturer who can make my ready-to-wear range, once I open my business.'

Mr Lewin studied the illustrations keenly then picked up several pieces of material. He could feel the superior quality of the cloth. The designs were fresh and innovative.

These dresses in this fabric will walk out the door, he thought to himself.

'So, you want to go into the *schmatte* trade?' he said with a grin. 'What made you come to us, if you don't mind me asking?'

'Your Miss Collins and Barbra Vance designs are some of the loveliest dresses I've seen here in Melbourne. I like the quality of your make and finish,' said Avril. 'There isn't another off-the-rack label that comes close to what you produce.'

A smile laced with pride spread over Mr Lewin's face. He recognised that Avril's compliments were genuine, and he liked her straightforward manner.

'Do you need patterns as well?' he asked.

'I've drafted my own patterns and worked out the lay-up plan for the fabric.' Avril took several pieces of paper from her satchel and placed them on the table. 'I believe this would be the most economical way to cut each style,' she said.

'I can see you're not new to the trade,' Mr Lewin said, regarding the professional and efficient young woman.

'I worked in Paris for the House of Dior for three and a half years, cutting and hand finishing, amongst other things. I arrived here in February,' said Avril, anticipating his next question.

'I came from Europe as well. Except it was February forty years ago,' he said, chuckling. Then, unable to resist asking what was on his mind any longer, he added, 'And your dress. It's one you've designed and made?'

'It is.' Avril reached again into her bag, pulled out a piece of leftover fabric from her dress and passed it to Mr Lewin. He ran the cloth slowly through his fingers, feeling the weft and warp of the fine wool crepe.

'Swiss?' he asked.

'British,' said Avril. 'I could only get six yards, unfortunately. You can imagine how scarce supplies were in Paris just after the war.'

Mr Lewin nodded and handed the piece of cloth back to Avril.

'Would you like to see our workrooms? We do everything on the premises. All our own pattern-making, cutting and sewing.'

'I'd like that very much,' said Avril eagerly.

As soon as Avril entered the production room, she could see that all the cutting and machining areas were spotlessly clean and well ventilated. A dozen machinists sat concentrating on their tasks as Avril followed Mr Lewin to the stock room at the back of the premises.

'Ah, Joshua,' said Mr Lewin. 'This is Avril Montdidier. We're going to be making some samples for her. Avril, this is my son.'

Joshua Lewin put down his clipboard and shook Avril's hand. Like his father he was smartly dressed and had the same dark brown eyes. He had an intense look about him, though he was happy to share his knowledge of the Melbourne clothing trade by telling Avril the best places to find hat blocks and top-quality millinery supplies. Then Mr Lewin and Avril left Joshua to complete his inventory checking.

An hour later, Mr Lewin gave Avril a price to make up her designs, which she happily accepted.

'I'll drop the patterns and fabric off in the morning,' she said.

'We'll have your order finished in five days,' said Mr Lewin as they shook hands at the front door.

As he watched Avril disappear down Flinders Lane,

Bert Lewin said to himself, *That one has real talent.* But the small order he had just taken from Avril was not on his mind. He was busy composing a job offer for a full-time women's wear designer – a position he hoped Avril Montdidier would find impossible to refuse.

CHAPTER 4

It was Josephine who suggested the idea.

'Duncan's taking two weeks off and going up to visit his sister in Sydney. I'm sure he'd be thrilled if you went with him.'

And he was. From the moment it was decided that Avril would be Duncan's travelling companion, the two of them had talked about little else. Duncan had even insisted on helping Avril choose her clothes.

'Sydney can be so humid this time of year,' he told her, as she pulled dresses from her wardrobe and offered them for his opinion.

'Take the pale blue and the black one for evening, but leave the other,' he pointed. 'That rayon fabric will stick to you like glue in the humidity.'

On the long train journey, Avril watched the passing scenery. She was looking forward to meeting Duncan's older sister Elizabeth and walking along Sydney's famous beaches. Autumn had brought a cool change to Melbourne but as Duncan and Avril stepped from their carriage at Central Station, Avril immediately removed her jacket and tied her hair back. Sydney was experiencing unusually hot weather and as the taxi weaved its way through the streets to Paddington, Avril wound down her window, allowing the warm air to blow against her face.

'This is it,' said Duncan as the taxi stopped in front of a Victorian terrace house. The front door flew open and Lizzy, as she was called, raced down the steps to greet them. At around five foot ten, Lizzy was shorter than her brother, and had titian-coloured hair and a peachy complexion. Lizzy gave Avril the same warm hug as her brother and ushered them inside.

In the comfortably yet sparsely furnished lounge room, a record player took pride of place in the centre of a sideboard under the front window. Lizzy explained that her housemate, Marion, was away for a week and Avril would be staying in her room. She told Duncan to show Avril upstairs while she made them tea.

Avril loved the homely bedroom immediately. A small attic window beside the bed provided an uninterrupted view over a sea of red-tiled roofs and stumpy brick chimneys. The floral bedspread was turned down and fresh towels placed near the pillows. Avril ran a brush through her hair, reapplied her lipstick and hurried downstairs, where she could hear Duncan and Lizzy's laughter.

Over clinking cups and sponge cake, Lizzy mapped out an itinerary for Avril and Duncan's visit: one that would show Avril the best Sydney had to offer before she returned to Melbourne in five days' time. A shopping expedition in the city was a must, as was a ferry trip to Taronga Zoo and Manly, and a few hours on the carnival rides at Luna Park.

'We have to see a floor show,' said Duncan. 'I'll get

tickets for your last night.' He placed his cigarettes on the kitchen table and Lizzy snatched them up.

'There's no smoking on my ward,' she said sternly.

'Once a nurse, always a bloody nurse.' Duncan laughed.

Avril couldn't help imagining Lizzy gliding down a spiral staircase in a burgundy-coloured satin dress, her red curls cascading down her back. If she ever wanted to give up nursing and become a model, she'd be snapped up instantly for parades and catalogue shoots.

Lizzy stared at her brother. 'You told me you'd given up this filthy habit.'

'Well, I haven't, sis,' he said airily.

'Avril, do you smoke these revolting things?' she asked.

'I used to,' said Avril. 'I'm French. Smoking is considered a pleasure. But you know, on the ship to Australia, I said to myself, no more smoking. I can't say I would never have another cigarette. Maybe. Perhaps. Who can tell?'

Avril placed her elbows on the table and rested her cheek on the top of her hand. It didn't seem to matter how much time Duncan spent with Avril, he never tired of her allure. He caught the expression on Lizzy's face and could tell she was equally mesmerised.

'Oh, don't you just love her?' Duncan cooed. 'She's *tray magnific*.'

Avril gave Duncan a gentle push on the shoulder. 'No, no, no. Your accent is appalling,' she said. 'No more attempts at sounding French, please.'

Lizzy laughed even louder than Duncan and tossed the cigarette packet back to her brother. 'I think it's time to start Avril's tour of Sydney. Go and get your swimmers on. We'll show her Bondi first.'

Gabriel had lent Avril a small box brownie camera and she used it constantly. *Capturing memories*, she called it. And there was no shortage of those during her stay in Sydney – she took photographs of Duncan and Lizzy in the surf, the view of the city from the ferry, people on the streets. Every scene in Sydney seemed to be lit by golden sun and blue sky; Avril had never known a place like it.

Her last day was spent shopping in the city. Avril had found a delightful twin set for Josephine and two pairs of shoes that had been calling her name. They were walking home across Hyde Park, Lizzy's arm linked through Avril's, Duncan ahead of them loaded with all the shopping bags which he insisted on carrying.

'It's a great comfort for me to know my brother has a good friend,' Lizzy said unexpectedly. 'Someone he can turn to. It's not always easy for him, making friends.'

'How so?' said Avril with genuine surprise. She hadn't met a single person who didn't warm to Duncan immediately, just as she had when they first met. 'Everyone likes him and he knows so many people in Melbourne.'

'Oh, I know he's popular. But you know how it is. True friends can be hard to come by.'

Avril knew the value of friendship. She was barely an adult when her mother died, and without friends she probably would not have survived. 'I do know how it is, Lizzy,' Avril said. 'And please, don't worry. Duncan will always have me in his life. Of that I'm certain.'

*

Avril knew she would see Lizzy again, and Duncan would be back in Melbourne in just over a week, but she was still a little emotional when they said their goodbyes. There had been so many highlights during her stay; Sydney had won Avril over. Duncan had outdone himself on her last night, booking one of the best tables at the Celebrity Club, and the cabaret dancers did not disappoint.

'One more photo,' she insisted, even though the taxi had already arrived. She quickly took a shot of brother and sister standing together on the front steps of the terrace house, arm in arm. As the taxi drove away towards Central Station, she looked back to see Duncan and Lizzy standing in the middle of the road, waving madly.

At the station, the last whistle for her train was blowing as Avril raced along the platform and wrenched open the door of the first-class carriage, scrambling in. A porter appeared and motioned for her ticket. 'You'd better hurry, Miss,' he said, 'train's about to leave.' When the porter had seen the smartly dressed woman running for the train, he assumed she was a first-class passenger. The wife or daughter of a grazier, up in Sydney for the Royal Easter Show. Then he frowned as he looked at her ticket and Avril worried that there was something wrong.

'I'm sorry to be a nuisance,' she said. 'I was simply trying to make the train.'

'I'm afraid they've overbooked the second-class carriages for the trip to Albury, again,' the porter explained, looking thoughtful. 'But I can put you in here,' and he gestured towards the nearby cabin door.

'My ticket . . . It's not for first class,' Avril stammered.

'You'd be doing me a favour,' he smiled, and tapped lightly on door 1A.

'Excuse me, Sir,' she heard him say to another passenger as he placed her case onto the rack above the seat. 'Morning tea will be served in an hour,' and he stepped aside to allow Avril to enter.

Avril was taken aback by the kindness of the porter. '*Merci beaucoup*,' she said, falling into her native tongue.

The porter touched the peak of his cap with his finger and hurried off as the train engines surged and it pulled away from the platform.

*

Henry Meredith looked up from his Inglis thoroughbred catalogue and stood, his tall solid frame instantly making the compartment seem smaller. His penetrating blue eyes swept over Avril, and he greeted her with a nod. 'Good morning,' he said.

'Good morning,' replied Avril.

Avril had caught him unawares and for a moment Henry was perplexed. The ticket master had assured him that the other seat had not been booked. He'd removed his light-weight wool jacket, hung it in the small coat cupboard and made himself comfortable. After the socialising and business dealings of the previous couple of weeks, Henry had been looking forward to travelling alone, but this unexpected intrusion was not an unpleasant one. Seeing Avril glance at him he looked away, conscious he was staring at his travelling companion.

He waited until the young lady had taken her seat by the window before he took his. Henry always made camp in the middle of the forward-facing seat, spreading his work documents to his left and right. He'd made his fortune from his ability to breed and run livestock: in particular, sheep and cattle. But his greatest passion was horses. There was no finer creature on earth, he would say. No animal with more courage, their beauty unsurpassed.

Henry gave the woman another cursory glance, then returned to his catalogue and retallied what he'd spent buying and selling colts and fillies at the yearling sales in Sydney. He'd been furious at being outbid on a chestnut colt by Midstream and had taken out his frustration by paying over the market value, considerably, for a Helios filly. Four of the yearlings from his own stud had set record prices. On reflection, he considered the sales a success and had come out of the entire proceedings in the black.

Avril rested her head on the seat and continued to look out the window. She didn't fidget or seem the least bit interested in making small talk, which Henry found refreshing. Nor did she turn her head when a folder of profit and loss statements slid from the seat and fanned out over the carpet. A calm temperament, self-assured and not easily alarmed, Henry thought as he assessed her demeanour. Henry Meredith credited himself with an innate ability to judge the character of both people and animals. Throughout his almost sixty years, his intuition had seldom let him down.

Henry continued reading as the train travelled south. Before too long, there was a soft tap on the door and the porter rolled in a small tea trolley, locked the wheels in place and retraced his steps. Henry closed the folder on his lap.

'*Excusez-moi, voulez-vous du thé ou du café?*' he said in perfect French, and he noticed a hint of surprise in his companion's expression.

'Coffee, please,' she replied in English, and her smile lit up her face.

'My name is Henry Meredith,' he said.

'Avril Montdidier,' she said. 'Pleased to meet you.'

Without fuss she secured the small fold-down table in place and took the cup and saucer from his hand.

'Your French is excellent,' she complimented him.

'I don't often get a chance to use it these days,' he said.

'Well, if it's all right with you, could we please use

English, then I'll be forced to concentrate,' said Avril. She picked up a plate of shortbread from the trolley and politely offered it to Henry. He declined and she placed a small piece on her napkin. Her eyes dropped to the cover of the catalogue next to him.

'Have you been buying horses?' she asked. 'Your catalogue. We have the same thing in France, although the sales are always in October.'

'Yes. I have. Buying and selling. I've been in Sydney for the yearling sales. Have you been in Australia long?' he asked.

'I arrived in Melbourne in February.'

'Did you sail from Marseille?'

'No. Plymouth, actually, then down to Lisbon.'

Much to Henry's surprise, and he had to admit delight, they fell into an effortless conversation. The questions Avril asked and the comments she made, Henry thought forthright and intelligent. He found himself discussing the time he'd spent in France as a pilot during the First World War, in a way he had not done before. His memory of the layout of Paris was excellent and he asked Avril about certain places he'd been to, wondering if they were still there after the destruction Paris had seen in the Second World War.

When she told him where she was living in Melbourne, Henry started laughing.

'You know Bistro Dubray?' she said.

'Yes. I've eaten there many times. My wife and sons as well. It's a particular favourite of ours whenever we're in Melbourne. In fact, I bred the winner of last year's derby, and we celebrated the end of the Spring Carnival at your aunt and uncle's restaurant. We had a marvellous night.'

'The Spring Carnival,' repeated Avril. 'Oh yes, my

friend Duncan was telling me about the horse racing in Melbourne.'

'So, you've heard about the Melbourne Cup then?'

'It is famous even in Paris,' said Avril. 'I hope to attend one day. Do you often race horses?'

'Yes. That's why I'm heading south. I have a thorough-bred stud just outside Melbourne, which I visit regularly. Do you ride?' he asked.

'Yes, I love to ride,' said Avril, 'but it's been a long time since I was on a horse.'

And for the first time since they'd started their conversation, Henry noticed Avril turned her face to gaze at the passing scenery. He refilled their cups and she thanked him, and they were quiet as they sipped their coffee.

Throughout the day the silence between them was, in fact, as comfortable as their conversation. Avril dozed off for a while and Henry went back to looking over the documents he'd told his Brisbane accountant, Eric Parker, he'd have finalised by the next morning. After their light luncheon was served, they both settled back into the comfort of their seats and allowed the conversation to flow as naturally as the rhythm of the train. He enjoyed listening to her talk about her childhood in the Loire Valley, and her account of her time living and working in Paris after the war. They spoke about horses, wine, the way Australia was changing, the Melbourne art scene and even a little bit about fashion.

But it was Henry's description of his cattle property, a 350,000-acre spread, located on Queensland's Darling Downs, that fascinated Avril the most. She was oblivious that daylight had all but disappeared as Henry explained the fundamentals of running 'the station', as he called it, the tasks carried out by the stockmen and the sheer number of people who lived and worked in and around the homestead. Henry didn't think Avril's questions impertinent when she asked how the sale price of livestock was regulated or what made a wool clip profitable. In fact, he found it uplifting to converse so easily about business matters with a woman less than half his age.

On their arrival in Albury, Avril and Henry, along with most of the other passengers, headed for the Railway Hotel. It was the only hotel in town and therefore the only place that catered for the Sydney to Melbourne train travellers, and Avril accepted Henry's invitation to join him for dinner.

'It will be steak and chips, I'm afraid,' he said, and so it was.

After dinner, Avril and Henry joined in a game of pool with a couple of locals who Henry was friendly with. Standing in the half dark thrown by the pool table light, Avril watched Henry concentrate on his next shot. *He's a handsome man*, Avril thought, *with his tanned face and greying hair line*. He had the look of a man equally at home on a horse or in a boardroom. There was a distinguished presence about him, and by the way that other men behaved and spoke to him, it was obvious to Avril that he had their respect. After the second game, Avril said goodnight and left the men to their drinks and banter.

It wasn't long before Henry climbed the stairs and, with a nightcap in hand, headed to his room on the first floor. It had been a long and pleasant day. Opening the tall narrow doors he stepped out onto the wooden balcony, into the cool night air. He sank down into the comfort of the large cane chair, stretched his legs forward and crossed his feet. Henry stared past the weathered edge of the bullnose veranda to the stars beyond. Thousands of sparkling dots against a blanket of ebony.

Savouring the peaty flavour of his drink, he let the whisky unlock events from long ago, replaying each scene in his mind as if it was yesterday. *What is a man and his life but a collection of memories?* Henry thought. The young French woman fascinated him. She'd somehow made the barrier between the past and the present fall away, leading Henry to look back at days long past. Which was something Henry Meredith rarely did.

Henry had everything a man could want in life – a wife he was still in love with after more than thirty years of marriage, three sons he couldn't be prouder of, a string of successful businesses – and he rarely thought about what might have been or what might be missing. Perhaps if he and Anna had been able to have a daughter, she might have been a bright light like Avril Montdidier.

The howl of a nearby dog brought him back to the present and to his feet as he drained his glass and went back inside.

*

A grey overcast Melbourne sky greeted the train as it rolled slowly into Spencer Street Station. By the time they'd reached the taxi rank, the drizzle had set in.

'Avril, you have been the most delightful travelling companion,' Henry said as they shook hands. 'If you'd ever like to see a bit of the country further north, you call this number,' and he handed her his business card. 'That's the homestead telephone line at the station. If I don't answer, the housekeeper or the housemaid will, and I'll return your call. You can also call this number and leave a message at my club here in Melbourne.'

'Thank you, Henry,' she said. 'How fortunate was I to be placed in your cabin?'

'We were both fortunate indeed,' smiled Henry.

And as natural and sincere as farewell can be, Avril reached up and kissed Henry on both cheeks.

'*Au revoir*, Henry Meredith. I hope we'll meet again,' she said, as she waved and stepped into a cab.

I certainly hope we do, Henry thought.

*

May had ushered in a chilly wind and by the end of June, the city streets were painted glossy black by the constant rain that had swept across the southern part of Australia. Melbourne headed towards a long cold winter. This didn't seem to deter the loyal customers who packed Bistro Dubray for dinner each night. Three nights a week, Avril worked as front-of-house hostess, freeing Josephine up to talk with the clientele, many of whom she'd come to know quite well.

Albert, on the other hand, was another matter. He hovered around Avril incessantly, checking everything she did. Avril rolled her eyes at Duncan as she showed a couple to their table.

'What's he doing now?' Duncan asked as he stood beside Avril at the front desk, his eyes scanning the bookings even though he already knew what they were.

'I wish he'd keep his hands to himself. Does he do this with the other staff?' Avril asked under her breath.

'Let's just stay the female staff never stay for long,' said Duncan. 'Don't worry. Use me as a buffer. He's less likely to annoy you if you and I are in close proximity.'

'Thanks, Duncan. But I think it might be a whole lot easier if I look for a part-time job elsewhere,' she said, moving to take the coats of four newly arrived patrons.

*

The six dresses Lewin & Son had made for Avril turned out better than she'd imagined. The quality of the stitching and the finish was outstanding. *I think I've found my garment maker,* she said to herself as she hung each design from the frame of her bedroom door.

When it was too wet and windy to venture out, Avril hunkered down at the table in her kitchenette and calculated the cost of setting up her business and producing her designs. She enjoyed the practical aspects of planning her enterprise as much as she enjoyed the artistic freedom of creating clothes. And while she'd been appreciative of the income she had from her nights in the restaurant, she knew Gabriel and Louise were right. She needed to find a suitable location for her shop and start something of her own.

There was also the issue of Albert, and Avril had had enough. Fortunately, he was seldom home and easy to avoid with Josephine around. At work, his hand on the sway of her back and her shoulders had decreased for a while but not enough to make her want to stay at the bistro. And despite Duncan's assistance and the manoeuvre he called '*dodge 'em*', where he'd try to intercept Albert as often as he could, he couldn't chaperone Avril around the restaurant while they did their work. As much as she wanted to talk to Josephine about it, Avril worried the situation would only cause trouble for her aunt.

For weeks now, Duncan had been encouraging Avril to move in with him. She could afford her share of the rent, and the more she thought about it, the more she realised it would be wise to take up his offer. The deal was sealed when Duncan told Avril about a part-time job that was coming up in a nearby restaurant in a few weeks' time. Avril was keen to apply for the position. The timing couldn't be better, and she decided to tell Duncan the night of Louise's party that she was ready to leave Collins Street and move to Carlton with him.

Everyone had been sworn to secrecy as Gabriel conspired with Duncan and Avril and planned a surprise party for Louise's birthday at the end of the month. The three of them took Louise out for a birthday breakfast, as a way of putting her off the scent. That evening, Louise hardly spoke to Gabriel as they rode the tram to Carlton. She was annoyed that they would be late for the movie he said he was taking her to see.

'I only have to pick up my jacket from Duncan's place,' he told her. 'It won't take long.'

Louise screamed when the lights went on in Duncan's lounge room and the assembled crowd started singing 'Happy Birthday'. It didn't matter that Louise and Gabriel had never met half the people before. Duncan was only too happy to play the party host. As the night wore on, the lounge room became the dance floor while the rest of the partygoers filled the hallway and kitchen.

In the early hours of the morning, Avril decided it was time to slip away and caught a lift back to Collins Street with Brenda, a work friend of Louise's. It was raining heavily as they left the party and by the time Avril got from Brenda's car to the shelter of the restaurant awning, her hair was soaked. Once inside, she removed her shoes and shook out her coat. Avril heard the faint sound of the lounge room clock chiming twice as she climbed the stairs and opened the door to Josephine and Albert's apartment. She placed her shoes down quietly on the entrance floor and, feeling her way in the dark, crept into the kitchen and hung her jacket over the back of a chair.

Avril opened the fridge door and took out a bottle of

water. The fridge light illuminated the surface of the table and Avril noticed three empty wine bottles in the centre. She could feel the presence of someone in the darkness. She jumped back and spun around.

Albert stepped out of the shadow, a wine glass in his hand. He was dressed in the same clothes he'd been wearing that morning, his shirt now crumpled and undone to the waist. He swayed slightly, placed his glass on the table and pushed his hands into the pockets of his pants. Then he took a slow step sideways and fell against the doorframe, blocking the only exit.

'Nice party? Did you have fun?'

Avril did not want to close the fridge door and lose her only source of light. She let the door swing wide open and went to the other side of the kitchen, picked up a glass and filled it with water. Any sense of tiredness had deserted her as a stinging tightness gripped her chest, and her senses were alert to every sound, every moment.

'I did,' she said. 'Early start tomorrow. Goodnight.'

She sensed something was about to happen and as she angled for the door, he was suddenly upon her, faster and stronger than she'd anticipated. He pushed her back against the kitchen bench and pinned her down. The glass she held flew from her hand, shattering on the floor. He held her by her wrists and brought his mouth down on hers, pushing his body into her breasts.

'Oh, come on,' he said, the repellent smell of his breath washing over Avril's face. 'Don't play the *vierge innocente* with me. Because I happen to know you're not.'

Avril lifted her knee swiftly, striking him in the groin. He doubled over and reeled back as she slipped from his grasp.

'You little bitch!' he shouted as his arm flew forward in

a desperate attempt to grasp some part of Avril's clothing. She dived through the door, across the lounge room and bounded up the stairs.

Her hands shook as she locked her bedroom door. She dragged a chest of drawers across and barricaded the doorway and felt the metal handles ripple down her back as she slid to the floor. Drawing her knees into her body, she held her hands across her mouth and muffled her crying. Tears streamed down her face. All she could hear was the sound of her own heart pounding. Her thoughts tumbled in myriad directions: Should she tell Josephine? Should she leave immediately and go back to Duncan's? How would she get past Albert?

Avril heard the front door slam with such force that it made her jump. She raced to the window and watched as Albert hurried to his car parked on the opposite side of the street. He stumbled as he grappled with the handle of the driver's door, then sped off, only turning the head-lights on some twenty yards down the street. *Run, you coward*, Avril thought. She was certain he would not return that night. Even so, this was not the time to leave. As soon as it was light, she'd go to Duncan's place. That's what she would do. She'd be safe there.

Her instincts told her to get dressed and to pack. Avril went to the bathroom and washed off her makeup. She scrubbed her hands, removed her clothes and tossed them in the laundry hamper. She never wanted to see that dress again.

Avril felt a switch flick inside her and her thoughts became ordered and clear. Practicality and quick thinking pushed aside any fear. She pulled on a pair of black pants, a turtleneck sweater and a pair of walking boots. She brushed her hair and pulled it back into a tight ponytail.

She knew she could not take all her possessions at once and would have to return to collect the remainder of her things. Into a duffle bag she quickly folded some clothes, gathered up her toiletries and two pairs of shoes. She yanked her navy wool coat from its hanger. Gloves and a beret, she rolled up and placed in the pockets of the coat. Her black notebook, passport, bank book and folder of personal papers she wedged down the side of the bag. From inside the wardrobe, she unhooked the tan leather bag which she'd worn the day she'd arrived. Some of her money she placed in the bag and some in the pocket of her pants.

Her hands shook as she made herself a pot of coffee. Then she found some writing paper and a pen and sat down at the desk. As precisely as she could, she recorded every detail of what had taken place, from the time she'd put the key in the front door to now. She reread what she'd written then dated and signed the four pages. Avril sealed the envelope and placed the letter underneath the tray in the cutlery drawer. When the time was right, she'd tell Josephine where to find what she'd written. It would give her aunt the privacy she'd need to process what she would read. But for now, Avril would slip a note into her aunt's handbag, telling her that she'd gone to stay at Duncan's for a few days.

The fear that had first consumed her shifted and morphed into anger. She sat in her room for the rest of the night and as soon as she saw the first tinge of daylight, she left. Once on Collins Street, she swung her duffle bag over her shoulder and walked briskly away without a second glance. She made her way down Russell Street and passed a milkman doing his rounds. It would take her thirty minutes at the most to walk to Duncan's place. *What will*

I say to Josephine? What other secrets lurk behind the closed doors of my aunt and uncle's life? she wondered.

The further Avril walked the stronger she felt and by the time she reached Duncan's house on Cooper Street, she was ready to smash the door down.

*

Duncan stoked the fire in the potbelly stove then refilled Avril's coffee cup. She told him what had happened without fanfare, and he said he was surprised but not shocked. Duncan lit a cigarette, crossed his legs and leant back in his chair. He stared at the small window of glowing coals that radiated from the stove for some time before he took a sip of coffee.

'Josephine gave me a job after the war when no one else would,' said Duncan. 'All I wanted to do as a kid was to get to the bright lights of the city.' He tapped his cigarette on the edge of the ashtray. 'And then that bloody war came along.' His eyes met Avril's. 'The army and I were not, shall we say, a good fit, by any stretch of the imagination. It was either that or the navy, and life on the high seas would have been the end of me.'

'I can understand your feelings towards the army,' Avril said as she smiled and took his hand. 'Khaki is definitely not your colour.'

Duncan lifted his head and blinked away the glassy sheen from his eyes and laughed.

'You really do remind me a lot of Remi. You'd like him if you ever meet.'

'Well, maybe we will one day. If you ever come good with your offer and take me to France with you,' Duncan joked.

Avril rested her elbows on the table and folded her

hands under her chin. 'They put on a good show, don't they, my aunt and uncle?'

'I'm not sure how much you know or have figured out but, behind closed doors, well, your aunt does not have it easy.'

'I'm assuming he hits her,' Avril said sadly. 'Does he?'

'There have been times. Yes. And I know what you're thinking. Why doesn't she leave him?'

'No, no. I wasn't thinking that at all,' she said. 'I understand the complexity of a relationship like that. They've been together since she was sixteen and he was twenty-three. He's all she knows and, besides, he controls the money.'

'I look out for her, as best I can,' said Duncan. 'There have been a few times when Josephine's stayed here. He's Mr Charm to everyone he meets. God, I'd like to knock that bastard down one day. And you know me, I'm opposed to violence.'

Avril moved her chair closer to the stove and warmed her hands. The thought of Josephine being hurt in any way repulsed her. She recalled the time she'd heard Josephine pleading with Albert to give her five pounds. And the nights Albert played cards, seldom home before the sun came up. The thrill of being in Melbourne had deserted Avril. She grabbed the steel poker, opened the door of the stove and pushed at the hot coals.

'I need to get away,' she said.

'Of course,' Duncan replied. 'You're moving in with me.'

'No, I mean, I need to get right away. Out of Melbourne, just for a little while. Maybe I'll go to Sydney. At least I'll know Lizzy. I know I said last night that I would like to share this place with you. But now I just want to get away – from him.'

'What about your plans to start your own business?'

Avril's mind was now racing as an idea had started to form.

She reached over and took Duncan's hand. 'You're such a good friend to me, Duncan. Believe me, no one is going to stop me from building my little fashion empire. I'm not giving up on that, but . . . I think . . . a little detour, maybe.'

*

Later that morning Avril walked to the phone box at the end of Duncan's street. The phone line crackled then she heard a voice loud and clear.

'Hello. Henry Meredith speaking.'

'Henry. It's Avril Montdidier,' she said calmly.

If he was surprised he didn't sound it. They exchanged pleasantries as if they were old friends, before Henry asked, 'What can I do for you, Avril?'

'I need a job,' she said with the forthrightness that he'd admired when they met. 'Do you have some work I could do on your property? I can clean or cook. Anything, really.'

They spoke for some time but Henry didn't ask why Avril suddenly wanted to leave Melbourne. The determination in her voice was enough for him to know it was a considered decision. Arrangements were made efficiently and Henry explained that her journey would mean staying a night in Sydney and in Brisbane, before catching a train to Toowoomba, the closest train station to his property.

'I have a friend I can stay with in Sydney,' she assured him.

'I'll book you a room in the Cook Hotel in Brisbane,' he said. 'It's next to the train station and I know the manager, so you'll be well looked after.'

She thanked him and, even though he knew that Avril Montdidier could look after herself, he made her repeat their arrangements to ensure she would arrive safely.

'So, we'll see you next Friday,' he said. 'My son, Jordy, will be there to meet you. Think of this as a new adventure. Your first visit to Queensland.'

On her return, Duncan opened the front door before Avril had a chance to knock. She hurried inside, back to the warmth of the kitchen.

'What did he say?'

'I'm leaving on the nine o'clock train on Tuesday morning,' Avril said. 'It seems I'm going to be a governess, just until December.'

'You! A governess!' Duncan roared with laughter. 'And how many kids do you have to look after?'

'Five, apparently.' She grinned at Duncan's amused expression.

'Well, all I can say is that this will certainly be an eye-opener for a girl from Tours via Paris. What's the name of this godforsaken place, anyway? Somewhere in southern Queensland, isn't it?'

Avril picked up the pen that was lying beside the crossword. She wrote the name of Henry's property in bold letters across the top of the newspaper and spun the broadsheet around for Duncan to see – *Monaghan Station*. 'That's where I'm going. Wish me luck.'

*

On Monday morning Avril returned to Collins Street to collect her belongings, relieved to know that Albert would not be there. 'Why he would suddenly need to go on a business trip to Adelaide with Max, I have no idea,' Josephine had told Avril on the phone the night before.

When Avril had told her aunt that she was taking up a job offer in Queensland, that she wanted to see more of the country, Josephine had asked all the standard questions, and pointedly avoided any personal ones. Avril sensed that her aunt knew there was more to her sudden decision than a desire to travel. She worried about leaving Josephine but reminded herself that her aunt had survived for decades without Avril, and besides, she had a true friend in Duncan.

'I'll miss you terribly,' Josephine said as she sat on the bed and helped Avril pack her clothes. 'You're a grown woman, with a life of your own, and Melbourne will always be here. Why not go off and do something different. I often wish that I'd . . .'

Josephine stopped short of what she was about to say, got up from the bed and walked towards the bathroom. 'I'll just check you've got all your toiletries.'

When her bags were packed Avril glanced around the room. *I can't tell her, I just can't*, she thought, staring towards the cutlery drawer where the whole sorry tale lay. *There will be a right time, but not now.*

'It's only until December,' she said, holding Josephine's hands. 'And then I'll be back.'

Josephine squeezed Avril's hands but couldn't meet her eye. 'This life. The bistro. Albert. It's all I've ever known,' she said. 'Please don't think badly of me.'

'Josephine, I could never think badly of you. Ever. Why would you even say that?'

For a moment, Avril feared that Josephine would cry. 'There are a lot of things I'd like to talk about with you one day, maybe when you come back,' she said. Then her aunt straightened her back and regained her composure. 'Now, let's get these bags downstairs. The taxi will be here any moment.'

Something had passed between Avril and Josephine. A knowing, and an understanding of stories yet to be revealed, of events yet to be spoken about. Avril felt closer to her aunt than ever before and she knew that when she returned to Melbourne, they would have that talk, honestly and without fear.

CHAPTER 5

Jordy Meredith leant against the Ford ute enjoying the warmth of the winter sun, his forearms resting on the top of the tailgate. He was deep in conversation with the station manager from Cathaway Downs as the midday train from Brisbane pulled into Toowoomba station.

'Dad's employed a new governess,' said Jordy. 'This one won't last long, they never do. The last one took off with a shearer. They all come, thinking they'll like country life, but they miss the bright lights sooner or later.'

Charlie Cassidy ground the toe of his boot into the dirt, killing what was left of his cigarette.

'It's not like you to be cynical,' Charlie laughed, extending his right hand. 'Anyway, it's been nice talkin' to ya, Jordy. Give my regards to Henry and tell him I'll get Stan to bring over those two mares he wants before the week's out.'

Jordy removed his hat, ran his hand through his thick dark hair and wandered over to the station platform, scanning the passengers for a young woman around his own age.

'Morning Jordy', 'G'day, mate', a couple of the locals said as they passed by.

Jordy's father had described Avril Montdidier like he would a filly at the Easter yearling sales – lean, carries herself well, nicely turned out. 'Don't worry. You'll know her when you see her,' Henry had said, and sure enough Jordy spotted her instantly. Down the ramp she walked, carrying two suitcases and a bag slung across her navy coat. Their eyes met and he nodded, returning her smile.

'Afternoon, Miss Avril. I'm Jordy.'

She put down one of her cases and they shook hands.

'It's nice to meet you, Jordy,' she said. 'Thank you for coming to collect me.'

'Here, let me take your luggage,' he insisted, replacing his hat then picking up the cases for the short walk back to the ute.

At a fraction over six feet tall, Jordy Meredith was a slighter and shorter version of his father. Though his warm brown eyes and thick eyelashes, Avril surmised, had been inherited from his mother.

'It's a two-hour drive back to Monaghan,' he said. 'I've done most of what I came to town for, so how about we get some lunch?'

At Banjo's Café on the main street, Avril and Jordy chatted over tea and toasted sandwiches. Avril could tell that Jordy was at ease in the company of women. Well spoken and polite, he was inquisitive about her life without being intrusive.

After lunch, Jordy parked the ute in front of Pigott's & Co department store. 'Just one more stop. I have to pick up some parcels for our cook,' he said. 'This is about as flashy as it gets around these parts when it comes to shopping. Why don't you have a look around the store and I'll meet you back here in half an hour?'

Avril didn't need any further encouragement. As far as she was concerned, this was an information-gathering opportunity. The ladies' fashion was a surprisingly large well-stocked department with a wide variety of Australian and imported designs, most of which she recognised. The shoe section was much the same and by the time Avril had finished browsing through haber-dashery and manchester, observing both the sales staff and customers, she could see that Pigott's was a well-run and profitable business.

Once they'd left Toowoomba, it wasn't long before the tarred road ended. Overnight rain had turned the soil burnt orange and as Jordy drove with one hand on the steering wheel, he casually navigated around the odd pothole.

'We're on dirt for the next ninety miles,' he said. 'And we might see a roo or two.'

'A kangaroo, you mean?' said Avril.

'Call them roos,' he grinned, 'and you'll sound like a local in no time.'

As he drove, Jordy gave her a brief history lesson on the region, explaining the livestock and crops that were farmed and pointing out landmarks.

Avril had learnt enough about the Darling Downs to know that the area was a prosperous farming district with rich soil and good rainfall, not unlike the Loire Valley. But unlike her verdant homeland, this country was a blend of green, grey and dark olive tones and it seemed to stretch endlessly in all directions. Avril found it beautiful, but also wild and exciting.

'Has your family been at Monaghan Station very long?' Avril asked.

'My great-grandfather came to Australia just over one hundred years ago. And we're still here,' Jordy chuckled, 'so we must be doing something right, wouldn't you say?'

Avril laughed with him. 'You've given me the short version,' she said. 'I'm interested. Truly.'

'I guess we have time to kill,' he said, and then proceeded to recount his family's story.

Samuel Meredith, Jordy's great-grandfather, was only twenty-two years old when he left the shores of Ireland on a sailing packet, knowing he'd never set foot on County Monaghan soil again. What Samuel didn't realise was that the decision he'd made on the toss of a coin in a tavern in Ballybay – to set sail for Australia – would lead to a life of happiness, prosperity and freedom beyond his wildest imaginings.

According to Jordy, the Meredith family motto, *Timing is everything*, was credited to Samuel. For shortly after he arrived in Sydney, gold was found in Ballarat and, like so many of that era, he headed south to try his luck. After two years of backbreaking work on the goldfields, Samuel found a large nugget of gold – it was worth a fortune, enough to buy his own land and livestock. When a 200,000-acre holding came up for sale west of the Great Dividing Range in Queensland, Samuel made a cash offer the owner could not refuse. The purchase of another 150,000 acres five years later confirmed Samuel's position as one of the largest landholders in southwest Queensland.

On the banks of the Condamine River, he built the first homestead – a rambling slab hut with a thatched roof. When the house was finished Samuel planed down a long piece of grey gum and secured the plank to the top railing of the home paddock fence. Then he dipped his brush in tar and wrote the name, *Monaghan Station*, in honour of the home he'd left behind and the new one he intended to create.

*

After an hour on the road, Jordy agreed with his father's description of Avril Montdidier as 'a bright and likeable young woman'. She was not, as he discovered, new to country life, and she seemed genuinely interested in the Merediths, the station and the day-to-day business of farming.

'Have you been a governess before?' Jordy asked as the ute rattled over a rickety old bridge, the water swelling precariously high.

'Never,' Avril said, laughing. 'I worked in a fashion house as a seamstress, before coming to Australia. So, teaching is something completely new for me. I'm looking forward to it, though.'

'Well, you'll have your hands full with a couple of them, but they're good kids,' he said.

'Whose children are they?' Avril asked.

'There's Sandra's twin girls. She works as a housemaid, and Col, our head stockman, he's got three boys,' Jordy explained. 'A local school's opening next year so they'll all be going there in February.'

'Has there always been a governess on the station?'

'"Staff can focus on their jobs when their kids are taken care of". That's what my father has always said. So yes, my folks have always employed someone to school the older kids or take care of the little ones.'

'What happened to the last governess?' Avril expected that perhaps the previous governess was a traveller, like herself.

'She didn't work out,' was all Jordy said.

*

Half an hour past Dalby, Jordy made a right-hand turn off the road. The sign on the gate as they rattled across a cattle grid told Avril they had arrived: *Monaghan Station.*

'Ten minutes to the homestead. Five if you're on a good horse and you know where to cut through the bush.' Jordy gave her a mischievous grin. 'My folks won't be back until late this afternoon, but our housekeeper, Mrs Carmichael, will be there to settle you in. Been with us forever. She's devoted to the family.'

Pockets of uncleared bush were scattered over the grass-filled paddocks that spread into the distance. The smoky blue hue of a jagged, low-lying mountain range dominated the background. Trees had been cleared ten yards either side of the road, creating a natural fence line of gums and wattle. Avril wound down her window and breathed in the eucalyptus-scented air.

At a bend in the road, the surrounding bush beside the driveway was replaced by a chest-height ficus hedge and neatly trimmed verge. Up ahead, Avril caught sight of a charcoal-coloured slate roof, peeking over the top of the green foliage. The ute slowed as they passed through a pair of elaborate cast-iron gates, gravel crunching underneath the tyres. Speckled sunlight flickered through the leafless branches of the giant jacaranda trees as a magnificent two-storey brick and stucco mansion came fully into view.

'Here's the homestead,' said Jordy. 'Or *The Big House,* as everybody calls it.'

The Georgian-inspired house sat peacefully in the centre of a sprawling manicured lawn, intersected by an array of pathways and flowerbeds. A heavy skirt of wisteria ran across the front of the house and down one side, anchored to the underside of the top balcony. Avril followed the white wrought-iron railing that framed the veranda on the upper level. The detailed pattern created an elegant line that drew the eye to the far ends of the building.

Three overfed labradors raced along the veranda, barking and wagging their tails as Jordy pulled up at the front of the house.

'What beautiful dogs,' said Avril, giving each dog the recognition they were seeking with a rub to their backs while Jordy retrieved her cases.

'Spoilt house dogs, that's what they are,' said Jordy. 'But don't tell Dad I said that.'

The glass-panelled front door swung open and Rosie Carmichael, stalwart champion of the Meredith family, bustled down the steps and called the dogs away from Avril's hem. She was short and slim, with grey hair pulled into a tidy bun, and although she was probably in her seventies, she was spritely.

'That's enough. Off you go,' she roused, clapping her hands. The inspection and greetings over, the dogs trotted back the way they'd come.

'Afternoon, Mrs Carmichael,' said Jordy.

'Easy run, was it?' she asked.

'Without a hitch,' said Jordy. 'This is Avril. Avril, our housekeeper, Mrs Carmichael.'

'Welcome, dear,' she said. 'How was your trip from Brisbane?'

'Very enjoyable, thank you,' Avril replied.

'I picked up all the orders you wanted,' Jordy told the housekeeper, 'and Jean's too. I'll unload around the back.' Then he turned to Avril and nodded. 'Mrs Carmichael will look after you. I'll see you later.'

'Thank you, Jordy, for picking me up from the station,' she said, adding, 'Let me know when you're ready for a race from the front gate.'

'Oh, I will,' he grinned. 'You can count on it.'

Mrs Carmichael lifted one of the suitcases and headed up the stairs. 'Come through and I'll get you settled.'

*

By the time Avril had walked from the front door to her bedroom on the other side of the house, she'd surmised that Monaghan was probably the most significant property in the region. The exquisite furnishings she saw as she followed Mrs Carmichael down the wide hall, past a large lounge area, dining room and library, emanated the same grand atmosphere as Chateau de Vinieres. Paintings, both traditional and modern, were hung throughout. Yet for all its grandeur, the house felt very much like a family home, welcoming and lived in.

'I hear you're not new to country life,' said Mrs Carmichael, opening the bedroom door. Avril looked around the generous yet cosy space and immediately noticed the rose garden beyond the tall windows.

'I grew up in a rural part of France,' Avril replied. 'Lots of crops, horses and cattle.'

'Well, it's lovely to have a governess who's a country girl,' the housekeeper said. 'Bathroom's through there. You'll eat with the family tonight. The governess always does on her first night, then you'll most likely eat with the rest of us around six o'clock in the evening. Now, let me show you the rest of the house and the school room before I introduce you to our cook.'

Avril was well aware that no one knew more about what went on at a country property than the housekeeper and the cook – the keepers of secrets. *If they're accepting of me,* Avril thought, *then my stay will most likely be a happy one.*

Mrs Carmichael led her to a large, weatherboard building, connected to the side of the main house by a covered walkway, which was the main kitchen and staff dining room.

The cook looked up and lowered the volume on the radio as Mrs Carmichael and Avril entered by the side door.

'Our new governess is here,' Mrs Carmichael announced eagerly. 'Avril, this is Jean.'

Jean Cooper was in her early fifties, with a trim figure, soft red curls that framed her face and sharp blue eyes that narrowed, sweeping over Avril from head to toe. She stood up slowly from the table where she'd been shelling broad beans, wiped her hands on her apron and lifted her chin. As culinary skills go, Jean was considered far above the average and the kitchen and vegetable garden were her treasured domain. She had worked in menial jobs her whole life until she'd come to Monaghan Station some twelve years before. She believed she'd met 'every type of critter God put on this earth'. Her childhood as an orphan had made her suspicious of most people, men and women, but particularly women, and she was never keen to have another about the place. *More trouble than they're worth*, she'd said to Rosie Carmichael many times over the years.

'It's very nice to meet you, Jean,' said Avril, extending her hand. 'Those beans look lovely.'

Avril's hand was soft, her nails painted a pastel pink. That combined with her smooth pale skin was enough for Jean to decide that the new governess had an easy life and knew nothing about a hard day's work.

'French then, are ya,' said Jean, returning to the broad beans.

'Yes. But Australia is my home now.'

Jean ignored her. 'Jordy pick up that bolt of cotton from Pigott's I paid for?' she asked Mrs Carmichael.

'And the stores you wanted,' Mrs Carmichael replied. 'I'll bring your fabric over shortly.'

'Needn't bother,' the cook said, untying her apron. 'Dinner's prepared. I'll come and get it myself. Besides, I could do with a stroll,' and she left the kitchen without a sideways glance.

Once Avril had been shown the schoolhouse, a generous-sized wooden hut with a low-slung veranda, Mrs Carmichael returned to the main house, leaving Avril to look around the homestead by herself. The large vegetable garden behind the kitchen teemed with winter crops that spread like a jewelled carpet in the late afternoon sun. Trellises groaned under the weight of the squash, surrounded by rows of leeks, cabbages, spinach and other greens. Hens pecked in the chicken pen that bordered the gardener's shed. A short distance from the big house was a large bungalow with a high-pitched roof. Through the huge windows Avril could see the workings of an artist's studio, a surprising yet delightful discovery.

Monaghan Station was a self-contained community, with myriad outbuildings, each one located according to practical or social considerations. Bob McIntyre was the station manager and the location of the house he lived in was an indication of the important position he held. Situated inside a fenced-off area with a well-maintained garden, the front veranda had a commanding view of a tree-lined section of the Condamine River that snaked its way south. Some distance away were the houses occupied by married couples and beyond that, further along the river, were the single men's quarters. Jordy had also pointed out the direction of the shearing shed on the drive in and explained that it was two miles from the home-stead, strategically placed to keep away the smell of sheep and the army of flies that accompanied them.

Beyond the mature trees and lawn that surrounded the homestead were numerous buildings and facilities, which were collectively referred to as 'The Yard'. Sheds for equipment and machinery fanned out across the yard, along with a workshop, the tack room and stables – the heartbeat of the station – and a little further out, the stockyards. Avril watched from beside a wood pile as a couple of stockmen rode in, flanked by their panting dogs, unsaddled their horses and let them go in a small paddock behind the stables. Two little girls peeked out from behind a tree, pointed at Avril, then ran off giggling.

Avril was heading back to the house when Jordy drove up alongside her.

'Hop in,' he called out. 'Got something to show you.'

He pulled up next to an enormous open-sided tin shed on the far side of the yard, just as the light was beginning to fade.

'What are we looking at?' asked Avril, as the only thing before them was a treeless flat paddock.

'You'll see. Shouldn't be long now,' he said. He'd no sooner checked his watch when a tiny dark speck appeared on the horizon. The blip grew closer and closer until a propeller aircraft came clearly into view.

'Who's flying the plane?' said Avril.

'Who do you think?' Jordy smiled.

The dirt flew up in a cloud as the plane landed on the airstrip then slowly taxied in, coming to a stop inside the hangar.

'That must feel incredible,' said Avril, 'sailing through the sky like that. Where has it flown from?'

'Rockhampton. North. On the coast,' said Jordy. 'Come and say hello to Dad and meet my mother.'

Inside the hangar, Jordy kissed his mother and relieved her of a briefcase.

'Avril, this is my mother, Anna,' he said, leaving the two women to talk while he placed a wheel block behind the front tyre of the plane. Anna Meredith pushed her sunglasses onto the top of her strawberry-blonde hair and greeted Avril with a welcoming smile. She wore tailored navy pants and a fine knit sweater, as if she'd just stepped out of a catalogue for the finest in country women's fashion.

'We're delighted you're here,' said Anna in a smooth and dignified voice. 'We were caught short when the previous governess left so suddenly.'

'Avril!' Henry called as he climbed down from the plane, clutching a bulging folder, his coat draped over his arm. 'Welcome to Monaghan. I trust Mrs Carmichael has shown you where everything is and has made you welcome?'

Avril replied that Mrs Carmichael had been most welcoming and explained that she'd been exploring the area around the house, while Jordy hoisted his parents' luggage onto the back of another ute.

'Has Reece arrived?' Henry asked Jordy.

'Got here on Monday. He left yesterday with Tim, Bob and Col to bring in those heifers from Jadamare. Said they'd be back by Friday next week.'

'Is Jadamare another property?' asked Avril.

'No,' said Henry. 'We name our larger paddocks here. Jadamare's a couple of days' ride away. My other two sons and the station manager are moving some cattle, bringing them closer to home.'

'We do the same thing in France with our cattle, but of

course it doesn't take a week to get there and back,' Avril said, and Henry was pleased to find her just as amicable as when they'd met on the train.

'Would you like a lift back to the house?' said Anna. 'You're welcome to squash in with us.'

'Thank you, but Jordy said he'd show me the shearing shed, before it gets too dark.'

'Which reminds me, Dad,' said Jordy. 'I ran into Charlie Cassidy in Toowoomba this morning. Said to give you his best and that Stan would be bringing over a couple of mares. What's that about?'

Henry rested his elbow on the driver's door as he started the engine. 'I thought one of them might be suitable for you, Avril. Both mares have been nicely schooled.' He smiled. 'One's a bit more *goey* than the other, apparently. You can take your pick. On Monaghan Station, everyone needs a reliable horse.'

*

Avril opened the French doors in her bedroom, stepped onto the wide veranda and spread her hands along the railing. The night sky was a maze of twinkling stars and in the distance, she could hear the low hum of the generator. A feeling of tranquillity and security swept over her as her thoughts turned to France.

Standing alone on the veranda of this beautiful home, Avril felt as though she'd fallen through time, and had landed in an Australian version of the chateau. She could not shake the sense of déjà vu she felt from the moment she arrived at the front steps earlier that day. She thought of Guy, and the wedding that never happened, and how their life might have been. Then, with practice honed over painful years, she pushed the thoughts aside and focused on her own future. *Five months working here will give me time to think and plan my business*, she told herself. It had been decided she'd move in with Duncan, Louise and Gabriel when she got back, as they were all keen to rent a house in Richmond or South Melbourne, and this would give her something to look forward to. Broaching the subject of Albert with Josephine on her return would be a completely different matter altogether.

How long she'd been staring up at the stars, she was not sure. But the sound from the bedroom clock told her not to be late for dinner on her first night. Avril suspected that although Anna, Henry and Jordy would not be formally dressed for dinner, they would still make an effort and she wanted to show respect for them. So Avril changed into a teal-coloured full circle skirt that hovered above her ankles and a dark grey fitted wool boat-neck top then decided to wear a pair of pewter-coloured court shoes. 'Where else are you going to wear these beautiful heels you bought in Sydney?' she said aloud to her reflection in the mirror. She quickly rolled her hair into a loose bun and applied a pale pink lipstick.

Avril could hear the music before she reached the doorway of the 'Front Room', as Mrs Carmichael had called it.

'I'm sorry I'm a bit late,' she said as she entered the room. 'I lost track of time, looking at the stars.'

Anna was perched on the arm of the sofa beside the piano, watching Jordy play. Henry was warming himself by the fireplace, a drink in hand. Avril caught her breath. How easily this could have been Madame and Monsieur Leon, Guy and Avril in the room. Jordy looked up from the keys for a moment and stopped playing. He smiled at Avril and returned to his piece by Cole Porter.

'Avril, how lovely you look,' said Anna. 'Henry! Stop roasting yourself by that fire and offer Avril a drink.'

Avril accepted a small glass of sherry.

'Cheers,' said Anna. 'Good health.'

*

Anna had been interested to meet Avril, ever since Henry had told his wife about their chance encounter on the train. Station life was essentially a male domain and although Anna travelled regularly to her hometown of Melbourne, there had been many times over the years when she'd longed for some more female company. It was no secret that, after Reece was born, Anna and Henry had hoped for a daughter, but it wasn't to be. Anna had often thought it was her sense of isolation – the boys away at boarding school, Henry's constant coming and going from Monaghan as he expanded his business interests in far north Queensland and the southern states – that had prompted her to explore her love of art more fully and develop her own artistic skills. As it turned out, painting had become her saviour over the thirty-one years Henry and Anna had been married. Not just because it filled her days, but because through her art, Anna had carved an identity which extended beyond her role as wife and mother. A gifted artist, her paintings were sold by two galleries, one in Brisbane and the other in Melbourne.

Throughout dinner, Jordy, Anna and Henry took turns retelling funny stories that had occurred at Monaghan Station over the years. Characters that had come and gone, mishaps and adventures, the drought years when the Condamine was reduced to a few muddy pools of water or, even worse, when the riverbed was bone dry. Anna sipped her wine, observing the natural banter between Avril and Jordy. She found Avril to be relaxed and charming company, frequently turning the conversation away from herself towards Anna, Henry and their family.

'And Reece, does he work on the property full-time?' Avril asked as dessert was served.

'Ha! The genius.' Jordy laughed. 'No, country life's not for my little brother.'

'But I thought he was bringing in cattle with your older brother?'

'Well, he is,' said Jordy, 'but being on a horse for a week is just a bit of fun for him while he's home.'

'Reece has just finished his law degree,' Henry said, with the note of pride he had whenever he spoke about his sons. 'He starts with a legal firm in Melbourne next month. Commercial law. That's his interest.'

'He's already asked for some leave so he can make it back for the first weekend in October,' said Anna. 'I can't see that they'd refuse him for such a special occasion.'

'It's Dad's sixtieth birthday,' Jordy said. 'It's going to be a very big night and a lot more formal than our Winter Dance.'

'Winter Dance. What's that?' Avril asked.

'A dance we hold in the shearing shed at the end of August every year,' said Jordy. 'Everyone who's anyone is there. Locals, and all the team here on the station. Friends and family come for the weekend.'

'You'll love it,' said Anna. 'It's a great night. Gives everyone a chance to dress up and celebrate with people they haven't seen for a while.'

Henry raised his glass. 'A toast, to celebration,' he said.

'To celebration,' they all responded in unison.

With dinner over, Jordy stood and placed his napkin on the table.

'Let's play some billiards,' he said. 'Avril and me against the two of you.'

'Come on,' Henry said to his wife, holding out his hand for her as she rose from the table. 'You used to be pretty good at billiards.'

'What do you mean, *used to be*?' Anna laughed and kissed him tenderly on his cheek.

CHAPTER 6

The week that followed was one of the coldest on record as the morning temperature dropped repeatedly to below two degrees. That didn't stop the yard from being a constant hive of activity. After breakfast, Avril spent each day in the school room with the children, now in her charge. Eight-year-old twins, Donna and Debra, were Sandra Whitman's girls, while Richard, Michael and Joe, or Little Joe, as he was called, were the sons of Col Bryce, the head stockman. Col, a local Jarowair man, was considered to be one of the best stockmen Henry Meredith had ever known. His calm temperament with horses and cattle, and his intimate knowledge of the land, made him an integral part of the team on Monaghan Station. At three o'clock the school day ended, and the children wasted no time speeding off on their bikes, eager to play.

'Just so you know,' Mrs Carmichael had said when she'd first shown Avril the school room, 'our cook's daughter, Sandra, works as a housemaid. Mrs Meredith gave Sandra a job after she lost her husband two months before the war ended. Such a tragedy.'

'And the boys' mother?' Avril had asked.

'She passed away, shortly after Little Joe was born,' Mrs Carmichael had said. 'It just about destroyed Col but he had to stay strong for his boys. Loves those kids like nothing else matters.'

In the corner of the school room, the wood-burning stove pumped out a constant stream of heat. Avril's little group of five were a compliant yet rowdy bunch and she tried to adhere to the school curriculum notes she'd been given. At first the children were polite yet somewhat wary, so Avril decided that building rapport was more important than learning the four times tables. She knew that, except for the stockmen, no one was more familiar with the geography of a country property, especially the immediate area surrounding a homestead, than the children who lived there. Avril glanced out at the cloudless blue sky and placed the lesson notes back on the table.

'Everyone, put your jackets on,' she told them. 'We're going on an adventure.'

'What are we doin', Miss?' Richard asked.

At nine years of age and the eldest, Richard was the self-appointed spokesperson for their little group. Avril drew the children into a huddle.

'We're going on a special science walk,' she said. 'You're going to show me how to catch frogs, butterflies and lizards, where to find interesting rocks and the best place to swim in the summertime. And if we find any wild-flowers, we'll pick them and then press them.'

Little Joe tugged on Avril's sleeve. 'Then, can . . . can . . . we play hide and seek in the shearing shed?' he stuttered.

'What a good idea,' said Avril. 'Let's go.'

The wicker basket Avril carried soon held an assortment

of sticks, leaves, rocks and feathers, and a perfectly preserved cicada carcass, all deemed important scientific finds. Avril asked the children to tell her the names of the birds they saw, and it wasn't long before kookaburras, finches, sparrows and magpies were pointed out.

At a narrow section of the river, Richard led the group across a wooden walk bridge to the paddock beyond. Clumps of dried reeds clung to the bottom railing, evidence of a waterline that had long since receded. Once on the other side, the older children charged off in the direction of some horses grazing near a windmill. Little Joe, who had clung to Avril's side since leaving the veranda, reached up and took her hand.

'Can we play hide and seek now?' he asked.

'Of course we can,' she said, hoisting him onto her back. 'Hold on tight and we'll catch up with the others,' and she pretended to canter while Little Joe laughed with delight.

*

The children had finished school for the day and Avril smiled as she watched them dash ahead of her to the kitchen for afternoon tea. Outside the laundry Mrs Carmichael was talking to Sandra, who had a basket of folded clothes under her arm. She waved as Avril approached.

'One of the boys will refill the school room wood box for you before morning,' Sandra said. 'I was just telling Mrs Carmichael how much my girls enjoy your lessons.'

'That's nice to know,' said Avril. 'I sometimes feel I'm learning more from them than they are from me.'

Sandra was about the same age as Avril, and had been welcoming and helpful, unlike her mother Jean who maintained an almost icy distance. She had the same red hair as Jean, and the clear blue eyes and lovely soft figure, but their temperaments could not be more different. Sandra clearly appreciated having another young woman around and she was fascinated by the clothes Avril had made for herself, while Avril was grateful for Sandra's practical advice on how the household and the station functioned.

'Who's this now?' said Sandra, turning her attention to the driveway where a truck towing a horse float was approaching. At the same time, there was the squealing of children from the kitchen. 'Can you go and speak to them, please, Avril? The men are out working on the fences. I'll sort out the kids.'

Avril walked across the yard as the truck pulled up next to the stables. A man in stockman's clothes jumped from the cabin and nodded at her.

'Afternoon, Miss,' he said. 'Jordy around? I've got a couple of horses for him.'

'Oh, you must be Stan. I'm Avril,' she said. 'I think Jordy's out checking fences.'

'Ah. You're the new governess,' Stan said. 'Well, I guess I'll get these girls off the float.'

'I can help you,' Avril said eagerly, then, noticing his hesitation she added, 'I'm good with horses.'

Stan glanced at the governess with scepticism, shrugged and unbolted the ramp. He backed the first horse out of the float, a tall black mare, and handed the lead rope to Avril. The mare whinnied and sniffed the air, ears pricked, muscles tense, but Avril just stroked her neck calmly. By the time he'd unloaded the second horse, a chestnut quarterhorse, slightly smaller, and they'd led them the short distance to the round yard and let them go, he'd changed his tune.

'You *are* good with horses, Miss,' Stan said.

Avril told him a little of her childhood, growing up

with horses and riding through the fields and woods near the chateau, and asked about the two mares he'd brought over.

'They're both about four,' said Stan. 'The black mare, she's a thoroughbred. She can be a bit hard to catch, and the chestnut mare's a guts for water, but other than that, they're trustworthy. No bucking or biting.'

'Well, they look to be settling in,' Avril said. 'We can leave them here until Jordy gets back.' Then she invited him to the kitchen for some afternoon tea.

Stan didn't have to be asked twice. Jean's scones were famous in the district.

Jordy returned as Stan was leaving for his hour-long drive back to Cathaway Downs. He found Avril in the kitchen, helping Jean with preparations for dinner.

'Feel like a ride?' he said with a grin. 'There's still enough daylight.'

'I'd love to,' said Avril. She excused herself from Jean and hurried to her room to change into her riding clothes.

*

At the stables, Jordy had both horses saddled up and tied to the hitching rail adjacent to the tack room. 'Which one do you want to ride?' he asked Avril. She chose the black thoroughbred, rather than the quieter chestnut. 'We might head up to the ridge,' Jordy called over this shoulder as they walked away from the stables. Without making it too obvious, he kept his eye on Avril, checking to make sure she actually could ride a horse, and was relieved to find that she knew what she was doing.

Water splashed about the horses' hocks as they crossed the bend in the river, where the water ran wide and shallow. They climbed the grassy bank on the other side and headed out into open country where Jordy suggested a canter. Without hesitation, Avril eased her mare forward, letting herself go to the rhythm of the horse's stride and rejoicing in the exhilaration and sense of freedom. She hadn't realised how much she'd missed riding; she thought of Guy and the hours they'd spent exploring the valley. For once, the memories didn't make her sad.

The climb to the top of the ridge tested the horses' stamina and they were breathing heavily as they finished the ascent. Jordy pulled up on a plateau facing out to the west and Avril stopped her horse alongside him, giving her mare a grateful pat.

The vastness of the view was breathtaking. The lush grasslands rose and dipped like a rippling rug until each undulation folded into the faraway hills. Cattle grazed on the pasture below, their butterscotch-coloured coats shining yellow, lit by the late afternoon rays.

'What a spectacular sight,' she said.

'Bunker's Ridge. That's what this place is called. I suppose our landscape's quite different from the French countryside.'

'There's a harshness to this countryside that you don't see in France. But there's a romance about this landscape as well, don't you think?'

'I'd agree with that.' Jordy nodded. 'I love the bush. Don't get me wrong, I have a good time when I go to Brisbane or Melbourne, but I'm a bushy at heart.'

'What's a bushy?' said Avril.

'A bushy is someone who lives in the country.'

'Bush–y . . .' Avril repeated, the word sounding strange with her accent.

Jordy laughed. 'That's another Aussie word I've taught you.'

Navigating their way down a sapling-filled slope tested the skills of both rider and horse. At the bottom of the descent, Jordy said, 'Nice work, Miss Avril. You sure can ride a horse.'

'You can just call me Avril, you know.'

'Nah. Miss Avril suits you,' he said with his cheeky grin. 'You're stuck with it now.'

They decided to change horses for the ride back to the homestead, so Avril could try out the chestnut. The mare's stride was strong yet smooth, and while she was quieter than the thoroughbred, she also seemed more alert, taking in her surroundings and carefully picking her way across the river.

'I thought the boys might have been back a day early,' said Jordy. 'They'll be bringing in about five hundred head when they get here. I'll probably ride out and give them a hand for the last few miles.'

'What happens once the cattle are in?' Avril asked.

'We'll hold them in one of the home paddocks nearby. Then they'll be picked up for market on Monday.'

'And the sheep. Where are they?'

'Well, all the shearing's been done for the year. The ewes and lambs have all been turned out into one paddock or another. We can ride out one day and take a look if you like?'

'I'd like that,' said Avril. She looked up as suddenly a flock of large black birds appeared overhead, their under-wings a startling bright red.

'Black cockatoos,' Jordy said. 'I guarantee we'll get some rain within a couple of days. Always do when you see the black ones.'

The light was all but gone by the time Avril and Jordy arrived back at the stable. They unsaddled the horses and turned them out in the stable paddock, then watched as they took their fill from the water trough.

'Have you made your selection?' said Jordy.

'I think I prefer the chestnut,' Avril said. 'What's her name?'

'I forgot to ask. You'd better give her one.'

After a pause, Avril said, 'I'll call her Piaf, after Edith Piaf.'

'Never heard of her,' said Jordy. 'Who's she?'

'A famous French singer. A strong woman, independent, defiant,' said Avril.

'Why don't you just call her Edith?' Jordy smiled. 'Easier to remember.'

'No!' laughed Avril, and as if in agreement Piaf walked over to the fence for a pat.

*

Avril soon fell into a pattern of having breakfast and lunch with Jean, Sandra and Mrs Carmichael in the staff kitchen, and dinner in the big house with the Meredith family. It was Anna's suggestion that Avril dined with them, as Henry and Jordy obviously enjoyed her company and it made a welcome change to have another woman at the table.

Each afternoon, once the school day was over, the Bryce boys were the first out the door, though sometimes Little Joe would stay and play with the twins. The three of them would set up a shop on the veranda and Sandra and Avril would be encouraged to fill their baskets with the empty cans, tea packets and boxes on display. Avril would then head to the kitchen for a cup of tea and offer to help Jean with dinner.

At first, Jean was hesitant to accept any help, but after

a week the cook softened somewhat, and was appreciative of the extra pair of hands, especially once she saw how competent Avril was. She was happy to do whatever mundane task Jean asked of her, fetching herbs from the garden, shelling the peas or cutting up the pumpkin. She worked with efficiency, too, wiping down the benches and clearing away the bowls and spoons, sweeping the kitchen floor, never shirking from the dirty work. *Perhaps I was a little quick to judge her. She certainly knows her way around a kitchen,* Jean thought to herself. And when Avril offered to make an apple tart one night, Jean was keen to see how '*the French*' made pastry.

*

Tim Meredith swung his horse to the right, cutting off the calf's impulsive dash, gently but firmly encouraging the youngster back in with the mob. His roan stallion fell into an effortless stride, moving the cattle ever forward. Bob and Reece flanked the herd left and right of Tim, Col was in the lead, while the rest of the stockmen acted as boundary riders, ever vigilant for breakaways. With less than fifteen miles to the holding paddock, the men knew that the cattle could smell the water, and the last thing they wanted was to lose control of the mob so close to home.

Despite the many hours in the saddle, Tim found solace in the time spent mustering that he no longer found at the Monaghan homestead. The constant stream of people and activity he'd once enjoyed now irritated him. The ever-growing lack of privacy had made him think about building his own place on a piece of land that overlooked the river, some miles away. Since the end of the war and his discharge from the Australian Air Force, he'd taken to riding longer distances on his own, staying out a few nights at a time, returning once he'd checked fence lines, water pumps or livestock. Increasingly he was drawn to the solitude of the bush and a campfire.

With the journey almost over, Tim turned his thoughts to the past week. The muster had been without incident and the excellent condition of the cattle was sure to be reflected in the price they'd bring at market. At the ten-mile tree, Jordy loped towards the mob and Reece peeled off to greet him. The three brothers and the station manager rode together until the cattle were inside the holding paddock and the gate firmly shut.

Nearly everyone who lived at the station had gathered excitedly to watch the cattle come in. The Bryce boys rushed to greet their dad. Col dismounted and hugged his sons, affectionately ruffling their hair then lifting all three off the ground at the same time. Col tipped his hat to Sandra, who was standing with her girls in the shade of the old gum trees.

One by one the weary stockmen filed in, unsaddling at the hitching rail. The dogs who had worked the cattle lay at the base of the trees panting, their pink tongues dripping into the dirt, their jobs done. Jean sent word that afternoon tea was waiting for the men in the dining room, something they had all looked forward to. The end of a muster always brought out the best in Jean's culinary talents and anyone who had ever worked on Monaghan Station would happily vouch for the quality and volume of food the cook provided.

Henry stood in front of the tack room and watched the men attend to their horses. He'd always felt a twinge of envy each time the team rode out with their swags and kits in tow. These days, he took more pleasure in their safe return, knowing all had gone well. He'd seen his share of dramas miles from the homestead and knew some of the best-laid plans could unravel quicker than a cheap rope. Tired, dirty and hungry, the men quickly fanned out in various directions leaving Henry leaning on the rail with his sons.

'Good to have you home, boys,' he said, patting his youngest on his back. 'You said the end of the week and here you all are.' Henry ran his hand down the sweaty neck of Reece's horse. 'How'd this old boy hold up? Still pull to the left like a right-handed batsman?'

'No. He went well,' said Reece. 'The Captain's got plenty of life left in him. To tell you the truth, it felt good to be out there, Dad. This time next month I won't be in a saddle, that's for sure.'

'Not you, genius.' Jordy winked at his brother. 'You'll be in a swish suit, pushing a pen instead of livestock. Know what I'd rather be doing.'

Once the horses were in the paddock and Jordy and Reece had headed to the house, Henry turned to Tim. His eldest son was exhausted, that he could tell, but Henry seized the opportunity to have a few moments alone with his 'top man', a term he never used in front of Tim's brothers.

'Happy with how things went?' Henry asked.

Tim removed his hat and wiped his brow with the side of his hand. His shock of wavy black hair, a throwback to his Irish heritage, shone with sweat. He rubbed the back of his neck and stretched his chin skyward. Father and son shared the same height, broad shoulders and deep blue eyes. Tim, being half Henry's age, was considerably lighter, his profile a natural blend of both Anna and Henry's attractive features. And when Tim smiled, his flash of white teeth added to his striking good looks, though he smiled less these days.

'I think Shady found the going a bit tough this time,' said Tim as he replaced his hat.

'Well, that's to be expected. Christ knows how old he is,' said Henry. 'Lighten his load but make him feel useful. Send him out with Col in the ute to check a few pumps.'

Tim nodded.

'And Reece. How did he go?'

'Well, it's a hobby for him,' was all Tim said. 'I'll see you at dinner,' and he headed for the tack room, a sure indication that their chat had come to an end.

For reasons Henry could not quite fathom, a void had opened up between the two of them and he didn't like it. It had been widening since Tim had left the air force. If they'd had some sort of disagreement, then perhaps he could understand, but there'd been none. Henry stopped at the front of the big house and turned back, looking across the lawn towards the stables where his eldest son was no doubt alone. *All in good time. Still waters run deep*, he thought to himself.

*

Bob McIntyre was the station manager, but Tim was the boss's son, and this set him apart from the rest of the team, whether he liked it or not. He was the middleman, the 'go between', for his father, Bob, the stockmen and jackaroos. The first one up in the morning and the last one to call it a day, Tim had carved out his own level of respect, through his work ethic and the fact that he never undermined Bob's decisions in front of anyone else. If Tim had an issue with something the station manager had said or done, he sorted it out with him in private, away from the eyes and ears of the other men.

'You can drink with the boys, but you can never get drunk with them,' his father had always said. And while Tim got on well with everyone who worked on Monaghan Station, he knew that one day the property, along with all the responsibly, would be his, including the hiring and firing of staff. Maintaining the right balance of camaraderie within the Monaghan community was crucial. Tim was quick to assess a stockman's character and anyone who slacked in their work or mistreated an animal was sent packing.

Tim walked slowly through the stables and his desire for a hot bath and a cold beer was pushed aside as he felt a cool breeze brush his face. Dusky pink clouds swept high above the airstrip and the fading afternoon sunlight caught the back of the plane, making the tail shine like silver foil. Instinctively, he wandered over, reached up and ran his hand along the smooth edge of the wing. The passion he'd once had for flying had deserted him. He hadn't flown in almost a year and despite Henry's encouragement to take the controls the last time they'd flown to Charleville, Tim had declined. The horrors of the war he'd witnessed from the air had not faded, and the freedom and exhilaration he once felt, twenty thousand feet up, now eluded him.

Halfway down the runway, a strong gust of air filled the windsock, catching Tim's attention. His focus fell on a horse and rider in the distance, the combination of which he didn't recognise. The woman, whoever she was, had collected up her mount nicely, the horse's head down and neck proudly arched, as she cantered along the grassy edge of the airstrip. She slowed to a walk just short of the gate and patted the chestnut on the neck. For a moment Tim thought he'd gone unnoticed as he stood motionless under the aircraft hangar, but the rider waved and trotted over. Tim saw that the horse's chest was white with foam as the young woman stopped in front of him and swept the hair from her face.

'Hello. I'm Avril. The new governess.' Holding the reins with one hand, she reached forward with the other. 'You must be Tim?'

Tim shook her hand, all the while studying her face. He recalled his father talking about a young French woman he'd met on the train to Melbourne and how he'd given her a job as a governess. *Typical Henry, as gregarious as his labradors*, Tim had mused at the time and then hadn't thought about it again.

'That's right,' he replied, and nodded in the direction from which she'd ridden. 'Looks like you've been out a while. Your horse has worked up quite a sweat.'

'She loves to run,' said Avril with a smile that lit up her eyes. 'And it was such a gorgeous afternoon, I must confess, I've cantered most of the way home.'

Something suddenly spooked the mare, sending her into a backwards dance, but Avril kept her seat. She turned the horse's head to the right and walked her in a large circle to settle her. 'Easy girl. Easy now,' she said.

Tim took in the white blaze down the centre of the horse's face. 'I don't recognise this one. She's not one of ours,' he said.

'Your father got her for me to ride. Stan, from Cathaway Downs, brought her over on Wednesday,' said Avril.

'What's her name?'

'I've called her Piaf.'

'After Edith Piaf, I take it.'

'Yes! You know her?' Avril couldn't hide her surprise.

'Not personally,' said Tim dryly, 'but I know who she is. I was in . . .' He stopped short of his last few words. 'Well, you won't go wrong with a quarterhorse out here. She's a beauty.'

Avril turned her face westwards towards the setting sun. Tim could see that small beads of sweat had gathered on her forehead and her cheeks were flushed. Wisps of sun-lightened hair blew across her face and her loose ponytail hung down the back of her black sweater. Tim quickly looked towards the homestead, aware that he'd been staring at her too long.

A lone magpie in a nearby tree chortled overhead, interrupting the silence.

'I'd better get going. I promised Jean I'd make a classic French dessert for tonight's dinner. Nice to meet you, Tim,' she said and tapped her heels against the mare's side.

Tim stood transfixed as Avril moved off. The silhouette of horse and rider blocked the last rays of the day, casting a long silky shadow over the ground that trailed behind them like a slow-moving veil.

*

Tim lifted the decanter and refilled Avril's glass. She smiled and thanked him, before turning to answer yet another one of Reece's questions. Tim had been watching her closely all evening, unable to look away. He couldn't remember the last time he'd enjoyed himself so much, and while he contributed to the evening's conversation, he took more pleasure in listening than adding to the talk around the table. Or perhaps his keenness to listen had more to do with the appealing sound of Avril's accent and laughter. Unlike most women he'd known, Avril's general knowledge about world affairs was extensive. Talk flowed easily from one topic to another – farming, Anna's new series of paintings, Reece and his life in Melbourne, along with the station's entries at the Brisbane Exhibition the following month. Henry described the annual ten-day event to Avril, explaining how it gave farmers a chance to show their produce and livestock.

'We call it the Ekka,' Jordy said to Avril, 'there's another new word for you.' They both laughed as if it was a private joke between them, and Tim felt a little jealous of his brother's easiness with Avril.

'And people come from all over the state to this "Ekka"?' Avril asked.

'Absolutely!' said Henry. 'Gives everyone from the bush a chance to catch up. Tim, you still keen to enter some of our heifers? You'll be going down anyway, I assume, to watch Rachel ride. I hear she's got a real chance of taking out the showjumping.'

Tim took a long slow sip of wine and stared expressionlessly down the table at his father. There were certain topics Tim preferred not to be quizzed on and his relationship with Rachel Stanley was one of them, despite her being his girlfriend. Why he felt so defensive, Tim wasn't exactly sure. He knew they made an attractive couple. She was right for him in many ways. He had almost asked Rachel to marry him before he'd gone mustering, but something had stopped him. Now, the thought was far from his mind.

'We'll enter two bulls,' was all Tim said, and went back to eating.

Anna, always more able to read her son than his father could, quickly changed the subject to Melbourne and the possibility of seeing Avril there when she returned. Anna loved visiting her hometown, and despite the boys having attended boarding school in Brisbane, they'd visited Melbourne regularly to see as much of her parents as possible. So the discussion moved on to their favourite places in city, before Henry brought up the Melbourne Cup. He became animated as he told Avril that every November they all went to Melbourne for the Spring Horse Racing Carnival.

'We have the most tremendous fun,' he enthused. 'It's a week-long party. Then we come back and get stuck into work before Christmas.'

'Have you been to the races in Melbourne?' asked Anna. 'You'd love the atmosphere of a big race day.'

'I went with some friends in March,' said Avril. 'I enjoyed seeing the horses but to be honest, I was more interested in the fashion.'

Henry leant back in his chair. 'That's right. You worked for a fashion house in Paris, didn't you?'

Avril told them about the clientele, the work she did as a seamstress, and the tasks carried out by the skilled artisans in the Dior workrooms. She explained how she'd learnt the trade from her mother when she was only a child. 'In my hometown of Tours, my mother ran a haberdashery business and was a wonderful dressmaker. And then, of course, the war came and well, everything changed, for all of us,' she said.

'You've had such an interesting life,' Reece said. 'So how did you end up here with us, being a governess of all things?'

'Stop with the lawyer questions,' Jordy said a little protectively.

Avril knew that Reece wasn't prying, but she wasn't sure how to answer him. She stared down at the delicate pattern woven into the linen tablecloth, aware that all eyes were on her. She decided to give them the most honest answer she could, without mentioning Albert.

'Well, after meeting Henry and hearing about Monaghan, I thought it would be a wonderful experience to see another part of the country before I start my new venture.'

'Which is?' asked Reece.

'I plan to start my own fashion business in Melbourne,' Avril replied. 'I've visited all the fabric suppliers and garment makers, and I think the time is right. I know I can make a success of it.'

'I'm sure you will,' said Anna. 'The skirt you're wearing is made of such beautiful fabric. Is this one you've made?'

'Yes, and I wish I'd had twenty yards of this wool crepe instead of only the five I brought with me from France.'

'We'll be sorry to see you go at the end of the year, but I'll be happy to help you with client introductions in Melbourne, any way I can,' said Anna.

Avril thanked her, then steered the conversation away from herself. 'That's enough about me. What I'd like to know is if anyone else flies, other than Henry?'

'Mum, Reece and I know the basics, take-off, landing, steering. We could take the controls in an emergency,' said Jordy, 'but Tim's the one with a pilot's licence.'

'He flew in the war, over Europe,' said Reece.

Tim gripped the arms of his chair and shifted slightly in his seat.

'You know I don't like to talk about the war,' he said curtly.

His tone silenced his family, but Avril was not afraid to meet his intense gaze. She, too, had experienced the war firsthand and knew the pain it caused.

The housekeeper entered the dining room, carrying the

apple flan, capturing the attention of Henry and the others and leaving Tim and Avril focused only on each other. Avril held Tim's gaze.

'On a beautiful sunny day, it must feel amazing to be flying high above the earth,' she said to Tim.

'Have you ever flown?' Tim asked, a smile forming in the corner of his mouth as he briefly recalled the joy of flying, the rush of speed lifting the plane from the ground, climbing ever skyward and leaving everything and everyone behind.

'Never,' she said.

'Well,' he said, raising his glass and pausing, 'something to look forward to.'

'Something to look forward to,' Avril replied.

CHAPTER 7

The first weeks of August brought nothing but cloud-less blue skies as the days started to draw out, ever so slightly. Avril took advantage of the extra daylight, riding Piaf before breakfast then riding again in the afternoon with Anna. Together, they'd cross the river where the water ran low and ride to the first fence line. Walking their horses home, Anna and Avril's conversation invariably turned to Melbourne and the many people Anna knew in the fashion scene. Growing up in a prominent political family, Anna Carrington, as she was then, was regularly photographed at social events in Melbourne. And most of her connections in the fashion and artistic world had become dear friends over the years.

'And you're sure it's all right if I borrow your sewing machine?' said Avril one evening as they unsaddled their horses. Josephine had sent Avril's sewing equipment and materials from Melbourne, and seeing it all again had given Avril a new rush of inspiration.

'Absolutely,' said Anna. 'It never gets used unless Jean or Rosie has something to mend. I'm sure you're longing to make up those beautiful fabrics your aunt sent you. There's a room you can use at the far end of the house. I'll get a couple of the boys to bring up a large table from the shed.'

Within a day Avril had converted the former playroom into her sewing space, and now spent much of her spare time there, designing and making patterns.

This particular Saturday morning, Avril stood at the window of the playroom and looked over the roof of the chicken shed towards the Bunya Mountains. The town of Tours and all she'd seen during the war seemed like a lifetime ago. And yet, there were times when Guy's face would appear in her dreams, or the scent of burning wood carried her back to the abbey, and she'd recall the velvety softness of her baby's skin. In these moments, Avril would let herself go where those memories took her and then, as if she was holding precious objects, she'd carefully wrap her thoughts in imaginary tissue paper and store them away.

She had settled in effortlessly to country life and was grateful for how the Meredith family had welcomed her into their home, their world. It had not been difficult to fall in love with the beauty of Monaghan Station – the graceful gardens that surrounded the house, the prolific bird and wildlife, and the vast open plains on which to ride.

Avril draped the tape measure around her neck and emptied the contents of her sewing box, looking for a particular piece of lace. To her surprise, hidden under the inner base of the box was a blue envelope she had never seen before. She carefully lifted it out and found that inside it were half a dozen photographs, wrapped in a piece of note paper. As Avril fanned through the images, tears welled in her eyes. There were pictures of Avril as a little girl, two images of her mother and one of the haberdashery shop with *1938* written on the back. Avril was overwhelmed with the thought of her mother placing these treasures in the sewing box: How long had the photos been there? How had she never known about them? She fell into the closest chair and sobbed into her hands. She wept for the senseless waste of life caused by the war. For the loss of her mother, Guy and their child. For the destruction of her country and the cruelty inflicted on so many. Everything came flooding back.

Jean stopped abruptly in the doorway, holding her dress with the broken zipper. She was taken aback to see Avril crying, as her demeanour was always cheerful – she brought smiles to everyone in the homestead, from the children to the stockmen. Jean moved quietly to Avril's side, placed the garment on the table and noticed the photographs, immediately understanding the cause of Avril's deep pain.

'Memories, hey. They'll bring us undone every time,' said Jean and wrapped her arms around Avril.

For quite some time, neither Jean nor Avril said a word. Then, when Avril's crying had eased, Jean took her handkerchief and gently wiped her reddened cheeks.

'I'm on my way into Dalby with Anna,' she said. 'Quick trip. We'll be back by five. I've just taken a fruitcake out of the oven. Why don't you go over to the kitchen and make yourself a cup of tea and have a slice?'

'Thank you. I think I will,' said Avril, squeezing Jean's hand briefly as Jean passed her the handkerchief. She had become very fond of Jean and learnt that under her no-nonsense exterior was a giving heart. She pulled the tape measure from around her neck and dabbed her eyes dry. 'I promised Col's boys I'd watch the plane take off with them. I'd better get moving.'

Jean patted her shoulder and left without another word. Avril looked at the photographs one more time, then tenderly placed them back in the envelope and returned them to their safe home at the bottom of her sewing box.

*

By the time Avril had hurried down to the fence line beside the airstrip, Henry and Jordy were taxiing from the hangar. The two older Bryce boys had climbed up on the fence and Avril lifted Little Joe onto the wooden railing next to his brothers. Henry waved from the cockpit as they passed by, Jordy returning the boys' thumbs-up sign.

'Where are they going again?' asked Little Joe.

'To the Ekka, in Brisbane,' said Richard. 'Remember? That's where our dad's gone.'

The propellers roared to life as the plane raced down the airstrip, lifted off the ground, climbed and banked to the left. The boys jumped down from their vantage point, collected their bikes and sped off. Avril watched until the aircraft was nothing but a tiny dark speck in the endless pale blue sky.

As she walked towards the kitchen, her thoughts turned to the day she'd been out riding before Tim and Col left to take the bulls down to Brisbane for the exhibition. She'd weaved her way up the trail to the top of Bunker's Ridge and was walking Piaf home when Tim had ridden up beside her. She didn't see much of any of them, Henry, Tim or Jordy, during the day, so Tim's sudden appearance took her completely by surprise. Henry and his sons were prone to leaving the station at the last minute, either by ute, horse or plane. Avril never knew who was going to be at the homestead and who wasn't. Jean, however, was a reliable source of who went where, when and why. 'Any one of the Meredith family are just as likely to be a thousand miles away as in the tack room,' she had said on more than one occasion.

Tim held the reins with one hand and guided his horse alongside hers. His eyes were shadowed by his hat, but she could still feel their intensity. For a moment, neither spoke. Tim Meredith oozed a reserved masculinity that Avril found intoxicating, no matter how much she tried to deny it.

'I saw you up the top,' he said. 'Great views. Jordy must have shown you that track. It's a hell of a descent, though.'

'The view's worth it,' Avril replied, aware that this was the first time they'd been alone together, away from the eyes and ears of the homestead.

'I hear you're riding twice a day. Hard not to when the weather's as good as this.'

They'd only spoken on a few occasions, but Avril had found herself paying closer attention whenever someone said Tim's name. And there had been times when she'd looked up from whatever she was doing and found that his attention was on her and she was compelled to return his gaze. She'd tried not to read into it, but in those moments she felt like something unsaid passed between them. She reminded herself that, according to Mrs Carmichael and Jean, Tim and Rachel were on the verge of announcing their engagement. 'I bet Rachel will want them to announce it at Henry's birthday party. Likes to be the centre of attention, that one,' Jean had said. Avril had to admit that she was curious to meet Rachel Stanley, to learn what sort of woman could win over Tim Meredith's heart.

Whenever Avril thought about Tim, she forced herself

to focus on the reality of returning to Melbourne. She'd asked Josephine and Duncan to look out for a suitable shop, and then during their last telephone conversation, Josephine had described a perfect place in Little Collins Street. The tailor who rented the site was moving to larger premises and the property would become vacant in February. The timing was perfect.

'You'll be glad to have a couple of weeks off while the kids are on school holidays,' said Tim, capturing Avril's attention.

'I enjoy being with them, but it'll be nice to have more time to myself,' she said. 'Are you ready to head off to the Ekka tomorrow?'

To her surprise, she caught a smile on Tim's face before he quickly looked away.

'What's so funny?' said Avril.

'Sorry,' he said, chastened. 'It's just when I hear the word "Ekka" said with a French accent, well, it sounds –'

'Ridiculous,' she suggested.

'No, not at all,' Tim quickly corrected her. 'Quite the opposite.' He paused, seemingly unsure of how to continue without offence, then said, 'It sounds musical.'

Avril glanced at him sideways. Tim was looking into the distance and seemed lost in his own thoughts. She straightened her back and shortened her reins.

'Race you,' she said. 'First one to the river,' and before Tim could reply, Avril's horse broke into a gallop and headed towards the Condamine.

Whether Tim had let her win, she wasn't sure. But since that day she'd lost the fight with herself and found herself thinking about him constantly.

*

Avril had almost walked back to the kitchen when Bob rode into the yard and slid from his saddle.

'Sorry you're not going to Brisbane?' she asked.

'Nah. I'm not much for the city,' Bob said. 'Always plenty to do here anyway. Got the boys moving stock and doing mill runs most of next week. The work never ends.'

He ran his hand down one of the horse's fetlocks and sighed.

'Second time this week she's been sore. Think I'll turn her out in the back paddock for a couple of weeks. That should set her right.'

Bob hesitated then busied himself with the buckle on the bridle before casually asking, 'Jean gone to town?'

'Yes. She's just left with Anna,' said Avril.

'Right. Ah, well, I've got something I'd like you to do for me, if you don't mind. Let me put my horse away and I'll come in.'

How mysterious, Avril thought, and wondered what he could want.

She was filling the teapot when Bob came through the kitchen door.

'Jean's baked a fruitcake this morning,' she said, and Bob's eyes lit up instantly.

They'd only just settled down at the table with their tea and cake when he pushed a wad of cash across the table at her.

'What's this?' Avril asked, surprised and perplexed.

'Well, you see, with the Winter Dance coming up and all, I'd like to treat Jean to something special. And I thought that maybe, seeing as you want to start a business in fashion, I could pay you to make something for her. I don't know anything about these sorts of things, but maybe something fancy, like a hat, with feathers . . .'

122

Avril didn't know whether to cry with the sweetness of it or laugh at Bob's discomfort. Not to mention his suggestion of a feathered hat, which simply wouldn't be appropriate for such an occasion.

'It would be my pleasure, Bob,' she said, and his weathered face transformed with the widest smile. 'But I refuse to take any money for it.' He looked downcast but she added, 'I'd love to do this for Jean, and for you. But I have one more condition . . .'

'What's that?'

'I get to choose what to make – and there won't be any feathers.'

Bob laughed and nodded his consent. 'But please, take the money and the next time you go to Toowoomba, pick up a fancy bottle of perfume, a lipstick and maybe a powder for Jean from me. I never go into Pigott's and even if I did, I wouldn't know what to buy.'

'All right. If that's what you'd like,' said Avril. She sipped her tea, smiling at the thought of creating something special for Jean. A wrap would be perfect and quick to make. She had a piece of bright blue silk that would complement Jean's eyes, and she would add some delicate embroidered daisies.

'Knew Jean when she was working as a barmaid in Toowoomba,' Bob said as he took a piece of cake. 'Sandra was just a slip of a thing.'

'You two go back a long way,' Avril said and hoped that Bob would tell her more. She enjoyed hearing about the history of the people who worked and lived at the station, and it conveniently helped to take her mind off Tim.

'She worked long hours to give that little girl a good life. Lived at the back of the pub. Room and board, came with the job. I'd see her behind the bar whenever I went to town. There was no husband to speak of, though she had plenty of admirers.'

'And you liked her?' said Avril.

'Oh, everyone liked Jean. She was kind and funny but she ran a tight ship. Had to, that pub could get pretty rough.' Bob slowly shook his head. 'Anyway, she wanted a better place to bring up Sandra so I got her a job here, and they've never looked back. Geez, that seems like a long time ago now.'

'You're a good man, Bob,' Avril said. 'Jean's lucky to have you.'

They were interrupted when one of the young jackaroos poked his head around the kitchen door.

'Can you take a look at the bay colt? Something's not right with his near-side hind leg,' he said to Bob, who was already standing from the table.

'That's my cue,' Bob said, and quickly downed what was left in his cup. His hat balancing in his hand, he stopped at the kitchen door. 'Thanks, Avril, for . . . helping me out . . . and for the chat, too.' Then he whistled up his kelpies and was gone.

*

While Henry, Tim and Jordy were away, Anna and Avril ate with the others in the main kitchen. Over dinner, Anna and Jean enthusiastically discussed the food arrangements for the upcoming Winter Dance. Mrs Carmichael said she was already preparing the bedrooms, knowing the place would be bursting with house guests for both the dance at the end of August and the weekend of Henry's sixtieth birthday celebrations in early October. An atmosphere of excitement energised the homestead.

At night, Avril replied to Duncan and Louise, who'd

kept her entertained with a constant flow of letters ever since she'd arrived. Mrs Rossi's correspondence read like an epic novel as she detailed all the goings on at Manton's department store and any other rag trade news she cared to share. Josephine sent regular letters and thoughtful packages – Avril's favourite tea, some ribbon which had caught her eye at Georges – and called Avril once a week, and noticeably, thankfully, only mentioned Albert in passing. In her latest package, her aunt had included the latest fashion catalogues from Myer, Georges and Foy & Gibson, to Avril's delight. Avril showed Jean a picture of one of the designs and suggested that rather than just replace the zipper on Jean's dress, with a few alterations, Avril could breathe new life into it.

'Oooh, that is lovely,' said Jean, running her fingers over the picture. 'But you don't think it's a bit, you know, too young for me?'

'Not at all,' Avril said, laughing. 'If you unpick the zipper and waist seam, I'll do the rest.'

Of course, she didn't tell Jean that the altered dress would be a perfect match for the wrap that Avril had made for her. Bob had been speechless when Avril gave it to him, his rough fingers running over the delicate fabric and embroidery. 'It's beautiful, just beautiful,' he finally managed to say.

*

Jordy and Col arrived back with the bulls along with a trophy for the Champion Bull of the Show, a prize they'd not taken out since before the war. Early afternoon, the aircraft made a victory dive over the homestead, and Anna and Avril ran outside in time to see the second pass. They walked down to the hangar and watched the aircraft taxi in, and to Anna's delight, it was Tim at the controls, not Henry.

'Please, say nothing about Tim piloting the plane,' said Anna as the engine fell silent. 'Let's not make a fuss. I was worried he'd given it up for good.'

Avril barely heard her, she was too concerned about concealing her pounding heart and the thrill she felt at seeing Tim again.

Henry strode over to Anna and Avril, while Jordy unloaded their bags and Tim was preoccupied with checking over the aircraft. He kissed his wife on the cheek then greeted Avril and flicked his head towards Tim and the plane. Anna responded with raised eyebrows. 'He wanted to,' Henry said quietly and neither of them said any more about it.

'How are the preparations for the Winter Dance going?' Henry asked.

Anna told him that the shearing shed had been swept clean and tables and chairs set out for the sit-down supper. All twelve guest rooms were taken, and she'd just finished the floral arrangements that afternoon. Avril had helped Sandra distribute the flowers throughout both levels of the house and had been awed by Anna's creations.

'Has Shady built the bonfire?' asked Jordy. 'All the kids love a bonfire.'

Anna ruffled her son's hair affectionately. 'You mean *you* love a bonfire,' she said, and Jordy grinned.

They started to walk back towards the house, Anna telling them about the eight-piece band, who were coming from Toowoomba to play, when Avril suddenly felt Tim beside her. Her heart, which had finally stopped pounding, now skipped a beat. He nodded at her, acknowledging her presence. Jordy and Henry were now engrossed in talking about the show, the number of entries, the standard of the competition, which of their friends were there. Tim subtly slowed down so that he and Avril were a little further back from the others.

'Let me know when you'd like a re-race,' he said, his face impassive except for a brief mischievous smile. 'I hope you've been training that horse of yours.'

'Did you let me win that day or did I outrun you, fair and square?' Avril replied.

Tim's eyes held hers and he leant a little closer.

'I don't think you could ever outrun me,' he said.

Avril laughed. 'We'll have to see about that.'

*

The Winter Dance had been a regular highlight on the district's social calendar for as long as anyone cared to remember. Graziers and pastoralists from surrounding properties gathered with the stockmen and their families for a night of feasting and dancing that went well into the wee hours of the morning. There was always a collection of last-minute attendees. Friends of friends and visiting relatives helped swell the numbers and these folk were always made welcome.

Before the sun had set, dozens of cars, trucks and utes flowed up the driveway and down to the shearing shed beside the river. Meanwhile, the homestead was a hive of activity as Mrs Carmichael showed the house guests to their rooms and Jean hustled over the final preparations for dinner, helped by Sandra, Avril and any other hands available.

For the women living in the country, the dance was an opportunity to don their finest party dresses. Avril had chosen a midnight-blue dress, the design simple yet elegant – full skirt with a wide covered belt, low-cut back and long fitted sleeves. At the last moment, she removed her jet necklace. 'That's better,' she said to herself in the mirror, securing her pearl earrings.

She was ready early so she wandered out to the upstairs veranda to take in the view. The tip of a glorious full moon began to rise and the first stars sprinkled the darkening sky in the horizon. *How fortunate am I to be in such a beautiful place*, she thought.

Avril heard the front door open below, and Tim flew down the steps, pulling on his jacket as he strode across the gravel towards his ute. Avril's breath caught. She'd only seen Tim in his work clothes, invariably a blue chambray shirt, khaki pants and riding boots, or dressed for dinner, which was just a clean version of his work clothes. In his dark blue suit he was undeniably handsome.

Since they'd returned from Brisbane, Henry, Tim and Jordy had thrown themselves back into station work, while Anna and the household were entrenched in preparations for the dance. Conversations around the dinner table were focused on their long lists of tasks, and Avril found herself enjoying the opportunity to observe the family going about their business. She was also learning more about Tim. In everything he did and said, he was a natural leader but there was also an aloofness about him. He didn't have Jordy's gregarious personality or the intellectual conversation of Reece. There was an inner strength to him, and an underlying warmth, that Avril found potent. She constantly reminded herself: *Tim is going to marry Rachel, and I'm returning to Melbourne. Nothing could possibly come of it. Let it go.* And yet he always returned to her thoughts.

From downstairs, Jordy called her name. 'Miss Avril. Come on. Let's get going.'

*

The shearing shed shone like a golden lantern in the darkness. Avril balanced the cream-laden pavlovas precariously on her knees as Jordy's ute rolled over the cattle grid that divided the sheep-holding paddock from the airstrip. As they pulled up at the back of the shed, Avril said, 'Thanks for the lift.'

'All part of the service, Mademoiselle.' Jordy grinned and his terrible accent reminded her of Duncan. 'And don't forget, you've promised me the first two dances.'

Jordy dropped the tailgate and lifted a large tray of carved beef from the back. Avril followed him into the makeshift kitchen area with the desserts. Jean and Sandra were busy directing the flow of food platters down two massive buffet tables. Avril had loved the smell of the shearing shed from the very first time she'd been there. The heady mix of wood and lanolin had her hoping that one day she'd see the shearing for herself.

'That's everything,' said Avril. 'I thought you were having the night off, Jean?'

'Chance would be a fine thing.' Jean laughed. 'Don't worry. I'll enjoy myself.'

With her hair softly curled and lips a vibrant red, Jean Cooper had made a surprising transformation. Her petite figure was enhanced by black stilettos, and the fitted satin floral dress that Avril had altered finished just below her knees. Her new wrap was draped across her shoulders.

Avril hoped that as long as she lived she would never forget the joy on Jean's face when she'd burst into the kitchen after receiving her gifts from Bob – perfume and an array of cosmetics and the silk wrap. 'No one's ever made me anything like this,' she said, her voice choked with emotion. The wrap had turned out exactly as Avril had imagined, and while she'd gained great satisfaction from making something for someone she cared about, she was also reminded of her purpose – to create garments that brought happiness to people's lives. This was her future.

'May I?' said Avril, reaching out to reposition the wrap so it fell a little lower across the shoulders. 'You look absolutely lovely.'

Jean blushed at Avril's sincere compliment. 'All thanks to you,' she said. 'I don't get much opportunity these days to put on the dog.'

'Put on the dog?' Avril was perplexed. 'What does that mean?'

'Oh, you know, dress up. Do my hair and wear makeup.'

Avril reached out and touched Jean's arm. 'Well, I think you should put on this dog more often. It suits you.'

Jean laughed then asked Avril to help her carry some platters to the tables. The shearing shed was unrecognisable, with lanterns and fairy lights strung across its rafters and Anna's floral arrangements on the tables. The band was playing on a makeshift stage in the corner and the dance floor was already filled with swirling couples. Anna and Henry stood at the main entrance to the shed, greeting the guests.

'Who's that?' said Avril, immediately noticing a tall, pretty blonde woman in a lemon dress.

Jean gave a small grunt of disapproval. 'That's none other than Rachel Stanley, Tim's beloved,' she lowered her voice. 'And they're the parents, Mary and Doug, talking to Henry. They own Cathaway Downs. They'll all be ooh-ing and aah-ing about Rachel taking out first place in the showjumping at the Ekka. Mind you, I think she sees Tim as a trophy as well. Unfortunately she seems to like the attention of most men. But it's Tim Meredith's ring she wants on her finger. If Tim had any smarts, he'd make a run for it while he still has the chance.'

'So you know her well?' Avril prompted, unable to contain her curiosity.

'I know enough,' said Jean. 'Let's just put it this way. That one doesn't lower herself to speak to the likes of me. She's snubbed me plenty of times since she started stepping out with Tim. And I'd watch out if I were you. She won't like you either, as sure as night follows day.'

Jordy appeared through the crowd and took Avril's hand.

'Excuse me, folks, but it's time for Miss Avril here to make good on her promises.' And with that, he pulled Avril towards the dance floor.

*

Doug Stanley patted Henry on the back, his laughter roaring above the rest of the group. For a rich man's joke is always funny, and Doug liked nothing more than to make a display of the friendship he had with his nearest neighbour. In contrast to Anna's understated grace, Mary Stanley's excessive makeup did little to enhance her matronly burgundy ensemble. The willowy bird-like creature was as gaunt as her husband was wide, his ill-fitting jacket straining at the centre button.

As the men laughed and exchanged commentary, Mary's close-set eyes fixed on her daughter's new silk brocade dress at it swilled about her long legs. Tim and Rachel were excellent dancers and the crowd around them parted slightly, giving the couple a pocket of space in which to display their talents. The moment they left the floor, there'd be a throng of people waiting to talk to Tim. There always were. The longer Rachel stayed in Tim's arms, the less chance she had of losing his attention to someone else: a practical skill Mary had schooled her daughter in. The band slipped into another song as Rachel was led reluctantly from the dance floor towards the bar.

'So, have you missed me?' Rachel cooed in Tim's ear, as he handed her a drink.

'It's always lovely to see you,' he replied, dodging a false answer.

At the edge of the dance floor, Jordy was attempting to teach Avril to jive, with little success. They laughed each time they stopped and started until finally Jordy conceded defeat and they opted for a waltz instead. Tim turned away, envious of his brother.

Rachel pressed her slender body into Tim's side and blew softly in his ear.

'Haven't forgotten I'm staying the night, have you? Three doors down from yours.'

Her smoky brown eyes looked him up and down as she recalled the numerous times she'd stayed at Monaghan in the past six months. At twenty-four there was no denying Rachel Stanley was an extremely confident young woman. Like Tim, she'd had a rural upbringing and city education. They'd bonded over their mutual love of horses and country life. Mary and Doug Stanley doted on their only child and no expense was spared when it came to funding her equestrian career, a commitment that had become a full-time occupation.

Tim enjoyed their physical intimacy, as did she. He was grateful for the professional advice he'd received on sexual health, while serving in the armed forces. He also had a father who was a pragmatist and a realist, advising his sons, 'Make sure the only reason to use the word "shotgun" is because you're going after rabbits.'

Rachel's outward display of affection had rarely displeased Tim but tonight, as his eyes searched the room for Avril, he felt uncomfortable, cornered and agitated. Tim spotted one of the local bloodstock agents and seized the opportunity to greet him. The two men fell into a robust conversation about cattle prices so Rachel drifted to a group nearby and was quickly asked to dance. As she took to the floor, she glanced over her partner's shoulder. To her annoyance, Tim was oblivious of her absence, and she watched as Bob and Col joined the discussion. *I won't see him for at least an hour*, she thought, as she concentrated on her twists and turns. But the quality of her performance was lost on Tim, for when she looked back, he was no longer at the bar.

*

Avril crouched in front of the bonfire with her arm around Little Joe. The twins threw small pieces of wood into the flames, their faces laughing with delight as sparkles flew skywards. Richard and Michael appeared out of the darkness with a fresh supply of sticks and a throng of kids gathered around and joined in. Tim watched Avril from the doorway. She wasn't responsible for the children tonight, but freely gave them her attention. He gathered up two glasses of champagne and wandered over to the bonfire.

'I thought you might like a drink,' he said. '*Santé.*'

'*Santé,*' she replied. The heat of the fire had banished the cold night air. They stood close to each other, staring at the flames. Tim was relieved to be outside. If he could have his way, he'd sit by the fire with Avril for the rest of the night. Finally, he broke their comfortable silence.

'Are you enjoying your first dance in a shearing shed?' he asked.

'Very much. Although, you travel a lot further to go to a party here than we did in France. I spoke to a lady who said she'd flown from a place called Clodcory, I think she called it, a thousand miles away.'

'Yes. That would be Dad's younger brother and his wife. But the town is pronounced Cloncurry,' he said, laughing, and Avril joined in. She never seemed to take offence at being corrected, in fact she sought it, always wanting to improve her knowledge of the country and its language.

'Do all property owners fly?'

'Quite a few, and it's becoming more popular,' said Tim. 'Flying certainly saves an enormous amount of time when you live where we do.'

Tim felt the touch of a hand on his back then Rachel slid into the small gap that existed between Avril and Tim, forcing Avril aside and bumping her arm so the champagne in her glass spilled down the front of her dress.

'Oh, I'm so sorry,' said Rachel. 'And on such a sweet dress.'

Then she wrapped her arms around Tim's waist and rested her head on his shoulder. 'So, this is where you've got to,' she said.

Tim reached over and lifted the champagne glass from Avril's hand. 'Let me get you something to wipe your dress,' he said.

Avril fanned the wet fabric. 'Oh, please don't worry. It's nothing, really.'

'Tim, we're about to sit down for supper,' said Rachel. 'Your parents are waiting for us.'

'Let them wait,' he replied with annoyance. 'I won't be a moment, Avril.' He turned and walked towards the back of the shearing shed.

Rachel was clearly unimpressed to be left alone with Avril and the children. Nevertheless, Avril extended her hand. 'We haven't met. I'm Avril. I'm working here as the governess until the end of the school year.'

Rachel briefly shook Avril's hand and introduced herself. They made awkward conversation, Rachel only providing a few words in response to Avril's attempt at pleasantries.

'Thank you,' said Avril when Tim returned and handed her a clean tea towel. She was grateful for his thoughtfulness but even more so for saving her from spending any more time alone with Rachel. 'You can hardly see the mark on the dark blue. If you'll excuse me, I promised Jean I'd help her with dinner,' and she turned and walked back inside.

'That was a little childish,' said Tim.

'It was an accident,' Rachel insisted, and hooked her arm through his.

*

Once everyone had taken their seats, Henry gave a rousing speech which did not disappoint. His wit and command of the English language was legendary, and he concluded with a couple of verses from the poem, 'The Man from Snowy River', and the guests cheered and clapped and banged on the tables.

The band was still going strong at midnight when Avril dropped down on the bale of hay next to Jordy and removed her shoes.

'I'm going to bed,' she said. 'I'm exhausted and my feet are killing me.'

'Take my ute,' Jordy insisted. 'I don't need it.'

Avril found her purse and slipped quietly through the makeshift kitchen and down the wooden steps. Tim was leaning against the tailgate of Jordy's ute, talking to a couple of stockmen.

'Goodnight,' she said, as she reached the driver's door.

'Did you have a good time?' asked one of the men.

'I did, thank you. But it's time to call it a night.'

Tim tossed his empty beer bottle into a nearby forty-four-gallon drum. 'Excuse me, fellas,' he said and with no hesitation, his drinking companions walked away.

'Would you like me to run you up to the house?' said Tim.

'No. But thank you.'

'It's a pity you're not staying longer. I believe you still owe me a dance.'

A feeling of irritation that bordered on exasperation overtook Avril. She hadn't expected to have any feelings for Tim. Was she jealous? Perhaps she was just tired. In frustration at herself, Avril pulled the car door open and turned back to face him.

'Actually,' she said, pausing for a moment, 'I don't believe I owe you anything.' And she slid into the driver's seat, closed the door and drove away.

When she reached the house, Avril turned the engine off and sat back against the seat. *Why did I act that way towards Tim?* she asked herself. But she already knew the answer. It was obvious to her that Tim and Rachel didn't seem at all like a match. It wasn't Rachel's shallowness or vanity that irritated her. She'd seen that in plenty of women. Why would Tim be attracted to someone who had such little regard for others? Who was Rachel to look down on Jean, or anyone else for that matter? The drink stain on her dress could be easily removed, but not the memory of Rachel's supposedly accidental nudge. *It's time you got your priorities in order*, Avril told herself. She got out of the ute and slammed the door. *Enough of this mooning over Tim Meredith. Come December you'll be gone from Monaghan. Focus on your plan.* And, sidestepping the labradors, she charged up the front steps.

CHAPTER 8

The garden around the big house burst into life with roses and daffodils as the warmer spring days rolled by. The Meredith men came and went in no fixed pattern, leaving Anna to coordinate the final arrangements for Henry's black-tie sixtieth birthday celebration taking place in early October. A hundred and fifty guests, friends and family were coming to celebrate what was expected to be the party of the year. The giant marquee complete with a parquetry floor was being trucked in from Brisbane a week before the main event. A silver and white theme had been chosen for the tables, lighting and decorations. Anna planned the menu with the caterers, while Henry had chosen the wines. On the same night, the shearing shed would be turned over to all the Monaghan Station staff, where they'd hold their own celebration. It would be a far more informal affair, but no less enjoyable.

Avril sat in Tim's office waiting for Josephine's Sunday night telephone call. She'd hardly seen Tim in the weeks since the Winter Dance. Tim and Jordy had ridden out to help with the branding of the calves and were away for more than a week. Tim had flown to Brisbane the day after they got back, without their paths crossing. From the window of the school room, Avril had watched Tim toss his travel bag on the back of the ute and drive towards the aircraft hangar. Now, as she sat spinning a pen on the top of his desk, she berated herself again for thinking about him so much. At eight o'clock sharp, Avril picked up the phone and the operator connected Josephine's call.

'What do you mean the owner won't rent the shop to a single woman?' Avril said in surprise. 'I have the money for at least ten months' rent and references from my time at Dior. What more does he want?'

'It's not just that,' said Josephine. 'He felt you were a risk, having never run your own business before.'

'Ha!' said Avril. 'And I thought the French were behind the times, not giving women the vote until six years ago. This is ridiculous.'

'C'est la vie,' said Josephine. 'It's just the way it is. Perhaps if Duncan took the lease in his name, it wouldn't be a problem.'

'Well, it is a problem for me,' Avril snapped.

The other end of the line fell silent.

'I'm sorry, Josephine. I didn't mean to speak to you like that. It's just very frustrating knowing a woman's not taken seriously when it comes to business.'

'That I know, Avril,' Josephine replied, and Avril was reminded that her aunt, and indeed many other women, faced worse problems than bigoted landlords.

'I know this place seems perfect, but there'll be other premises,' Josephine continued. 'Sometimes missing out on what you want can be a blessing in disguise. Duncan and I will keep looking. The right place will turn up.'

'Yes, it will.' Avril might have been defeated on this shop, but it only made her more determined to find the perfect premises. 'Thank you for all your help and support,' she added, feeling humbled by Josephine's wise words and kindness.

'Now,' said Josephine, her voice taking on a lighter tone, 'tell me what you've made to wear to Henry's birthday party.'

*

Avril heard the cheery sound of chatter as she came around the corner. Henry had specifically wanted an informal gathering the night before his sixtieth celebrations. But low key at Monaghan could mean up to forty people. Friends and family moved easily through the four sets of open French doors between the front room and the wide veranda, where the bar and buffet table stood.

Avril wandered over to the piano and listened to Jordy's rendition of 'Some Enchanted Evening'.

He looked up and winked. 'Evening, Miss Avril.'

She was becoming very fond of Jordy. He worked as hard as anyone on the station but he was quick with a joke and a smile, and quite the maestro on the piano. They'd formed an easy friendship since she'd arrived, and Avril realised she would miss him terribly when she returned to Melbourne.

'Are you the entertainment for the night?' she said.

'Always!' He grinned before returning his focus to the keys.

Avril drummed her finger against her wine glass, enjoying the rhythm of the music. She noticed Rachel outside talking to Reece. In a low-cut crimson dress, Rachel's choice of outfit was anything but casual. She stood out among the other guests who were informally dressed, as no doubt she intended to.

'Have you been avoiding me?' Tim's voice was quiet and close over Avril's shoulder.

She hadn't seen him approach and she didn't look around.

'Not at all.' She took a sip of wine and kept her eyes on Jordy's playing.

'Good. Because if I've upset you in any way, I want to apologise.'

'There's nothing to apologise for,' she said.

'I'd like to talk to you. This place will be teeming with people all weekend and we might not get the chance to speak in private. There are eyes and ears bloody everywhere right now.'

She turned around at this and noticed that Tim looked tense.

'Is everything all right?'

Tim lowered his voice. 'Not exactly,' he said. 'Will you meet me out at the windmill in the home paddock at first light?'

'Of course.'

'Thank you,' he said. 'I'll see you there,' and he stepped away to intercept Doug Stanley who was making a beeline towards Tim with a beer in each hand.

*

Shortly before midnight, Tim bid the last of the guests goodnight, as one by one they headed off to bed. He carried his brandy down the front steps, out into the garden and leant against the giant trunk of a jacaranda tree, now in full bloom. He studied the sky ablaze with stars and turned his thoughts to Rachel. The enjoyment he'd once felt in her company had disappeared. In fact, he now found himself avoiding her.

A long slow crack had formed in the centre of his chest, which burned like hot coals on a winter's night. From the moment he'd shaken her hand, Tim hadn't stopped thinking about Avril Montdidier. He'd never felt such an intense and instant attraction to any woman. It was much more than just her beauty that drew him. It was also the life experiences which had made her who she was, her considered opinions, and her genuine interest in other people. He felt like he could talk to her about anything. And, he wanted her passionately. It was no good trying to deny that. *You're being a bloody idiot*, he told himself. *She's going back to Melbourne and you're staying here.*

Station life was in Tim's blood and he always imagined he'd settle down with a country girl. There wasn't only Monaghan to think about. The family had cattle properties in the Gulf of Carpentaria, a substantial real estate portfolio, mining interests and, his father's pride and joy, a thoroughbred stud outside Melbourne. Tim wanted a family of his own one day, but how this would eventuate felt more uncertain than ever. Rachel was a beauty and the life of the party, for sure, but those qualities no longer seemed appealing or enough. How easily they'd fallen into a relationship. How vacuous the time he spent with Rachel now seemed. If he was honest with himself, he didn't know if Rachel and he had much in common at all.

What he did know was that tomorrow, Monaghan Station would be packed with friends and relations celebrating Henry's birthday milestone, but also anticipating that something else might be announced. Tim and Rachel had been together for almost two years, and Tim knew what the rumour mill was saying about them.

He raised his index finger and traced the pattern of the Southern Cross above. It would be a joyous gathering for his father's sixtieth birthday, but Tim had made his decision, and he felt like a crushing weight had been lifted off him. Swirling the contents of his glass, he downed what was left of his brandy and stared out into the night. There would be no engagement announcement; of that, he was absolutely certain.

*

A chorus of kookaburras chortled as a blast of tangerine broke over the skyline to the east. If she hadn't thought about Tim all night, and wondered what he might want to say to her, Avril would have felt more awake as she rode to the windmill at first light. From a hundred yards away, she could see that Tim was waiting for her, his horse tied to the rail. She dismounted, tied Piaf and sat down on a nearby log next to him.

'Thank you for meeting me,' he said. 'This probably seems rather strange. But I wanted to talk to you. I haven't been able to discuss what I'm about to tell you with anyone and, well, I thought you'd understand.' His voice was unusually hesitant as he gathered his thoughts.

'Not even Rachel?'

'Especially not Rachel,' he said, casting his eyes towards the horizon. 'Rachel, I'm afraid, has never had to think about anyone other than herself. Her parents have denied her nothing and, well, I can't see . . .' He didn't finish what he was saying but leant back against the wooden mill stand.

Avril studied the soft lines that had formed around Tim's eyes. 'Whatever it is, Tim, it won't go any further, I assure you.'

'I know, I trust you,' he said. *That's why you mean so much to me*, Tim said to himself. He took a deep breath and, before he had any more second thoughts, said, 'You've heard that saying, *It never rains but it pours*? Well, I'm dealing with a deluge right now.'

Avril knew that all she had to do for now was listen.

'Dad's not well,' he said finally, turning to look directly at her. 'He's been having abdominal pains for some time. I've been back and forth to Brisbane with him these past weeks, seeing specialists, having tests.'

Avril was surprised to hear this. The Henry Meredith that she had come to know and respect seemed, well, invincible. 'What are the doctors looking for?' she asked.

'They're not sure, exactly. We'll know more next week.'

'I'm so sorry, Tim. There's probably very little I can say to give you any comfort, but I'm pleased you've told me.' *More than pleased*, she had to admit to herself – for the first time, she felt close to him, and wanted him to be close to her.

'That's only the half of it,' he said, and the contours of his face showed the seriousness of what he was about to tell her next.

'Dad invested heavily in a mining venture that Doug Stanley's involved in and the whole operation is shaky, to put it mildly. The venture is highly speculative.'

'How heavily?' Avril knew it was none of her business, but she cared too much about the Meredith family to not show her concern.

'A ridiculous amount of money. It's quite complicated, I'm afraid, and I can't for the life of me figure out why he's done it. He's left himself exposed, financially. It's a reckless gamble and so unlike him. He's broken his own cardinal rule – never mix friendship and business.'

'Why didn't you talk him out of it?' asked Avril.

Tim hesitated. His hypnotic blue eyes locked on hers. 'Because I wasn't consulted,' he said, and she saw the flash of hurt across his face. 'Not until a week ago when Dad found out that the coffers are almost empty, and the board is trying to raise more capital.'

'What does this mean for your family?'

'It means that very quickly we could be land rich but cash poor, as the saying goes. It takes a lot of money to keep this show on the road, Monaghan and the other stations, and once you start borrowing to stay afloat, well, it's the kiss of death in our sort of game.'

He explained that if the mining company failed, they'd have to start liquidating assets. The two cattle properties up north would have to be sold, possibly their house in Melbourne, and his father's beloved thoroughbred stud.

'You couldn't lose Monaghan, could you?'

'Christ, I'm hoping not.' He ran his hand through his hair and shook his head. Losing Monaghan Station was clearly what worried him the most. 'That would destroy the old man, not to say what it would mean for Jordy and myself. And for everyone else who works here.'

Avril took a moment to think about all the people who relied on Monaghan for a roof over their heads and food on their tables, people like Bob and Mrs Carmichael who'd spent most of their lives here. And the children. Where would they all go?

'And what about Doug Stanley?' she said. 'Is he in the same position as Henry?'

'He piled in big time, apparently along with his brother-in-law. Lords knows what the ramifications will be for them.'

Avril asked if it was possible for Henry to trade his way

145

out of the situation and Tim was again struck by her intelligence and business sense.

'It might be doable. We've got the lawyers and accountant working on it. I think that's why Dad wanted to have this big hooray for his birthday. In case it's his last one here. I doubt we'll all be making the annual trek to Melbourne for the spring racing in November. It's simply not a priority right now, even though Dad's got horses nominated for the Derby and the Oaks.'

'What does Anna say?'

'That's another bone of contention between Dad and me. She doesn't know. We've argued about it so many times and I've pleaded with him to tell her, but he refuses to. He keeps saying that he doesn't want to worry her.'

'Tim, he has to tell her!'

'I know. He's making decisions based on pride at the moment. He can be a stubborn bugger when he wants to be. Anyway, firstly, we need to sort out Dad's health and then how we're going to fix this mess we've landed in.'

'I'm not making light of any of this, Tim, when I say you'll get through this. Believe me, there've been many times over the past ten years when I didn't know if I'd make it to the next day, let alone the next week. And here I am.'

'Funny, isn't it, the family motto: *Timing is everything*,' said Tim. 'I guess the Meredith clan have had a pretty good run, but with all that's happening, I can't help wondering if timing has nothing to do with anything in life. Does it simply come down to luck?'

'I don't know if I believe in good luck or bad luck,' said Avril. 'Unexpected things happen to us all. And sometimes the worst possible situations bring hope and a second chance. I wouldn't give up on your motto just yet.'

For the first time since they started talking, Tim smiled. 'Yes, here you are,' he replied.

The sun had started to rise and Tim sighed then slowly stood, offering his hand to Avril. 'We'd better get moving, big day ahead.'

Avril took his hand and they walked together to the horses. 'Thank you, Avril,' he said. 'You don't know how much it means for me to be able to tell you this.'

'Thank you for trusting me.'

They were still holding hands, and Avril fought the urge to wrap her arms around him. He reluctantly let go of her fingers and drew himself into his saddle. They pulled their horses up just short of the river.

'How about you ride in ahead of me?' suggested Avril. 'No need to give those eyes and ears you mentioned anything to gossip about.'

'I'll see you tonight,' he said, and cantered away without looking back.

Avril watched as Tim's horse crashed through the water and up the bank on the other side. The gravitational pull they felt towards each other was impossible to deny and almost as hard to resist. 'He has the weight of the world on his shoulders right now, Piaf,' she told her mare. 'The weight of the world.'

*

Henry and Anna greeted their guests as they entered the spectacularly decorated marquee. Station owners, businessmen, politicians and newspaper proprietors and their partners took their seats along with members of the Meredith clan for what was going to be a party like no other. Avril partnered Jordy, and they were both surprised to find they were seated at the same table as Tim and Rachel.

'I don't know how this came about,' Jordy whispered to Avril. 'I thought we were sitting with Col and Sandra, and Jean and Bob. That was my preference.'

Rachel wasted no time in greeting the others at the table with an array of compliments. 'Oh, what a lovely dress, Hazel. That colour looks magical on you.' And, 'Doctor Lambert, you look younger every time we meet.' Her eyes swept over Avril, and she gave her an icy smile then turned instantly to Jordy.

'No one dances quite like you, Jordy, so I hope you'll whisk me onto the dance floor for the jive,' Rachel cooed.

'Oh, I'm sure I can find a place for you on my dance card,' he replied neutrally.

The conversation throughout dinner was lively and varied, though frequently dominated by Rachel. Avril and the art dealer from Melbourne who was seated on her left spoke about many subjects, including his love of dining at Bistro Dubray.

All eyes were on the host and hostess as they opened the dancing. Henry looked debonair in his tuxedo, Anna a picture of style and grace in a long white georgette gown. Avril thought about the many beautiful events held at the chateau before the war as Jordy led her to the dance floor. For the rest of the night, she was rarely without a dance partner as the band play one hit song after another.

The tempo of the music slowed as Henry's brother was about to claim his second dance with Avril. From amongst the crowd Tim appeared and tapped his uncle on the shoulder. In an instant, Avril was in Tim's arms as the band started to play 'Chances Are'. She could feel the tautness of his body and the strength of his arms as his hand pressed firmly against her back. She wanted the song to never end, but as the final notes played she saw, out of the corner of her eye, a cloud of peacock blue move towards them from the other side of the room.

She was not going to wait for Rachel to stake her claim.

'Thank you,' said Avril and she pulled her hand from Tim's and left the dance floor.

*

By two o'clock in the morning, most of the guests had left but those who were staying at the homestead danced on. The band was still in fine form as Avril reached the front steps. She'd danced and drunk more champagne than she could ever remember. Anna had made a heartfelt speech, as had Tim, and everyone drank to Henry's good health. Henry's response was punctuated with eloquent anecdotes and hilarious tales which received a standing ovation and a rousing rendition of 'For He's a Jolly Good Fellow'. *It has been a truly wonderful party*, Avril thought, as she removed her shoes, pulled the pins from her hair and shook it loose. She hummed a tune as she strolled the length of the veranda, her shoes swinging from her fingers, and turned the corner and continued towards the far side of the house. She stopped at the railing opposite her bedroom door and looked out over the rose garden. The light of the moon threw a hue of pale blue over the lawn.

At the corner of the veranda, Tim leant against a pillar. He'd seen Avril leave the marquee and had circled in the opposite direction, hoping they'd meet halfway. Rachel had long since gone to her room and he had no desire to join her.

Avril turned, suddenly aware of the shape in the shadows. She knew it was Tim, even before he started walking towards her. He'd removed his bowtie but was still wearing his dinner jacket. He stood close to her and placed his hand on the balustrade. A smile crossed his face and he looked down the length of the veranda, to nowhere in particular.

'It's no use, Rachel and me,' he finally said. 'It's never going to work, I can see that now. I think perhaps you can, too.'

'Well, I know it's wise to listen to your intuition. I do,' said Avril.

'The thing is,' said Tim as he took Avril's hand, 'you've awoken me from a very long sleep.'

'And that's a good thing?' she asked.

'Yes, a very good thing.' And he brought his hand slowly to Avril's face and stroked her cheek.

Without a word, Avril smiled as Tim led her from the veranda onto the lawn, where low-light shadows were thrown by the branches of the jacaranda trees. He placed his hand around her waist and her hand found his shoulder. Ever so slowly they started to sway to the sound of an absent tune.

'I'm not a very good dancer,' Avril whispered.

'Well, we'll have to do something about that,' he said and tenderly pulled her closer. His lips pressed against her cheek as he gently lifted her face to his. She leaned into him and his body folded around hers and he kissed her passionately.

For Avril, it was like a key turned and a lock opened, releasing every thought, every wish, every dream she had ever had about Tim Meredith.

*

It was still dark when Tim left the big house a few hours later. He'd hardly slept. He saddled his roan stallion, crossed the river at sunrise and rode towards an outlying paddock where he knew a mob of cattle were grazing. He needed to get away from the homestead for a while before the onslaught of the recovery lunch, followed by a procession of drawn-out farewells.

Tim knew he'd have to tell Rachel, but his father's birthday weekend wasn't the time nor Monaghan Station the place. He felt like he was about to take a giant leap into the abyss, and he relished it. Longed for it. He had no idea what would happen between him and Avril. That was a separate conversation. Could he have built a life with Rachel? Possibly. Could they have made it last? Maybe. But he wasn't in love with her and knew he never would be. He did care about Rachel, and he saw how sociable and spontaneous she could be, but that wasn't nearly enough to build a marriage on.

He poured the boiling water from the billy into the tin mug and swirled the tea leaves. The camp space, protected from the wind by a small rocky outcrop, was one Tim used regularly. He placed a small log on the fire and worked it down amongst the orange coals then sat back against the trunk of a grey gum and watched the faint wisps of steam rise from the cattle in the early light.

He couldn't have predicted any of this. How could he? Avril had swept into his life as unexpectedly as a fast-moving current. And now with all that was happening with his family, Tim wondered if somehow destiny was lurking in the trees, calling to him, *Sink or swim. What's it to be?* He knew what he had to do. *I'll swim*, he said to himself and he finished his tea and doused the fire.

Tim was not expecting to see Avril at the hitching rail when he rode back into the yard, but he was delighted. He pulled up beside her and looked around to see if they were on their own.

'You're up early,' she said, tightening the girth strap. 'That was quite a party. I'm just about to head out.' She spoke casually, as if nothing had changed between them, but Tim sensed tension beneath her words.

He gently tucked a loose strand of hair behind her ear.

'I'm flying Dad down to Brisbane in a couple of days. His test results will be back, and we'll finally know what we're dealing with.'

Avril said nothing, putting the bridle on her horse and toying with the straps. She'd replayed their kiss in her mind endlessly throughout the night but the magic of it was tainted by a dark thought: Rachel.

'I was thinking,' Tim continued, 'once I'm back and if everything goes well for Dad, how about you and I pack a couple of swags and head off for a few days? There's some beautiful country I'd love to show you, and this is the perfect time of year. No heat, no flies.' He smiled.

Avril felt like she was tumbling hopelessly between joy and despair. She couldn't wonder any longer.

'And Rachel,' she said, trying to keep her voice from breaking. 'How does she figure in all of this?'

'She doesn't,' he said. 'It's over. We're not a good fit. I've known that for some time.'

'When will you tell her?'

'I don't want to do it today, or here at Monaghan. It wouldn't be fair to her. I'll be seeing her in Brisbane; I'll tell her then.'

A wave of relief washed over Avril, so powerful it felt like her legs would buckle. She steadied herself.

'Well, if it is truly over between the two of you, let's talk about this when you get back.'

It took all her willpower not to throw her arms around

him, so instead she swung herself up into the saddle, smiled and rode away from the yard. She felt like she was floating, her heart rejoicing. And for the first time it crossed Avril's mind that she might not be going back to Melbourne quite as soon as she had planned.

*

A few days later, Tim and Henry touched down in Brisbane at Archerfield Aerodrome. Once the logbook entries were completed, they took a cab to the Royal Hotel in the city, dropped off their luggage and went straight to Henry's specialist appointment. They barely spoke throughout the journey but as they left the specialist's office, father and son couldn't stop smiling as they hugged and patted each other's backs.

'Christ, that was a close call,' said Henry.

'You've still got a very nasty ulcer, Dad. And your blood pressure is still too high, and you're going to have to watch your diet,' he said. 'You heard him. Lay off the wine and port. No bacon.'

'All the same, it's a relief to know I'll be around for a little longer,' Henry said. 'The doc's a bit harsh, though. No port, no bacon . . .' He sighed. 'Well, that's one drama sorted. Let's hope we do as well tomorrow.'

The cab pulled up at the hotel and when Henry got out, Tim stayed seated.

'Not coming in?' Henry asked.

'No. I have something I need to take care of. I'll see you for dinner. And I'll be vetting what you order.'

Henry rolled his eyes and tapped the roof of the cab with his hand.

*

When Rachel was in town, she had the run of an old Queenslander in St Lucia, on the banks of the Brisbane River, a house that once belonged to her grandparents. Considering what he was about to say, Tim thought a meeting at lunchtime seemed like the most appropriate time.

The morning after the party, Rachel had gone straight back to Cathaway, to take delivery of a warmblood gelding her father had recently bought her. After her success at the Brisbane Exhibition, she'd entered in a showjumping event at Roma and wanted to start training the new horse immediately. She'd made it clear to Tim that she wouldn't be hanging around for a drawn-out Sunday goodbye. As always, her training schedule was her priority.

Rachel opened the front door before Tim reached the top step.

'You're here, finally,' she said, throwing her arms around his neck. She stepped back and looked around. 'What? No luggage?'

'Not this time,' he replied.

'What's wrong?' Her smile had been replaced with a look of concern.

Tim didn't like to drag things out at the best of times. He'd decided to deal with this as swiftly as possible.

'Let's sit down,' he said.

*

As worldly as Tim was in many ways, he was no match for the likes of Mary Stanley or her daughter when it came to sheer manipulation and outright scheming. *Two years and no ring.* Mary had watched Tim the entire night of the Winter Dance, but she'd studied the governess even more closely, and she hadn't liked what she'd seen. There wasn't a man in the shearing shed that night who hadn't noticed the beautiful brunette in the dark blue dress, her own husband included. Hidden by the darkness, Mary had scrutinised the expression on Tim's face as he chatted with Avril by the bonfire. The chemistry that existed between the two was obvious, and a contingency plan was needed.

When Rachel arrived back at Cathaway Downs the day after Henry's party, Mary was quick to pull her aside, and in no uncertain terms, told her daughter what she had to do. 'You're not going to make a scene if he tells you it's over. Any theatricals, any at all, and you will lose him. No man wants a woman weeping hysterically. You will stay calm and agree with whatever he says. We'll let him have his fun with that French tart. It will all be over in a month.'

Rachel listened with annoyance to her mother's lecturing. She was already ten steps ahead, and had no intention of losing Tim to Avril, or any other woman. Eventually Rachel held up her hand.

'Enough of this, Mum,' she said. 'Tim's not going anywhere without me. Of that I can assure you.'

*

Tim shifted uncomfortably on the sofa despite its plushness. It looked new, and he wondered how much it had cost Doug Stanley. He clearly wasn't curtailing his lifestyle, despite the financial ruin they faced. Plus, there was the new horse.

'Whatever it is, Tim, just tell me,' said Rachel, dragging his attention towards her.

He took a deep breath and ran his hand through his hair.

'There's no easy way to say this, but I need to be truthful – our time together as a couple has come to an end. You and I need to go our separate ways.'

There. He'd said it. It was done.

Rachel looked at Tim then got up and walked calmly to the sideboard.

'Would you like a whisky?' she said. 'Because I certainly would.'

Tim stared at her in disbelief then nodded. He'd half-expected some sort of showdown. She handed Tim his drink, sat down, stared into her glass then took a sip.

'To be honest, Tim, I think we've been drifting apart for some time. This hasn't come as a complete shock.'

Tears welled in Rachel's eyes and he reached out, took her hand and squeezed it gently.

'You're so involved in your family's business interests,' she continued. 'I hardly ever know where you're going to be. And I'm, well, you know me. I'm determined to go to the Olympics. There's never been a woman on the Australian equestrian team, I want to be the first.'

Tim had always admired Rachel's ambition and her dedication to her sport. He would have supported her, one hundred per cent, but he knew she was right. His family, and their business, was his priority.

They spoke for a little longer, small talk but it was comfortable. Tim asked Rachel about the new horse, and even teased her about the number of suitors that would be at her door. She seemed unaware of her father's financial troubles, which Tim fully expected. Tim declined a second drink and called a cab, relieved that things had gone so smoothly.

'You'll always be very special to me, no matter what,' Rachel said as they stood at the front door. She kissed him softly on the cheek before watching him walk down the drive.

Rachel stood on the wide wooden veranda, waving as the cab drove away. She took a deep breath and let the tears stream down her face. Then she went back inside, closed the front door, opened all the kitchen cupboards, and smashed every piece of crockery she could find.

*

The following day, after Tim and Henry finished their meetings with Eric Parker, the accountant, and their lawyers, Tim walked into Regal Fine Jewellery on Queen Street, and bought a gift for Avril, then Henry and Tim went to the aerodrome for their midday departure. Tim had decided to wait until they were home to tell Anna and Henry together about him ending it with Rachel.

The aircraft lifted effortlessly off the ground and rose rapidly through a bank of low-lying clouds. Tim settled back into the pilot's seat and when he looked across, Henry was fast asleep. The second nature of flying had come back to him over the past few months, the feeling of freedom, the quiet space it provided, all the things he missed about being in the air. He retreated into his thoughts. Regardless of what might happen between him and Avril, he knew his decision to break up with Rachel had been the right one. Her revelation about them drifting apart had come as a surprise, but what did it matter. He admired the way Rachel had been so mature about the end of their courtship. They were bound to run into each other from time to time and he wanted to think they could remain on friendly terms.

Before they landed, Henry asked Tim to make a slight diversion, sweeping over a paddock twenty miles from the homestead, so he could see the water level in the dam for himself. And for the first time in years, Tim was overcome with an unexpected sense of excitement about touching down at Monaghan Station. It was good to be home.

Jordy wood-blocked the front wheel as Tim pulled the bags from the cargo hatch.

'Welcome back, Dad,' said Jordy, 'and you too, ugly.'

A heartfelt smile broke across Tim's face. 'Good to see you too, mate.'

That night, behind closed doors in the front room, Anna and Henry sat together as Tim told them about his visit with Rachel and the end of their relationship. Neither of his parents were surprised; in fact, they seemed relieved.

'Is this because of Avril?' Anna said without preamble. Even though he was a grown man, there were still times when she knew her son better than he knew himself.

'Yes, and no,' said Tim.

'What do you think will happen between you and Avril?' Henry asked.

'I have no idea,' Tim replied truthfully. 'We need some time on our own so I've suggested we take a few days off and get away. Camp out for a few nights. There are places I'd like Avril to see.'

'Good place to start,' Henry said. 'It'll give you time to talk about what you both want to do.'

'Are you in love with her?' asked Anna, her eyes scrutinising Tim's face.

'Yes. Yes, I am. Very much so,' he answered without hesitation.

'And is Avril in love with you?'

'Well, that's what I need to find out.'

Henry refilled their glasses and dropped back in his chair.

'Well, we're proud of you, son. Lord knows how this will all play out, but your mother and I support your decision, and we think Avril is a wonderful young woman.'

'We just want you, all of you, to be happy,' Anna added.

Henry suddenly grinned. 'Geez! I know one person who won't be happy – Mary! I think she'd already picked out her mother of the bride outfit,' and he laughed heartily.

CHAPTER 9

Avril helped Tim pack the truck with all the gear they'd be needing for a three-day camp. Since returning from Brisbane, Tim had found a whole new level of energy and enthusiasm for life. He'd given Avril a detailed account of his conversation with Rachel and said they'd been able to part on good terms – friends, even. Now, loading the last of her belongings, she looked towards the milky blue haze of the distant hills and her excitement grew. Tim and Avril exchanged private smiles as Col and Shady approached.

'All packed?' said Col.

'And ready to go,' said Tim.

Col and Shady would drop off the equipment and supplies below Mount Kiangarow a day ahead. Sandra was happy to take over as teacher for a couple of days, and early on the Thursday morning, Tim and Avril rode out and headed northeast towards the Bunya Mountains.

Spring had chased away the biting winds of winter. They traversed the gently undulating ground and came across a mob of kangaroos feeding in long grass as they stopped to water the horses. A large male drew himself up proudly, statue-like, watching the intruders. His ears twitched, then his interest waned and he hopped forward and bent down to eat.

Three hours later they stopped at a clump of scented gums and tethered the horses. Tim quickly had a fire going and water on the boil. Avril dropped her hat on the log and unwrapped the sandwiches.

'Smoko!' said Avril. 'I love that word.'

She cradled the hot tea in her hands and stared off into the distance. The clear blue sky stretched to the horizon above a vast open plain, a landscape peppered with a patchwork of green. The sweet smell of burning leaves and bark drifted through the low flickering flames. Other than the occasional passing bird or the isolated call of the cattle, they were completely alone. Tim rested his elbows on his knees and rolled his mug between his hands.

'It's as if the rest of the world doesn't exist when I'm out here with you,' he said.

Avril turned and smiled. 'I was just thinking something similar. Are you a mind reader, Tim Meredith?'

It was the first time Avril had said his name like that, *Tim Meredith*, and without any hesitation, he leant over and kissed her.

By mid-afternoon they'd reached their campsite just below Mount Kiangarow – an elevated stretch of land looking southwest, protected on either side by an arboretum of grey gums. Avril shut the horses in the holding yard – a piece of station practicality that had been maintained since Tim's great-grandfather's day. No one wants to lose their horse thirty miles from the homestead. For the lone rider camping out, the small yard provided surety that the horse would not wander off during the night. A short distance away stood a water trough and windmill.

Tim and Avril set up a tent then scouted the area for firewood, creating a makeshift wood pile that could easily supply their needs for the next few nights.

'If we head off shortly, we'll be able to catch the sunset from a plateau not too far away,' Tim said, glancing at the mountain range behind.

They changed into walking boots and Tim pulled a rucksack from the supply box and swung it over his shoulder.

'Lead on,' said Avril, breathing in the mint-like aroma that drifted from the edge of the trees.

The path into the cool green rainforest quicky narrowed and steepened as they trekked in single file. The fine shards of sunshine that drilled down through the thick forest canopy provided just enough light for Tim and Avril to find their way. Fifteen minutes later, the vegetation fell away and a large flat rocky outcrop opened up before them, providing an even grander view than the one seen from the ground.

Tim spread a small rug on the ground and opened a bottle of wine. Avril pulled the collar of her jacket up to her ears as she took the glass.

'*A votre santé,*' she said.

'*Santé,*' Tim replied.

He took her hand and they sat on the rug. Avril drew her knees up to her chin and leant back into his chest, his arms wrapped around her. They watched the citrus-coloured glow of the sun setting in the west.

'What a spectacular sight,' she said. 'The space. The beauty of it all. Thank you for bringing me to such a beautiful place.'

'I wanted to share this with you; it's a special place to me,' he said. 'But I also wanted us to have some time together, alone. So we can learn more about each other.'

'Well,' she said, taking a sip of wine. 'My story is a long one, but I can skip over the dull parts if you like.'

Tim gently ran his finger through Avril's hair. He was aware that her levity was a deflection. He knew how France had suffered. He'd been there. He'd been part of the whole goddamn tragedy.

'I don't want you to skip over anything,' he said. 'Not one single thing. Will you do that for me if I do that for you?'

'No secrets then. Is that what you're saying?' said Avril.

'I think it's the best way, don't you?'

'Okay then, Tim Meredith.' She said his name, enjoying the sound of it again, and he smiled. 'You tell me your story and I'll tell you mine. No secrets.'

Tim kissed her, tasting the sweetness of the wine. And before the fading light disappeared completely, they worked their way back down the hillside to their camp.

*

That night by the campfire, Tim and Avril's laughter echoed over the flames as they swapped tales of happy times.

'Two-up with Jordy. Don't get roped into that. He'll lose none of his money and all of yours,' said Tim, unable to contain his laughter.

'Jordy,' said Avril, grinning with deep fondness. 'We clicked from the moment we met. I'm surprised there's no special girl in his life. He's such fun to be with. And so kind. Surely someone local is keen on him?'

'Oh, the girls all love Jordy. But he's a free spirit, that's for sure. I've never known Jordy to have a steady girlfriend.'

A pool of hot coals had grown underneath the tower of burning logs and a light wind sprung up, spurring on the flames. Tim pushed himself out of the canvas chair and arranged the embers with a stick then he piled on more wood. He brushed his hands together and sat back down. Avril rested her elbows on the table and stared into the flames. With only the crackling of the fire and the shimmer of the stars to witness this moment, Tim began to talk.

'The smell. That's what I remember so vividly. That, and the noise of the gunners and the whistle of the bombs. Relentless,' he said. 'Coming home was just as bad. I was expected to trade my air force uniform for my saddle and return to running the station as if I'd been on a school camp. It wasn't until about a year after I got back that I started to unravel, and I couldn't cope. I guess I blamed the old man for a lot of things. But it wasn't his fault. It wasn't anyone's fault.'

As Tim recalled his experiences as a pilot during the war, Avril sat silently and listened, allowing his memories to tumble forth. He'd rarely discussed his time in Europe during the war, and certainly not with Rachel, but he found that he wanted to tell Avril everything. All of it. It was his journey to where they were now. Eventually he reached across the table and took both her hands. 'I've never told another living soul what I've told you tonight,' he said.

'Thank you for letting me in. We all carry scars, Tim, and with time, they do fade. They're still there, but they do fade.'

Later, after Tim had made sure she was comfortable and they'd said goodnight, Avril lay in the tent, thinking about what Tim had told her. The appalling waste of life he'd witnessed. *It's very hard to talk to someone about what really went on over there,* Tim had said. *It's impossible for anyone who has never lived through the violence, the chaos, the sheer idiocy of war, to truly understand.* But Avril understood. She had lived it. And when he described his feelings of depression that would come and go for the first couple of years after the war – *I felt trapped in a vortex for so long* – Avril knew how that felt too. She had told Tim that it was brave of him to tell his story, but now she wondered if she would have the courage to reveal hers. *How much truth is too much truth?* Avril thought. Did she really want to tell Tim everything? And, more importantly, what would he think of her? But if they were to have any chance together, she knew she had to. There could be no secrets.

*

For the first time in years, Tim had slept right through the night, waking only when he heard Avril making the morning fire. He'd climbed into his swag the night before, consumed by thoughts of making love with Avril. And the idea that Avril was sleeping only a few yards from him felt torturous. But Tim was relieved to have spoken to Avril openly and honestly. Having done so, it was not the right moment for any passionate encounter, even though their day and night together had felt magical.

After breakfast and with supplies in their saddle bags, they mounted up and headed west. Tim wanted to show Avril a different kind of terrain to the open plains that surrounded the homestead. Her hat was pulled slightly forward, blocking the morning sun, and her hair fell loose across her back. Together they collected up their reins and eased their horses into a gentle canter along the foothills of the mountains. As they reached the crest of a hill, a large mob of kangaroos grazing on a rich grassy plateau below burst into motion. The joeys ricocheted left and right in the rush to seclude themselves amongst the trees.

They slowed to a walk as the landscape changed around them. It now rose and fell in a series of twisting grassy valleys that tested the skills of both horse and rider. Thick grass was suddenly replaced with patches of rock-strewn topsoil and at one point Piaf stumbled, almost tossing Avril out of the saddle.

'Do you ever get lost out here?' Avril asked as she carefully guided her horse over the rough ground.

'It's a bit hard to. Sun rises in the east, sets in the west and the Darling Range and the river are natural landmarks. Plus, there isn't a part of Monaghan that I haven't ridden over.'

They stopped for lunch at a river, tying their horses in the shade. After they ate the picnic that Tim had packed, they leant back against the base of a big old gum tree and stretched out their legs. On the other side of the river, some cows and their calves waded in at the water's edge and began to drink. *It is so peaceful*, Avril thought, and her mind drifted back to where her life had started.

'I was born in Tours,' she began. 'Tours is such a pretty town in the summer. The wildflowers and sunflowers and the long sunny days.' She talked about her mother's shop, the Resistance movement, living at the chateau with Madame Leon, her love for Guy.

'The day after Paris was liberated, Guy asked me to marry him, and I said yes. We'd planned to marry the following month. But the week before our wedding day, he was abducted and killed.'

It was the first time Avril had ever spoken the words

aloud, they'd always been too painful. But with Tim beside her, their hands clasped together, she found the strength to tell her story. She held nothing back.

*

The day after Avril buried her son, her temperature soared to one hundred and four and she drifted in and out of sleep. When Brigette arrived at the abbey, Sister Marguerite sent her back down to the village to find the doctor. He did not take long to make his diagnosis and he told Sister Marguerite to expect the worst.

'She's in a bad way,' said the doctor. 'And there won't be any more children, I'm afraid.'

For three weeks Sister Marguerite nursed Avril day and night, until she was well enough to be moved. A week later, the doctor collected Avril and drove her back to the chateau, where Brigette was waiting for her.

'The war had ended but there was still so much confusion,' Avril explained. 'The lights would suddenly go out and we'd be plunged into darkness, never knowing when the power would return. Everything was in short supply – food, clothing, candles. We were lucky to have the vegetable gardens and orchards, a dozen hens, some goats and a few cows.'

She didn't find out what happened to Madame Leon and Guy until November. Monsieur Fortin, who had been searching for them since they disappeared, telephoned with the news. He'd learnt that Guy and his mother had arrived in Paris the day they left the chateau, but some extremists within the Resistance were waiting for them. Madame Leon was arrested, accused of being a collaborator and imprisoned. She told Monsieur Fortin that she watched as Guy was beaten and dragged down the street.

She was pushed into a car and driven away. She never saw her son again.

'So many people, looking for someone to blame,' said Avril. 'The charges were false, of course, and eventually Madame Leon was released. When she returned in July of 1945, Madame Leon, Brigette and I lived on at the chateau, trying to pick up the pieces of our lives, like everyone else. There wasn't a minute of my day when I didn't think of Guy, hoping by some miracle he'd walk through the door.'

Avril sighed and broke off a long stem of grass, twisting it between her fingers.

'Still, we were better off than most,' she said. 'And then, the following autumn, Madame Leon came back from a few days in Paris and told me she arranged an interview for me, if I wanted it, with a new fashion house that was opening. They were handpicking a staff of eighty-five, cutters, seamstresses, hand finishers, and Madame Leon knew the director of the design studio personally. That's how I came to work at the House of Dior.'

'Madame Leon sounds like a wonderful woman,' said Tim.

'She was. She still is. They all were. Brigette encouraged me to not give up on my sewing skills in the months after the war. And Madame Leon managed to get some linen, quality damask and English tweed. I made each of us a dress and a tailored suit for Madame. Sewing again – it kept me sane.'

'And did you like living in Paris and working at Dior?'

'Oh, yes. I was one of the lucky ones. I had work I loved, and a very tiny but safe apartment I shared with another seamstress.'

Avril had never lived in the city and those first few months in Paris were a whirlwind, she recalled. Monsieur

Dior was bringing together his first Spring/Summer collection and the workrooms were not properly completed, so they worked wherever they could. By the windows, on the stairs, anywhere they could sit as they attached buttons and sewed hems. Avril's job was to hand-finish the lining on suits and day dresses, sew hems and insert zippers. She could still imagine the feel of the exquisite materials, smell the coffee drifting up from the nearby café and hear the laughter of her workmates, their camaraderie brightening every long hard day.

'And Guy?' Tim asked.

'In Paris, I looked for him everywhere. I never stopped. I'd turn a corner hoping, praying, that he'd come walking towards me. He never did. It seemed everyone was looking for someone.' Avril sighed. 'Monsieur Fontin was doing all he could. He kept me informed but there was nothing, and then, a year after I moved to Paris, Monsieur Fontin received confirmation that Guy had died the same day he'd been abducted. Such a pointless, pointless death.'

Avril wiped the tears from her eyes. Tim reached out and took her hand in his.

'Please, don't be sad for me, Tim. I feel so lucky to be here and so many suffered far more than I did.'

It was hard not to feel sad, but more than that Tim felt admiration for Avril, everything she had been through and the dignity with which she'd told her story. 'I'm honoured that you've taken me into your confidence,' he said.

'I guess I wanted you to know all of this because, Tim, I can't have any more children. I can give you my love, but no children.'

They sat in silence under the big old gum tree. 'Life rarely goes in the direction we think it will,' he said. 'When I was at boarding school, there were two brothers in my house,

Sam and Robert, only one year apart. I was good mates with Sam. Hell of a tennis player. I could never take a set off him. Anyway, the brothers, they looked so alike you'd almost swear they were twins. And yet, they were both adopted. Completely different parents. What I'm trying to say is, there's more than one way to make a family.' He hugged her tightly. 'I adore you, Avril. Let's take this one step at a time.'

The sun was starting to sink towards the tree line as they made their way back to camp. As they reached the open plains again, a warm breeze swept up behind them, willing the horses to run. Avril felt a lightness and she pushed her mare into a canter and raced towards the water tank. She raised herself high in the saddle, let go of her reins, looked up at the sky and spread her arms as if she were flying.

*

Tim had the fire burning strongly long before the sun completely disappeared. He'd skinned and dressed the rabbits he'd shot and opened a bottle of red wine while he waited for Avril to return from the shower that had been fashioned beneath the water tank. The calls of the kookaburras echoed overhead as once again Tim and Avril were treated to a luminous blend of burnt peach and deep saffron on the horizon.

Avril could smell the aroma of the meat and sweetcorn as she emerged from the tent. She tossed a lightweight wrap around her shoulders, taking the glass of wine Tim handed her. Over dinner their conversation waxed and waned between the present and the past, sharing stories of their childhoods, discussing Tim's plans for Monaghan and what Avril planned to do in Melbourne. After dinner

Tim pulled a harmonica from his bag and placed it on the table.

'Ah! Dinner and entertainment,' said Avril, delighting in the surprise.

She relaxed into her camp chair as Tim brought the instrument to his mouth and started playing. The vibrato of the notes drifted soulfully out into the darkness, searching for somewhere to rest. The light from the fire lit Tim's tanned skin and his thick black hair fell about his face. With each breath Tim took, the notes rose and fell. In the intimacy of the moment Tim closed his eyes as the last note sailed away and he finished the tune.

'Come on,' he said, taking Avril's hand and helping her out of her chair. 'You know you've set a precedent, don't you? Dancing with me under the stars.' He placed his hand around her waist. 'Though I can't hold you in my arms and play the harmonica at the same time, I'm afraid.'

Avril began to hum a tune and by the light of the fire, they danced. Tim's embrace was a heady mix of strength and tenderness she no longer wanted to deny or resist. Under the blanket of stars the nocturnal sounds of the bush folded around them as Avril closed her eyes, savouring the moment that was only theirs. She brought her eyes up to meet Tim's, his strong arms wrapped across her back.

'Bring your swag,' she said softly. With one easy sweep Tim picked up his bedding and, still holding her hand in his, they walked towards the tent.

Tim's kiss and touch was pleasure beyond anything Avril had ever known. She helped lift his shirt over his head, and as he undid the buttons down the centre of her blouse, his eyes didn't leave hers. His kiss found the back of her neck, her shoulders, her face. The straps of her camisole fell away as he guided her to the floor of their shelter, and under the light of the full moon their passion broke free.

*

Tim and Avril woke in each other's arms to the sounds of the bush. Magpies chortled from nearby trees and the call of the cattle carried over the hills. By early afternoon they had started their trek up the mountain to a place Tim called 'The Falls'.

The climb was exhilarating if somewhat arduous. Where the incline was sharp, Avril took Tim's hand so she could pull herself forward. The floor of the eucalypt forest was lined with ferns and exotic-looking plants. Halfway up the climb, Tim stopped.

'Look! Just there,' and he pointed a few feet ahead.

A large blue-tongued lizard lay in the centre of the track. To Avril's surprise, the beautiful creature remained motionless as they stepped slowly around it and continued up the slope.

Avril could hear the roar of the waterfall long before they reached the swimming hole, halfway up the mountain. Dense bush surrounded the rock formation which held the large body of dark green water. Sunlight poured down through the gap in the canopy. Water mist drifted over Tim and Avril as they sat on a flat rock that overhung the naturally formed pool. They drank from their water bottles, taking in the natural beauty in all its wonder.

'How many times have you been here?' asked Avril.

'I've come here ever since I was a kid. It was Col who first showed us this place – Jody, Reece and me. Growing up, Col was always teaching us stuff. He's only six years older than me so he's been like a big brother to all of us.

He'd teach us where to find bush tucker, food that is. How to find water and the easiest way to start a fire.'

'It really is magical,' she said.

'It's a special place to Col and his people.'

Avril leant over the edge of the rock and scooped her hand through the water.

'I'm game if you are,' she said with a cheeky smile.

They stripped off their clothes, held hands and plunged into the deepest part of the waterhole. The water was more refreshing than cold, and their laughter echoed off the rocks as they dived and swam. As they waded out, Avril stopped and pulled Tim towards her. She felt his lips on her neck as her hands worked their way down the muscles of his back. Her body clung to his as once more, they rejoiced in their mutual passion.

After dinner Tim took their swags from the tent and spread them by the warmth of the fire. They lay side by side and finished off the last of the wine while they talked. Tim suggested they make an early start back to the homestead in the morning so he could show Avril a spectacular section of the river she hadn't seen.

'How do you think things will be, between you and me, once we're back at the homestead?' said Avril.

'Fantastic!' Tim laughed and kissed her hand. 'No, seriously. As much as I often feel Monaghan is like some sort of hotel with a permanently rotating guest list, the homestead can also be a sanctuary. And it will be for us as well.'

Tim pushed himself up and rested on his elbow.

'You must have noticed that the sheer size of the house allows all of us to live in relative privacy,' said Tim.

'What are there? Forty-two rooms?'

'Forty-six, to be exact,' he replied. 'There's a freedom to living on a station that you won't find anywhere else.

I love the fact that you and I can come out here alone, and no one bats an eyelid.'

'What do you think Anna and Henry will make of us?' Avril asked.

'They already know how I feel about you, so our relationship won't be a surprise.'

Avril turned on her back and stared up at the full moon hovering above them. She had not raised the subject of returning to Melbourne, and nor had Tim. There was no denying that she was in love with Tim, and she loved being at Monaghan, but she also had plans and dreams of her own. And financial independence was on the top of her list. As for marriage, Avril wasn't even sure she wanted one, now or in the future. Avril had always known she wasn't like other women of her age and she cared little about conforming to the expectations of others. She had seen relationships in all their complexities when she lived in Le Marais – men living with men, women living with women, and every combination of relationship in between. Everyone trying to find some form of happiness out of the rubble and chaos that was post-war Paris.

Is it possible to have both? A life with Tim and my independence? she wondered.

Tim sat up and pushed a log into the heart of the fire.

'You look deep in thought,' he said.

It wasn't the time to raise her concerns; they'd agreed to take it one step at a time and she was jumping too far ahead. 'Have you heard about the Harvest Moon?' she said, pointing above them to the moon which was glowing golden. 'That's what we called it when all the crops are in, and families and farm workers come together to celebrate the end of the harvest.'

'That's a rather auspicious sign,' he said. 'The two of

us, out here together under the light of the Harvest Moon.'

They sat staring up at the night sky, accompanied by the crackling fire, then Tim said, 'Close your eyes and hold out your hands.'

Avril did as he asked.

Tim reached into his swag and placed the square black velvet box into Avril's palms.

'What is this?' she said in surprise.

'Something for you from me.'

Avril lifted the lid to find the box contained a wide yellow gold bangle, and an inscription on the inside that read, *Timing is everything.*

'Think of us and this night when you wear it.'

'Oh, Tim. This is beautiful. Thank you.'

He took the bangle and slid it onto her left wrist.

'So, you're a romantic, Tim Meredith?'

'With you, Avril Montdidier, how can I not be?' and he moved closer to Avril and kissed the nape of her neck.

CHAPTER 10

Just as Tim had predicted, life at Monaghan Station went on without so much as a raised eyebrow after they arrived back from their three-day camp. The only thing different about Avril was the precious gold bangle she constantly wore on her wrist. Anna and Henry had gone to Melbourne, where, Henry had assured Tim, he would tell Anna about his financial predicament, once and for all.

Avril returned to the school, having thought up a variety of inside and outdoor learning activities her five little students would enjoy. Tim, Jordy and the stockmen came and went on horseback or ute for one task or another. Cattle and sheep were moved, fences repaired, and windmills checked. When Tim wasn't on his horse, he could be found in his office, which was as well appointed as Henry's, with a Chesterfield sofa, oak desk, swivel chair and telephone. The telephone was the lifeline to the station, with incoming calls starting early each day then peaking again late afternoon. Anna had taken on a new housemaid, Katie, and while Sandra still did some domestic work, her main role was office support, which she excelled at. Col and his boys were now having dinner each night with Sandra and her twins, at the cottage she called home. In the evening, Avril would often see the two of them sitting on Sandra's veranda, talking as the five children played around the house.

Tim's decision to move into the self-contained set of rooms at the northern end of the grand old house, affectionately known as 'The Aviary', gave Tim and Avril the space and privacy they needed and was also close to Avril's bedroom and sewing room. The suite had all the amenities of a small house and was once occupied by Henry's parents. It had been redecorated after both Mr and Mrs Meredith senior had passed away, and all its rooms were now bathed in soft tones of blues and creams. Most of the time it stood empty, only used for house guests. Its corner rooms on the ground floor overlooked a vine-covered large wire enclosure, built to house injured birds while they recovered, hence its name.

'I can't believe I didn't move in here ages ago,' Tim said, as he dropped down next to Avril on the sofa one evening. With an entire section of the house to themselves, Avril delighted in using the little kitchen to cook for the two of them as often as she could. The days were longer since October blurred into November and they would often end up on the secluded corner of the veranda, idly talking about whatever was on their minds. The matter of Avril returning to Melbourne was the only subject they avoided.

*

Avril stood at the top of the airstrip and waved Tim off once again. Unlike his father, Tim rarely enjoyed his business trips and even though he was only away for three days on this occasion, he couldn't wait to get back to Monaghan, and to Avril. He'd started with a short visit to Bundaberg then flew down to Brisbane to see the lawyers again. He had just taken off his jacket and opened the window in his room at the Royal Hotel, when the telephone rang. Expecting it to be a call confirming his dinner reservation, he was surprised to hear Rachel's voice.

'There's some important business I need to talk to you about,' she had said before asking if he would have time to come by the house that evening for a quick drink. He thought it might have been about the mining company, and suggested they have dinner together instead. Strangely, she said that she'd rather not and so they agreed on six o'clock.

It was a warm Brisbane night and an orchestra of cicadas were in full pitch as Tim knocked on Rachel's front door at St Lucia.

'Come in. It's open,' she called.

Tim found Rachel in the lounge room, and she greeted him with a hug. They sat and chatted for a bit and then, without warning, Tim felt the walls close in as the words Rachel had just uttered circulated around the room.

'Are you sure?' A vice-like pain gripped his chest.

'Yes, Tim, I'm certain. I'm ten weeks along. I have the doctor's report,' she said, and picked up a long white envelope that was sitting on the coffee table. 'A copy for you.'

He read the contents and dropped the letter on the polished rosewood.

'How? When?' he said in complete amazement. 'We were always so careful.'

'I'm just as surprised as you are,' she replied. 'But it's happened. A couple of weeks before the Winter Dance, by my calculations.'

Tim felt as though his life was being sucked into a black hole, from which there was no escape. It didn't seem real; it couldn't be real. And yet he knew it was.

'What are we going to do?' Rachel said. 'It's not what either of us expected, but I can't have a baby if I'm not married. It would be . . . dishonourable.' She let the last word hang.

Tim walked to the window. A wave of regret flooded his body. Regret. Nothing but regret. He felt as if his legs were about to give way, so he steadied himself and sat down again. She placed a glass of whisky in front of him.

'I don't know what to do right now, Rachel,' he said. 'I'm going to need time to think about what you've just told me.'

Rachel studied the anguish on Tim's face as she sat in the chair opposite. She watched and waited like a sleek cat slowly cornering her prey. Then she played her trump card.

'I've had more time than you to come to terms with this, and I think there is a way through it.' She had his full attention now.

'How?' He was prepared to listen to anything that might be a solution.

'Well, it's not exactly conventional, then again neither am I . . . But I thought we could get married before our baby is born and then, when the child is a year old, we go our separate ways. I know divorce is not an option for most people, but it is for people like us. We both have money and legal connections.'

'Who knows about this?' said Tim.

'No one,' Rachel lied. She had, of course, discussed it all with Mary. 'I really think my idea could work, Tim. Of course, to divorce, we'll have to have grounds. I'll need to accuse you of something. That's probably the most likely angle to take.'

Tim downed the whisky and pocketed the envelope. 'This is a complete shock, Rachel, as you can imagine.' He struggled for words. 'How are you feeling?' he asked awkwardly.

'I'm a little nauseous in the morning, but apart from that I'm fine.'

'And how do you feel about having a baby, about us?'

'I would prefer not to be in this situation, to be honest, but it's happened, and we have to make some wise decisions. I'm not trying to ruin your life, Tim. But we need to do the right thing. And we need to do it sooner rather than later.'

'And your riding career?'

'I'll have to take a break until the baby is born, but I'm not giving it up for anyone or anything. Look, Tim, I truly believe there's a way through this. And when it's all over, we'll have a beautiful son or daughter, and we'll be free to continue our lives.'

'You make it all sound so straightforward, which we both know it isn't,' said Tim.

Rachel sat down next to him but she deliberately didn't touch him, as if to prove that she respected his space.

'We can get through this, Tim. I know we can. You just need to trust me.'

*

Tim flew back to Monaghan Station in a state of utter confusion. Avril sat motionless as he told her what had taken place in Brisbane. Her initial shock quickly gave way to disbelief, and finally a wave of grief overtook her. She dropped her head in her hands but there were no tears.

There simply weren't any. *Loss. Again. Loss.* The words rang in her ears as a fury rose inside her.

'Our beautiful dream is at an end, Tim,' she cried. 'It's over. Every dream, every plan. Over.'

'Don't say that,' he pleaded. 'Please, don't say that.'

'How can it not be?' she said. 'Life! It never goes in the direction you think it will.' Then her anger fell away as quickly as it had overtaken her. She breathed deeply as the door to her heart slammed shut.

'I'll be returning to Melbourne in a couple of weeks and you, well, you've got a lot to sort out.'

'I understand that you're angry,' Tim said. 'But we can get through this.'

Avril got up, went to the window and sat down on the wide ledge. *Rachel can give you the one thing I never can. A child you have fathered. How could I ever stand in the way of that,* she thought.

'No, Tim,' she said. 'I'm not angry. Anger doesn't even begin to cover it. I'm devastated. I'm completely heartbroken. I find someone I love, and who truly loves me, and what we could share is torn from me. From both of us. What's your family motto? *Timing is everything.* You're going to be a father. Something you and I could never experience together. Well, not in the conventional way at least. We're finished, you and me. Fate has other plans for both of us.'

The tears were now streaming down Avril's face. Tim crossed the room and sat beside her, taking her hands in his.

'In two years, Rachel and I will be divorced, without any dishonour to her, and then you and I can be together, forever.'

'Two years is a very long time, Tim, with an ocean of possibilities in between.'

'Avril, I can't live without you. I don't want to live without you.' His blue eyes, so like the sky in summer, were wet with tears and full of such pain that Avril could hardly bear to look into them.

She brushed her hand down the side of his face.

'I'm sorry, my darling, I don't know how all of this will play out. What I do know is that I'll always love you, and the time we've had together. But for now, we'll both have to live without each other.'

*

Tim asked Avril if she would let him fly her to Melbourne and she accepted his offer. The day before she left, Avril worked her way around the station and said her goodbyes. There were heartfelt tears from everyone, from the children to all the women of the homestead. Bob and Col's farewell was equally genuine.

That night, Henry poured a glass of wine for Avril and himself, as they waited for Anna and Jordy on the front veranda. He tenderly put his arm around Avril's shoulders.

'I didn't think it would end like this, Avril. You'll always be part of our family. Always.'

And despite everything that had happened, Avril believed that she would. Her bond with Henry, Anna and Jordy was stronger than the adversity which was currently driving them apart.

Tim had asked Avril what she'd like to do on her last night at Monaghan, and she'd replied that she wanted them to eat dinner together under the stars. So in a clearing on the bank of the river, not too far from the homestead, he set up a campsite. The long grass caught the hem of Avril's blue cotton dress as she made her way to the clearing. She stopped short of the camp and drank in every detail, to be locked in her memory forever.

Tim stood, his back to the table and chairs, and stared across the water. The sun dipped in the western sky while birds called their evening songs. The crystal glasses on the table caught the rays of the setting sun. Between the plates was a platter of cheeses, cold meats, olives, roasted tomatoes and bread.

'Are you trying to impress me, Tim Meredith, with your European food skills?'

Tim turned and looked at Avril. His half smile carried despair and his eyes showed only sadness. Avril moved forward and kissed him on the lips.

'Please, let's not be unhappy tonight. No matter how difficult that might be.'

Despite their best intentions, their normally free-flowing talk was more like a series of pleasant statements as they skirted around the subject of the nuptials between Tim and Rachel, which would need to take place in a matter of weeks.

Before the fire had burned away, Tim picked up his harmonica. The haunting sound of the notes filled the air as Avril closed her eyes. She floated back to the base of the Bunya Mountains and pictured their little camp, the waterfall where they'd made love, riding together across the undulating hills, the night sky and the glow of the coals. *I can't do this again*, she thought. *Finding love and losing it, the pain is too much. Perhaps this is the universe pushing me in the direction I'm meant to go. Alone.*

The following morning as the plane lifted off the airstrip at Monaghan Station, Avril saw the landscape from the air for the first time. Tim made a low angled turn over the homestead that gave Avril an uninterrupted view in every direction. The plane climbed through a bank of clouds and levelled out into the infinite blue sky beyond. Something deep inside Avril told her that she would return to Monaghan Station one day. Her hand found her wrist and as her eyes followed the meandering silver path of the Condamine River below, she rotated her gold bangle around and around.

PART 2

It is not in the stars to hold our destiny but in ourselves.

William Shakespeare

CHAPTER 11

A week before Christmas, Avril weaved her way through the morning pandemonium that was Flinders Lane towards Lewin & Son. If ever there was a day Avril needed to be busy and have her mind fully occupied, it was today. She sidestepped a delivery boy, almost dropping one of the rolls of fabric from under her left arm while managing to hang on to her patterns with the other. It had just gone ten o'clock and already the summer heat was trapped between the cars, trucks and narrowness of the constantly busy thoroughfare that was simply called The Lane.

Since returning to Melbourne, Avril had worked at a frenetic pace, scouring the city for suitable fabrics, buttons and trims during the day, returning home to design and make patterns until midnight. Each landlord she'd spoken to had knocked back her request to lease their premises, as they considered her to be an unsuitable tenant.

Duncan, Louise and Gabriel had moved into a rambling old cottage in Coben Street, South Melbourne, at the end of November. In preparation for Avril's return, they had converted the sunroom, a covered-in veranda at the back of the house, into a production space. Duncan had given the airy north-facing room two coats of white paint and procured a large table, ideal for laying up fabric. Well used but in good working order, the black Singer sewing machine that had once been Duncan's mother's only reliable source of income sat patiently in the corner.

At the very moment Avril was charging towards Lewin & Son, Tim and Rachel stood side by side in an old stone church sixteen miles from Cathaway Downs and said their marriage vows. With only immediate family members in attendance, the Monday nuptials were carried out in a pleasant yet perfunctory fashion. The bride wore white; the groom, a look of irreverence. Afterwards, the party of eighteen would drive to Cathaway for a wedding breakfast and then the married couple would return to Monaghan Station to commence life as husband and wife.

'Good morning, Avril,' said Mr Lewin warmly as she entered the showroom. 'You've returned to us from your adventures beyond.'

The offer of employment Mr Lewin had made Avril before she left for Monaghan Station had been an attractive and generous one, particularly in terms of the salary. Although Avril had been flattered, she had respectfully declined the position and Mr Lewin said he wasn't surprised. He admired her drive and determination and said he would leave his offer 'on the table' should she change her mind.

Avril showed Mr Lewin the fabric swatches of the alabaster, oyster and crimson duchess satin she'd carried in. Enough material to make up six dresses.

Mr Lewin studied Avril's sketches. It was evident to him from the way the designs had been drawn that Avril had an excellent understanding of garment construction.

Bert Lewin knew these designs would be flattering to any customer, regardless of height or shape.

'So, you're moving into cocktail wear, I see. Very nice, Avril. Very nice,' he said, holding the sketch of the crimson dress up to the light.

He said he was able to supply the covered belts for the dresses and once the pick-up date for the order was confirmed, Mr Lewin poured two tall glasses of cold water and they sat down.

'What's the matter, Avril?' he said. 'If you don't mind me asking?'

'I looked at three vacant shops last week. Each one perfect for my needs, and not one of the owners thought I'd make a suitable tenant. Their first question, all of them, was, "Are you married?" Their second question, "Are you planning on getting married soon?" If I hear the term "too risky" one more time I'll scream.'

Mr Lewin placed his elbows on the arms of the chair, drew his hands to his shirt front and interlocked his fingers. 'Disappointing,' was all he said.

Avril continued, 'I told them I could pay four months' rent in advance, even six months, but it didn't make a bit of difference.'

'Do you have any plans for the next hour?' he asked.

'I was going to have a look at the stock in Myer and Foys, nothing in particular. Why do you ask?'

'I have something I'd like to show you,' he said, standing up and slipping his arms into his jacket. 'It won't take long.'

Ten minutes later Bert Lewin and Avril entered the Block Arcade from the Collins Street side. They worked their way down to a shop on the left at the far end, where the sign-writing on the window read, *Chapman's*

China & Crystal. The shop was devoid of customers and much of the stock Avril considered rather old-fashioned.

'I happen to know these premises will become vacant the first week of April,' said Mr Lewin. 'Thirty yards square. Rates and electricity payable quarterly. Wonderful location. It would suit you perfectly, I believe. The owner is looking for a two-year lease with an option to extend.'

Avril quickly calculated the monthly outgoings on the premises.

'I can meet all those costs,' she said excitedly. 'Including what I'd need to spend on stock, fittings and fixtures.'

Avril's nose was almost touching the glass as she stood in front of the large picture window and started to mentally redesign the soon-to-be empty space. She was deep in thought, assessing the opportunity this little gem of a shop represented. The display cabinets were all free-standing and could easily be removed. Except for two shelves attached to the wall behind the cash register and telephone, there were no other permanent structures. There'd be no need for the conservative dowdiness of the costumery chaise longue and heavy velvet curtains she'd seen in many of the made-to-measure salons. Avril's ideas were fresh and innovative, much like the clientele she knew her designs would attract with her ready-to-wear range.

'Well, I've got nothing to lose by at least trying,' she said. 'Do you know who I need to contact?'

'As a matter of fact, I do,' Mr Lewin said. 'The shop's owned by a private company. If you're serious about securing this premises, and can provide a month's rent as a deposit, I'm sure the paperwork can be ready to sign by this afternoon. Are you interested?'

Avril paused for a moment.

'I only have one question,' she said. 'Is Albert Dubray the owner or in any way connected with these premises?'

'The restaurateur?' said Mr Lewin with genuine surprise. 'Not at all. I can assure you he is not the proprietor.'

'And do you know the owner?'

'I know him very well.'

'In that case, if he accepts, I'd be delighted to sign the lease today if it can be arranged.'

'He accepts, and I'd be delighted to have you as my tenant,' Mr Lewin said, smiling warmly.

It took Avril only a moment to process what Mr Lewin had said, before they both started laughing. 'Really? Oh, thank you, Mr Lewin!' Avril could scarcely believe her luck or contain her joy. She hugged Mr Lewin spontaneously then stepped back. They shook hands and their agreement was sealed.

And, on the same day that Tim Meredith signed a contract of his own, Avril secured her first business premises in the heart of Melbourne.

*

Avril could not stop smiling when she left Lewin & Son later that afternoon. By the time Louise and Gabriel had returned around six o'clock, she had set the table in the back courtyard and laid out an antipasto platter with mortadella, prosciutto and olives and had a loaf of crusty bread warming in the oven. She was doing anything to keep herself busy and her mind off Tim. Once the celebratory hugs and laughter had died down, the conversation turned to the task of promoting Avril's new business and the shop she'd decided to call 'le Chic'.

They were still celebrating when Duncan arrived home after his dinner shift at the bistro.

191

'That's a terrific retail site,' said Duncan, once Avril explained the location and size of the shop. 'So, you're definitely not going to do couture?'

'I've done my research and I think there's enough couturiers in Melbourne already. Running an atelier takes a lot of money, the garments are expensive to make, you need to employ at least six full-time staff and, to be honest, I don't want to do that sort of work anymore.'

'So, all ready-to-wear. Is that what you're saying?' asked Gabriel.

'I'll offer a *soft* made-to-measure service, so to speak,' said Avril. 'One of my designs cut in a specific fabric for a customer or altered slightly to flatter her figure. I'm not going to try and compete with the existing couturiers in this town. They're too well established and besides, there's a gap in the market for beautiful off-the-rack dresses that have the look of couture, without the price tag. And what's the most popular social outing for young women?'

'Dancing!' cried Louise.

'You know the halls and venues all over the city and in the suburbs are full every Friday and Saturday night with people wanting to dance. Not to mention private parties and balls. There's also this new square dance craze that's taken off. So many events for women all needing a fabulous dress.'

'And what about all those weddings,' said Louise, regretting her words the moment she spoke.

'Yes, and weddings,' said Avril, glancing at her friends gathered at the table. 'And before anyone asks, I'm fine.' She'd tried not to think about Tim all day, but hadn't succeeded.

'It will be my pleasure to take whatever photos you need. I can get you a couple of models,' said Gabriel.

'Between Louise and I, we'll get you some free publicity.'

'Gabriel, who do you know at *The Australian Woman* magazine?' said Avril, relieved to change the subject from weddings.

'I get on well with the senior editor. She keeps putting work my way and if it keeps up, I'll be able to go freelance by this time next year.'

When Louise and Gabriel had gone to bed, Avril turned to Duncan. She explained that initially she was going to be doing everything herself. Overseeing the orders with Lewin & Son, running the shop, designing, sourcing fabric and making the patterns. 'But eventually, not too far down the track I hope, I'll need someone to work with me,' she said. 'Someone I can trust.'

'Are you trying to poach me away from the hallowed halls of Bistro Dubray to be your right-hand man, Miss Montdidier?' Duncan gasped, feigning offence. 'Well, I never!'

'I'm serious,' Avril replied.

Duncan's smile disappeared from his face. He placed his arm gently around Avril's shoulder.

'I'm a double act, I'm afraid. As much as I'd love to say yes, and tell Albert where to stick his menu, I won't leave Josephine there on her own.'

'Well, that's the thing,' said Avril. 'I thought I might be able to persuade her to help out one day a week. At least that way she'd have some of her own money and she wouldn't have to plead for every cent from Albert. Monday's the slowest day in the bistro. It makes no difference if she's not there. What do you think?'

'Why don't you ask her?' said Duncan.

'I'm going to visit her tomorrow evening. I'll let you know what she says.'

Avril sat in the courtyard for some time after Duncan said goodnight. Through the warm night air came the chorus of the crickets. A thin curve of silver shone brightly, announcing the start of a new moon cycle. The last time Avril had looked at a waxing crescent moon, she'd been standing on the veranda outside The Aviary with Tim, his arms around her, his breath soft on her neck. Avril blew out the cluster of candles on the table, and just as Tim was doing that same night, went to bed alone.

*

Avril hid in the doorway across the street and watched Albert drive away from the bistro. She hadn't been back to Collins Street since returning to Melbourne as Josephine was only too happy to visit Avril at her place. But tonight, with Albert out for a night of cards, Josephine had wanted Avril to visit her. 'Curl up on the sofa and talk like we used to when you first arrived,' she'd said on the phone. Avril had been looking for an opportunity to tell Josephine about the letter, hidden in the kitchen drawer. The truth weighed on her mind but at the same time, she worried about the impact it would have on her aunt.

Josephine was all smiles as she greeted Avril and as far as outward appearances went, Madame Dubray was French chic from head to toe as always. But the charm and elegance of the entrance and living area had disappeared. Instead, the modern furniture and abstract paintings seemed staged and artificial.

Her aunt couldn't contain her excitement as Avril told her what had transpired the previous day.

'The Block Arcade! How marvellous,' she said. 'When will you get the keys?'

Avril explained that the current tenants would be out by

the end of March, possibly earlier, and as soon as they'd gone, she'd be able to move in. It would take a couple of days to paint the interior and bring in the fittings and stock. The floor was covered in large black and white square tiles and all it needed was a thorough clean and polish. 'It doesn't look like it has been done for years,' Avril said.

'Of course, the bistro will provide the food for your launch. When will that be?'

Avril had chosen the first Monday in April to open her business. 'A bit of a celebration at the end of the first week would be nice,' she said. 'Just for those close to me so I can thank everyone for their help.'

Josephine insisted on opening champagne to toast le Chic then they discussed Avril's plans for the decor and the range she was creating. Her aunt immediately connected with everything Avril described and was a font of brilliant ideas and enthusiasm. Avril realised how much she had missed her. Curled on the sofa, just as Josephine had wanted, Avril relaxed in the comfort of the only family she had.

'There is one thing I'd like to ask you,' said Avril. 'Would you consider working in the shop with me, say, on a Monday? This is a paid position, Josephine. I couldn't have you work for nothing. I'll need someone to serve customers when I'm out choosing fabric or picking up garments from Lewin & Son, and you'd be perfect. Beyond perfect. What do you think?'

Josephine's hands touched her face as she beamed.

'Oh, Avril. What a wonderful idea. I'd love to.'

They clinked their champagne glasses and toasted le Chic again.

'What do you think Albert will say about you working somewhere else?' Avril asked.

'I couldn't care less!' Josephine snapped.

The tone of Josephine's voice took Avril by surprise. It was a sign of strength not previously displayed by her aunt, which Avril was delighted to see, but it also concerned her. *What has happened to Josephine while I was away to make her speak like that?* Avril wondered.

'I'm sorry, Avril,' Josephine said. For a moment, Avril thought her aunt wanted to tell her something, but then she asked, 'Are you all still happy to come here on Christmas Eve?'

'Absolutely,' said Avril, sipping her champagne. 'Duncan, Louise and Gabriel are looking forward to it.'

A knot formed in the pit of Avril's stomach at the thought of having to sit down to a meal and celebrate Christmas with Albert. *I'm doing this for Josephine's sake*, she said to herself. It would be the last time Avril would ever voluntarily see that revolting man again. She did not want to make a scene, but if push came to shove, Avril had made up her mind to tell Josephine what had happened.

*

Avril stopped at the Elizabeth Street entrance to the Block Arcade and looked up at the late Victorian sandstone facade. She was on her way to pick up some millinery supplies when the excitement of seeing her shop overtook her. She took her time as she worked her way forward, manoeuvring between the parcel-laden shoppers until she stood opposite shop number seventeen. To the left of Chapman's China & Crystal was a chocolate shop and the other side of that, a stationery store. To the right of her soon-to-be business premises was a large eveningwear boutique called Star Gowns.

Avril knew exactly how many garments she'd need to sell each week to cover all her overheads and production costs. Beyond that point, it would be pure profit. And it wasn't just clothing Avril wanted to stock. Ultimately le Chic would dress the customer from head to toe. Shoes, handbags and jewellery. The wrapping and packaging, like the interior of her shop, would be distinctive and easily recognisable. Customers would provide free advertising, simply by having the le Chic pink and white striped carry bag over their arms.

*

Avril could hear the music and laughter the moment she got out of Duncan's car. The heat of the day had not abated and all the windows on the first floor had been pushed wide open in an attempt to capture even the slightest of breezes.

'I thought it was going to be just the four of us,' said Louise.

'So did I,' said Avril in surprise.

She opened the front door with her original key and let Duncan take the lead. Avril felt stronger than ever before and her nervousness while getting dressed for the Christmas Eve celebrations had disappeared. Perhaps it was a case of force in numbers. She wasn't entirely sure. But with Duncan as her partner, she knew she had a knight in shining armour at the ready.

'Welcome,' Josephine called over the beat of the music. 'I know. There's a few more than we expected. Word got out. What can I say? Come in, come in.'

Avril scanned the crowd and saw Albert standing by the bookcase, his back to the rest of the room. Avril turned to Duncan and whispered, 'With a bit of luck I'll be able to avoid him all night.'

'Don't worry,' said Duncan, 'it won't be a late night. I'll make sure of it.'

The drinks flowed, and platters of canapes circulated constantly throughout the room. Two hours on, and Avril had had enough of the social chit chat and had succeeded in avoiding Albert.

'Let's get out of here,' she said to Duncan, who gave Louise and Gabriel the nod that meant, *We're leaving.*

The minute Duncan stepped away to say goodnight to Josephine, Albert was at Avril's side. When he said hello, she straightened her back, stared across the room and didn't respond.

'Come now, Avril,' he said, his voice laden with insincerity. 'We'd both had a fair bit to drink that night. I can forgive you if you can forgive me.'

Avril couldn't bear to be near him one moment longer. She moved swiftly to Josephine's side, wished her a Merry Christmas, and with Duncan, Louise and Gabriel close behind, headed for the door.

Back at Coben Street, Avril told Duncan what Albert had said.

'He really is a total bastard,' said Duncan. 'Are you all right?'

'Yes, I am,' she said, taking a deep breath. 'But he won't be. Not by the time I'm finished.'

Avril folded her arms and stared out the window. She wasn't after revenge. That lay in the hands of some higher power, she believed. It was the thought of her aunt being trapped in a marriage with a man who mistreated her that filled Avril with rage.

'I've got to get Josephine away from him,' she said. 'Working one day a week in the shop is a start. God knows what he must put her through.'

The Midnight Mass bells from Saint Francis's church rang out. Avril reached over and took Duncan's hand.

'Merry Christmas, my dear friend,' she said.

He smiled and kissed her hand.

'And a very Merry Christmas to you, too,' he said. 'What a year 1951 is going to be.'

'There's a bottle of champagne in the fridge,' said Avril. 'Come on, let's open it.'

CHAPTER 12

On New Year's Day, Avril was back in her workroom making hats. Adept with the basic millinery skills her mother had taught her, Avril let the steam from the boiling pot of water seep into the cherry-coloured buckram. With both hands she moulded the limp material over a hat block to form a flat brim. Pinning the buckram in place, she set the creation aside to dry and started work on the dome-shaped piece that would form the crown of the next hat.

When the holidays were over and her housemates had returned to work, Avril delighted in having the cottage to herself during the day. Before moving in, Gabriel had insisted they install a telephone. He didn't want to have the magazine editors, who were now booking him for photo shoots on a more regular basis, contacting him at the *Melbourne Times*. It also meant Avril could check on fabric availability and other incidentals with a simple phone call, rather than race over to Flinders Lane once a day. Lewin & Son would soon start production on her first Autumn range. A collection of sophisticated day and evening dresses, elegant and understated, suitable for a cross-section of social events. How many times had she hoped she'd pick up the receiver to hear Tim's voice? *Impossible*, she always reminded herself.

Avril was sitting at her table working on some designs when there was a knock at the door. *Who could that be?* she thought, putting down her pencil. She had no intention of opening the front door, not knowing who it was, so she went to the corner window in the lounge room and craned her neck to look out.

'Reece!' she cried as she ran to the door.

She gleefully threw her arms around him and he returned her hug.

Avril recalled the first time she had met Reece, after he'd returned from the muster, in her first weeks at Monaghan Station. She had been surprised to find that the youngest Meredith son didn't resemble his father or older brothers, with their dark hair and tall build. Reece clearly took after Anna, and had inherited her strawberry-blond hair, warm brown eyes and a lean frame. Jordy always joked that Reece was born a 'city slicker', and now, standing before her, she could see why. In his immaculate pin-striped dark grey suit and polished shoes, he was the sophisticated young lawyer in every way.

'I probably should have phoned,' he said, giving a shrug. 'It's so good to see you, Avril.'

'This is such a lovely surprise. Please, come on in. Do you have time for some lunch, or at the very least, tea?'

In the kitchen, Avril put the kettle on and cleared away the morning newspapers from the round table.

'Your cottage looks quite small from the street, but it's actually spacious in here,' said Reece as he looked around.

'I know. Deceiving, isn't it? It has four large bedrooms and an inside bathroom. Toilet's out the back, I'm afraid.'

Reece removed his jacket, placed it over the back of the chair and sat down. Avril, chatting as she set about making a pot of tea, soon realised there was something on his mind. She hadn't seen Reece since they met for coffee, just before he went home for Christmas. And now he'd just turned up, in the middle of the day, when he should have been at his desk at Carter, Carmody and Wainwright.

'Whatever's the matter?' said Avril as she sat in the chair opposite him.

Reece stared at his cup as he rotated the teaspoon on the saucer.

'I have some sad news and I didn't think you'd want to hear it over the phone,' he said.

Avril instantly saw the faces of everyone she knew at Monaghan Station – the Meredith family, Jean, Sandra, the children and particularly Little Joe. Her mind raced with imaginings.

'Two days ago, Rachel had a fall,' he said.

'From a horse?'

'No. Not from a horse.' Reece swallowed and took a drink of his tea. 'She fell down the back stairs. You know, the ones that go from the house kitchen up to the first floor. Broke her arm.'

Avril sat perfectly still. She'd taken those stairs many times herself. She could see the steep rise of each narrow wooden tread and the smooth rosewood banister that had felt the touch of countless hands over the years.

'There's been such a carry-on back home,' he said.

'Where was Tim?'

'Off somewhere. You know Tim. Bob and Col had to ride out and find him. He'd been camping out near the Bunya Mountains for a couple of nights. Left after he and Rachel had a shocking row, so Mrs Carmichael said.

Mum was there at the time, but Dad was up north. All hell broke loose, as you can imagine. The Stanleys arrived not long before the Flying Doctor Service landed. Mary fainted when she saw Rachel.'

'Rachel and the baby – are they all right?'

Reece dropped his eyes and shook his head.

'No. She lost the baby. The Flying Doctor Service took Rachel and Tim down to Brisbane the next day. Not sure when either of them will be back at Monaghan.'

Avril placed her elbows on the table and pressed her hands together. For a moment she closed her eyes. She knew there had to be more to the story. As well as being beautiful, Rachel was strong and athletic from all those years of training and competing in showjumping; someone like her didn't just fall down the stairs.

'How did it happen?'

'Rachel was plastered, apparently. Mrs Carmichael got up around one o'clock and went to make a cup of tea because she couldn't sleep. She found Rachel at the bottom of the steps. Lucky, really. We could have lost them both. There was one empty bottle of whisky in Rachel's room. My guess is she was going down for another bottle but who knows.'

'This is a tragedy,' said Avril with genuine empathy. 'For Tim and for Rachel. There's nothing anyone can say that will give them any comfort. It will take time, and then some.'

Reece had to get back to work so he only stayed a little longer. It was impossible trying to talk about anything else after that. They said their goodbyes at the front gate, Avril thanking him for coming to speak to her in person, and he assured her that he would be in touch if there was any further news from the station. Avril had no desire to return to her workroom. Instead, she slung her leather bag across her body, put on her sunglasses and headed off for a walk through the Fitzroy Gardens, her heart and head in turmoil.

*

Throughout February and March, Avril frequently thought about Tim and as much as she longed to hear his voice, she never telephoned. What would be the point? She wouldn't wish the loss of a child on any woman or man. This was not her heartache to work through. It was Tim and Rachel's, and the best Avril could do was to leave Tim alone and get on with her own life. But despite her busy schedule, the image of the peach tree and the small white cross where she'd laid her own child kept floating into her mind.

*

With only a week to go before the opening of her boutique, Avril scrutinised the finished dresses from her first ready-to-wear range at the Lewin & Son showroom. Each garment was made to exacting standards, the stitching first class and the application of zippers, buttons and buttonholes all beautifully finished. All that remained was for the garments to be carried over to the Block Arcade and hung on the racks ready for Monday's opening.

Joshua Lewin raced through the door and fanned out some fabrics on the table.

'Quick. Look at these,' he said excitedly. 'They're the colours of the wool crepe I've had dyed especially for the Miss Collins label. What do you think?'

For a man of thirty-five years, Joshua often had the exuberance of a teenage boy when excited by a design or piece of fabric. Avril always enjoyed visiting Lewin & Son, especially when Joshua was around. They had bonded through their mutual love of the fashion industry and talked constantly about manufacturing, selling and a marketing concept Avril had been reading about called 'branding'. Avril believed, just as Joshua did, that the fashion industry would undergo some monumental changes in the years ahead and they speculated about what those changes would be.

'There are many lovely fabrics available in Melbourne but I struggle to find certain types of material,' Avril had said during one of their discussions. 'I remember the beautiful fabrics my mother used to sell in her haberdashery. Irish linens, Swiss cotton, French laces and those soft cashmere tweeds from England. Surely those companies went back into production after the war?'

'The factories are producing again, but there was such a shortage of cloth during the war, the manufacturers can hardly keep up with demand,' Joshua had explained. 'Our government's put a limit on the amount of fabric that can be brought into the country. What I wouldn't give to get my hands on a large volume of some top-quality European textiles.'

Avril ran her eye over the colours of the crepe and picked up the muted fuchsia pink.

'I bet you a lunch at Pellegrini's this colour will sell out first,' said Avril.

Joshua's eyes lit up and he smiled.

'I have to disagree with you this time. I think it will be this charcoal grey,' he said as he folded up the samples. 'I didn't take you for a gambler, Avril.'

Avril slipped on her lightweight jacket and picked up her satchel.

'Oh, I'm not,' she said, 'but I know what women like, and that this colour here,' she said, passing him the piece of fuchsia material, 'is the winner.'

*

Duncan was applying the final coat of white gloss paint to the skirting boards when Avril opened the glass door of her shop and stepped over the drop sheet. Wide pale pink and white stripes covered the back wall from ceiling to floor, while the side walls had been painted white.

How many times did I deliver those beautiful striped boxes of Mama's to customers all over Tours? Avril thought to herself, as she admired Duncan's artistry.

'You've done the most fabulous job,' she said, as she approached the back wall. 'The straight lines are so perfect.'

Duncan placed his paintbrush in a pot of turpentine and wiped his hands.

'What do you think?' he said as he pulled the cover sheets from two pieces of furniture.

Avril rushed over and ran her hand over the glass top of the counter which was in the style of Louis XVI. A matching glass-fronted armoire stood nearby. With their detailed carved legs and door frames, the cream and silver cabinetry pieces were exactly the sort of fittings Avril had wanted to find for her first boutique.

'Duncan, they're wonderful, but I can't afford this sort of furniture,' she said, turning the key in one of the two tall display cabinets.

Duncan beckoned Avril over to what was to be the sales counter and pulled open the top drawer.

'Things are not always what they seem,' he said with a smirk. 'Feel the weight of the drawer. See, it's made

206

of lightweight pine. It's what's called *prop furniture*. Reproduction furniture they make for stage productions. Looks like the real thing but it's not. A friend of mine makes them for the theatres here in Melbourne. It's not designed to take a lot of weight, but then, you won't be putting anything heavy on the shelves.'

Avril threw her arms around Duncan.

'Thank you, thank you! It's just how I imagined everything would look.'

'The floors have already been cleaned,' said Duncan. 'Your free-standing racks arrive this afternoon. That leaves Thursday and Friday for the place to air. You don't want the smell of paint putting customers off. Then on the weekend, in between my shifts at the bistro, I'll help you set out all your stock ready for Monday.'

Avril showed Duncan where she wanted the shelving to go. It had been her idea to paper over the windows, keeping the interior a surprise until opening day.

'And is everything organised for the launch party at the end of your first week?' Duncan asked.

'I'd like to know I've sold a few dresses before I can think about celebrating,' she said. 'But as soon as I close the door at lunchtime on the Saturday, we can open the champagne.'

*

On the Sunday before the shop was due to open, Louise and Duncan removed the paper and began polishing the windows either side of the front door. By the time Avril had swept the floor and wiped every surface for the third time, the interior of the boutique radiated an atmosphere of modern Parisian charm, which for any discerning shopper would be impossible to resist. Gabriel had been taking photos for the best part of an hour, capturing even the smallest detail of the fit-out and merchandise, close-up shots of the dresses and accessories that Avril had skilfully displayed on the shelves and in the cabinets.

Avril had visited every shop in the Block Arcade and introduced herself the week before opening. If there was any way she could support another business, she did. From the stationery store she bought pens and paper, and from the perfumery, a floral scent she sprayed over the change room curtains. From the chocolate shop next door, she ordered one hundred small boxes filled with sugar-coated almonds to give away to customers.

'Nice touch,' said Gabriel, as he rearranged the small boxes before taking some shots.

'It's called building goodwill,' Avril said with a smile.

The combination of a small chandelier and cleverly placed mirrors made the interior of the boutique seem much larger than it really was. Three generous-sized change rooms, each one accessed through a hinged mirrored door, had been installed on the far-right wall. A chair and a small convenience table for a customer's handbag and parcels had been positioned in each dressing space. She'd also had two ceiling fans installed which she'd deemed essential, knowing how hot Melbourne could get in the summertime.

Not only was Avril excited to see how customers would respond to her designs, she was also constantly thinking of things to do that would set her business apart from all the other fashion shops in the city. Any customer who had made a purchase was given a card entitling them to a small discount on their next purchase, and a fresh glass of water was always available, regardless of whether a purchase was made or not. Avril had often thought how soulless many of the shops she'd visited felt, so she bought a small record player so music could be played constantly throughout the day. She was sure these little touches would make her business unique and help to build a loyal clientele and the le Chic brand.

When the cleaning equipment had been stored away and there wasn't a single thing left to do, Avril, Louise and Duncan stood at the front door, striking a series of poses while Gabriel took photos. It was almost dark by the time Avril turned off the lights and locked the door. She stood staring up at the dainty pink and white canvas awning over the entrance and noticed her reflection in the glass. Even though she was yet to sell a single dress or accessory, her heart was full of gratitude and pride. She would often stand in the very same spot in years to come, remembering this moment. *Not bad for a girl from Tours,* she'd think to herself. *Not bad at all.* How she wished Tim were here to share this with her.

CHAPTER 13

A vril had hardly slept and was at the boutique by seven-thirty in the morning. Josephine arrived shortly after, and they changed immediately into the crimson-coloured dresses Avril had made especially for both of them – another one of her innovative ideas. While Avril didn't want to outshine her customers, she saw no benefit in wearing a dress made by another label. And she didn't want to emulate the head-to-toe black outfits worn by the women in the large department stores. The understated yet stylish clothes Josephine and she would wear while on the shop floor had to be designed and made by Avril.

Louise had managed to get her articles about the opening of Avril's shop into three of the weekend papers. The previous week's edition of *The Australian Woman* magazine had featured an editorial piece about Avril and her ready-to-wear designs, 'French Chic for the Fashion Conscious'. A full page had been given over to Gabriel's colour photos showing the models standing on the steps of the Royal Galaxy Ballroom, wearing the le Chic label.

By eight-thirty a queue had formed at the door of the

shop that snaked all the way down the arcade. Duncan, who had come by to wish Avril well, suddenly found himself thrust into the role of maître d', moderating the number of customers allowed in at one time. Three large bouquets of flowers were delivered by mid-morning, but Avril had no time to even open the cards. At lunchtime she phoned Joshua Lewin to see if anything from her most recent order was ready. She explained how the racks were almost bare and of the twenty small buckram cloche hats Avril had made, only six remained.

'I have thirty dresses finished in the small and medium sizes,' he said, 'but nothing in extra small. I'll bring them over myself straight away.'

'Thank you!' Avril said but he'd already hung up.

Avril and Josephine worked together like a well-oiled machine, efficiently ferrying garments in and out of the change rooms and ringing up the sales. Each time a tissue-wrapped purchase was carried from the shop in a glossy pink and white striped rope-handled le Chic bag, an over-whelming sense of joy and relief washed over Avril.

By the time she finally closed the door at five-thirty, she'd taken more in her first day of trading than she thought she'd take in a week. Avril phoned Joshua, as even with the extra garments he'd brought over she had little stock left, and he assured her that she'd have plenty by the morning, even if he had to make the garments himself.

'What a day,' said Josephine as she stepped out of her shoes and sat down on the padded ottoman. 'The wonderful things people said, "These designs are so modern", "Such value for money", and my favourite,' Josephine smiled, '"At last, an armhole that doesn't cut you in half".'

Avril placed the day's takings and sales ledger book in her satchel and gathered up the flowers. When they left the shop together, smiles broad across their tired faces, the arcade was deserted.

*

As their cab pulled up outside the bistro, Avril said, 'Josephine, I couldn't have managed without you, and besides,' she squeezed her aunt's hand, 'there's no one I'd rather share this with.'

'I knew you'd be a success,' Josephine replied. 'But you can't keep this up every day. You're going to need to find a full-time assistant, and fast.'

Avril had thought about this but wanted to let the initial rush of business settle before she made any commitments. 'I need to find my feet first, but I'll start looking straight away. It might take time to find the right person.'

'I can help you for three hours each day this week,' Josephine said. 'The bistro doesn't need me in the mornings.'

Avril gratefully accepted her aunt's offer and they embraced before Josephine stepped out of the cab. 'See you tomorrow morning!' she called out from the front door, waving gaily.

Back home in the kitchen, Avril kicked her shoes off and placed the flowers in water. The lilies were from Anna and Henry with a note of good luck and congratulations, the peonies from Mr Lewin and Joshua. The envelope attached to the two-dozen pink roses, Avril opened last and smiled as she read what was written.

Congratulations. Ride like the wind! Love Tim

Even the heartache of their separation couldn't diminish the joy she felt. At least this dream, le Chic, had come true, and no one could take it away. Avril slept sweetly that night.

*

Two days after le Chic opened, the manager of the Block Arcade was quoted in the fashion section of the *Melbourne Times* newspaper:

In the fifteen years it's been my privilege to be the manager of this historic shopping precinct, I've never seen such a positive response to the opening of a new business. Avril Montdidier and her exciting new fashion label, le Chic, are a glamorous addition to the Block Arcade.

Throughout the first week the local press, ever keen for someone new to write about, descended on Avril, requesting interviews and photographs. At the close of business on Friday, Louise came by the shop and told Avril she needed a publicity plan.

'You'll need to map out when you'll be releasing your seasonal ranges, and what events you want to hold, and especially how to get your designs seen at the most important events. You'll have to do something spectacular for the spring horse-racing carnival in October and November. Everyone who's anyone will be there.'

Avril knew Louise was right, but the way she was feeling, there simply weren't enough hours in the day to do everything she wanted to do. Louise had been incredible stirring up publicity to promote le Chic and its opening, writing articles and hustling newspapers and magazines. 'You truly are wasted in that typing pool,' Avril said.

Louise couldn't contain a broad smile. 'Actually, I was planning to wait until the weekend to tell you all . . .'

'What?' Avril perked up.

'As of yesterday, you're looking at the new assistant editor for the fashion section at the *Melbourne Times*.'

Avril squealed and threw her arms around Louise.

'Congratulations!' said Avril. 'Why didn't you tell me you were going for this job?'

'It came up suddenly as the previous assistant editor is getting married. And I would have been heartbroken if I didn't get it, so I didn't want to say anything until I saw my name on the door.'

'You have your own office?'

'It's a cupboard, really. But yes. My own office, my own desk, right next door to the formidable Nancy Cameron,' said Louise.

Nancy Cameron was the Chief Fashion Editor of the *Melbourne Times*, one of the most powerful people in the fashion industry, with the ability to make or break a business with a few well-chosen words. 'I hear she's a little scary,' said Avril.

'Nancy's not scary – she's terrifying! But she liked the articles I sent her enough to call me last week to say she wanted to see me in her office immediately. Plus, she's a self-confessed Francophile.' Louise laughed.

'Right, we need to go home and celebrate,' Avril said and started tidying up the shop.

Louise lit a cigarette and blew away the smoke. 'During the war, would you ever have believed that one day we would have all this?'

Avril looked at her friend and felt, yet again, grateful that fate had put them on the same boat to their new lives. 'I hoped life would be good, but no, I didn't always believe it,' she said.

'Life is good,' said Louise.

And timing is everything, Avril thought.

*

With Saturday trading over, Avril restocked the shelves with hats and hair flowers and straightened all the hangers. As hectic as it was, Avril had managed despite not having

Josephine with her that morning. She'd called in saying she had a shocking headache and Avril had insisted Josephine stay home and rest. Avril was surprised and disappointed, though, that her aunt would miss the launch that she'd so meticulously organised.

At one o'clock, as planned, Louise and Gabriel arrived with drinks for le Chic's official launch celebration. When Duncan hadn't arrived thirty minutes later, Avril assumed he'd simply been held up. Mrs Rossi arrived early, followed by Reece who presented Avril with a bottle of French champagne. Mr Reynolds, the arcade manager, and the other shop owners chatted as Louise passed around the food.

Bert Lewin arrived and stopped a few yards from the door. His eyes swept over the shop, taking in every detail, from the awning to the window display and the layout of the shop itself. *She's started a little goldmine*, he thought. Mr Lewin knew practically everyone in fashion, not just in Melbourne but in Sydney as well. They'd come, they'd go. Some would make a decent living. Others would disappear in the night leaving accounts and rent unpaid. He had seen it all. But in all his years, he'd never met someone quite like Avril Montdidier. Not only was she an outstanding designer but her business acumen was equally impressive. Avril, he'd discovered, didn't run thirty-day accounts with anyone on The Lane. She operated on a strictly 'pay as you go, cash on delivery' basis, and in a short period had gained a good name amongst all the wholesalers.

When Avril saw Mr Lewin, she excused herself from the owner of the shoe shop who she'd been speaking with and headed for the door.

'Congratulations, Avril,' he said. 'What an incredible achievement.'

'Thank you, Mr Lewin. Please, won't you come in for a drink and something to eat?'

'That's kind of you to ask, but I need to be getting home. I just wanted to stop by and see your shop for myself. Joshua has been talking about nothing else all week.'

'I couldn't have done it without you and Joshua,' Avril said.

Duncan appeared out of nowhere, out of breath and looking flustered.

'Now, I must be off,' said Mr Lewin. 'And once again, congratulations, Avril.'

The moment Avril and Duncan were on their own, he took Avril by the hand.

'I hate to break up your party, but I need you to come with me right away,' he said in a low voice. 'It's Josephine.'

'Where is she?'

'At our house.'

Avril quietly pulled Louise aside and handed her the keys to the shop.

'Could you wrap this up in thirty minutes and lock up for me?' whispered Avril. 'Something's happened to Josephine and I need to go now.'

'Of course,' said Louise, concern in her eyes. Josephine's troubles were no secret at their home in Coben Street and she was like family to them all.

Avril grabbed her satchel and, pausing for a moment, announced that she had been called away unexpectedly and that everyone was to enjoy themselves. As soon as they were out of sight of the shop, Avril and Duncan ran to his car that was parked on Elizabeth Street and took off for the cottage.

*

Josephine was lying on her side on Avril's bed, her face to the wall, a rug pulled over her back.

'It's me,' Avril said softly as she opened the door. Avril sat down on the edge of the bed and placed her hand gently on her aunt's shoulder as Josephine began to sob into the pillow.

'I'm here now. I'm with you,' said Avril and she stroked the back of Josephine's hair.

'I'm never going back,' said Josephine. 'I thought he was going to kill me this time.'

When Josephine turned over and looked at her niece, Avril tried not to flinch when she saw the injuries Albert had inflicted. The purple blackness spread from around her eyes and down the sides of her face. Her bottom lip had split open.

'You never need to go there again,' said Avril. 'You're going to live with us. I'll take care of you. We'll all take care of you.'

From under the pillow, Josephine pulled a crumpled envelope and handed it to Avril. Avril recognised it at once.

'The pest control man found this when he took your kitchen apart. It was still sealed. That's how I know what happened to you. I know it all now,' she cried. 'Such a nice man, he was,' Josephine stammered through her tears. 'Said I wouldn't believe some of the things he finds in houses when he goes to spray for pests.'

Avril placed the crumpled envelope on her bedside table.

'I couldn't stop shouting at Albert. I was so angry. I can't even remember what I said exactly.' Josephine buried her face in the pillow.

'You're safe now. You're with me. With Duncan. You're safe here,' Avril reiterated.

'I'm so sorry. I feel so ashamed,' said Josephine. She gasped for air as she curled into a ball and cried.

A little later, Avril helped Josephine into the shower and as her aunt removed her blouse, the bruises across her back where Albert had struck her were plain to see.

While Josephine was showering, Avril stripped her bed and made it up with fresh sheets and turned the covers down, then placed a small vase of flowers and a glass of water on the bedside table.

Louise and Gabriel arrived home and hurried into the kitchen, where Duncan explained what had happened. He was just about to leave for the party when there was an almighty banging on the door and Josephine literally fell into his arms. She told him that Albert had beaten her last night, and she had waited until Albert left after lunchtime, then hailed a cab on the street.

Avril came in and joined them at the table.

'She's gone back to bed, and I've given her some more headache tablets.'

Josephine had told her that Albert was going to burn everything she owned. 'I don't care about what's in the apartment,' Josephine said, 'but I want my clothes, my personal belongings.' Avril was determined to get them for her.

'Louise, could you stay here with Josephine while Duncan, Gabriel and I go and collect her things?' she said.

'I won't be leaving her,' Louise said. 'You do whatever you need to do.'

As Duncan's car hurtled towards Collins Street, they agreed there was only one objective, and that was to get in and out as quickly as possible. Duncan would wait in the foyer of the apartment in case Albert returned, while

Gabriel and Avril would grab as many of Josephine's personal effects as they could carry.

'And whatever either of you do,' said Avril, firmly, 'if Albert turns up, don't get into a slinging match with him. If you hit him, he'll go straight to the police station and have you up on an assault charge.'

'It's bullshit,' Duncan said. 'A man beats up a woman and kids and nothing happens to him. I ought to know, growing up with my old man.'

While Duncan stood guard just inside the door of the apartment, Avril lifted Josephine's clothes off the rail, hanger and all, and threw them into a large duffel bag. As she gathered up the shoes, Gabriel took toiletries, cosmetics, jewellery and other personal effects from Josephine's dressing table. Once they had as much as the four bags would hold, they bolted down the steps and out to Duncan's car.

A black car pulled up as they were loading the duffle bags into the boot. Albert jumped from the front seat of the cab and rushed forward, waving his arms, his face red with fury.

'Avril, get in the car, now. Gab, take the wheel,' said Duncan, stepping up to block Albert's advance. But Avril wasn't going to let Albert think he could intimidate her. She stood beside Duncan.

Albert's furious charge stopped short of the gutter. He stood, feet wide apart, with his hands on his hips, shouting obscenities.

'You're fired,' he yelled at Duncan. 'You'll never get another job in this town, ever. I'll make sure of it. And you, you shitty little whore. Who do you think you are, sticking your nose into my business?'

Arrogantly, Albert took one step closer and stabbed his

index finger in Avril's direction. 'She'll be back. She always comes back. It's none of your business what happens between my wife and me.'

'Well, I've made it my business,' said Avril.

And then suddenly, Duncan took two large strides forward and towered over Albert. Avril had never seen him angry before, the time bomb of his past exploding. He grabbed Albert's shirt front.

'Don't you ever touch her again, you miserable, pathetic excuse for a man.' Duncan flicked his hand away, turned and he and Avril got into the car.

Gabriel sped off, leaving Albert standing on the road, waving his arms in the air.

'She's nothing without me,' he yelled. 'Nothing!'

'Can we go back and run him over?' Gabriel said under his breath, as he glanced in the rear-view mirror.

Josephine started crying again when she saw that they'd brought her belongings. She hugged each of them in turn before Avril insisted her aunt needed to rest. Avril had set up a bed for herself in the sunroom, so Josephine could have the bedroom to herself.

Later that night Avril opened the black velvet case and ran her fingers over the gold bangle inside it. She'd taken it off on her first night back in Melbourne, and there were times, in her darkest moments, when she never wanted to see it again, let alone wear it. She felt that maybe the bangle was a bad omen. But as she looked at the inscription on the inside, *Timing is everything*, she wondered if Samuel Meredith had been right all along. If, perhaps, everything in life was about timing, being in the right place at the right time, or possibly the wrong place at the wrong time. With such strong sales and reviews in her first week of business, Avril felt confident that le Chic could not only employ Josephine full-time, but Duncan as well. She took the bangle from the box, slipped it back on her wrist and ran her hand over the smooth gold finish. She decided she was wrong about the bangle being cursed. *I think this bangle was always meant to bring me luck*, she said to herself.

*

The same week Avril opened le Chic, the shearing team arrived at Monaghan Station. The shearing contractor supplied his own cook, who worked out of the kitchen facility attached to the shearers' quarters. The searing heat of summer had abated, making the next three weeks of back-breaking work, penning, shearing and wool classing, slightly more tolerable.

Tim sat at his desk and tapped the tip of his pen on the documents in front of him, listening to what Eric Parker had to say. He didn't like any of his proposals. *Conservative, short-sighted solutions to solvable problems*, Tim thought. Confident they could trade their way out of the current impasse with proceeds from wool and cattle sales, Tim ran his eyes down the columns of figures.

'Look,' said Eric. 'You can easily liquidate some assets. There's no shame in that. The house in Toorak will be the easiest property to sell. Or a parcel of shares.'

'I don't like having my hand forced,' said Tim. 'Shearing's about to start. This year's clip should put a decent dent in the debt. Combine that with cattle sales and the horses Henry will sell at the yearling sales, and we should be out of the woods.'

'I can only advise you, Tim. In the end the decision is Henry's and yours. But the fact of the matter is, the bank wants its money and Henry hasn't got it.'

'Why is the bank pushing us so hard on this?' Tim asked. 'Christ, we've banked with them for long enough. I can't help thinking there's more to this than we're aware of. I'll come down to Brisbane next week and see if I can get the bank to give us a bit more time.'

As he put down the phone receiver, Tim was surprised to see Rachel standing in the doorway, dressed to go riding. How long she'd been standing there, and what she had heard, he didn't know, but he didn't like the smirk on her face as she took the seat opposite him.

Rachel hadn't been on a horse since her arm mended. In fact, she'd rarely left the house these past few months, except on a couple of occasions to drive over to Cathaway and see her parents. Since the loss of their child, Rachel showed no interest in spending time with Tim and any desire Tim had once felt for Rachel was long gone. To the casual observer, Tim and Rachel Meredith looked like any other newlywed couple, aside from the horrible loss they were still grappling with. Except their union was in name only. They slept in separate rooms and only spoke when they had to.

'This is nice,' said Tim, 'seeing you in your riding gear.'

'I thought I might work that bay gelding in the arena for a bit,' she said, as she flicked some lint off the leg of her pants. 'I've decided to go down to Brisbane for a while. A couple of weeks, maybe more.'

They both knew there was nothing binding them to each other, as there had been before they lost the child, yet Rachel refused to discuss the subject of divorce.

'Rachel,' said Tim, 'we need to –'

'Need to what?' she snapped. 'Need to what, Tim?'

'We need to talk. Really talk,' said Tim. 'We can't go on like this. What we have, it isn't a marriage. It isn't even a life.'

Rachel stared at Tim with a look of disdain he'd never seen before.

'I don't know,' she said calmly, resting back in the chair. 'I'm your wife. I'm wearing your wedding ring. I have your surname. Looks like a marriage to me.'

'Rachel, regardless of how it looks, you know this isn't a real marriage.'

'Don't you at least want to see if we can make it work?' asked Rachel.

Tim was stunned by what she'd just said and could see that the conversation was sliding into dangerous waters.

'That's not what we agreed,' said Tim. 'There's no reason for us to keep this charade going any longer, Rachel. I want to get on with my life and you need to get on with yours. You can't want both of us be miserable, surely?'

As soon as the words left his mouth, Tim knew he'd well and truly declared his hand.

'Miserable? Is that what you are, Tim?' she said. 'From where I sit, you've got nothing to be miserable about. A wonderful family, wealth, a privileged life, and me.'

'When you talk like that, Rachel, I realise I don't even know who you are.'

Rachel stood and walked over to the window. She looked across the lawn and watched the labradors lolling in the sun. *Your misery hasn't even begun, Tim*, she thought to herself.

'Yes. I think I will get the train to Brisbane in the morning. We can talk about this when I get back.'

Except Rachel didn't intend to come back any time soon. What she did intend, however, was to be Mrs Tim Meredith for a very long time.

CHAPTER 14

Two weeks after moving into the cottage in Coben Street, Josephine stood in front of the bathroom mirror and gently ran her fingers over her cheekbones. The bruising and swelling had subsided and each day, with Avril's help, she could feel her confidence returning. Once her hair and makeup were done, she slipped on a work outfit, a cream skirt and jacket, and secured a black Juliette cap in place. Josephine heard the toot of the cab's horn and picked up her gloves and handbag and took one last look at herself in the long cheval mirror.

'No looking back,' she told her reflection bravely. For the first time in her adult life, she felt she didn't have to pretend she was happy. *She was happy.* She couldn't care less about the bistro, and the expensive paintings and furnishings in the apartment in Collins Street that had once meant so much to Josephine now seemed trivial, irrelevant. 'No looking back,' she said one more time and with just a hint of trepidation, the manager of le Chic boutique left for work.

*

The amber and tangerine leaves of autumn that carpeted Melbourne's streets soon gave way to cold winter days and grey skies. August winds whipped off the Yarra River and hurtled through the city streets as the hat and coat wearing workforces alighted from the trams and made their way to department stores, offices and the factories that bordered the city centre.

Any doubts Avril might have had about her business acumen quickly disappeared. From the time the shop opened to when it closed each day, there was a regular flow of customers. With lunchtimes being overwhelmingly busy, Avril made sure she was at the store by midday to help out, as secretaries and shop assistants used their precious one-hour break to try on the latest designs and accessories le Chic had to offer. Word quickly spread about the service the boutique offered called 'Hold and Pay'. For one pound, a garment or accessory could be set aside, as long as it was paid for and collected within four weeks.

Constantly on the lookout for new fabrics and accessories, Avril began to do the rounds of the wholesalers each morning with Duncan. Just like Avril, he had a keen eye for spotting an unusual fabric, button or trim, that little bit of individuality that could transform a design into something spectacular. Duncan had quickly morphed into Avril's *Right-Hand Man*, a turn of phrase they joked about frequently and fondly, remembering the day they met. Collecting orders from Lewin & Son, racing down to Bloomfield's for buttons or delivering a roll of pattern-making cardboard back to Coben Street in his car, Duncan loved the newfound freedom his role as Design Assistant gave him.

The window displays, however, were Duncan's forte. He scoured the weekend flea markets and second-hand furniture shops for any unusual bric-a-brac to use in his increasingly elaborate displays. Bike wheels, umbrellas, even wooden fruit boxes were part of his ever-growing collection of props. After closing time on a Saturday, Duncan would stay for as long as it took to bring his visual stories to life. For his first winter display, he spray-painted willow branches silver, suspended them from the ceiling, and hung leather gloves and berets from the crossing branches in a falling raindrop formation.

The newspaper and magazine coverage about Avril and her store was constant. Louise's article, titled, 'Singing in the Rain – Window Display Visionary', accompanied by Gabriel's photographs, was given a half-page colour spread in the weekend section of *Melbourne Fashion*. The article detailed the popularity of Avril's designs and Duncan's creative artistry. The following Monday, an unprecedented number of shoppers filed through the arcade just to see the window display at le Chic.

A week later, Avril was working on a calico sample at home when the telephone rang.

'Get over to the arcade right now,' said Louise anxiously. 'Nancy Cameron is on her way to le Chic. She's looking for designers to showcase at her Spring Gala fundraiser. She'll be choosing three couturiers and half a dozen ready-to-wear designers for the parade. It's one of the most sought-after tickets on the fashion calendar.'

'I'm on my way,' said Avril.

'And whatever you do, don't call her Mrs Cameron. It's Nancy,' Louise warned her.

Avril telephoned Josephine then a cab, changed her outfit and was racing through the Block Arcade less than forty minutes later. She recalled the many stories Louise had told her about the formidable Nancy Cameron.

It had just gone closing time when Avril opened the glass door and greeted Nancy with a kiss on each cheek. She was not intimidated by Nancy Cameron, despite her reputation.

'Welcome to le Chic,' said Avril. 'My name is Avril Montdidier. How many designs would you like me to create exclusively for your fundraising gala? I take it that's why you've called by?'

Dressed in a black suit and matching turban, the doyenne of the Australian fashion media smiled indulgently and introduced herself. Her husky voice was like that of a jazz singer, each syllable rolling effortlessly off the tongue. She glanced over the shop with cool violet-coloured eyes that didn't miss a detail, but then something – or someone – caught her attention. She studied Josephine's face.

'I have the strangest feeling we've met before,' said Nancy.

'We have,' Josephine replied. 'At Bistro Dubray. You like the corner table near the window, and you always order the duck.'

Nancy peered at her over the top of her cat-eye shaped glasses, assessing the scenario.

Josephine lifted her chin slightly and pulled herself up a little taller.

'My name is Josephine Dubray. I used to help my ex-husband, Albert Dubray, run our restaurant,' she said. 'I left him recently. Now, I manage le Chic for Avril, who is my niece.'

With a directness that Nancy herself was renowned for, Josephine had told her all she needed to know.

'Good for you,' Nancy said, and patted Josephine on the arm with a touch that was full of kindness. 'I left my swine of a husband two years ago. Should have done it long before that. You think things will improve, but darling, they never do. It only gets better when you leave.'

*

Twenty minutes later and Nancy had seen enough. The clothing and accessory designs were unique and stunning, the shop fit-out and window display original. The business was soundly run. As far as Nancy was concerned, Avril Montdidier had what it took to succeed.

'Get your notepad, Avril, because you're going to need it,' said Nancy. 'I want to shake things up a bit for this year's gala. Do something different from the usual fashion parade format. Got any ideas?'

Avril tapped her pencil on her notepad while she thought. 'Group the outfits into recognisable categories and send the models down the catwalk in complete head-to-toe styling, as if they were attending a specific type of event,' said Avril. 'A luncheon, the races, a wedding, cocktail party or a ball. Give each category a name. *Off to the Races, Dance the Night Away* or *Chapel of Love*.'

'Go on,' said Nancy. 'I like what I'm hearing so far.'

Encouraged, Avril said that she believed a fashion parade was not just about looking at beautiful clothes, it was about showing women how fashion can be a form of self-expression.

'Break away from the same old-fashioned parade routine where the audience has to sit through one model after the other walking silently down the catwalk. Add music. Two models could stop at the end of the catwalk and study the race book together. Or one model holds up a hand mirror while the other touches up her lipstick.'

'Brilliant,' said Nancy. While she enjoyed listening to Avril's innovative ideas, she didn't need to hear any more to be convinced – le Chic would be the making of the Spring Gala.

'I'll have to give the bridal finale to one of the top couturiers,' she said with a dismissive wave of her hand. 'But if you can give me a dozen original designs for, say, *Off to the Races* and *Dance the Night Away*, then those two categories can be exclusively yours.'

'When would you need all the garments?' said Avril, her mind already designing the range.

'The gala's always held two weeks before the Melbourne Cup. I'd like to see everything at the beginning of October,' said Nancy. 'Now, as much as this visit has been most pleasant, I must leave as I'm already running late for my next appointment, but one more thing . . .' She turned away from Avril.

'Josephine, would you consider joining my planning committee for this event? I've been looking to recruit someone new, and I think you'd be perfect.'

Josephine didn't need to think twice. 'I'd be delighted,' she said.

'Fabulous,' said Nancy. 'Why don't you come to my place for dinner next Saturday night if you're free? I'll send a car for you.'

And with a swish, Nancy Cameron draped her boucle wrap over her shoulder and left.

Avril collapsed onto the ottoman.

'What a coup,' said Josephine. 'She's given you the two best categories!'

'They're the ones I wanted. I mean, I would have taken anything, but those categories would best showcase our designs. Sales from this event will carry me for the next year.'

Avril took three deep breaths, letting the whirlwind encounter with Nancy Cameron sink in.

'And she certainly took a shine to you.' Avril looked at her aunt with pride. 'You're now on one of the most influential fashion planning committees in Melbourne and you've been invited to dinner. She must think you have quite a bit in common.'

'Yes,' said Josephine as she repositioned hats back on the shelf, 'I think we probably do.'

*

On a cold and wet Monday in June, James Carmody stood at the window of his corner office and looked down at the umbrella-filled intersection of William and Collins streets. He listened carefully as Reece Meredith summarised the details of a contract they were working on. Over the past year Reece had proven himself to be a valuable addition to Carter, Carmody and Wainwright, of which James was a founding partner. It hadn't been Reece's degree with first-class honours that caught James's attention at the job interview, but Reece's well-worn, yet perfectly polished leather boots. No flashy new brogues for this young buck.

After Reece had left the interview, James said to his colleagues, 'There are any number of straight-A graduates out there we could employ. Most of them have never been further than Portsea and couldn't defend themselves in a fight at a picnic, let alone go head-to-head when tough negotiations are needed. The kid from the bush gets my vote.'

James Carmody's near photographic memory and obsessive desire for a better life had been his passport out of the Melbourne slum into which he was born. At forty-seven years of age, the streetwise University of Melbourne graduate was considered one of the sharpest corporate lawyers in Australia. He was a rare breed. Highly intelligent, ruthlessly ambitious and, at the same time, scrupulously honest. His specialty was mergers and acquisitions, predominantly in the resources industry, but his personal interest was commercial property development, and between the two activities, he had amassed a sizeable fortune.

'Those documents need to be submitted by next Wednesday,' he said as Reece closed his folder. 'Where are we at with the Lampoon Thomas deal?'

'Just waiting on the final audit from the accountants.'

For a lad from a privileged background, Reece's work ethic impressed James, along with the respect he showed everyone, regardless of their position. Reece was just as comfortable in the company of the tea lady as he was with high-net-worth clients who frequented the practice, and over the past year James had begun to give Reece responsibilities not usually allotted to someone so young. James could see that Reece had the qualities to become a highly successful lawyer.

'I'm having a casual lunch on Sunday if you're free,' said James as Reece gathered up his files. 'Roast lamb with all the trimmings. You should come. Meet some new people. There'll probably be about twenty of us. And please feel free to bring a guest.'

Although Reece worked closely with James, he knew very little about his private life nor that of the other two partners. And as it would be considered inappropriate to ask questions on the subject, Reece never did.

'Thank you. I'd love to come, and bring a guest,' Reece said, then added with a smile, 'You knew the lamb would hook me in, didn't you?'

'Go on. Get out of here. I'll see you Sunday,' James said.

'Who's the lucky girl, by the way? Alison from accounts or Patty?'

'You don't know her,' said Reece, 'so you'll have to wait and see.'

*

The midday winter sky was a pale lavender blue as Reece and Avril walked up the path towards the Kooyong mansion. The house, which had once been the governor's residence, had recently been renovated. Small shrubs and leafless rose bushes yet to bloom for the first time filled the newly planted garden. The dark ivy that clung to the walls and surrounded the freshly painted window frames made a homely yet stately impression.

'It was so kind of you to invite me to this lunch, Reece,' said Avril. 'I can't remember the last time I took a day off. What's James's wife's name?'

'I don't know. I've never asked,' Reece replied. Then in true Meredith style he teased her, 'Knowing you, you'll be best friends with her by the time you leave.'

They were nudging each other and grinning as James opened the front door, his arm opening wide in a gesture of welcome, though his eyes keenly took in the couple before him.

'Ah! Reece, you've made it,' he said warmly. 'Please, come in.'

'James, this is my friend Avril. Avril, this is James.'

'Lovely to meet you, Avril. Let's go through and I'll introduce you to everyone.'

It was the most sophisticated 'casual lunch' that Avril had ever attended. The guests, a number closer to forty than twenty, were gathered in an elegant glass atrium that overlooked a tennis court. They seemed a relaxed

and interesting mix of individuals, and as James introduced Reece and Avril, it was clear he had a wide circle
of friends, from those in the legal profession and business owners, to writers, artists, and a publisher who
was visiting from America. The waiters replenished the
buffet table – Reece declared the lamb to be as good as
Jean's – and kept everyone's glasses filled throughout the
afternoon, as the music changed from hit songs to jazz
then swing.

James was the perfect host. Avril noticed that he
carried himself with confidence, but without arrogance
or superficiality. He was a handsome man with fair
hair swept slightly to the side, modestly but impeccably
dressed in a navy crew knit sweater and sand-coloured
pants. Avril could see that he thought very highly of
Reece, and that told her that he was a good judge of
character.

Late in the afternoon, she struck up a conversation on
the veranda with the friendly publisher from New York
who introduced himself as George.

'And how do you know James?' he asked Avril.

'I've never met James before today,' she said. 'My friend
Reece, the young man I came with, works at James's law
firm. How do you know him?'

'I went to college with Beth, James's wife. That's how I
met James. Beth and I used to be great friends.'

'You're not friends with Beth anymore?'

George looked at her strangely then said, 'You obviously
don't know?'

Avril shook her head. 'I'm sorry. Know what?'

'Beth was killed in a car accident three years ago this
Christmas. It's tragic. They'd only been married two years.
Someone was saying this is the first time James has done

any entertaining since her death. She was from New York. That's where they met.'

'That's very sad,' Avril said and, seeing that James was headed their way, changed the subject, asking George about his visit to Melbourne.

*

In the four hours since he'd opened his front door, James had quietly engaged Reece in conversation and discovered as much as possible about Avril Montdidier. An immigrant from France, governess on the Meredith family's property, niece of the owners of Bistro Dubray, fashion designer and business owner who was driven to succeed, Miss Montdidier had a curriculum vitae James found interesting.

Her hair was twisted into a loose bun on the top of her head, her face framed by the high neck of her chunky cable sweater. The hem of her black tailored pants skimmed the top of her patent leather boots. She could have stepped off the ski slopes in Switzerland, he thought. The attraction he'd felt when he first saw Avril was a sensation he had not experienced in a long time. He wasn't an impulsive man, and yet he'd always been drawn to confident yet unconventional women.

When George moved away to get a drink, Avril asked James if he would tell her about the various paintings in the room. He was only too happy to oblige.

'Are you a collector?' she asked as they stopped in front of a landscape.

'I'm hoping to be,' he said. 'There are a few Australian artists I particularly like. I have a few pieces by William Dobell and Arthur Boyd. And I've just bought a very interesting portrait by Joy Hester. Have you heard of her?'

'Yes. Actually, Reece's mother has one of her works. Have you always loved art? Did you paint or draw while you were growing up?'

At the thought of his childhood, James could instantly smell the damp odour of the one-room shack he'd called home for the first fourteen years of his life. The curtain-less windows, the bare floor and the sight of his mother bent over the washing board, the skin of her hands tinged red, as she did laundry for those who didn't have to.

'No. Not at all,' he said. 'We were very poor and had one book in the house I grew up in, and only because it was given to my mother by some well-meaning distant relative. It was called *The Children's Book of Art*, and I loved that book beyond anything. I would have turned those pages thousands of times. Still do, sometimes.'

Avril was taken aback by his openness and humility, though she wasn't completely surprised. James had the manner of someone who had overcome hardships but never forgot their lessons – a quality which Avril respected and hoped to emulate – and there was genuine warmth in his hazel-coloured eyes. She liked him already.

'Why don't we visit the national gallery together, and then I could take you to lunch afterwards, if you'll let me?'

'I'd like that,' said Avril. 'Very much.'

They agreed to meet at the gallery at one o'clock on the following Saturday, as Avril would be working at the shop until midday. Avril found herself looking forward to it. James had made the invitation without fanfare, or any strings attached. There was no reason why she shouldn't enjoy the company of a very charming and intelligent man.

*

When the last guests had finally left and every plate and glass had been cleared away, James switched the lights on in the library and kicked off his leather loafers. Picking up a silver photo frame, he stared for a long time at the image of him and Beth, taken by the skating rink in Central Park the day he'd proposed. It had felt like an eternity since the house had sounded like a home, but today the place had come alive again and so had something inside of James. The sound of laughter, clinking of glasses and music had drifted through the place, chasing James's solitude away. Above all, it was good to be around people he could call friends, eclectic bunch that they were. And Avril – what a pleasant surprise she'd turned out it be. These days, James was too pragmatic for love at first sight, even though Avril did take his breath away when she walked through the door, but he was hopeful that one day he might love again. A beautiful French woman who he felt comfortable with was certainly a good place to start.

James ran the tips of his fingers over the image of Beth's hair and down the side of her face. The love he'd felt for his wife would never die.

'I like her, Beth,' he said, continuing to stare at the photo. 'Do I risk my heart again?'

He placed the frame back on the shelf, reached above it for his well-worn copy of *The Children's Book of Art*, lay down on the sofa and began to turn the pages.

*

Nancy Cameron's Spring Gala fundraiser was like nothing Melbourne had ever seen before. Every newspaper and fashion magazine ran front page stories the following day and into the next week, about the innovative and sophisticated way the parade was organised, from the live music to the theatrical presentation of the parade itself. Leading up to the big event, Duncan raced between the suppliers and Lewin & Son, transporting the finished garments back to Coben Street and taking the current winter stock to Josephine at le Chic. In the evenings, he visited the set designer at the Prince Theatre, overseeing the construction of a garden gazebo that was to be assembled in the great ballroom of the Capital Hotel.

The morning before the gala, Avril took delivery of a massive bouquet. She opened the card and her heart sank when she saw the flowers weren't from Tim. *Why would they be?* she berated herself. She reread the card. *Can't wait to see you tomorrow night. Good luck! James.* Since their gallery and lunch date the previous month, James and Avril had gone out several times, to dinner, to the pictures and a late-night supper club in St Kilda. He was handsome, charming and fun to be with, and yet, it was always Tim she dreamed of when she closed her eyes. Running her business would be her saving grace. She knew that now. *I can't take another heartache. I won't expose myself to such vulnerability ever again*, she'd decided. The openness and lightness of spirit she'd felt all those months living at Monaghan Station would never return. A solid wall had come up around Avril's heart that not even the sweet fragrance of roses and lilies could penetrate.

*

The day of the Spring Gala, Avril was backstage with Josephine by five o'clock, checking the garments and accessories. They dressed the models, making sure every detail of their le Chic outfits was perfect. Avril had invited Lizzy to the gala and she didn't hesitate to make the trip down from Sydney. When one of the models fell ill the day before the event, the willowy redhead was happy to take her place.

'I've always thought you'd make a wonderful model,' Avril told her as she zipped up the dress.

'It will be fun,' said Lizzy, unfazed as she stepped into her shoes.

Unlike many of the other designers, Avril stayed away from garish overworked floral prints and the excessive use of fabric, preferring to showcase a new material she'd been working with called rayon. Woven with silk or cotton, the rayon blended materials had the look and feel of luxurious fabrics but were a fraction of the price. Wearing fresh peonies pinned in their hair and dresses the colour of summer sorbet – peach, mint, rose and honey – one by one the models took to the catwalk in Avril's *Dance the Night Away* collection. The audience murmured their approval. And when the first three models stepped out in the outfits for the *Off to The Races* category, dressed in black and white from head to toe, there was instant applause.

Once the parade was over, Avril changed into an aqua satin dress ready for the second part of the evening: the sit-down dinner and dance which would go until the wee hours of the morning.

'I don't even know who's at our table,' said Avril as she applied her lipstick and Josephine secured her earrings. 'James, Reece, and Lizzy, of course, but I left it to Duncan to fill the other seats.'

By the time Avril and Josephine entered the ballroom, the catwalk and gazebo had been removed and the band was already playing.

'We're over here, next to the dance floor,' said Josephine as they weaved their way past the crowd of glamorously dressed guests. When Avril saw who was standing at the table, she gasped and threw her hands in the air.

'Anna! Henry!' she cried, hugging them both. 'I can't believe you're here. It's so good to see you. Why didn't you let me know?'

'Then it wouldn't have been a surprise,' said Anna, hugging Avril again.

'*Toutes nos félicitations*, Avril,' said Henry. 'What a show.'

'*Merci beaucoup*, Henry,' said Avril. She felt a tap on her shoulder and a voice said, 'First dance is mine, Miss Avril.'

'Jordy!'

In true Jordy style, he picked Avril up and spun her around and around, the light reflecting off the sheen of her dress.

'Who else knew about this?' asked Avril, as she looked from Louise to Gabriel and back to James.

'Guilty as charged,' said Duncan. 'We all did. And now if you will all raise your glasses . . . To Avril.'

Once everyone had drunk to Avril's good health, Jordy wasted no time in leading her onto the dance floor for a slow waltz. There was a wonderful familiarity to be dancing with Jordy again. *All the Meredith men are good dancers*, she thought, as the memory of Tim and her swaying under the stars at their camp flashed before her. But tonight she would not be sad about Tim, her heart was too full of joy and love for her dearest friends.

'I've missed you so much, Avril,' said Jordy. 'The station isn't the same without you.'

'Tell me everything that's happening at Monaghan,' she said. 'It will be impossible to talk once we sit down.'

'Well now, let me see,' he said, his face lit up with his

irrepressible smile. 'Jean and Mrs C send their love. Col and Sandra are now officially an item. And the money we got from this year's wool clip will keep the banks off our backs for a while. At least we didn't have to sell any property.'

'You knew about the financial difficulties your father was in?' asked Avril in surprise.

'Geez, Avril. I know Dad and Tim don't think I have their business smarts, but I can read those two like a book,' said Jordy. 'Plus, when we didn't all high-tail it down to Melbourne for the racing carnival last year, I knew something was up.'

'And Tim. How is he, really?' asked Avril.

'I don't think I've ever seen him work so hard. He's going north with Bob to bring down about three hundred head of cattle. Said he didn't want to come to Melbourne this year for any of the racing. He told me Rachel and he are going to try and make a go of it, if they can. But she spends most of her time in Brisbane, and when she's at the station, well . . .' Jordy tailed off.

'Well what?' said Avril.

'I'm not saying she has a problem, but the gin flows pretty freely most nights when Rachel's at Monaghan.'

Jordy nodded in James's direction.

'And the good-looking blond,' he said. 'What's the story there?'

'Oh, James. I'm not sure,' said Avril with the natural openness she'd always felt with Jordy. 'I like him, very much. We'll have to wait and see.'

'I wish you could come up to the station, even if it was just for a few days. Sometime when Rachel's not there, perhaps?' he suggested.

'Jordy, you know I can't, but that's a lovely thought.

Besides, what would I do without my faithful Piaf to ride? I take it she's been sent back to Cathaway?'

'And not for the first time, Miss Avril, you'd be mistaken,' smiled Jordy. 'Tim bought Piaf off Doug. Said he didn't want her sent back. He takes her out most mornings. Never thought I'd see Tim prefer a mare over a stallion, but there we go.'

She smiled at the thought of Tim on a horse smaller than what he usually rode but she was grateful that he had kept her dear Piaf.

Henry was in fine form that night, entertaining the table with his anecdotes and taking to the dance floor with Anna. James conversed easily with everyone, though it was noticed that he was most attentive towards Avril. 'A true gentleman, that one,' Anna had whispered to her. The Meredith brothers were, of course, sought out by a bevy of women eager to dance with them. Gabriel didn't leave Lizzy's side the whole night.

'Why have you been keeping this gorgeous creature a secret from me?' he demanded of Avril. 'And I thought we were friends!'

As the party finally started to wind down, Duncan found Avril walking towards their table. 'Are you and James coming with us?' he said.

'Coming with you where?' said Avril.

'Louise, Jordy, Lizzy, we're all going with Gabriel to a nightclub. It'll be fun.'

'You should ask James but I'm going to stay here,' said Avril. 'I want to spend more time with Henry and Anna.'

She said goodbye to her friends, hugging each of them tightly, then sat down next to Henry. James had politely declined the nightclub invitation and Anna and he were deep in conversation about their mutual love of art.

'So,' Avril said to Henry, 'tell me about your plans for this year's racing carnival.'

Henry didn't need encouraging. 'We have our usual box at Flemington,' he said. 'Why don't you join us, at least for one day? I have two runners on Oaks Day. You're most welcome to bring James. He's a very interesting fellow.'

'You know, Henry, I think I just might,' said Avril and she let Henry replenish her champagne glass.

CHAPTER 15

First thing Monday morning after the Spring Gala, Avril walked into Hoffman's Accessory Importers and bought four hundred pounds' worth of stock. Never one to make a rash business decision, Avril intended to take advantage of the publicity she was receiving since showing her two collections at the gala. Customers didn't just want garments from le Chic, they wanted the complete look, which included shoes and handbags. The headwear Avril was already making herself and, by her calculations, she was better off making her own hats than buying them in. She selected two styles of shoes and four handbags that weren't being stocked by any other retailer.

'We'll have your order delivered by lunchtime,' the sales assistant told Avril.

Avril looked back at her sales and operating costs for the last six months. With no debts and a tidy sum in the bank, she had even started to think about where she'd open her second shop. A larger shop this time, not in the city but somewhere close by.

A week later, Avril sat at the table in the atrium and

watched James clear away their dinner plates. He had cooked simple but delicious steaks on the barbeque for them. Their relationship had not progressed beyond a lingering goodnight kiss on the night of the gala, and as much as Avril enjoyed James's company, it was still Tim who filled her heart. She knew she wasn't ready to admit that it was truly over between the two of them.

'What's on your mind?' James asked, as he placed a pot of coffee on the table. 'You've been quiet all evening.'

'Have I? I guess I have. I'm sorry,' she said. 'There's just so much happening with my business now.'

'Anything you want to talk about?' he asked.

'Actually, if you don't mind, I'd like to get your thoughts about the ideas I have for growing my business and investing in other businesses.'

'Sure,' said James. 'I'm happy to help you in any way I can.'

Avril retrieved her ledger from her satchel and passed the book to James.

'Would you mind looking at the figures and telling me what you think?'

James picked up his reading glasses and ran his eyes over the columns – rent, electricity, telephone, wages, fabrics, production and sundries. Every conceivable expenditure had been accounted for, with sale totals broken down into days, weeks and months. Cash on hand was recorded at the bottom of the page.

'And this is your turnover and net profit,' he said, a little astounded, 'in only six months?'

'That's right,' she said.

'And you've done this without any borrowings or carrying any monthly accounts? You have no debts outstanding?'

'That's correct.'

'Avril, this is an incredible achievement, and if I were you, I'd form a company. It's not to your advantage to be operating as a sole trader. I'm happy to execute the paperwork for you, free of charge, of course.'

'That's a gracious offer, James, but one I can't accept,' Avril said. 'I'd feel more comfortable paying my way and besides, it's time I found myself a lawyer. Would it be all right with you if I were to engage Reece?'

'That's an excellent idea.'

James leant back in his chair and as he ran his hand through his hair, Avril flinched, the gesture was so reminiscent of Tim.

'I look at businesses all the time that don't have this sort of profit margin. Here's the big picture question,' he said, looking intently at Avril. 'What is it exactly that you want to achieve?'

Before Avril had time to think the word tumbled straight out of her mouth.

'Money!' she said. They both laughed and she explained, 'Not because I need to buy expensive things, as nice as they can be. Money gives you freedom. The freedom to help others. The freedom to make your own choices.'

'You won't get any argument out of me on that score,' said James.

'You know, I caught myself the other day, squashing two pieces of half-used soap together just like we used to do during the war,' she said. 'I can't change the past, but I can create my future. Being financially independent is very much a part of that.'

'In my experience, it's a common concern with women in business, and who can blame them?' James drummed his fingers on the table. 'They have as much right to succeed as any man.'

'I see these young women come into my store all the time. Bright girls, smart girls, working in retail, secretaries as well. They have jobs they like and that they're good at. They earn their own money and yet, the moment they get married, it's all over. They're expected to give it all away. They become totally dependent on their husbands and when things go wrong, which so often they do, they're left with no money and nowhere to go. Look at what happened to my aunt. Forced to leave just so she could be safe, and with nothing after working for all those years. It's so unfair. I want to be able to help women who are in this situation.'

James closed the ledger and slid the book across to Avril.

'You don't want to get married and have children?' James asked.

'Not particularly,' said Avril. 'You may think I'm being harsh but that's how I feel.'

'I don't think you're being harsh at all. I think you're wonderful,' he said, and he reached across the table and took her hand. 'I completely understand your desire to expand your business. And you're right, money buys you choices.'

'How can a woman be paid half of what a man earns, even when they do the same job? It makes me so angry,' said Avril.

James smiled and lifted his coffee cup.

'What's so funny?' she asked.

'You and Beth would have got on very well. We used to talk about things like this all the time,' he said.

This was the first time James had mentioned his late wife and Avril could see he did so with pride.

'What would she have said?'

'If she were here, she'd say it was because men make the rules. And she'd be right.'

'Was she a lawyer as well?'

'No. Beth was one of the few female doctors in private practice here in Melbourne. She qualified in America. That's where we met. Our backgrounds couldn't have been more different.'

Throughout the evening, Avril and James talked easily about property, commercial and retail, shares and other money-making ventures. Avril knew that to really succeed financially, she needed to invest in other businesses. To take the money she made from le Chic and find new ways to grow her capital.

'If you keep going the way you have been, in a couple of years you'll have enough cash to diversify into all sorts of ventures.'

But Avril told him she was in a hurry and two years was longer than she wanted to wait. James laughed heartily but he understood her ambition full well as it matched his own. There were so many things he admired about Avril Montdidier.

Later that night after James had taken Avril home and kissed her goodnight, she went straight to her production table in the sunroom. For the following three hours she constructed a plan, her 'Road Map', she called it, detailing where and when she'd open other stores, revenue projections and, more importantly, what she was going to do with the money she knew she could make. Avril went to her sewing box, took out the envelope of photos and looked at them, one by one. The photo of her mother standing in front of her haberdashery store, she put into a frame that Louise had given her. Years later, Avril would say she believed it was divine intervention that gave her the name of her very first company, A Y Holdings Pty Ltd – *A* for Avril and *Y* for Yvette. In the male-dominated business world of the 1950s, A Y Holdings would give Avril the anonymity she needed from the prevailing attitude that believed a woman's place was in the home and not in the boardroom.

*

Two days after the Melbourne Cup was run, the gates at Flemington opened again as racegoers gathered for the Oaks, a prestigious race for three-year-old fillies, and the social event known as Ladies Day. Elegance was the order of the day with men in classic cut suits or tails and top hats, and women in calf-length skirts and tailored jackets. Dressed in a red coat dress with wine-coloured shoes and small handbag, Avril's bewitching fine veil fascinator drew looks of admiration as she and James made their way through the bookmakers' ring towards the members' stand. For the first week in November, the day was surprisingly cold. The pale blue sky was scattered with clusters of clouds as a chilly breeze rolled across the racecourse.

Anna greeted Avril and James warmly and introduced them to the other guests in the Merediths' private box in the members' stand, one of whom was a client of James's.

'Henry, Jordy and Reece have gone down to look at the horses,' said Anna. 'We've got Pure Bliss running in the second race.'

With James engaged in what looked like a lengthy conversation, Avril slipped from the box and walked, down the stairs and across to the horse stalls. It didn't take her long to find Henry and the Meredith boys, and after a quick hello and a pat of the big grey gelding, she left them talking tactics with the trainer.

Avril worked her way over to the mounting enclosure and stood at the fence as the runners in the first race, led by their strappers, paraded past. She opened her race book and looked at the names of the sixteen runners. She smiled as she saw the name of horse number two, Silk Sash, a chestnut mare with a white blaze down her face, just like her darling Piaf. Avril took it as a good omen and decided she'd have a pound each way, just for the fun of it. She was eyeing off another horse when she felt the touch of a hand in the small of her back.

'What do you like in the first race?' Avril heard him say. Her breath wicked from her body, her pulse raced.

She turned slowly to see Tim's deep blue eyes staring straight into hers. He stood so near she could feel the warmth of his body and see every detail of his face.

'Hello, Avril,' he said. 'It's so good to see you.'

Their embrace was instant. Tender and lingering. The world around them stopped as Avril felt Tim's body press against hers, and she didn't want to pull away. Their hands spontaneously found each other's waist, their touch as natural as breathing. There would never be another man on earth she could love the way she loved Tim Meredith.

'What are you doing here?' The delight in her voice was impossible to hide. 'Jordy said you weren't coming down this year.'

'I decided Col could go with Bob to move the herd,' he smiled. Then he added matter-of-factly, 'Besides, Rachel and I have been invited to a list of parties as long as your arm.'

'She didn't go through with her promise of a divorce, did she?' said Avril. There was no point avoiding the subject.

'No,' said Tim. 'She wanted us to give our marriage a chance first, put some effort into it. Then if it doesn't

249

work, she'll divorce me. Or so she says. She could change her mind next week. I never know with Rachel. Who knows what will happen in the future?'

Avril felt her heart crack again, though she was grateful for his honesty. Their lives had to move on, in different directions. 'Where's Rachel at the moment?'

'Oh, she'll be up in the members' stand somewhere, having a good time. If she's got a drink in her hand, she's happy.'

Avril thought how sad that sounded.

'Did you know I was going to be here today?'

'What do you think?' He smiled. 'Dad said he'd invited you and I had to see you, Avril. And where better than in plain sight of everyone. I hear you've brought a date. Is it serious?'

'It's serious as far as a friendship goes. He's a lovely man, Tim, but he's not you.'

Tim took her hand and as he did, he saw the bracelet on her wrist.

Avril removed her hand and steered the conversation back to safer ground, asking how long they were staying in Melbourne.

'We're heading to Brisbane on Sunday. Rachel's riding competitively again, and she's got a couple of horses stabled at Eagle Farm.'

Sensing the wall between them, Tim congratulated her on the success of her business, adding that he was not at all surprised. They spoke about the financial issues that he'd been dealing with and Avril was relieved to hear that the situation had improved.

'There's been a restructure of the board, amongst other things,' said Tim. 'We're not completely in the clear, yet.'

'And Doug? How did he fare in all of this?'

'Well, let's just say they don't call him *Dodgy Doug* for nothing. If he took a hit financially, he's not showing it. Mary's driving around in a brand-new Mercedes and Doug's just bought two new tractors, so the money has to be coming from somewhere.'

The trumpet sounded as the horses moved onto the track and Avril, suddenly feeling overwhelmed by Tim's presence, seized the opportunity to be on her own. She needed some space to think, to breathe.

'I'm going to have an each-way bet on number two,' said Avril. 'I'll see you upstairs.'

*

The bookmakers' calls could be heard across the betting ring as racegoers rushed to place their bets.

'Carnival Lights, twelve to one, Neptune, odds on,' a bookie shouted.

Avril stowed her ticket in her small purse and looked up. Albert Dubray was standing not two yards away, counting out a wad of twenty-pound notes into the bookmaker's hand. She heard the penciller say 'Cameo Charm' as he thrust Albert his ticket. Avril tried to move but was caught in the crush of jackets and hats. Their eyes met as Albert took a swift step forward and, trapped in the crowd, Avril couldn't move. She could smell his beer-soaked breath as he pushed his face up close to hers.

'You stole from me,' Albert spat out through clenched teeth. 'My wife, my employee. I know where you live. One of these days, you might have an accident, you . . .'

Avril shoved her hand into Albert's chest, forcing him back as she drove her heel into his shin. She spun around and shouldered her way through the mass of bodies as quickly as she could and headed straight to the members' stand.

'Ah, there you are,' said James as Avril took her seat. 'I was wondering where you'd got to. Did you run into someone you know?'

'You could say that,' she said. James listened carefully as Avril told him what had happened with Albert. He took her hand.

'Are you sure you're all right? We don't have to stay. I'm happy to leave,' he said.

'I wouldn't give that creep the satisfaction of making us leave. And thank you. I'm fine. Really,' said Avril.

'You don't happen to know the name of the bookmaker he placed his bet with, do you?' said James.

Avril, with her eye for details, was able to answer him. 'Arthur Mallard. Do you know him?' asked Avril. 'You seem to know just about everyone I ever mention.'

James gave the slightest hint of a smile as he lifted a lock of Avril's hair that had fallen across her face and gently pushed the strands under her headpiece.

'Well, it's a friendly town. It won't take me long to find out all the dirt on Albert Dubray. If he's betting big, he's probably betting with only one or two bookmakers,' said James.

'Ha!' said Avril. 'And he's likely to make credit bets when he's not so flush with funds, I take it.'

'Precisely,' said James. 'My guess is he probably has a gambling problem. And as all bookmakers know, you can win, but you will lose. Leave this with me. I'll see what I can find out.'

As the horses thundered down the home straight, every person in the grandstand was on their feet, cheering the jockeys and horses on. Silk Sash came second, and James put his arm around a beaming Avril. When she turned around, Tim and Rachel were standing right behind them.

There was an awkward silence then Tim extended his hand towards James. 'Tim Meredith,' he said. 'And this is Rachel.' He didn't call her his wife.

James introduced himself as they shook hands.

Rachel tilted her head and smiled at James.

'Have we met? I'm sure I know you from somewhere,' she said.

'Ah, I don't think so,' replied James. 'I must have a face people think they recognise. I get that from time to time.'

'Well, I'm going down to collect my winnings,' said Avril.

'Let me get a bottle of champagne,' said James. 'Back in a moment,' and Avril and James disappeared, leaving Tim and Rachel side by side, looking in opposite directions.

*

Avril was back at the mounting enclosure watching the runners in the next race parade when Tim came up beside her and leant against the railing. Not a word was spoken as they watched the strapper lead Henry's two-year-old filly, Pure Bliss, her black coat shining like wet coal. The jockeys began to mount up, before trotting their horses onto the track and cantering slowly down to the starting barriers.

Avril glanced up to see Rachel, champagne in hand, standing at the edge of the balcony with James. They were looking across the racecourse towards Footscray as James was pointing at something in the distance. James noticed Avril and motioned to her with a smile as if to say, *Help me out here.* Avril waved slightly, acknowledging their exchange. Rachel laughed and tossed her head skywards, pressing her back against the railing and downing her drink.

'I miss you terribly,' Tim finally said.

'And I miss you, Tim.' *More than I can say*. But she couldn't bring herself to speak the words. 'Tim, I need to get on with my life and you need to get on with yours.'

'I know,' he said. 'Most days I feel like I'm living in some sort of haze, some warped kind of dream I can't wake up from.' He touched Avril's bangle affectionately.

'Life is long and full of surprises,' she said. 'Come on. Let's go up and cheer on Henry's horse.'

*

Avril took her seat next to James as a hush fell over the crowd.

'He's got his hands full with that one,' James whispered into Avril's ear. 'Thank goodness you came back when you did. One more drink and I think she was going to start unbuttoning my shirt.'

'A bit forward, would you say?' said Avril.

'That doesn't even begin to cover it,' said James. He placed his arm across the back of Avril's seat. 'She doesn't seem the least bit interested in spending time with her husband. I've met dozens of Rachels before today, and I can tell you this. If one man's not enough, then ten won't be too many.'

'You think she takes other lovers?'

James leant closer to Avril, making sure no one could hear. 'Let's just say, in my experience, past performance predicts future behaviour. So to answer your question, yes, I'm sure she does.'

As Pure Bliss crossed the finish line two lengths ahead of the nearest rival, Avril and James, along with everyone else, were on their feet shouting. After the race Henry proudly accepted the owner's trophy and at the end of the afternoon, despite being asked to join all the other guests at Anna and Henry's home in Toorak, Avril and James respectfully declined the invitation. Avril said her fare-wells to all the Meredith clan with a kiss on both cheeks, and as Tim said goodbye, he gently squeezed her hand.

James adjusted the car radio while Avril unpinned her hair and wound down the window, letting the wind blow against her face.

'Did you enjoy yourself today?' he asked. 'Apart from what happened in the betting ring?'

'I did,' said Avril. 'Very much.'

'I know this might be difficult but try not to worry about Albert. By the time I've made a few phone calls, I'll know everything about him, from his shoe size to what he ate yesterday for breakfast.'

James didn't need to ask about Tim Meredith. He'd seen by the way Tim looked at Avril that there was obviously a story between them, but as far as he was concerned, it was none of his business. Tim was married and Avril was single and that was all James needed to know.

The sun had almost set as he swung his Jaguar into the driveway. He turned off the engine, leant across and kissed Avril and this time, for the first time, she returned his kiss fully, passionately and with intent. Something had shifted in Avril. Her perspective, her expectations. She didn't want to be on the sideline of life anymore as far as intimacy was concerned. But she wasn't about to go falling hopelessly in love, either. She was through with such foolish ideas. *Love. It never works out.* She couldn't wait for Tim. What was there to wait for?

She stroked James's face. 'Let's go in,' she said.

Upstairs in James's bedroom, Avril eased his jacket from his body as he removed her coat dress. His touch was strong yet sensitive, his kiss erotic. Avril thought only of this moment. She never imagined that pleasure with James would feel so natural. Her passion was not like the intense, all-consuming love she felt for Tim. But a different form of love, and in its own way, beautiful. A tenderness they both needed and desired. And in that moment, James and Avril set one another free from the past, and opened the door to an unknown future.

*

With the Christmas and New Year's celebrations over, women in summer cotton dresses and smart hats poured into the city for the department store sales. Every floor, from haberdashery to manchester, women's shoes to children's wear, saw stock reduced to make way for the Autumn/Winter collections. Avril decided not to hold a sale for one simple reason. She didn't need to. Since opening, she'd limited her production to only six garments per size. Seldom was a dress, skirt or jacket on the rack for more than a week. Same went for her quirky yet stylish accessories. The buses and trams loaded with parcel-carrying shoppers rumbled away from the city each day, and as the long sun-soaked days of the Australian summer stretched on, Avril worked seven days a week to bring about the next phase of her plan.

The first week of March saw Avril, James and Duncan standing on the footpath outside her new shop on Chapel Street, South Yarra. The space was four times the size of her shop in the Block Arcade with a large room at the back of the store. Avril opened the door of the storeroom and flicked on the light. The wide wooden shelves that lined the walls would be perfect for storing Avril's ever-growing supply of fabrics.

'Time to work your magic,' she said to Duncan.

'As the lady wishes,' Duncan replied, but he was already measuring the shop dimensions with his eyes.

'How long do you think the fit-out will take?' she asked as they walked around the shop floor. 'I'd like to open at the beginning of April.'

'The painters can start tomorrow, the furniture will be finished by the end of this week and the racks and shelving I can do myself,' said Duncan. 'If your stock's ready, you could probably open before the end of March.'

James, who had been engrossed in the contract papers, looked at his watch and swore. 'I'm due in court in an hour. I'll see you tonight, honey,' he said as he dropped a kiss on Avril's forehead. 'Cheers, Duncan,' he called as he closed the door.

'Honey, is it now?' Duncan teased.

'Oh, stop it,' Avril smiled. 'Back to business.'

*

Duncan was constantly amazed at Avril's ingenious ideas for displaying merchandise and how best to encourage customers to linger in her store. Avril, on the other hand, was always impressed and delighted by Duncan's ability to transform a space. From the practicalities of hanging racks, to lighting and of course his beloved window displays, he was a genius. Together, they were a dream team.

'You didn't tell me how you got on at Hoffman's,' said Duncan as he wrote down the measurements of the front window.

'Hoffman's will supply us with an exclusive range of shoes and bags, all bearing the le Chic label. I'm also trialling a small range of belts,' said Avril.

Selling shoes and handbags had been one of the smartest

decisions Avril had made since opening her business. At the Chapel Street site, Avril wanted one area of the shop to be specifically for accessories, with floor-to-ceiling mirrors and generously sized padded bench seats. Avril wanted to make her customers feel like they were walking into a mini department store.

'Have you got someone to run the store?' asked Duncan.

'Not yet. I'll start interviews next week. Now, I must go. I'm visiting Gabriel's new studio. I think I'm the only one who hasn't seen it.'

'Would you like a lift?' Duncan asked, assuming Avril had arrived by cab.

'No thanks,' she grinned. 'I have something to show you.'

She dragged him out the front and patted the bonnet of a white VW Beetle.

'What do you think?' she said. 'She's only a few years old and in great condition.'

'Oh my goodness!' said Duncan as he gave Avril a celebratory hug. 'Can you even drive?'

'Of course. And I have a driver's licence to prove it.'

Avril waved Duncan goodbye and looked back at the shop through her rear-view mirror. He had his hands over his eyes in mock despair.

Avril loved the freedom of owning a car. She could go wherever she wanted whenever she wanted. And in the same way as when she was riding a horse, her thoughts could flow with the forward motion. Lately, she had been thinking about other ways to expand her business: *If I can create a second le Chic store in Melbourne, what's stopping me from doing the same in Sydney and Brisbane?* The only problem Avril envisaged was getting a regular supply of quality fabrics as the government had put a quota on fabric imports. *What if there was some way of getting an exemption from the import quota?* she thought. And by the time Avril pulled up outside Gabriel's new studio, she'd already formed her next money-making venture.

*

Josephine cradled the phone to her ear with her shoulder as she straightened the jewellery in the glass cabinet.

'That's wonderful news, Nancy. Congratulations,' she said. 'Oh yes. The Chapel Street store's opening in a week. You're still coming to the launch party the following Saturday afternoon, aren't you?'

Josephine looked up as Avril came through the door carrying some boxes. She waved as Josephine mouthed the word, *Nancy*.

'She's just walked in, so I'll tell her straight away. I'll see you for cards this Saturday. Bye, darling.'

Josephine put down the receiver and clasped her hands.

'Nancy's been offered the role of Editor-in-Chief for *The Australian Woman* magazine.'

'Is she taking it?' asked Avril.

'Of course she's taking it. It's what she's always wanted. She starts in a month.'

'I'll send her flowers and champagne from you and me,' said Avril.

'Make sure they go to her home,' said Josephine. 'The word's already out and apparently her office at the *Melbourne Times* looks like a florist. Her boss is furious, of course. They don't want to lose her, but he understands what a wonderful opportunity this is.' Josephine eyed off Avril's straight skirt and jacket. 'You look lovely,' she said.

'I'm having dinner with Henry Meredith at the Café

Florentino tonight,' said Avril. 'I haven't seen him since we were all together at the races last November. I'm so looking forward to seeing him and eating there.'

'Oh yes, Florentino. Tony's place. One of the few restaurants in this city to own a liquor licence,' said Josephine. 'Every time Albert applied for one, he was knocked back.'

Josephine rarely mentioned Albert and Avril was surprised by her comment. Avril walked over to her aunt and put her hand on her shoulder.

'Is everything all right?' said Avril.

'I don't know why I even mentioned him,' she said, looking out through the window of the shop and down the arcade. 'Perhaps it's because I thought I saw him the other evening when I was crossing Bourke Street. I had the strangest feeling I was being followed. When I turned around, there was a man close by, but he looked nothing like Albert.'

'In the boxes are some new handbags, but don't worry about them now. Put them out in the morning,' said Avril. 'Why don't you lock up and head home?'

She kissed Josephine goodbye and left for her ten-minute walk to the restaurant.

Keen to see the latest items, Josephine cut open the box, removed the tissue paper and placed a green velvet and burgundy lace clutch on the counter. She was looking at the detail on the clasp when she heard the door open.

'What have you forgotten this time?' Josephine said jokingly.

There was no reply and as the silence lingered, she turned. Albert stood with his back pressed against the inside of the closed door. Ever so slowly, Josephine's hand tightened around the scissors she'd been using as her other hand glided towards her large crystal ashtray on the counter.

'Get out! Get out this instant,' she said, as possible outcomes raced through her mind.

'Or what?' Albert leered. 'Who's going to hear you?' His eyes locked onto hers.

Slowly, deliberately, Albert stepped forward, the soles of his shoes squeaking on the black and white tiles. Josephine's only thought was to get out of the store. She hurled the heavy ashtray at Albert. It skimmed his ear and smashed through the door, showering glass in every direction.

Mr Reynolds, the arcade manager, stepped from the nearby elevator and, hearing the commotion, ran in the direction of le Chic.

'What's happened?' he called, stopping short of the door, the sound of glass crunching under his shoes. 'Is anyone hurt?'

In a few quick strides Albert was out the door and down the arcade, disappearing into the street, leaving Josephine ashen-faced as she leant against the counter. Mr Reynolds took one look at Josephine and nodded.

'An unwanted visitor, I take it,' was all he said as he picked up the phone and dialled a number. 'Are you all right, Josephine?'

'I will be.'

'Jim. It's Tom Reynolds,' he said. 'Yes. A glass door. Shop seventeen. Terrific. Thanks Jim,' he said and hung up the receiver. 'The glazier's on his way. I'll sort this out. Don't you worry, love.'

'Thank you,' she said, and Mr Reynolds noticed she was now shaking.

'I'm going to call you a cab, which I'm paying for, then I'll walk you to the street and wait with you until the driver arrives. Will there be someone at home when you get there?' he asked.

261

'I'll call now and see,' said Josephine.

Louise answered the phone. They spoke briefly and then Josephine said to Mr Reynolds, 'Yes, there's someone at home. They know I'm on my way.'

Mr Reynolds stood watch as Josephine put on her coat and gloves and collected her handbag then he walked her to the cab. He opened the cab door and Josephine hesitated before getting in. She looked up at Mr Reynolds, who at six foot four towered over most people, and tried to smile.

'I'll sort this out,' he said. 'Don't worry about a thing.'

*

Despite Avril insisting Josephine take the next day off, she refused. They had just arrived at the shop together and were removing their coats when a young police officer came striding down the arcade. Avril unlocked the newly repaired door.

'Can I help you?' said Avril as the constable removed his hat.

'Are you Josephine Dubray?' he asked.

'No. I'm Avril Montdidier, the owner of this business. This is Mrs Dubray,' said Avril as she motioned towards her aunt. 'What's this about?'

The policeman flipped open his notebook.

'A Mr Albert Dubray has reported that he was attacked by you yesterday evening with a heavy object and narrowly escaped injury. Is this correct?'

'My husband, from whom I'm separated, is a devious and violent man,' said Josephine. 'He came to this store to attack me. Not the other way around. He blocked the doorway and was preventing me from leaving. I threw the ashtray to smash the door window, hoping someone nearby would hear. And someone did. Fortunately for me, Mr Reynolds, the arcade manager, was close by, and he came to my rescue. I suggest you speak to him.'

When the officer had finished writing his notes and thanked Josephine, Avril followed him outside.

'Surely you can see the situation, officer,' said Avril. 'Albert Dubray is a dangerous man. He hit his wife many times during the course of their marriage.'

'Did she ever press charges?' asked the constable.

'It's not as easy as that for a woman to get justice through the legal system, whatever you might believe,' said Avril. 'You'll find Mr Reynolds's office on the second floor.'

Avril watched the officer take the stairs, turned and went back into the shop, thinking nothing would come of the visit.

'What a plain-faced liar Albert is,' said Avril. 'James tells me he owes quite a bit of money to a bookmaker and that the restaurant's been going slowly downhill since you and Duncan left. Albert's changed chefs twice in the last year and he can't keep staff.'

'And there's his drinking,' said Josephine. 'I think his world is unravelling around him. I don't like having to watch over my shoulder all the time. I mean, he knows where I am every day.'

Avril straightened some hangers, then stopped suddenly, aware of a solution.

'I don't know why I didn't think of this sooner,' said Avril. 'I'd like to offer you the position of General Manager. You could oversee the running of both stores, manage the sales staff and work with Duncan on any promotional activity. The business is ready to have someone in this position and this way, Albert won't know where you're going to be. What do you say?'

Josephine didn't need convincing, and Avril already had the names of four sales assistants from Foys and Buckley & Nunn, who were all keen to work at le Chic.

'That's an excellent idea. I think that would work perfectly.'

'Now we have that settled, I have to run,' said Avril as she kissed Josephine goodbye. 'If all goes well with this meeting this morning, we'll be celebrating tonight.'

CHAPTER 16

Joshua Lewin was waiting on the footpath outside the offices of Carter, Carmody and Wainwright as arranged. He greeted Avril with a warm smile and she kissed him on both cheeks before they headed inside. James showed Avril and Joshua into his office while Reece followed, carrying the documents.

'Please, take a seat,' said James, his manner the very essence of professionalism. 'Reece and I have moved heaven and earth in the last ten days, but it looks like it's been worth it. I'm delighted to report that your application for an import licence and a lifting of the quota embargo on importing textiles from Europe and the UK has been successful.'

'That's incredible!' said Joshua, a smile spreading across his face. 'I'm in shock. How did this all happen so quickly?'

'Well, to be completely honest, Avril had told me some months ago about the difficulties all manufacturers have getting a regular supply of fabrics. So I did a little digging and felt there was a case to be made for granting an exemption to the quota ruling. Turns out, no one had tried to test that law. So, congratulations. You're now free to start your textile import business.'

'I know you said you had warehouse premises, Joshua, but have you and Avril decided on a business name?' asked Reece.

'We have,' said Joshua.

A few days before the Chapel Street store opened, Avril and Joshua had signed the contracts for their first business venture together. Lewmont Fabrics was a fifty-fifty partnership which would operate from a warehouse owned by Bert Lewin. Avril had committed nearly all her capital into the business which would see Joshua embark on a month-long buying trip in Europe. Certain fabrics would be used exclusively by Avril for her le Chic range, while Joshua was keen to import suiting fabrics for his own menswear label. The rest of the range would be sold to fashion houses, department stores and fabric shops across Australia. Before the year was out, Lewmont Fabrics would be open for business. After that Avril and Joshua would focus on the next phase of their enterprise: a garment factory of their own.

*

The white bubbles lapped at the edge of the bath as James turned off the hot tap. He stroked the back of Avril's neck with a water-filled sponge.

'I'm a bit surprised Joshua Lewin didn't want to go into the fabric importing business with his father,' said James.

'He wanted to achieve something on his own,' replied Avril, 'without his father's help, but he didn't have enough capital to do it without a partner. We both recognised how difficult it is to get great fabric. We got talking and we both knew that wholesaling fabrics was a good idea.'

'Does he know how lucky he is to have you as a business partner?' said James as he soaped her arms.

Avril laid back and rested her head on James's chest and draped her feet over the edge of the bath.

'Of course he does. But I'm also lucky to have him. We work so well together. He has his life and I have mine, but we talk the same language when it comes to business and that's the main thing. Besides, Bert leased me the shop when no one else would and they've been with me all the way.'

'And does Joshua know about us?' said James.

'I'm not sure. I don't talk about my private life to anyone, you know that. It's my business how I choose to live my life. No one else's.'

'When are you going to marry me and let me make an honest woman of you?' James teased.

Avril spun around and looked at James, sending the water surging over the sides of the bath and across the marble floor. She smiled and pushed his wet hair back off this forehead.

'I'm already an honest woman,' she said. 'Just not the marrying kind of honest woman,' and she placed her hand on the side of his face.

'Yes. You are an honest woman and I love you for that,' he said as he leant forward and kissed her.

*

To celebrate the opening of Avril's second le Chic store, James threw a party at his home. It started early, finished late and at one point almost one hundred people filled the atrium and back veranda. Avril and Louise sat on the bottom step of the sweeping staircase that dominated the grand entrance, sipping champagne.

'A little bit more stylish than the top deck of the *Harmony Prince*,' said Louise, nudging Avril's arm.

Avril smiled and stared at the intricate pattern of the parquetry floor.

'That seems like a lifetime ago now, doesn't it? Joshua leaves next week for Europe,' said Avril. 'France, Belgium, then Switzerland and back via London. I can't wait to see what he orders.'

'You didn't want to go?' Louise asked.

'We talked about it. But I've got too much going on here and, to be honest, I'm not ready to go back.'

'Me neither,' Louise said.

Duncan arrived with a huge bunch of roses and a bottle of champagne.

'For you,' he said. 'Oh, I hope you don't mind, but I found this lost and lonely soul wandering up the driveway, so I invited him in.'

'Where does a man put his horse around here?'

'Jordy!' Avril screamed. She jumped up from the step and they threw their arms around each other, laughing. Then Jordy lifted her off the ground and spun her in a circle, their standard greeting.

'It's so wonderful to see you. I can't believe it. When did you get here?'

'This morning. Dad's gone out to check on the stud and Mum's having an exhibition,' he said. 'They would have loved to have been here. They said to congratulate you and said they would see you soon.'

'Yes. Anna sent me an invitation to the exhibition opening. I'm looking forward to it,' said Avril. 'Can you stay the night?'

'I'd love to, but I've made other arrangements,' said Jordy. 'Thank you anyway.'

'James is holding court on the back veranda,' said Avril. 'He'll be happy to see you.' And he was, proudly introducing Jordy to the partygoers and encouraging him to take to the dance floor in the atrium.

Avril always delighted in watching the interaction between Jordy and Reece. Their appearance and personalities were so different, and yet they were similar at the core. Even though the evening air was cool, the brothers preferred to stand outside. They leant against the veranda railing and stayed in the same spot, just like they did at Monaghan Station, deep in conversation, breaking out in laughter, occasionally poking each other in the ribs. Although Reece was now entrenched in Melbourne and Avril marvelled at his business acumen, at times he would still have the look of country life about him. Reece was at ease with who he was, and Avril admired him for it.

Later in the night Avril and Jordy sat on the bench swing in the garden and looked back at the house. It didn't look like the party was going to wind up any time soon.

'I asked you this the last time I saw you,' said Jordy, nodding in the direction of James. 'Is he the one?'

'Who can say,' said Avril. 'We're happy with the way we are. And James respects my dedication to my work, as I do his. I know our situation is unconventional, but it works for us.'

'I saw you and Tim caught up on Oaks Day last year. How was that?'

'Quite strange with everyone else around but it was good to see him, Jordy. It also made me realise that I had to move on with my personal life. Now, tell me about everything that's happening back home,' she said, eager to talk about other things.

Jordy gave Avril the rundown on everyone from Mrs Carmichael and Jean to the children and the various stockmen. He talked about what crops had been sown and all the comings and goings. Avril closed her eyes as he spoke. She could almost smell the freshly cut grass that surrounded the homestead, hear the kookaburras calling and feel the wind on her face as she cantered up the airstrip.

'Tim and Rachel seem to each be happier these days,' said Jordy, startling Avril out of her pleasant memories. 'I have no idea what really goes on between those two. She's hardly at the station and when she is, well, at least they're not fighting the way they used to.'

'I thought they might try and start a family?' said Avril.

'I don't exactly see Rachel as the mothering type. From what Mrs Carmichael's indicated, it would be an immaculate conception if it happened. Tim still stays in The Aviary, while Rachel's taken over the corner guest room upstairs. I sometimes wonder if she's got someone down in Brisbane.'

'What makes you say that?'

'Just a hunch. Tim's always been blind where Rachel's wandering eye is concerned. He's not stupid, but he doesn't always see what's obvious to others.'

'Life. It's a funny thing, isn't it?' said Avril. 'And you? Is there someone special in your life?'

'There might be,' Jordy grinned.

'Well, if you're happy, that's all that matters,' said Avril, and while she wondered who the lucky girl might be, she had no intention of asking and Jordy had no intention of telling her.

*

By the time the year was out, Avril had secured a retail site in Pitt Street, Sydney, and Queen Street, Brisbane. Reece reviewed the lease agreements and once the documents were signed, Duncan set about organising the shop fit-outs while Josephine interviewed and selected the staff. Avril wanted both shops opened by the end of summer, ready to transition into autumn with her new range. With the help of her 'team' as she affectionately called them, Avril's two new stores received a vast amount of publicity in the broadsheets as well as *The Australian Woman* magazine.

Nancy Cameron ran a three-page article on Avril with images by Gabriel Dupont. Lizzy, who'd quit nursing and moved to Melbourne to try her hand at full-time model-ling just before Christmas, graced the cover of February's twenty-fifth issue of the magazine, in a strapless raspberry-coloured taffeta cocktail dress by le Chic. Gabriel and Lizzy had become the darling duo of the fashion set since her arrival and their relationship had moved from profes-sional to personal in only a matter of weeks.

Louise had introduced a regular feature to the bottom of her weekly fashion page in the *Melbourne Times* – 'Ask Avril', a witty one-paragraph response from Avril Montdidier to the readers' fashion dilemmas. The responses, usually concocted by Avril and Louise over dinner on a Sunday night, dispensed advice on everything from suitable necklines, how to dress formally in the hot weather without melting away, and what accessories to buy.

The first container of European and British textiles had arrived before the end of winter. Avril had been ecstatic when she saw the brocade, satin, crepe, faille, taffeta and fine woollen suiting Joshua had selected. By the time the orders from local fabric makers had been delivered – bolts of printed cotton, damask and linen – and Avril and Joshua had opened their doors for business, Lewmont Fabric was the largest dress fabric wholesaler the country had ever seen.

Avril swung her white VW into her allotted space in the Footscray car park of Lewmont Fabrics and checked her watch. Running slightly early, as she always did, she sat for a moment and closed her eyes. She'd flown back the previous day after attending the opening of both the Brisbane and Sydney shops and for the first time in weeks, Avril felt as though she could fall asleep at any moment. She shook off her tiredness, gathered up her things and was greeted at the reception desk by Eliza, Joshua's cousin, who ran the showroom. The smile on Eliza's face said it all.

'Every appointment has been taken for the first week of showing,' Eliza beamed, 'and the buyers from Foys and David Jones have booked double timeslots.'

'That's excellent news,' said Avril.

'Joshua's in his office. He's waiting for you.'

His door was wide open, but Avril knocked and waited for Joshua to look up.

'Ah! Here she is. Did you see the write-up you got in *Rag Trade Weekly* yesterday? Very impressive,' Joshua smiled. 'Coffee?'

'Oh, yes please. How long have we got?' said Avril.

'Half an hour. First appointment's at nine o'clock,' he said, handing Avril a cup and saucer.

Avril and Joshua discussed the inventory on hand and the incoming fabrics that were expected to arrive later that month. They'd drawn up a strict set of guidelines by which to operate their business. These included minimum customer orders and a seven- or fourteen-day bill of sale, only for those orders over a certain amount. Every other order was to be strictly cash on delivery. Customers wanting exclusivity on fabrics had to be prepared to buy the whole consignment and pay upfront.

'You know our terms are going to ruffle a few feathers,' said Joshua.

'We're not a credit service,' said Avril, 'and besides, where else are the designers, fabric retailers and department stores going to get fabric like ours?'

'You know it's only a matter of time until someone else is granted an exemption and starts doing what we're doing, don't you? And they're likely to give thirty-day accounts, which we won't,' said Joshua.

'Of course. And we'll let them. We're not going to carry anyone. If a business can't pay us when they place their order, what's to say they'll be able to pay in three months' time?'

Joshua had nothing but admiration for Avril's reasoning when it came to business decisions. He knew that some in the rag trade considered Avril to be a *tough cookie*, simply because she was a shrewd negotiator, able to obtain exclusivity on many of the accessories she sold.

'I agree,' he said. 'We need to have this business cash flow positive as soon as possible so we can start the factory.'

'I have some news where our manufacturing site is concerned,' she said.

Avril walked over to the window and motioned for Joshua to follow.

'What do you see?' she said, pointing to the red-brick building on the large block of land across the street.

Joshua stood with his hands on his hips and looked at the abandoned premises. Once a biscuit factory, the windows had been boarded up a year ago when the business relocated to a modern facility west of the city.

'I see a building that's owned by a company who doesn't return my letters of inquiry,' he said.

'Do you know what's going to happen this time next year?' Avril asked, not taking her eyes off the building for a moment. 'This country will be in the grip of royal fever when Queen Elizabeth and Prince Philip arrive for their very first tour of Australia together. Can you imagine the number of parties, dances, balls and afternoon teas women and their partners will be attending? Thousands upon thousands of women wanting to emulate the elegant style of the young queen. And we're going to give then all the style and glamour they want, all manufactured by us.'

Joshua sat on the window ledge and crossed his arms and Avril joined him.

'What are you suggesting?' he said.

'I've been informed that the old biscuit factory goes up for auction next month and I think we should buy it,' said Avril.

'How on earth do you know this?' Joshua said in amazement. 'I've been trying to find out who owns that site for the past three years. Some obscure company with only a post office box.'

Avril explained that she had asked Reece to look into it. The sale of the property had come up out of the blue. The owner needed money and he needed it fast. Which meant he was desperate. The building was structurally sound, the plant and equipment had been removed leaving all the electricals in place, and the lighting was excellent.

'Best of all,' Avril said, 'it's across from our fabric warehouse.'

'Well, you'd better give me the figures,' Joshua said, knowing Avril would already have a file prepared.

'You won't be sorry,' she said enthusiastically as she passed over the manila folder. 'I know it's a little sooner than we'd planned but this is too good to miss.'

'How did you raise the money?' asked Joshua, thumbing through the paperwork. 'I thought you used all your cash for our wholesale business.'

'I did. I've borrowed against my share portfolio,' Avril replied confidently. 'We could have the factory up and running within a month, six weeks at the most, once the sale is finalised.'

'When do you need an answer?'

'You've got right up until the fall of the hammer. I hope you're able to come in with me on this, Joshua. If you decide not to, I'll understand. Either way, I'm going to be the winning bidder on this piece of real estate, come what may.'

'Well, I'll certainly see if I can raise the funds. But I'll be happy to manufacture out of your factory, Avril, if that's how this all plays out. There'll be no hard feelings if you're the sole owner of the property. Business is business.'

Joshua sat down and read the name of the seller on the sale contract. 'Ah. That's them, Premise Holdings. So, you obviously know who's behind this company then?'

'As a matter of fact, I do,' she replied. Avril stared back out the window across to the brick building. 'There's only one owner. His name is Albert Dubray.'

*

At the fall of the hammer, lot 74 was sold. Albert snatched up the pen and reluctantly signed the sale documents, knowing the building had been purchased for much less than its true value. Reece, who attended the auction and bid on behalf of Avril and Joshua, completed the sales transaction, handed over the deposit cheque and phoned the new owners with the good news. Even Reece had to concede, Avril and Joshua had got themselves a bargain.

Leading up to the sale, Avril and Joshua had lined up all the tradesmen needed to convert the building into a modern production facility. Cutting tables, sewing machines and other equipment had been placed on hold, ready for purchase should the sale go through.

Avril had insisted that Monash Manufacturing, the name they'd chosen for their garment production business, would provide facilities and benefits to their employees that were not offered anywhere else. Avril began to feel that she could really start to implement positive changes where women and their working conditions were concerned. Changes that extended beyond what she had already implemented for the employees in her four le Chic shops.

'You can't put a price on loyal staff who are happy,' she said to Joshua as they drew up the terms of their business agreement.

Once word started to circulate about the wages and conditions being offered by the new factory, a long queue of pattern makers, cutters and machinists had formed by six-thirty in the morning, the first day of interviews. Avril had already offered Mrs Rossi the position of Production Supervisor, with a salary and hours she found impossible to refuse. After fifteen years at Manton's department store, Bella Rossi handed in her notice and, for the first time in her life, took a month's holiday, at Portsea.

In the factory, a modern cafeteria was installed, and all employees had access to shower facilities. Women and men were granted time off work without loss of pay to look after a sick child or to attend a medical appointment. And all employees worked a nine-day fortnight, something previously unheard of in the rag trade. Within a week, Avril and Joshua had sixty applications for twenty-two positions.

Despite James's suggestion to take a weekend off here and there, Avril's dedication to the running of her shops, Lewmont Fabrics and the garment factory meant she was busier than ever before, and she loved it. She thrived on it.

CHAPTER 17

The months rolled by. Winter transitioned into spring and as the new summer fashions hit the stores, sales reached unprecedented levels as women across the country readied themselves for the plethora of social events they would attend in the new year once the Royal Tour began. Every prediction Avril had made about consumer demand for affordable yet stylish fashion was realised. Not only was Monash Manufacturing producing the le Chic range and Joshua's menswear label, but Avril had also cleverly tapped into the younger women's market with a label she named 'Summer Princess'. Sold exclusively to certain department stores, the designs were simple, fresh and modern and at a price every salesgirl and secretary could afford.

James stood in the doorway of his bedroom in his tails and white tie and watched as Avril turned in front of the mirror checking her dress from behind. Her midnight-blue strapless gown hugged her torso and billowed from her waist in deep pleats. Avril's hair had been cut into a sophisticated bob with a long fringe that hovered just above her eyebrows.

'You look breathtaking,' he said, as she fastened her earrings and picked up her evening purse.

'You don't look too bad yourself,' she smiled.

'Come on. We'd better down our drinks, honey, or we'll be late.'

*

The City of Melbourne Ball, where Queen Elizabeth II and His Royal Highness, The Duke of Edinburgh, were to be the guests of honour, was the social event of the decade. With four thousand people invited to the event at the Exhibition building, Avril and James planned to attend for a couple of hours then head to Anna and Henry's home, for a party the Merediths were hosting.

Avril tinkered with the clasp on her purse, irritated that she couldn't stop thinking about Tim as the car pulled up near the main entrance. Most of the time, Avril's mind was filled with matters concerning work and Tim rarely came into her thoughts during the day. It was times such as this, when the Meredith family came together, that Avril found her heart raced and the anticipation of seeing Tim sent her into a spin.

James reached over and gently squeezed Avril's hand. 'Ready?'

'Ready,' she replied.

Avril stepped from the chauffeur-driven car, and members of the press called her name. The white lights of the photographers' cameras flashed in every direction.

By the time Avril and James arrived at Anna and Henry's home in Toorak, the party was in full swung. Avril's friends had also been invited, and the first people she saw were Gabriel and Lizzy. One look at Lizzy's face and Avril knew something was up. It only took a moment for Lizzy to extend her left hand and proudly display a sapphire and diamond engagement ring.

'I'm the luckiest man in the world,' Gabriel announced, as he kissed his fiancée.

'Congratulations. What a wonderful surprise,' said Avril, in between the hugs.

'When's the wedding?' said James.

'We'll wait until spring,' said Lizzy. 'I couldn't stand a winter wedding. And Avril, I'd love for you to design my wedding dress.'

'It would be my absolute pleasure,' said Avril, taking Lizzy by the hands.

Avril broke away and wandered past a sea of stunning floor-length gowns and handsomely dressed men to the candlelit balcony beyond. Her eyes searched the room for Tim, but he was not to be found.

'Miss Avril,' came a familiar voice. Jordy, Reece and Duncan stood on the steps that led down to the pool and garden. Avril was greeted with much affection as Jordy insisted she twirl around so he could see her dress.

'What would those stockmen say if they could see you now?' he said.

Avril and Jordy were shortly on their own when Reece was dragged onto the dance floor and Duncan went to replenish his glass. They caught up on what each had been doing, reminisced about a few memories, and avoided the topic of Tim and Rachel. But it was no use; they were a fact of life for Jordy. He turned his back to the crowd and leant on the square pillar.

'Tim runs the station like a man possessed these days,' said Jordy. 'If it's not one project it's another. Decided the tennis court wasn't up to scratch. Had the whole thing ripped up and built again. Rachel seems to lead her own life, socially, shall we say, down in Brisbane. Practically given up on her riding, despite Tim's encouragement.'

The thought of Tim. The mere utterance of his name. And still in a loveless relationship, when Avril and Tim had so much to give each other . . . Suddenly Avril's mind started to spin and she took hold of the railing.

'Are you all right?' asked Jordy as he guided her towards a chair.

'I'm fine. I think this dress might be too tight. I'll be back in a moment.'

Avril made her way down the hallway towards the guest bathroom, and as she did, the door to Henry's office opened and there stood Tim. He hesitated for a few seconds, a crystal tumbler in his hand, then he reached out, took hold of Avril's wrist, pulled her into the half-lit room and closed the door.

Without speaking their bodies came together. Tim kissed her and in that spontaneous moment, every rational thought, every wall that kept them apart, dropped away. There was only Tim, his lips on hers, on her neck, his hands caressing her back, her body pressed hard into his.

'I can't bear being without you, Avril,' he said. 'All I've ever wanted is for us to be together.'

She pressed her hand on Tim's chest and pushed herself away. 'Tim. I can't. We can't. No matter how much we might want to.'

She went to the window and adjusted her dress and fixed her hair. Tim placed his hands gently on Avril's shoulders and turned her to face him.

'Rachel says she'll never divorce me. But I won't give up, Avril. There has to be a way out of this facade of a marriage. This hell I'm living in.'

Tim ran his hand through his hair. Avril took his hand and kissed it.

'Goodbye, Tim,' she said. 'It's time I went home.'

'Please, stay. I don't want you to leave on account of me.'

'Of course I'm leaving on account of you,' she raised her voice. 'I can't be around you. It breaks my heart. I wish you all the love and luck in the world, Tim. I always have.'

Avril opened the door, walked swiftly down the hallway and into the lounge room where James was standing by the piano.

'I'm happy to leave if you are,' she said. 'I've seen everyone I needed to see.'

'Fine by me,' he said. 'It's been a long day.'

As they started down the road, Avril told the driver her address in South Melbourne. 'I'm so tired,' she said to James. 'I'd prefer to be at my place tonight.'

'Is everything all right?' James asked, studying her face in the half light.

'Everything's fine,' she replied as she felt the shape of the gold bangle through the fabric of her evening gown.

You tell yourself you won't let him in but you always do. Brick your heart up as much as you like, it will always crumble.

James saw Avril to the door and for the first time, she felt awkward in his presence. 'Goodnight,' she said and kissed him briefly on the cheek.

'I'll call you in the morning,' he said. She turned the key in the lock and went inside. James stared at the closed door for a few moments, concern etched on his face, before walking away.

*

The following February, Duncan and Avril sat together in his newly decorated apartment as he sang her 'Happy Birthday' and she blew out the candles on her thirty-first birthday cake. Gabriel and Lizzy were away on their honeymoon – as it turned out, theirs had been a summer wedding – and with the owner of Coben Street putting the old cottage up for sale, Louise and Josephine had moved into a flat together.

'It's a pity the girls couldn't be here for your birthday high tea,' said Duncan.

'I know, but it's wonderful for Louise to be doing so well.' Since taking over as the fashion editor for the *Melbourne Times*, Louise was travelling frequently for work and that week she was in Sydney for a society wedding.

'When's Josephine back from Brisbane?'

'Next week. The manager of the store left to get married so she's been trying to find a suitable replacement.'

Avril took a bunch of birthday cards out of her satchel which she hadn't had time to open that day. She smiled as she read them and passed them on to Duncan, but one she placed back into the envelope with its embossed crest of Monaghan Station on the back.

'Sends one every year, doesn't he?' said Duncan.

'Every year,' she said.

Duncan raised his glass.

'To love,' he said.

'To love, my dear friend,' said Avril.

They were silent for a while, Avril lost in thought, twisting her fork over the icing of the cake.

'Are you going to tell me what's on your mind or do I have to drag it out of you?'

Avril took a deep breath and put the fork down on the plate.

'I think it's time I ended it with James,' she said. 'Romantically, I mean. He's a kind man, a wonderful man and I still want him in my life, but . . .'

'But you're not in love with him,' said Duncan.

'I've tried to be. I've wanted to be. But I'm not,' she said, then added, 'I want to be on my own for a while. I can't tell you why. It's just how I feel.'

'What's brought this on, do you think? A birthday perhaps?'

'Possibly. Or maybe it's because I've decided to buy Coben Street myself,' said Avril.

'What! You want to live in that dump on your own?'

'I don't plan to live there. I'm going to renovate the whole place. I want to turn it into a safe house for women who have nowhere to go. God only knows what would have happened to Josephine if we hadn't been there for her.'

'She would still be with Albert,' Duncan said, 'and she'd still be his victim.'

'There's this young girl,' Avril went on, 'a machinist at our factory, who turns up regularly with bruises down her arms. She wants to leave home, but she has nowhere safe to go. Nowhere she could afford.'

Duncan thought of the bruises on his mother's arms, on Lizzy's, on his own. The pain so much more than physical. 'This doesn't just happen to the women, their children often suffer too.'

'Exactly,' Avril said. 'Only last week I came across a young woman and her two small boys in Fitzroy Gardens. They'd been there all night. Shelly was her name. She had no money, no food. Nothing. Not so much as a toothbrush. I brought the three of them back to Coben Street. Got her and her boys clean clothes and made them a hot meal. She stayed for two days and then I gave her money and put them on the bus to Sydney. She said she could stay with her sister there. I have to do something to help these women, Duncan. I can't stand the thought of going to another gala dinner knowing women like Shelly or the machinist who works for us have no one to turn to.'

'And can you afford to pay the price they're asking for the cottage? Plus renovations. Plus the cost of having people live there.'

'Yes, I can. I've done the sums. And I'll just look for a little place for myself, maybe not too far from you,' she added with a small smile.

'You know, a lot of people will say what goes on behind closed doors is none of your business,' said Duncan. 'That's how people think.'

'Well, I intend to make it my business. I have the full support of Nancy, Anna and Josephine and a lot of other women. We won't be hanging a sign out the front advertising what we do. Women who come to Coben Street will need to know they're safe staying there. It will be a service for women, supported by women.'

'Well, I think it's bloody marvellous. You're a remarkable woman. If my mother had been able to get away, she would have packed up Lizzy and me and we would have been out of that life like a shot.'

Duncan refilled their glasses and placed the bottle back in the ice.

'So, when do you see James?' he asked.

'I'm having dinner at his place tonight. I can't put this off any longer,' said Avril. 'It's time.'

*

James surprised Avril with a spectacular dinner he'd prepared and cooked himself, and a pair of diamond earrings. The gift, Avril felt awkward accepting, considering what she was about to say to James, but as they curled up on the sofa the words formed in her mind. She placed her coffee cup down and took his hand. *He knows,* she thought to herself. *He already knows.*

'You have been the most wonderful friend, lover and companion over these past years, James, but it's time for us to call it a day. I –'

James brought his index finger to Avril's lips briefly.

'Please. Don't say another word. I've felt this coming for some time. In fact, I've known since the night of the Royal Ball. I don't know what took place between you and Tim that night, but something obviously did. I've watched you drift away from me over these past months. No, not drift. Grow. Expand. Become even stronger and more independent than ever.'

'I couldn't have grown without you,' Avril said sincerely.

'Look how blessed we've been, Avril. After I lost Beth, I never thought I'd love again. We've been able to love freely, without judgement or the limitation put upon most couples by society. You've just turned thirty-one and I'm now in my fifties.'

'What difference does that make?' she asked.

'None, as far as you and I are concerned. In many ways I'm not that conventional, and you certainly aren't. You're the most liberated woman I know. There's a world out there for you to discover, Avril. You have so much still to do.'

Avril leant over and hugged James tenderly and kissed him on the cheek. 'You understand me like no one else.'

'And now I have some news for you.' James swirled the

red wine in his glass and took a sip. 'I hadn't made my decision before tonight but now I have. I've become very involved with a major company in the United States that specialises in what's called shopping centres or shopping complexes.'

'Shopping centres,' repeated Avril. 'I've heard of those.'

'I've been offered a twelve-month contract in a senior advisory position in the company. I'm going to accept. I'd be based in Los Angeles, but there'd be quite a bit of travel to New York as well.'

'Tell me about the shopping centres,' she said. 'They sound like something I'd very much like.'

'Oh, you would.' James laughed affectionately. He described a vast complex, the size of a football field, specially designed to accommodate a whole host of retail shops, from department stores to small boutiques like le Chic. The centre would have hair salons, restaurants, even a picture theatre. And they would be built throughout the suburbs.

'These shopping centres are going to change retailing completely,' said Avril. 'Do you think customers will still shop in places like main cities?'

'They will, but we're going to see huge changes in the retail space over the next ten to twenty years in this country. My trip to LA is part legal work, part research and development. I've just invested in a new company here in Melbourne, looking to build the first large scale shopping complex in Australia. If you're interested in investing, I can show you the details?'

For the next hour James answered every question Avril asked, explaining the size and scale of the conceived shopping complexes, the time they'd take to build, and the returns investors were looking to make.

'So, do you think I should keep my leases short and not lock myself in?' asked Avril.

'I think that's wise,' said James.

'What sort of money will retail spaces in these shopping complexes rent for? Will they incur other fees, based on turnover or takings?'

'You never cease to amaze me, Avril,' James smiled. 'A shopping complex won't be suitable for all retailers, but for those in fashion, it could be profitable beyond belief.'

James explained that he wouldn't be leaving for another couple of months, and he planned to come back for the Olympics next year. 'Do you still want Reece to put an offer in on your behalf for Coben Street?'

'I do,' said Avril. 'Every woman deserves to have a place she can go in a time of need and feel safe and receive food and a warm bed.' She had already decided to call the house 'Marguerite's Place', in honour of the woman who was there for her when she desperately needed help. She wished Sister Marguerite and Madame Leon could see her now. Avril knew they would be proud.

'I'd like to donate on a regular basis to your cause,' said James. 'And I'm sure I can persuade some of my clients with deep pockets to do likewise.'

'Thank you,' said Avril. 'That means the world to me, James. And your beautiful home. What are you going to do with it while you're away?'

'I thought you might like to live here,' he said. 'I don't want to rent the house out or lock it up. This way I won't have to worry about packing everything up and putting it all into storage. You'd be doing me a huge favour.'

'It is a spectacular home,' said Avril. 'I do love it here.'

'The gardener will still come once a week and the pool man during summer. Betty will do the cleaning and make the odd casserole. Eat that at your own peril,' he said, laughing.

As much as Avril had liked the idea of buying a place for herself, she liked the idea of investing her money into this new shopping centre concept even more.

'All right. I'm sure I can force myself to live here until you get back,' she said, smiling.

'Fabulous! Dessert?' he asked, pushing himself out of the soft cushions. 'It's your favourite and your recipe. Apple tarte tatin.'

Avril reached out and took James's hand and stopped him from standing.

'I'll never forget this birthday. Why are you always so understanding about everything I do?'

'It's the way I choose to be, Avril. And I suppose, in the end, you and I are very much alike. We care about what's really important. Not the nonsense most people carry on about.'

He placed his other hand on top of hers. 'We were never a conventional couple,' he said. 'And now, if you'll excuse me, I have cream to whip.'

CHAPTER 18

Duncan held Lizzy and Gabriel's son as the priests baptised baby Michael. As the other godparent, Avril looked on while the formalities concluded, then the assembled friends made their way to the feast waiting on the balcony of Lizzy and Gabriel's house in Port Melbourne.

Eight months on, the city was still revelling in the triumph which had been the thirteenth modern Olympic games the previous November. Lizzy delighted in showing Duncan the brand-new television set which took centre stage in their open plan lounge room. Saturday nights had become wine and fondue night at the Duponts. The comperes of *In Melbourne Tonight*, *Pick a Box* and *Juke Box Saturday Night* quickly became the most talked about celebrities in the country.

James swung his bottle green Jaguar into the driveway and alighted with champagne and flowers. His one year in LA had morphed into almost two, with only one trip back for the Olympics as he said he would do.

Josephine sidled up next to Avril and placed some quiche on her plate.

'Well, he's been back six weeks,' said Josephine, with a slight inflection in her voice. 'When are you moving out or is it all back on again?'

'No! It's not back on again, and I've been looking for a place of my own, but I haven't seen anything I like as yet.'

'If you had any sense, you'd get back with that dream boat called James, standing there,' Josephine teased.

James waved Avril over and they stood on the balcony, taking in the view of the water. They chatted about their various businesses and Marguerite's Place, which had been taking up a large proportion of Avril's time.

Since opening more than two years ago, they'd helped hundreds of women. Some with children, some without. The women heard about what they offered through the 'petticoat grapevine', as it was called. Women talking over the fence, on a tram or bus, or with someone they knew at work. Their stories broke Avril's heart every time. Marguerite's Place was helped by the services of a few medical professionals but they needed to be careful who they engaged. Avril was amazed by how many educated men seemed to think it was acceptable to 'give the wife a little slap from time to time', as one director of a company board had joked with her.

'We need ten houses, not one,' said Avril. 'It's a disgrace that we need them at all.' She sighed and shook her head.

Unexpectedly, James leant over and whispered in Avril's ear. 'Let's take a stroll on the sand. We need to talk in private.'

Down at the water's edge, James stopped and looked out across Hobsons Bay.

'I thought you might be interested in acquiring a piece of real estate in Collins Street that's about to come on the market.'

Avril followed the gliding path of a pelican and watched as it turned and landed gracefully on the surface of the water.

'Fallen on hard times again, has he?' she said, not taking her eyes off the magnificent bird.

'He owes Arthur Mallard thirty thousand pounds and that's just for starters. The restaurant hasn't made a profit in over a year. His suppliers will only sell to him if it's cash up front, he's sold off any other property he had, and Arthur's boys will shortly be paying Albert a visit. And that won't be pretty.'

'I've been doing a bit of my own research,' said Avril, 'and apparently certain sections of the city are about to be rezoned retail and residential. The Paris End of Collins Street is one such area. I'll be able to have twelve apartments built on that site and keep the street level for retail.'

'You certainly don't let the grass grow under your feet. Why am I not surprised?' said James. 'Would you like me to come in on this one with you? Share the purchase and development costs?'

'No. But thank you. I think I'd like to make this investment myself. Besides, I'm doing this so I can give any profits I make to Josephine. She won't know, of course, not until the redevelopment's finished. It's the least I can do for her.'

'So, Miss Montdidier, are you instructing me to proceed?' said James, grinning.

'I am, Mr Carmody. The owner of A Y Holdings would like to acquire the Collins Street premises where Bistro Dubray is located. I want to buy him out and get him out. When's the auction?'

'Friday week,' said James.

'Perfect,' said Avril. 'What a lovely way to round out the month.'

*

Avril and James took their seats at the back of the room. Albert sat in the front row, twisting the real-estate brochure in his hand. Avril ran her eyes down the list of commercial properties for sale. The property was second on the docket. Avril couldn't help noticing that she was the only woman present. She read the side glances of the other attendees. *The boss and his pretty secretary* was written all over their faces. *Let them think what they like*, she thought. She didn't care.

'Now we come to lot 257, Collins Street, Melbourne. A five-storey sandstone building in a prime city location, often referred to as the Paris End of Collins Street,' the auctioneer announced.

He read out the terms of sale and other formalities. What the auctioneer didn't say, and what Avril knew, was that there was no reserve. The building would be sold on the fall of the hammer. The bidding opened slowly. Those who had raised their hands early, most likely associates of Albert's, were soon silent and it quickly became apparent to Avril that there were only two other interested parties.

The price rose slowly in increments of two thousand pounds until one of the bidders dropped out. The remaining bidder turned, smiling, and whispered something into the ear of the man sitting next to him.

This was the first time Avril had attended an auction herself. Previously, she'd been happy to let Reece carry out purchases on her behalf, preferring to stay anonymous. But this was different. She wanted the satisfaction of seeing Albert's reaction when he realised the building had been sold to her. He did not disappoint.

'Do I hear any advance on thirty thousand pounds?' called the auctioneer.

Albert sat motionless, his shoulders slumped forward.

'Any further advance in the room? This property will be sold. Going once, going twice . . .'

Avril lifted her hand.

'Thirty-five thousand pounds,' she said loudly and clearly.

Every head in the room spun around, including Albert Dubray's. His dark eyes locked onto Avril's face as he stood quickly. For a moment Avril thought he was going to speak. The once elegantly dressed Frenchman had the look of a man of desperate means, his cheeks were hollowed-out and his hair uncut.

'Ah. We have a new contender,' smiled the auctioneer.

The previous bidder and his companion spoke back and forth and increased the bid by two thousand pounds. This was the sign Avril was looking for. It told her all she needed to know. A low bid made in consultation towards the end of the auction process indicated they were at their limit. She wanted this over with.

'Forty-five thousand pounds,' said Avril.

The room fell silent.

'Do we have an advance on forty-five thousand pounds? This property will be sold, ladies and gentlemen,' the auctioneer said. 'At forty-five thousand pounds, going once. At forty-five thousand pounds, going twice . . .' The bang of the hammer reverberated throughout the room. 'Sold. At forty-five thousand pounds, and good luck to the buyer.'

'Congratulations, Miss Montdidier,' said James. 'Would

you like to complete this deal yourself or shall I enact my power of attorney on this one?'

'Sign away,' smiled Avril. 'Meet me at Café Florentino at one o'clock. I'm taking you to lunch to celebrate.'

*

The opening night of Anna's abstract exhibition, a late September storm rolled over Melbourne's Port Phillip Bay, releasing a deluge that lasted for two hours. Umbrellas were no match for the furious winds as guests scurried through the water that gushed down the footpath and through the doors of the Mitchel's Gallery. Earlier that day, the chief engineer of the Rallyside Shopping Complex had given Avril and James a personally guided tour of the almost completed facility. Even though she had reviewed the architectural plans many times over the previous two years, nothing could have prepared Avril for the excitement she felt as she stood in front of what would soon be a le Chic boutique, on the mezzanine level of the complex.

'Thank goodness it wasn't like this earlier today,' said Avril, as she handed James a catalogue.

'Are you going to be joining Henry and Anna for the Melbourne Cup this year?' he asked. 'I'm assuming they've invited you. They have in the past.'

'I'm going to be up in Sydney the week of the Cup for a television show. I managed to catch up with Henry and Jordy on Monday, and finally got around to showing them through Lewmont Fabrics and our factory across the road.'

'Well, it looks like the whole family's here tonight to support Anna,' said James, as Jordy, Reece and Duncan made a beeline towards them.

Not all the family, Avril thought to herself, having

already ascertained that Tim and Rachel would not be attending.

'Excuse me, gentlemen,' said Nancy Cameron as she slipped her hand through Avril's. 'I just need a quick word with Miss Montdidier for a moment.'

Nancy scooped two glasses of champagne off the tray and nudged Avril into the corner.

'Business first,' she said. 'I thought you'd like to know that your le Chic and Summer Princess labels are going to be featured in the special edition fashion booklet we're producing to coincide with the opening of the Rallyside Shopping Complex. *The Australian Woman* magazine has so many exclusives my head's spinning.'

'That's wonderful news, Nancy. My design team will be so thrilled.'

'But more importantly, what's really going on with you and James Carmody these days? After all these years, you're still the hot topic of dinner party gossip. You know, living together, never marrying,' she said, rolling her eyes. 'Of course, all the other women are pea green with envy. So tell me. What gives? If you're not together, why haven't you moved into a place of your own?'

Nancy Cameron, formidable as ever. Avril grinned at the woman who had become a dear friend and mentor and fanned herself with the catalogue.

'For starters, you know I don't care what people say about me at dinner parties or anywhere else. And to answer your question – off the record, of course – any romance between James and I was over a long time ago. He's one of my closest friends. And my trusted business advisor.'

'And the sleeping arrangements?' Nancy said with a trademark arch of her eyebrow.

'Oh. Stop it. You're too much.' Avril laughed. 'Seriously, Nancy, I just haven't got around to moving out.'

'Lucky you,' she cooed.

It had become a peaceful, mutually happy co-existence that Avril shared with James. Without any formal discussion, they'd divided the house up into their own spaces. Avril had rooms that she liked to use, including the atrium which provided perfect light for her design work, and James preferred his library. They had dinner together if they both happened to be home, which was rarely, and the occasional hit of tennis on the weekend, but they did tend to meet in the kitchen each morning where they made coffee for each other and shared their plans for the day or anything else on their minds.

'Sounds like the perfect relationship to me,' Nancy said, making a mock wistful face. 'So, he's definitely single and on the market?'

'You'd have to ask him that, but as far as he and I are concerned, we're strictly platonic,' Avril replied, then added cheekily, 'Why are you asking, Nancy? Have you got your eye on James?'

Nancy chuckled so loudly that many heads in the hushed gallery turned to stare. But no one dared disapprove. She was, after all, Nancy Cameron, one of the most influential women of her time. 'Good heavens, no,' she said, bringing her champagne glass to her lips. 'I guess the eager young journalist in me can't resist the thought of a scoop.'

'Sorry to disappoint you,' said Avril with a laugh. 'Now, let's go open our chequebooks and buy some art,' and she hooked her arm through Nancy's.

*

It was well past midnight when Avril and James got home to Kooyong. Avril dropped down on the kitchen stool and fanned her arm across the cool marble bench top. Behind her was the whirl of the machine and the smell of the freshly roasted beans. Coffee before bedtime was another shared habit that Avril and James enjoyed together, talking about their days, winding down.

'I won't need any rocking tonight,' she said over the top of a yawn. 'I'm so tired. I think I'll push my meeting with Joshua back to the early afternoon tomorrow instead of first thing in the morning.'

'Hah! I knew it,' smiled James. 'Can't do those long days like you used to.'

Avril suddenly leapt from her stool, as the sound of someone pounding heavily on the front door blasted through the house. James and Avril rushed through to the entrance and James looked out through the side windows towards the front steps.

'Jesus Christ,' he yelled. He flung the door open.

Duncan and Jordy were slumped together on the step, their faces and shirts covered in blood.

'Help me get him inside,' said Duncan. 'I'm all right but I don't know if he's even conscious.'

Avril raced into the lounge room and pulled a woollen throw from the sofa and spread it on the carpet.

'Avril, call an ambulance,' said James as he positioned cushions either side of Jordy's head.

Duncan reached out and grabbed her by the wrist.

'No. Not an ambulance. That means hospital and a police report. We can't have that.'

The look of fear and sadness in Duncan's eyes was enough for Avril to know what he was worried about, and why.

'All right. But he needs a doctor,' she said, looking up at James.

'I have just the person,' said James and he left the room.

'His pulse is steady and his breathing is strong,' said Avril. 'Fetch some warm wet cloths and a couple of towels from the bathroom, Duncan.'

Duncan's eyelid was split open, as was his top lip, but his injuries were nothing compared to Jordy's. Blood oozed down the side of his face to his shoulder. His hands were misshapen, as if they'd been trampled on, and his collarbone protruded through his ripped shirt. Avril gently wiped his face and stroked back his hair. Gregarious, kind-hearted, loving Jordy was almost unrecognisable.

'It's me, Jordy. Miss Avril,' she said quietly. 'It's all right now. You're at our house. Duncan's safe, he's here too.'

Having collected the linen Avril requested, Duncan slumped on the floor against the wall, his hand covering his eyes as he began to cry.

'John's on his way,' said James as he crouched down and carefully checked Duncan's face. 'He's a surgeon and a good mate of mine. He'll take care of Jordy. You can be sure of it.'

Within twenty minutes John arrived with his wife Rhonda, a nurse. They rushed straight into the lounge room and Avril, James and Duncan waited in the kitchen. After they had treated Jordy, Rhonda stayed with him while John joined the others. He examined Duncan's face, declared there were no breaks, and as he cleaned the wounds he asked Duncan what had happened.

'After the exhibition, Jordy and I went to a club in South Yarra.'

'Stella's, I take it,' said John.

'Yes,' said Duncan.

'This is not the first time those pricks have set upon men leaving Stella's. They seem to get some kind of kick out of it,' said John, shaking his head.

'We had a couple of drinks, a bit of a dance and then decided to leave. We were only there about an hour. They jumped us from behind as soon as we left the club. There were three of them, maybe four. It all happened so quickly.'

'And how did you get from there to here?' asked John.

'A car came down the street, saw what was happening and pulled up. The thugs took off and the bloke in the car helped us. He drove us here. I don't know who he is. He might have worked at the club or been a patron.'

'A good person is what he is,' said James.

'Well, the bastards have given Jordy a good going over,' said John. 'He's taken a nasty knock to the head, and they've made a bit of a mess of his hands, but he'll be all right. He's got a broken collarbone, which I've iced and strapped. He'll need to wear a sling for a few weeks. He needs a couple of days in bed initially. Preferably here, so we don't have to move him too far.'

'He can stay as long as he needs to,' James said. 'And you, too, Duncan.'

Rhonda emerged from the lounge room and introduced herself.

'The sedative's kicked in and he's sleeping soundly,' she said. 'Let's put him to bed.'

The men carried Jordy down the hall and into one of the guest rooms. Avril helped Rhonda get him out of his clothes. Then they washed him, Rhonda treated some more minor injuries she found, and finally they pulled the bedcovers up around his chest and left him to sleep.

'I can't thank you enough,' said Duncan, as he shook John and Rhonda's hands.

'Rhonda will pop by in the morning and I'll come on my way home tomorrow night,' said John. 'And before you make the honourable gesture of insisting on paying, we refuse to accept. We're happy to be able to help.'

Then John gave James a solid whack on the chest and smiled.

'If this lug gives me a one set advantage next Thursday at tennis, we'll call it even.'

James opened the door and patted John on the back.

'Thanks again,' said James, following them down the front steps.

'Stay right there, James,' Rhonda said. 'We can see ourselves down your glamorous driveway. I've staggered this path often enough. Night all.' She waved.

Avril, James and Duncan stood in the doorway of the room where Jordy lay sleeping.

'Thank you, both of you. Thank you for everything,' said Duncan.

'The ensuite's right there,' said James, placing his hand on Duncan's shoulder. 'Try and get some sleep. I'll leave a few lights on so you won't be stumbling around in the dark if you get up.'

The moment James had climbed the stairs, Duncan fell into Avril's arms and cried again.

'You're here now. You're both safe,' she said, holding him tightly. 'I'm only down the hall. Please, come and get me if you need anything. Anything at all.'

'Where would I be without you, Avril?' Duncan sobbed, then he turned and went into the bedroom where Jordy was sleeping soundly.

*

Avril peered through the half-opened door. They were both still asleep, side by side. Duncan's hand was touching Jordy's swollen fingers. She pulled the door closed and made her way to the kitchen.

'What a darling man you are,' Avril said aloud to the empty kitchen.

James had already left for work but on the central bench was a fruit salad with fresh bread and condiments laid out next to the cutlery and china.

It was mid-morning before Rhonda left and Duncan walked into the atrium dressed in some of James's clothes. Avril looked up from her paperwork and patted the cushion beside her.

'How's the patient this morning?' she said.

'Rhonda's given him some more painkillers and he's sitting up, in striped pyjamas if you please,' said Duncan through a half smile. 'I've taken him a cup of tea. He wants to see you.'

Avril tapped lightly on the door.

'I hear it's visiting hours,' she said.

Avril bent down and kissed Jordy softly on his forehead, careful to avoid a large bruise that had erupted, and lowered herself onto the bed.

'Now my reputation's really shot to pieces,' Jordy said through his black eye and puffy lips. 'A boy from the bush gets taken out by a couple of city slickers. We'd better say there were ten of them, not three or four.'

'Definitely ten,' Avril said, smiling and stroking Jordy's arm.

'Are you wondering why I've never said anything to you?' said Jordy.

'Not at all,' Avril replied.

'Are you disappointed in me?'

'Oh, Jordy. There's nothing to be disappointed in or about,' Avril said. 'I love you. I've loved everything about you from the moment when we met at the railway station, to the first time we rode to the top of the ridge, even the annoying way you always make me dance with you when you know I'm hopeless at it.'

Jordy tried to smile at her but it came out as a painful grimace. He took a deep breath. 'I think Mum knows. The old man doesn't have a clue. Well, if he does, he's never let on.'

'Tim and Reece?' said Avril.

'Tim's always known. Probably even before I did. But you know Tim. He respects the choices and privacy of others and doesn't want anyone interfering in his business. Reece, well, typical lawyer-to-be, he came straight out and asked me one day when we were mucking around with a couple of horses, jumping fences and barrel racing. He was only about sixteen. *Thanks for being honest*, was all he said, then he pushed me out of the saddle.'

'What will you say happened last night?'

'Oh, the usual. I've got a dozen go-to stories to cover my tracks. I asked a girl to dance and her boyfriend didn't like it. Got into a fight in a pub in St Kilda. Left a card game carrying cash and got rolled. You name it, Duncan and I have spun it. People like us are used to having to defend ourselves.'

'You and Duncan. How long has it been?'

'You mean, how long have we been seeing each other?' he replied.

'I guess so.'

'Ever since the night of the gala, back in '51. We hit it off right from the start.'

'The world can be a cruel place, Jordy, but there's also

plenty of good out there. And you'll always have your family, everyone at Monaghan, and me.'

Duncan came into the room with a bowl of fruit salad and some toast and placed it on the bedside table.

'Have you decided what story we'll go with?' he asked.

'Went to the aid of an intoxicated sailor and got set upon. How does that sound?' said Jordy.

'The drunk in the street it is,' said Duncan, and he rubbed Jordy's foot through the covers.

CHAPTER 19

'Back a bit further,' said Avril. 'Now, a little to the left.'
'Make up your mind, woman,' said Duncan, as he, Reece and Jordy manoeuvred the ten-foot Christmas tree into the corner of the atrium.

'Perfect!' she said. 'Now for the decorations.'

'Anyone for a drink?' said James. 'Give 1959 a send-off. I don't know where this year went.'

'We've earned a drink,' said Duncan. 'Don't know how you live with this woman.'

'I haven't done this since I was a kid,' said Reece from the top of the footstool. 'Mum used to wait until we were home from boarding school, then we'd all do the tree together.'

'Are you upset that you're not going back to Monaghan for Christmas?' asked Avril.

'Can't see the point. The folks want to go to Noosa, and I'm not sitting down to Christmas lunch with Tim and Rachel. You can imagine how exciting that would be.'

Avril didn't comment as she held the decoration box aloft.

'Who's coming Christmas Day?' asked Jordy.

'The whole gang. Josephine, Nancy, Louise. You know Lizzy is pregnant again?' said Avril.

'I know. Twins. Can you believe it?' said Jordy.

'If anyone can handle three kids under five, it's our Lizzy,' Duncan said.

James drew Avril away from the others with a tilt of his head.

'I wanted to let you know that I transferred the funds from the sale of the apartments in Collins Street yesterday,' said James. 'You've told Josephine then? She's going to be a very wealthy woman, all thanks to you.'

'It was never really my property,' said Avril. 'I was just the go-between to make sure she got what was rightfully hers. And yes, I've told her and naturally she's thrilled. She couldn't believe it at first, but it didn't take her long to start contacting a few real estate agents. You can imagine how excited she is at the thought of decorating her own home. I keep telling her she should design a range of homewares. I believe there's going to be a huge market for that sort of thing in the future.'

'I believe you're right, as usual,' James said.

'And Albert. Have you heard anything about him?'

'Not surprisingly, I've been told by a reliable source that he skipped town, still owing Mallard money. Gone to Western Australia, apparently. It will all catch up with him one day. It always does with blokes like him. It's a shame. Bistro Dubray did the best roast duck I've ever tasted.'

*

Tim strode onto the top veranda of the big house at Monaghan, a mug of tea cradled in his hand. The once lush garden and paddocks had been reduced to a lifeless brown haze. Endless months of cloudless skies had rolled into three years of drought, depleting every dam and water tank for thousands of miles. The Condamine River that ran through Monaghan Station, once brimming with clear flowing water, had been reduced to nothing more than a few muddy pools and a labyrinth of twisted tree roots that were exposed for the first time in twenty years.

A hot wind fanned Tim's face as his eyes fixed on a brushstroke of movement in the distance. A herd of wild horses had banded together and were back near the homestead again, desperately scouring the plains for anything to eat and tearing up the powdery topsoil. When Tim came downstairs, Henry was standing near the staircase, an envelope and letter in his hand. He peered over the top of his glasses and shook the pieces of paper angrily.

'I've only just opened last week's mail. Did you receive any correspondence from our lawyers?' he asked.

'No. What does it say?' said Tim.

Henry cast his eyes up towards the first landing on the stairs and spoke with his voice lowered.

'My office,' he said, and turned sharply and paced down the hall. He closed the door behind Tim, handed him the documents and stood with his feet apart, his broad tanned hands on his hips like he was ready to draw a gun.

Tim's eyes travelled down the pages.

'That slimy, shifty bastard,' he said. 'Ha! That explains why he was flush with funds a while back.'

He handed the documents back to his father.

'So Doug knew all along the company was going to go under,' said Tim.

'Not a goddamn word,' said Henry.

'And he didn't declare the other holdings he had to the board. A blatant conflict of interest with a good dose of insider trading, all rolled into one. He made a killing, while all those years we struggled to keep our heads above water.'

Henry brought his first down hard on the top of his desk.

'Goddamn it,' he shouted. 'How could I have been so bloody stupid?'

Loyalty and trust were everything to Henry Meredith. Once lost, they were virtues Henry believed could never be retrieved.

'You know we have grounds to take him to court over this, don't you?' said Tim.

Henry let out a heavy sigh and ran his hand over his chin.

'Where's your mother?'

'In her studio.'

'And Rachel?'

'She has a hangover, so Mrs Carmichael tells me.'

Henry tossed the papers onto his desk. 'Let's get out of here,' he said. 'I need some air.'

'I've just seen those wild horses again, out to the north,' said Tim. 'We can bring them into the home paddock. They must be skin and bone by now, the poor beasts.'

'Give me ten minutes and I'll see you at the stables,' said Henry.

The sun was midday high when Tim and Henry crossed the bend in the dry riverbed. They rode silently, Henry consumed with rage over Doug's deceit and betrayal. Sheer jealousy was all Henry could put it down to. Doug Stanley had been in competition with the whole world his entire life. Trying to impress people who couldn't care one way or the other what Doug Stanley did or didn't do.

Within the hour they'd found the horses, eighteen of them, sheltering in a valley.

'Let's push them along the fence line and up and over Quaker's Spur,' said Tim.

'Right you are,' said Henry, and he broke away, circling slowly behind the ragged creatures.

They hadn't gone more than a mile when Henry cried out. Tim watched as his father slumped forward over the neck of his horse and rolled from the saddle, hitting the ground hard. In less than a dozen strides Tim was at Henry's side. He leapt to the ground and threw his arm behind Henry's head.

'Dad. Dad! Can you hear me, Dad?'

Henry's eyes were closed but his chest rose and fell, and he moved his hand and took Tim's forearm.

'The pain. My chest. Down my arm,' he said, the effort to speak making his voice a whisper.

Tim released the girth buckle on his father's horse, flung the saddle to the ground and pulled away the saddle blanket. He tented the stiff blanket, shading his father's face.

'I have to go for the truck, Dad. Hang in there, mate. I won't be long.'

Horse and rider flew across the paddock, over the stony riverbed and down the airstrip. Bob McIntyre was sitting on his veranda and saw Tim racing towards the yard. The body line of his stallion was flat from nose to tail. He sprang from his seat knowing such a gallop only brought bad news.

'Get the truck. Get some men. Bring a mattress,' Tim bellowed. 'Dad's had a heart attack.'

Henry was still conscious as the men carefully lifted him into the back of the truck. Tim held his father's hand, not releasing it until he was carried into The Aviary and placed on Tim's bed. The men left the room, leaving Tim, Anna and Bob at Henry's side.

'Two doctors are on their way from Dalby,' said Anna as she sat beside her husband. 'They'll be here within the hour.'

Tim looked down at this father's face and wondered if in an hour, it would be too late.

'The flying doctor's been alerted but the aircraft's on an emergency in Longreach and won't be here until tomorrow.'

Henry was breathing steadily now but was unresponsive.

'A minute,' said Bob quietly to Tim, and nodded in the direction of the outer room.

Once through the door, Tim read the look on the station manager's face.

'We've just had word that smoke's been spotted west of the Cleary Downs and that fire's flared up again north of the Bunya. I've got the boys fuelling all vehicles and priming the generators. We'll put all the fire-fighting equipment on the utes, and I'll let Jean know so she's fully prepared for what might happen.'

'For pity's sake,' said Tim, running his hand through this hair.

Bob put his hand on his shoulder. 'We'll get through this. I know we will.'

'Tim,' Anna called.

Tim raced into the room to see that Henry's eyes were open.

'He's been trying to say something, but I can't make out what it is,' said Anna.

Tim knelt down beside the bed and took his father's hand.

'What is it, Dad? Whisper if you need to.'

Henry's eyes were barely open. 'I want to see my boys,' he gasped. 'Get them home. Avril too.' Then he closed his eyes as his head rolled to one side.

*

'Could you turn that music down a bit?' said Avril as she answered the phone.

'Hello, Avril speaking.'

'Avril, it's Tim.'

Avril knew immediately by the tone of his voice that something was wrong. She listened as Tim explained what had happened, instinctively reaching for a pen and note pad, taking down the information.

'He wants Jordy and Reece here right away. You too, Avril. He was very definite about that. All of you. Can I leave you to sort it out?'

'Of course, Tim. I'll make the arrangements now.'

At the sound of their brother's name, Jordy and Reece looked up.

'I'll pass you over to Jordy. Reece will pick up the other phone so you can all talk together.'

*

Avril, Jordy and Reece were in the air that afternoon, on the only flight from Melbourne to Brisbane on a Sunday. Tim had called a pilot mate and arranged for him to fly Avril and his brothers out of Archerfield Aerodrome later the same afternoon.

The ravages of drought, clearly visible from the air, tore at Avril's heart as the Beechcraft came in to land at Monaghan Station. Bob and Col were waiting beside two vehicles at the end of the airstrip as the pilot taxied in and

the engines closed off. Avril came down the steps behind
Reece and Jordy and as she did, she looked across at the
stables to see Piaf standing in the shade of the scented
gum. The chestnut lifted her nose and sniffed the air. In
nine years the filly had grown into a grand mare, her head
just as regal as the day Avril first saw her. She forced back
the tears and was greeted by Bob and Col with firm hugs
and welcoming words.

'Firstly,' said Bob, to the assembled group, 'Henry's
going to pull through.'

Avril brought her hands to her face, and this time the
tears flowed while Jordy and Reece threw their arms
around each other.

'He's got to take it easy, very easy, for some time and he
may need an operation in the new year, but he's all right.
He's asleep at the moment, so is Anna. She's wrung out.
Mrs C asked if you could see yourselves in. Everyone's to
meet in the front room at seven tonight.'

'You all go ahead,' said Avril. 'I'd like to walk up.'

Only the previous day Avril had been fussing over
which decorations to hang. And now, as she looked
around and drank in the smell of the scented gums, she
couldn't quite believe she was back at Monaghan Station.
Avril closed the small gate as Piaf came up behind her.
She ran her hand along her back and over her withers
and rubbed the side of her face. Her coat was covered in
dust and her mane and tail had long since seen a brush,
but she was in good condition and her eyes were bright
and clear.

'How are you, old friend?' she said as Piaf lowered her
head into Avril's hand.

Avril took her time walking up from the stables, past
the tack room and workshop, and along the veranda that

led to the staff dining room. Despite the emergency that had brought her here, it was good to be back. Better than she had even imagined.

From the veranda she could see Jean fiercely grating a carrot on the chopping board.

'Got time for a cuppa?' Avril said as she opened the kitchen door.

'Avril!' Jean cried, dropping the grater, drying her hands on her apron and bounding forward in one swift movement.

The women hugged, then hugged some more. Jean brought the edge of her apron up to her eyes, dabbing away the moisture.

'I said I would cry when I saw you and look at me. Well, don't just stand there, girly, put that kettle on. You know where the cups are. Nothing's changed. Or would you prefer a sherry?' Jean said with a smile.

'Let's have a sherry,' said Avril.

With glasses in hand Avril and Jean sat at the kitchen bench, just like old times. Avril reached over and took Jean's left hand and admired her ruby and diamond ring.

'Went down on one knee and all,' said Jean, giggling like a schoolgirl.

'Jordy told me. Said Bob was more nervous than a teenage boy at his first dance. When's the wedding to be?'

'Lord! It took him near on ten years to propose. We don't want to go rushing these things, do we,' she chuckled.

'Can I give you a hand in here?' Avril asked as she looked around at the kitchen benches, every available space filled with food and utensils.

'I'm making sandwiches and the like,' Jean said. 'In case these winds and temperature rise. The country's as dry as a wooden god. A tinderbox as far as the eye can see.'

'I'll go find Mrs Carmichael and say hello then I'll come back,' said Avril.

'She's here, you know,' said Jean as Avril reached the door. 'Rachel, that is. She'll probably keep to her room. Tends to do that these days. Although she might go over to see her folks at Cathaway. As unpredictable as a dice game, that one.'

Mrs Carmichael clasped Avril to her. The housekeeper had refused to retire, despite Henry's assurance that she would have a home at Monaghan for as long as she wanted, and while she had relinquished some of her duties, she was efficient as ever. She showed Avril through to the bedroom on the other side of the house, just as she had done the first day Avril arrived, a lifetime ago. The bed had been repositioned on the opposite wall, but other than that, everything was the same as Avril remembered it. A spray of newly picked blue gum had been placed on the dressing table. Avril kicked off her shoes and laid down on the bed, overcome with exhaustion. She must have fallen asleep for she woke when she heard someone knocking on the door.

'Can I come in?' said Anna. 'There you are. I'm so happy you're here at last.'

They embraced then Avril held both Anna's hands in hers, studying Anna's pale and drawn face, the dark shadows under her eyes. 'How are you holding up?'

'Oh, you know me. I'll be all right,' said Anna. 'Henry wants to see you.'

The moment Avril saw Henry, sitting up supported by large pillows, she realised how much he'd aged since they'd last met. His eyes were as blue as they'd always been, but his hair was now completely grey.

'Pushing into my first-class cabin again, are you?' he said in a low gruff voice.

Avril bent down, kissed Henry on both cheeks and sat on a chair next to the bed. Henry weakly squeezed Avril's hand.

'Seems I've given you all a bit of a scare,' he said.

'You did. I bet you're sick of being asked, but how do you feel, really?'

'How do I feel? Like a single malt whisky if I'm being truthful. Unfortunately, my lovely wife won't hear of it. I'm to survive on a ration of water and tea, so I'm told. No red wine for me this Christmas,' Henry said. And a dry smile twinkled across his lips.

*

Avril finally made it back to the kitchen but Jean waved her away, as Anna, Jordy and Reece were already in the front room. Mrs Carmichael had laid out a buffet style dinner, though not one of them seemed the slightest bit hungry.

'What a day,' said Jordy. 'I've called Duncan and James and given them an update. How does it feel to be back?'

'It feels a bit strange, but wonderful too. I had no idea how bad the drought has been. I got a bit of a shock as we flew in. And this heat. How long do you expect it to be like this?'

'Summer's only just starting. Two, maybe three months,' said Jordy.

Tim stopped in the doorway and his eyes met Avril's. The last time she had seen him, they'd both let their guards down and for a few precious minutes they'd allowed their feelings to flow freely. Now, even though he hugged her tightly, she could feel the walls all around him. Drought and despair could do that to a man.

The five of them sat together at the dining room table,

talking quietly and barely picking at their food. Shortly after Mrs Carmichael had cleared away the plates, Rachel sashayed into the room, and went straight to the decanter on the sideboard and poured herself a drink.

'Welcome to Monaghan Station,' she said, almost losing her balance as she executed a curtsy. 'The governess has returned.'

Tim stood and was at Rachel's side in a few strides.

'Get a grip of yourself,' he said to her. 'At least have something to eat if you're going to drink.'

'Why so hostile, dear husband? That's no way to address your *wife*.'

Rachel crossed the room and took the seat next to Jordy and draped her arm around his shoulder.

'Rachel, it's best you go to bed I think,' said Anna, but the suggestion was ignored.

'Now, isn't this lovely. All of us together for Christmas. What are you considered these days, Avril? Staff or family. Must be staff, surely.'

'That's quite enough,' said Tim, and he took Rachel by the arm and lifted her out of her seat. 'If you'll excuse us, Rachel's not feeling the best.' But she broke free of his hand, clutching her brandy balloon, and staggered over to the sofa where she pulled herself up and drew her shoulders back. Tim crossed the room, but she anticipated his move and slipped alongside the piano and hit a couple of keys.

'I want to help you, Rachel,' said Tim as he slowly moved in her direction. 'We all want to help you.'

She hit the keys again, only this time louder and she didn't stop. 'I can't hear what you're saying,' she said in a sing-song voice.

'The truth is, Rachel, you have a serious drinking

problem,' said Tim. 'I want to help you, but I can't if you won't let me.'

She dropped the lid of the piano with a crash. Anna stood.

'That's enough, Rachel,' she said. 'Jordy, Reece. Give Tim a hand and get her upstairs.'

'Truth! Did you say truth?' Rachel shouted. Her eyes were ablaze with pure malice.

'I'll give you the truth, Tim Meredith, if that's what you want. You've been screwing that French bitch all along, haven't you? I know what you're really like. I know a lot more about this stinking family than you think I do. And you, Jordy,' she spat, 'I know all about your sordid little secret.'

Avril stood up and put her arm around Anna.

'Don't do this, Rachel. Have some goddamn consideration for what Dad's been through today. What we've all been through.' Tim was beside her before she had a chance to move. He prised the glass from her hand. 'I'm not going to argue with you. This isn't the time or place for any of this,' he said.

'It's the right time. In fact, it's way beyond the right time,' Rachel screeched. 'Time you heard the truth. The whole truth and nothing but the truth. Isn't that what they say?'

Rachel had displayed some spectacular behaviour over the past decade, but Tim had never seen anything quite like this.

'She's delusional,' Anna said quietly.

Rachel looked Tim straight in the eye. She pushed her body into his and walked her fingernails down his chest. She pressed her lips against his ear.

'You want the truth?' she purred. 'Well, here it is.' She

stepped back, glaring at Tim then casting her eyes slowly over Anna and Avril to Jordy and Reece.

'You were never the father of my baby. There's the truth for you, Tim. It was never you.'

Tim stood, anchored to the spot. A force of anger overtook him. He tried to speak but the words failed to form.

'You're lying,' he finally blurted out. 'You're drunk and you're lying.'

Rachel laughed hysterically.

'Oh, my goodness. It was worth waiting all these years just to see the look on your stupid face. Yes, Tim, I'm drunk. But I'm not lying. Well, not anymore. And I know what you're thinking,' she cooed. 'If you weren't the father then who was?'

'You vile creature,' said Anna. She shook her head, her face pale with anguish. 'What's wrong with you?'

Tim had never been so repulsed by anyone or anything in his entire life. He knew in a handful of strides he could be out of that room, but he had to see this through to the very end. He had to know.

'Want to take a guess? I bet your mind is racing.' Rachel gave him a lopsided smile, enjoying her moment. 'Time's up,' she shouted and threw her hands in the air.

'Why don't you just tell us, Rachel?'

'Oh, there, there, don't be angry at me. What was I to do? My riding instructor and I got a little friendly.' Her bloodshot eyes narrowed. 'I had to get pregnant somehow if I wanted to keep you, didn't I? You were always so responsible, so careful, but we ended up having a wedding in the end, didn't we?'

'Stop!' Avril screamed. 'Stop!' But Rachel wouldn't stop.

'Either way, Tim, it definitely wasn't you. I was already

six weeks pregnant by the time the Winter Dance came around. And I can assure you, you were not the father.'

Tim towered over her, his stance wide, but he looked like he would buckle any moment. Then a hammering bang sounded on the door and Bob McIntyre and Col Bryce raced in.

*

'Quick. You've got to come. Now. All of you.'

'Henry!' Anna cried.

The station manager turned and faced the group the moment they were in the front entrance.

'No. It's not Henry,' said Bob. 'A massive fire's broken out north of the Bunya Mountains and is heading south. It's come out of nowhere. It's bad. Real bad.'

Henry bellowed from his bed in The Aviary nearby. 'What's happening? Get in here.'

'I suggest we all have this conversation in there with Dad,' said Tim.

Anna took her husband's hand as his sons, Avril, Bob and Col gathered around Henry's bedside. Rachel had slinked away.

'The roads to the north have been closed and it's a suicide mission to try and head for Dalby,' Bob said. 'We have to light the home paddock now and backburn using every man we have.'

'I agree,' said Tim. 'We don't stand a chance if the fire gets within five miles of here. The riverbed will make a barrier and give us some reprieve, but not much. Are the boys ready to go?'

'They're ready,' said Bob.

'One rifle per vehicle,' said Henry. 'I won't have any injured animal suffer on my land.'

'We'll use the generator and pull water from the reserve tanks if we have to fight to save the homestead,' said Tim. 'Bring the horses into the stables so we know where they are. At least they'll be safe from the smoke and embers. But if the fire gets too close, open all the gates and let them go.' He looked around the room. 'And no heroics, from anyone.'

The stockmen and station hands mobilised like a well-drilled army and took off in the night. Tim left with Col in one of the water trucks headed to the northeast, while Jordy and Reece took off north with Bob. The kangaroos could be heard bounding from the paddocks and straight through the homestead yard as the smoke and ash began to drift closer. Most of the birds had already taken flight and the suffocating air rang only occasionally with the desperate calls of those few left behind.

Within minutes Avril had changed into a long-sleeved shirt that belonged to Jordy, thick cotton pants and boots and brought Henry's precious labradors inside. She helped Mrs Carmichael close every window and door at the big house' and pack wet towels and blankets under the doors. Then she rushed to the stables to bring the horses in.

Avril had just caught a black gelding and was leading him into the stable when Rachel pushed her aside.

'Get your hands off my horse,' Rachel demanded and snatched the rope.

There was no spare time or energy to argue with Rachel, even if Avril had wanted to, so she turned and raced back to the paddock to catch Piaf, who was now whinnying and running the fence line in panic.

By the time Avril led the mare in, Rachel had saddled up her horse.

'What are you doing? You can't take a horse out in this,' Avril pleaded.

Rachel swung up into the saddle and glared down at Avril. 'There's a stallion a mile away my father paid five thousand pounds for, and I don't intend to lose him.'

'Don't do this, Rachel,' said Avril. 'This is madness.'

'How dare you tell me what to do,' Rachel spat.

'I'm begging you,' said Avril as a gust of warm wind chased the dust into the air. 'You can't go out in these conditions. Tim explicitly said no one was to ride out from the homestead.'

Rachel circled her horse on the spot, forcing Avril back against the wall.

'Tim doesn't always get what he wants, Avril,' she said through clenched teeth, then she drove her heels into the belly of her horse and took off into the darkness.

*

With one ear on the local radio station and the other on the two-way radio, Jean and Sandra replenished each food box with freshly made sandwiches and drinks.

'Fill all those water bottles and put them in the box in the coolroom,' Jean said to Avril the second she entered the kitchen.

'I've just tried to stop Rachel from going out to bring in a horse, but she wouldn't listen to me. She's gone,' Avril said.

'Stupid girl. You'd think she'd have more sense, growing up out here,' said Jean. 'I'll try Tim on the two-way and let him know.'

Throughout the night the trucks and utes came and went, refuelling and taking back food and water for the men. When Bob pulled up, Avril rushed out with supplies.

'Tim and Col aren't picking up on the two-way,' she said. 'Rachel's taken off to find her stallion.'

'On a motorbike?'

'No. On her horse.'

'Bloody hell. What's she thinking? There are no spare men to go look for her. It's a bloody nightmare out there for hundreds of miles. Let's hope she's back soon.' One of the men whistled, signalling to Bob that they were ready to head off again. 'I have to go. If I get in contact with Tim, I'll tell him.'

*

Early the next morning, Tim and Col were the first men to return. Avril raced across the yard.

'Have any of you seen Rachel? Have you come across her anywhere?' Avril shouted over the wind.

'Isn't she here at the house?' said Tim.

Avril explained quickly what had happened at the stables.

'Jesus Christ!' said Tim. 'You can't see thirty yards for the smoke out there.'

'Where did she think the horse was?' asked Col, as he took a swig of water.

'A mile or so away,' said Avril.

Col wiped the sweat from his brow.

'The bloody horse got taken back to Cathaway last week. I watched as she loaded it onto the float herself.'

'Rachel doesn't always remember things so clearly these days,' said Tim. 'This is all we need. I'll have to go and look for her.'

'No. Let me go,' said Col. 'I'll take my ute. I know where she is.'

*

By late afternoon all the rooftops, verandas and railings were covered in a thick coating of fine pale grey ash. The wind picked up and as the temperature climbed three separate fires became one, forming an unstoppable inferno razing everything in its path. Embers carried through the air for miles, igniting the parched undergrowth. During the day the skyline was painted with a thick band of charcoal that sat beneath an eerie milky orange fog.

Monday night came and went with no sign of either Rachel or Col. Hour after hour, the homestead was the scene of a never-ending cycle of men and vehicles returning to refuel and replenish their food and water supplies, as one of the worst Queensland fires in fifty years roared across the southern corner of the state.

Avril ran from the kitchen towards Bob's ute as soon as he pulled into the yard.

'Did you hear Tim's message on the two-way?' she yelled before he'd even opened the door.

'What message?' Bob shouted back, competing with the wind to be heard.

'Tim radioed in a few minutes ago saying that he and Jordy are near Bunker's Ridge and the truck won't start. He said they'd go on foot and follow the line of the river and for someone to bring two horses straight away as there's no vehicle access this side. The wind's in the other direction so they'll make it no problem. But they need the horses immediately.'

Bob's two-way crackled to life.

It was Reece, telling him that they had Monaghan's home paddock under control, but the fire was bearing down fast on Cathaway and their neighbour urgently needed more men.

'I'm on my way. Over,' Bob yelled into the receiver.

Between a rock and a hard place. Bob looked at Avril; there was no one left to take the horses out and get Tim and Jordy.

'I'll go,' said Avril without hesitation. 'I've ridden out to Bunker's Ridge dozens of times.'

Bob took a deep breath. There was no other choice.

'No heroics. If you have to turn back, then do it.'

Avril put water bottles in each saddlebag and soaked her shirt. With wet cloths tied loosely around her neck, nose and mouth, she crossed the lifeless Condamine River and used the faintly visible tree line as her guide. She trotted Piaf cautiously, the other two horses tethered to a lead rope off to one side. The curve of the river provided the natural landmark she needed to hold her course. It was more frightening than she ever imagined. *Slow and steady, Avril,* she repeated to herself. *You just have to get there.*

Tim and Jordy saw Avril before she saw them. They appeared in the distance, their arms waving slowly above their heads as Tim's loud whistle pierced the air. The men were up in their saddles as soon as she reached them, and they turned immediately for home. They galloped in unison, not sparing the horses, knowing that if the wind suddenly turned there'd be nowhere to go.

Tim, Jordy and Avril jumped from their mounts at the hitching rail and Avril led the horses into the protection of the stable.

'Get on the two-way and tell anyone who responds that Jordy and I are on our way,' Tim said to Avril. 'We'll take the motorbikes.' He paused for a moment, his eyes locked on hers. 'Thank you,' he said with a nod before disappearing in the haze.

*

On the morning of the twenty-third, the winds suddenly dropped, and every man, woman and child looked to the sky as dark clouds drifted in from across the coast. By mid-afternoon the heavens opened up, and rain fell steadily throughout the night. *It is over,* Avril said to herself as she stood on the veranda and breathed the sweetest air she'd ever known.

One by one, the trucks and utes crawled back up the driveway, the exhausted men tumbling out of the vehicles to be greeted by their mates and loved ones with hugs and slaps on the back. But Rachel and Col had still not returned to the homestead by the time Tim and Bob, the last of the crew, drove in. And when Rachel's black thoroughbred limped into the yard, still saddled but riderless, every able man and vehicle was refuelled and immediately sent back out again, searching.

*

At daybreak on Christmas Eve, it was Tim who first spotted the outline of the burnt-out bonnet of the ute in the distance. He knew immediately. Bob stopped the truck at a respectful distance from the scene and placed his hand on Tim's arm.

'Not this time, mate,' he said. 'While I'm still the station manager, you'll respect my decisions. You don't want to see this, Tim. You can't remember anyone this way.'

Bob walked slowly to the blackened carcass of the vehicle, looked inside and turned away. It took only seconds to register the charred remains of two people. He removed his hat, his head dropped and he brought his hands to his face. Tim was standing beside the truck as Bob approached.

'It's them,' he said, breathing deeply as he wept.

Tim collapsed, his arms and head falling onto the bonnet, and he bellowed like a wounded beast. His body convulsed as his tears flowed. He cried, knowing the horrific death Col and Rachel had suffered. The kind of deaths he'd seen in the war, in his nightmares. He cried for all the dead men he'd known, and all of those he hadn't known. For Col's boys, now without their father. For Rachel and the madness that had consumed her. And for all those long, lonely, wasted years. Tim cried for all of it.

*

Rachel Meredith and Col Bryce's funerals were held two days apart. Mourners for Rachel's service packed the same stone church near Cathaway Downs that Tim and Rachel had been married in almost ten years earlier. Doug and Mary Stanley were inconsolable; their raw grief echoed throughout the church. They would never recover.

At the request of his three sons, Col was laid to rest at Monaghan Station. Richard and Michael, now growing into fine young men, bore the coffin with Tim, Reece, Jordy and Bob, while Sandra and Joe walked behind, hand in hand. A stillness descended over the station, like the motionless leaves of a lemon-scented gum on a frosty morning. Even Henry's labradors lay still, heads pressed against their paws on the front veranda.

Unlike some of the surrounding properties, the homestead and outbuildings on Monaghan Station had survived the worst of the flames yet again and would stand as a testament to the bravery and perseverance of the men and women who fought the three-day battle. The homestead at Cathaway had been razed to the ground in a matter of minutes as, in the middle of the night, the wind changed direction and hurled the flames forward, the fire front obliterating everything in its path.

After the funerals Avril had flown back to Melbourne with members of Anna's family on a privately chartered plane. Jordy and Reece stayed on. The Meredith family, the workers and their families, all knitted together in tragedy. And for the first time in living memory, the front gate to Monaghan Station was closed for a fortnight and a wreath placed upon it.

In the days that followed, Tim and Henry discussed how they'd replenish the livestock, fences and wind-mills that had perished in the merciless fire. But it was Tim who threw himself into the financial and logistical side of running the station, allowing Henry and Anna to spend as much time together as possible while his father convalesced.

And as the months passed, the land to the west of the Great Dividing Range would begin to recover. The flames of destruction that had swept the earth bare would bring forth new growth, new life. The birds and wildlife would return and the winter rain would feed the dams and the channels and replenish the Condamine River.

CHAPTER 20

Pale Melbourne sunshine filtered through the window as Avril emerged from the bathroom with a white towel wrapped around her head. She tied the belt of her bathrobe around her waist as she made her way past the lounge room. The removalist boxes were still scattered throughout the house. It had taken all of ten minutes to decide that this elegant Victorian terrace was the one she wanted, and she'd pushed for the settlement to take place quickly so she could be in by the first week of May. Close to the city and a short drive to the factory and warehouse, Prahran proved to be the perfect location. The ever-increasing number of flights she was taking to Sydney and Brisbane meant living any further away wasn't an option.

She'd planned to have the whole place beautifully organised before Tim arrived, but any thoughts of the house being completely set up had been forgotten the moment she'd heard Tim's news. He'd phoned the previous day to say he'd rescheduled most of his meetings and would be leaving Brisbane four days earlier than expected. He was booked on the last flight out on Friday afternoon and would be going to the airport as soon as his meeting with Eric Parker was over.

'I'll be at your place around six o'clock Friday night,' he told her. 'I can't wait to see you, my darling. I may have to take the controls if the pilot's too slow,' he joked.

Most of the furniture was in place, which was the main thing, and Avril had delighted in setting up her bedroom with the cushions, linen, towels and toiletries she'd ordered from Georges department store. She made coffee, dried her hair and looked at her wristwatch for the umpteenth time. It was only seven in the morning. *The next eleven hours will be the longest of my entire life*, she thought to herself.

After flicking through her wardrobe trying to decide what she'd wear for Tim's arrival, and holding up multiple outfits and finding nothing suitable, Avril gave up and went back to taking in the view of the garden. She leant against the windowpane and closed her eyes. 'Can this really be happening?' she said aloud. 'Please, please let nothing go wrong today.'

Eventually she started unpacking, in a fervour, to give herself something to do. She listened to all her favourite music, record after record, while she sorted out the boxes, checking the time constantly.

In the late afternoon Avril dressed and went downstairs and poured herself a glass of red wine. She changed the record and curled up on the sofa to wait. The moment she heard the cab pull up she raced to the front door. All the lights were on across the front of the house and down the pathway that led to an arched gate. She stood, shaking, holding the doorhandle, and waited for the cab to drive away. Avril wanted to savour this moment. A moment she had thought would never happen. Then she opened the door of her own home.

Tim walked towards her, his coat and briefcase in one hand, his travel bag in the other. As he came up the handful of steps, Avril's eyes drank him in and his face lit up. Finally, he was standing right in front of her. Once inside he immediately dropped his luggage and pushed the door closed. He pulled Avril into his body as she wrapped her arms around his neck. Theirs was the kiss of lovers who had waited a lifetime for this moment.

Tim kissed her face, her neck, her lips.

'You're here, you're finally here,' said Avril. Then he picked her up and carried her up the staircase, two at a time.

*

The following day it was almost eleven o'clock before they decided they really should get up, take a shower and have something to eat. Tim pushed open the curtains and looked out onto an elegant rose garden and a fine Saturday morning. He glanced back at Avril lying in the white cotton sheets, her dark hair falling over her face, and went straight back to bed.

'How badly do you want coffee?' he teased as he kissed her neck.

'Badly. I think I deserve my coffee, don't you?'

He rolled over onto his side, propped himself up on his elbow and made an obvious performance of looking around the bedroom.

'Hmm. Nice camp you've made here. I think I could get used to this sort of set-up.'

Avril reached over and touched his face with her fingers. 'Tell me this isn't a dream.'

He weaved his fingers in hers and kissed the back of her hand.

'Oh, it's a dream all right,' he smiled. 'A dream come true.'

*

Their plane tickets and the maps of Europe and the United Kingdom were still on the kitchen table where Tim had left them the previous night. Eight weeks away together. Did they ever think this could happen?

'October is a perfect time of year to arrive in France,' she'd told Tim. 'The heat of summer has gone and it won't get colder until November.'

Avril sipped her coffee and thumbed through the book Tim had bought from the local bookshop. *A Beginner's Guide to Discovering France.*

'Bonjour,' said Tim as he sauntered into the kitchen. 'There. I can speak French.'

Avril grimaced then grinned at him. 'Don't forget we have our vaccination appointment at nine,' she said.

'I hate needles,' he said. 'Are you sure this is necessary? We've already had the blood tests. Won't that do?'

'You're sounding like a child.' She shook her hair loose. 'I'm going to get ready.'

As Avril was walking past him, he pinned her against the kitchen bench, kissing her passionately.

'Happy?' he asked.

'Very happy. Couldn't be happier. And no!' she squealed, as he ran his hand up her leg and under her robe. 'You'll make us late.' She wiggled out of his grasp and went to get dressed.

Recommended by Nancy Cameron, Dr Marion MacManus had been Avril's doctor for the past seven years. She was straight talking and progressive, and with every consultation Avril had enjoyed increasing her understanding about her own anatomy and health.

'Well, now,' said Dr MacManus as she opened the folder on her desk. 'You're both here to have the vaccinations required for travelling abroad.'

'That's correct,' said Tim. 'We leave for Europe next month. But I have to tell you, I'm terrified of needles. All those shots I endured at boarding school.'

'I promise to be gentle,' smiled Dr MacManus. 'However, there's a slight problem.'

Tim and Avril looked at each other askance.

'I'm not going to be able to give you your shots today, Avril, as I've reviewed your blood work, three times actually, and I'm happy to report that you're expecting a baby.'

'A baby!' Avril gasped. 'A baby.' Her face was a picture of complete disbelief. 'No, that's not possible.' Avril shook her head. 'I'm thirty-six years of age. I can't be pregnant. I can't have children.'

She looked at Tim, her eyes wide with shock, and back at the doctor.

'I can assure you,' Dr MacManus said calmly, 'that you are most definitely pregnant. You're twelve weeks along.'

'How could it happen?' Avril said without thinking.

'Darling, I think we both know how it happened,' said Tim, not bothering to hide his delight.

'But I was told when I was twenty years old, after the birth of my son, that I could never have any more children,' Avril said to the doctor.

'Well, medical science has come a long way since then. It is possible that the physician who attended you back then may have been incorrect in his assessment. At the time, and for many years after you arrived in Australia,

Avril, you were still experiencing the effects of ongoing malnutrition.'

Dr MacManus looked down at her notes.

'There were occasions when you said you didn't have a period for months, sometimes more than twelve months.'

'Yes, that's correct.'

'And over the last couple of years, your cycle has been more normal than previously, but still irregular. Is that correct?'

'Yes.'

Dr MacManus suggested a quick examination to check that all was well, which Avril submitted to willingly. After providing Dr MacManus with some additional medical details, the doctor informed the couple that everything was progressing as expected.

Tim took Avril's hand and held it in his.

'I'm definitely having a baby then,' she said. 'You're absolutely sure?'

'Avril, you are most definitely expecting a baby next February,' Dr MacManus repeated. 'I suggest you put your travel plans on hold for a while.'

'What happens next?' Avril asked.

'I'll see you each month and then each week closer to your due date. I've prepared some information for you both to read,' she said, handing Avril a folder. 'And we'll need to book you into a hospital for your delivery. I'd like to see you in two weeks. In the meantime, I advise you to avoid alcohol and cigarettes, follow a nutritious diet and enjoy your pregnancy. And finally, congratulations.'

*

Tim couldn't stop looking at Avril and wanting to hug and kiss her. She kept saying she was in shock and couldn't quite believe what she'd been told. As soon as they were back at the house, Avril dropped onto the sofa and hugged a cushion to her chest.

'I have to sit for a while and let this news sink in,' she said.

Tim made them a cup of tea and sat by Avril and took her hand.

'Do you think you could handle another surprise on the same day that we find out we're expecting our first child?' said Tim.

'Sure. Why not,' she said, laughing. 'It can't be as ground-breaking as the baby news.'

'You are the love of my life. I adore you,' said Tim. 'Will you do me the honour of becoming my wife? I know in the past marriage hasn't been a priority for you, but I'd be so proud to be your husband.'

Tears welled in Avril's eyes, and she simply couldn't think of any reason to say no. She knew she loved Tim beyond measure. She always had.

'Yes, my darling, I will,' and she sealed her promise with a kiss.

Tim pulled a small black velvet box from this pocket and opened the lid. In the centre was a large emerald cut diamond with a smaller diamond either side.

'Oh, Tim, it's magnificent,' she said as he lifted the ring from the box and placed it on her finger.

'I picked it up from the jewellers last week. I was planning on proposing somewhere in France, but this wonderful news makes this moment all the sweeter.'

*

A week later, Avril, Tim and Reece landed at Monaghan Station for a weekend visit. The excitement was almost too much for Tim and Avril to contain. Once they were all gathered in the front room and Jordy had entertained them with a couple of tunes, Tim asked for everyone's attention. With Avril by his side, he picked up his glass and turned and looked at her and then at his parents, Jordy and Reece.

'I'm delighted to announce that Avril and I are getting married.'

As the cheers rang out, Anna jumped up, almost spilling her champagne, she was the first to embrace Avril.

'Oh, what fabulous news,' said Anna, as more hugs and kisses followed from the boys and Henry.

'And about time,' said Henry.

Tim retrieved the ring from his shirt pocket and ceremoniously slipped it back onto Avril's left hand.

'Congratulations, Miss Avril,' beamed Jordy. 'When's the wedding?'

'Before the year's out,' said Tim, giving Avril a wink.

During dinner Henry offered to fill Avril's wine glass several times.

'This is one of my best reds,' he said. 'That's not like you to turn down a Chateau Margaux.'

'Darling, you shouldn't even be drinking red wine. Remember what the specialist said,' remarked Anna. She rolled her eyes and shook her head.

'Our eldest son has just announced he's getting married to the love of his life,' said Henry. 'And I'm the one who introduced the wonderful Avril into our lives. Tim, you should be toasting your old man. I'll lay off the grape for the rest of the week. How's that?'

Avril and Tim exchanged glances. She smiled and gave a little nod.

'We also have some other exciting news to share,' said

Tim. Silence fell at the table as everyone's cutlery hovered in midair. 'We're expecting a baby in February.'

More cheers filled the room and this time Henry was the first to shake Tim's hand and hug his daughter-in-law to be.

'Believe me,' said Avril, 'no one is more surprised about that news than me.'

Throughout the rest of the dinner, no one could talk about anything other than the wedding and the baby.

'What are you and Tim thinking of doing for your wedding?' asked Anna.

'We'd like to be married here, at Monaghan,' said Avril. 'And we were thinking we could combine the wedding with Henry's birthday. We thought Saturday the twenty-ninth of October could be the date?'

'Why not,' said Henry. 'What a birthday present.'

'Who will you get to perform your marriage service?' asked Reece.

'We'd like a celebrant to marry us,' said Tim.

'You know James is a licenced celebrant,' Reece said.

'Oh, yes, I'd forgotten that,' said Avril. 'He would be perfect. I'll ask him.'

'Fine by me,' said Tim. 'He'll be coming to our wedding anyway.'

Later that night as they were curled up in bed, Tim asked Avril if everything was all right.

'What's on your mind? You look miles away,' he said.

'It's just hitting me how much I have to sort out. I'm responsible for a lot of people's livelihoods and need to make sure my business interests will still run smoothly. I've also given over a day a week to working with the team at Marguerite's Place. Even with our four safe houses now, each one is full every night. I guess it comes down to

336

working out how to divide my time between Melbourne and Monaghan.'

'If you want my advice, I'd suggest you talk to James about any concerns you have about your businesses. He's always had your best interests at heart and he's one of the smartest men I've ever met.' He smiled and placed his arm behind his head. 'But feel free to ask me anything you like about the latest cattle or grain prices. I'm your guy in that department.'

'You're hilarious,' Avril quipped.

'Darling, please don't think you need to sort everything out in one week. I'm not going anywhere, except with you,' and he reached across and turned out the lamp.

*

Anna and Mrs Carmichael had created a spring wonderland in the white marquee. It sparkled with tiny lights, flowers and round tables elegantly set with fine crystal and china. Friends and family started arriving the Wednesday before the wedding, and in true Meredith family style, the house was full to brimming over. Anna had had the shearers' quarters repainted and ceiling fans installed in every room. A truckload of furniture, rugs and linen brought up from Toowoomba completed the transformation.

'My giddy aunt,' Jean said when she saw the finished results. 'Anna's turned this place into the Monaghan Hotel. Those bloody shearers will never leave if they see all this.'

A second, smaller marquee had been set up in an open space beside the river. The night before the wedding, Anna and Henry hosted a casual evening barbeque which brought together everyone who had come for the weekend festivities. A cheer went up as Tim and Avril came out onto the front veranda, Tim in a deep blue, open-neck shirt and dark pants, Avril in a low-backed cream A-line dress that skirted her ankles.

Avril sidled up to Gabriel and put her arm around his waist.

'You're supposed to be having the weekend off,' she said. 'Put that camera away and come and have a drink.'

'Ah, *ma chérie*. You should know by now that nothing will give me more pleasure than to record some precious moments at this special time. I promise, just a few more shots and I'm done.'

And what precious images Gabriel captured. The smiles of Avril and her dearest friends, Louise, Lizzy, Josephine, as they stood beneath the blooming jacaranda trees. Avril and Duncan embracing, their eyes bright as they looked at each other. A quiet moment between father and son as they stood side by side, their arms stretched across each other's shoulder. Joshua and his wife deep in conversation with Henry and Anna. Tim placing a frangipani flower behind Avril's ear, and the laughter between Duncan and Jordy as they played croquet on the lawn.

Tim kissed Avril on the hand.

'All ready to walk down the aisle tomorrow?' he asked.

'As ready as I'll ever be. And you? Are you happy?'

'I'm so happy, I could burst,' said Tim.

*

The guests were seated and the handsome groom, standing in his dark suit and white bowtie, smiled broadly when the string quartet began to play, announcing the arrival of the bride. The congregation stood in unison and spontaneously drew breath as Avril appeared on Henry's arm at the flower-filled doorway of the marquee chapel. Avril wore a garland of white flowers, her short bob skimming the top of her shoulders, and she carried a bouquet of pink and white peonies, lovingly assembled by Jean that morning. Her sleeveless, white silk chiffon gown draped softly to the ground, and the transparent train floated effortlessly behind her.

There wasn't a dry eye in the room as Avril walked slowly towards Tim, and he took Avril's hand. They stood facing each other as they said their vows, exchanged wedding rings and were finally pronounced husband and wife. Together they joyously signed the marriage register James placed before them, Josephine witnessing on Avril's behalf and Jordy on Tim's.

The sky shone a vivid blue all day while intermittent calls from the kookaburras rang out overhead throughout the afternoon. Avril and Tim stood on the lawn, thanking their friends and family for their good wishes, sharing in the happiness of a day they both thought would never happen.

Avril and Tim had asked Jordy to play 'It Had to Be You' for their wedding dance. Anna, having had six stockmen carry the grand piano into the marquee from the big house, had the beautiful instrument hidden behind a flower-filled screen until Jordy was sitting at the keys ready to begin. He surprised all the guests by playing the song through a second time, only this time, he sang the words, note perfect, as Tim and Avril continued to swirl around the floor.

Shortly before two o'clock in the morning, Avril and Tim slipped quietly from the marquee and into their rooms in The Aviary. Unbeknown to either of them, Anna, Jean and Mrs Carmichael had turned down the bed and placed a garland of jasmine on each pillow and vases of flowers throughout their rooms. A cluster of pink candles had been lit in the bathroom, chilled champagne and a platter of fruit, cheeses and chocolates were on the table.

'Give me your hand,' Tim whispered, as they lay naked in each other's arms.

He intertwined his left hand with hers and stared at their wedding bands, and ever so tenderly, kissed Avril's hand.

*

As any Australian bushy will tell you, the best-laid plans often go awry. As was the case on the Sunday morning in January when Tim and Avril were due to fly back to Melbourne to await the arrival of their baby the following month. Whether it was fate, or the gods had a hand in it, no one would ever know. When Tim turned the ignition switch on his brand-new twin-engine Beechcraft, it wouldn't start. There was nothing. Not a single sound. He reviewed the flight manual while Henry and Anna watched from beside the aircraft hangar, trying to figure out what on earth was going on.

'We might be staying a bit longer than we'd imagined,' said Tim, once they were back at the big house.

'I know I said I wanted to have the baby in Melbourne,' said Avril, 'but to be honest, now that we're here, what's wrong with the local hospital?'

*

For the next couple of weeks Avril waddled around the homestead, her feet swollen and her back aching, being fussed over by everyone. She woke about seven in the morning and touched Tim on the shoulder.

'I don't want you to panic, darling, but my waters have just broken.'

340

'Are you sure? You're not due for another week.'

'Trust me.' She winced. 'As you so often say to me, this isn't my first rodeo.'

'Does this mean you're about to have the baby?'

'Not at this very moment but, yes, the baby is on its way.'

And on its way it certainly was. For at five past two that afternoon, on the tenth of February, 1961, an eight-pound ten-ounce baby girl, with a shock of jet-black hair and a set of lungs that would start a stampede, came kicking and screaming into the world.

With Tim at Avril's side, and Jean assisting the local doctor, who'd been summoned by Anna the moment they realised what was happening, the birth had gone as smoothly as anyone could have hoped.

While Avril slept, Tim held their daughter. He could not bring himself to put her in the bassinet. Just before midnight Avril woke and together they marvelled at the child they'd created.

'She's so beautiful,' said Tim. 'A little miracle. Our miracle.'

Avril looked up at her husband as he gently swayed back and forth with their precious daughter in his arms.

'You know, I think your great-grandfather was right. There really are moments in life when timing is everything,' said Avril, as Joy Yvette Anna Meredith reached out, took hold of her father's finger, and would not let go.

ACKNOWLEDGEMENTS

My heartfelt thank you to the wonderful team at Pan Macmillan Australia who do the heavy lifting behind the scenes – Cate Paterson for giving *A Remarkable Woman* the go-ahead, Candice Wyman for her marketing expertise and for the editing skills of Brianne Collins and Susin Chow.

A special thank you to Claire Craig, for believing in this story right from our initial discussion over coffee in 2020, and for all your ongoing professional guidance.

To Bernadette Foley, who's been there for me as a mentor and advisor from the start of my writing career. Thank you. And to fellow writer, Catherine Greer, who continues to traverse this creative road with me, providing inspiration, friendship and chocolate brownies in spades.

The feedback provided by Cindy Jones, Mishelle DelCaro and Melanie James, as they read and commented on the initial drafts of the manuscript, was invaluable. A massive thank you each of you.

Bella Harmer and Nick Van Mil – thank you for all your encouragement and for celebrating every milestone of this journey with me, from story concept to published book.

Graeme – this work of fiction couldn't have been written without the constant love and support you give me, and always have, in everything I do.

And for every reader of *A Remarkable Woman* who, having experienced the many challenges life can present, finds their way forward to happier times.